BASTION

O-MEN: LIEGE'S LEGION, BOOK 2

ELAINE LEVINE

Published by Elaine Levine
Copyright © 2019 Elaine Levine
Last Updated: January 25, 2020
Cover art by The Killion Group, Inc.
Editing by Arran McNicol @ editing720
Proofreading by Jenn @ sidekickjenn.com

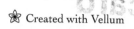

✻ Created with Vellum

BASTION

O-MEN: LIEGE'S LEGION, BOOK 2

The Matchmaker's Curse says if the mutant accepts the match, then his fated mate must die. If he doesn't accept it, then he must die...

No one has yet survived the curse.

The threat coming for Selena Irving has been stalking her family for years, ruining her parents' lives and pushing her onto the warrior's path. She's the only female yet to qualify for the elite dark ops unit in the Army called the Red Team, and while that shielded her for a little while, the nightmare's begun again. Now she's caught the eye of an alpha male with superpowers—her definition of trouble. Sexy-as-hell Bastion loves easily, laughs often, and cooks like a master chef. He's also the only man to see through her defenses to the person she used to be...the woman she might have become had her past been different.

Bastion, changed against his will into a mutant warrior, is on a mission to find those responsible for stealing his life, intent on stopping their plans to unravel humanity. He wasn't looking for a mate, but he bonds with Selena the first time he sees her, activating a curse neither of them can escape. His only chance to break it is to ruthlessly burrow into her secrets, forcing her to face her hidden scars, helping her heal before the danger headed her way can use her past to take her down—and everyone she loves with her.

OTHER BOOKS BY ELAINE LEVINE

Sleeper SEALs

Romantic Suspense/Military Suspense

Men of Defiance Series

Historical Western Romance

(This series may be read in any order.)

ABOUT THE AUTHOR

Elaine Levine has a simple life and a twisted mind, both of which need constant care and feeding. She writes in several different subgenres of romance, including romantic suspense/military, historical western, and paranormal suspense. Her books are sexy, edgy, and suspenseful, but always end on a happy note because she believes love gives everything meaning.

Be sure to sign up for her new release announcements at http://geni.us/GAlUjx.

If you enjoyed this book, please consider leaving a review at your favorite online retailer and Goodreads to help other readers find it.

Get social! Connect with Elaine online:
    Reader Group: http://geni.us/2w5d
    Website: https://www.ElaineLevine.com
    email: elevine@elainelevine.com

OTHER BOOKS BY ELAINE LEVINE

Sleeper SEALs

Romantic Suspense/Military Suspense

Men of Defiance Series

Historical Western Romance

(This series may be read in any order.)

DEDICATION

Barry —
I love everything about our life.
Because of you.

1

Wolf Creek Bend, Wyoming
The Red Team Headquarters
Early December

The moon was late rising. Not quite full, it spilled cold light over the quiet mansion Bastion was charged with infiltrating. An orange glow radiated from somewhere around the front of the garage. It was steady, not flickering like a fire, but it was orange, not red like taillights.

That light was a summons, pulling at Bastion. He'd avoided it for weeks, but tonight, he could no longer resist its call. He cautiously made his way around to the garage wing of the house, keeping his energy shield in place, effectively hiding himself from technology and humans alike.

He knew what he was looking at—he'd known all along. It was the specter of the Matchmaker. The fiend had no balls; he never delivered his curses in his corporeal form. No, he brought his terrible messages the coward's way, through an astral projection, sparing himself the blowback he deserved.

The orange glow wasn't coming from the Matchmaker's bright red hair or glowing eyes; it was a light that emanated from his entire body. Bastion rushed the mirage, wanting to touch its energy to get a sense of who was behind the Matchmaker persona.

Of course, he couldn't get close enough. The thing's projection moved with Bastion, keeping just out of his reach.

When Bastion gave up, the Matchmaker lifted a hand and pointed at the house. One of the four overhead garage doors opened. Bastion shielded the screeching sound from being heard by anyone inside.

Briefly, the reality of what was happening registered; the experience Bastion had both yearned for and feared was at hand. He froze in place, staring into the black void of the open garage.

If he accepted the Matchmaker's pairing, shit was going to get real—and fast. He was ready for it, but was the female who'd been selected for him ready?

How could she be?

Legend said if the male mutant accepted the chosen female, she would die. And if he didn't, he would die.

Maybe that was all bullshit. Neither Liege nor Summer had died...but it had been a close miss for Summer. And their relationship was still new, so it was anyone's guess as to what was yet to come. Now that

Liege's woman was changed, was she spared from the curse?

Merde, there was so much they didn't know.

Bastion spun on his heel, intending to continue yet another pass around the estate. He stared at the hill in front of the garage that provided the house privacy from the road, and though he willed himself to move forward, he couldn't go in that direction.

Bastion looked at the glowing fiend watching his struggle, still pointing toward the open garage door.

The Matchmaker's red eyes looked victorious. And he was—Bastion's only way out of this clash of wills was surrender.

Baise-moi. How satisfying could a relationship be if it was forced on both participants? This was unacceptable, but there was nothing for it but to pretend to yield. Bastion headed into the shadowy garage, making a show of giving in.

He'd seen in the time he'd been surveilling the compound that many females lived here. How was he to know which was his?

After only a few steps into the oversized garage, the Matchmaker's bright glow blinked out. Bastion pivoted, intending to make his getaway, but once again he found he was physically blocked from going in any direction that led away from the house. The garage door slowly lowered—even as the house door unlocked itself and opened inward.

This was fucked up. No way could the Match-maker force Bastion to do anything. But for now, for show, he had to make the fiend believe he'd accepted his fate.

Bastion stepped inside. The door closed behind him. Though he'd been prowling around the property for some time, this was the first he'd been in the house. He'd studied the blueprints for the sprawling mansion—it was essentially a big X with an elongated middle section—so he knew basically where the public rooms and bedrooms were located.

He pulled the shadows in around him so no human could observe him. No animal either. The mild electromagnetic frequency he was emitting hid him from recording devices, making him invisible. He wasn't a man, wasn't a ghost. He was nothing. He went through the public rooms on the ground floor. The house slept, unaware of the shadow moving within it, the mutant hunting the woman that legend had preordained was his.

Temporarily abandoning his mission to find evidence of this mercenary group's allegiance—and the scientists they hid—Bastion was now on a different scent, driven to find the woman fated to be his. He made a brief pass through the southern end of the main floor, where some of the bedrooms were. Without entering any of the rooms, he knew she wasn't there. He briefly considered making a ruckus, summoning all the occupants of the house into the living room so he could walk among them and find her more easily. He didn't because the anticipation was delicious. Heady. Each step closer to her deepened his hunger. He wanted her as he hadn't wanted another female — not just in the time since he was changed, but in his entire life.

And this was a female he'd not yet met.

Upstairs, the sprawling mansion contained only bedrooms. Three in each of the suites at either end of the house, eight in the long middle, with a break between both sides for a bridge that crossed over the foyer. The smell of lumber was strong coming from the basement. Likely there were more rooms down there. Why were they expanding the already sprawling mansion?

He'd find out soon, but not now. Tonight was his time to meet his woman — if he chose to accept the curse. He made a brief pass through the second floor's southern bedroom wing. She wasn't there. He started down the main hall, holding his palms inches from each door.

She was near. His heart beat faster. His woman, his light, his life. She was here. His hands vibrated as they hovered at her door.

This was a moment like no other. He didn't want to rush it, but nor could he stand the anticipation. He opened her door with just the power of his mind and stepped inside, closing it behind him.

A short hallway passed between the bathroom on one side and the closet on the other, then opened into a large space. Her room was tidy, decorated in the masculine style of a mountain lodge. It wasn't to her tastes, he realized, but he also knew she held no attachment to it; it was merely a place to sleep, nothing more.

She was on the bed, sleeping soundly. He stopped,

stunned by the white glow coming from her. Liege could see auras, but Bastion had never before seen light of any color surrounding a human.

If he needed any confirmation that the Matchmaker had indeed found his light, Bastion was staring right at it. He forced his focus to go deeper, inside the light, to the woman it covered.

Her face was peaceful. Angelic. Streams of dark brown hair spilled down her shoulders, over her green tank top. She was half in, half out of the covers. One long, supple leg was bent over the blankets that covered the other half of her. He couldn't quite determine her skin color. White or olive, he supposed. Her lips were lush, rounded. Her lashes were long. Her brows arched artfully over her eyes. He wondered what color they were. Brown? Green?

He reached a finger out to stroke along her bare arm. The next thing he knew, he was on his back on her bed, a knife at his throat, his woman straddling his waist. Her strong thighs gripped his sides as if he were a horse she meant to ride.

Her dark hair curtained her face as she leaned close to snarl, "Who are you and what are you doing in my room?"

He roared with laughter.

God, his woman was full of bravado. The knife nicked his skin.

"This is but a dream," he said. "You have nothing to fear from me. And you won't remember any of this." His comment was part compulsion. He wasn't ready for her to meet him yet. He had to get a better understanding of who she was and what her people were up to before he let himself be known to her.

Her legs eased their grip. She set the knife aside, but still held him down on her mattress. "I don't know you."

"Not yet. We'll meet soon." He pushed her dark hair back over her shoulder. "You are beautiful."

"You need a shave."

"Perhaps I do." He smiled, then drew her down close so he could taste her mouth. Fuck, her lips were as delicious as he knew they'd be. He caught the upper one in his teeth, releasing her slowly and gently. "Tell me your name."

"Selena. Selena Irving. Who are you?"

"Bastion." He kissed the side of her jaw, near her ear. "Say my name."

"Bastion."

Shivers prickled his skin. "I like how it sounds when you say it." He lifted her fists from his shoulders and kissed her knuckles. Her breasts were perfection—heavy globes against his chest. "Tell me everything about you." He wanted to hear her voice. He wanted to know her story. He wanted to fuck her senseless.

He yearned to let her remember him, but knew that wouldn't happen because he wasn't going to let her keep this memory. Maybe one day he would give it back to her—one day long in the future, when she no longer carried knives.

Selena looked suspicious. "Why do you care?"

"Because you fascinate me." He caught her chin in his teeth and raked them lightly over her skin.

She moaned, but pulled free. "You haven't earned the right to know me yet."

"But how can I earn it without getting to know you?" He could simply compel her to reveal her secrets, but he didn't. He wanted her to bring forward what was most important to her of her own accord.

"That's not my problem," she said.

He rolled her over, slipping his legs between hers, still holding her wrists. As soon as she was on her back, he felt the panic that slammed into her. Instantly, he released her and rolled off her to lie on his back. With all of her gusto a moment earlier, Bastion felt broadsided by her reaction. It hurt that his woman held fear so close that, even in her sleep, it was a go-to emotion.

She didn't mention it, so neither did he.

They both stared up at her flat ceiling. Bastion played an image for her, a star-scape with translucent clouds floating under a bright moon. The trees at the edge of the vision shifted in a slight breeze.

Selena was captivated.

So was Bastion, watching her.

As gifts went, this wasn't much of one. Merely a vision to bring her peace. He suspected that just as he hadn't earned the right to hear her story, nor did he have the right to give her a tangible gift.

He sighed. He was going to have to do this on human time.

Slow as fuck.

"If you won't tell me the story of you, then at least tell me one thing you wish for."

Selena turned from the shimmering vision and met his eyes. "What are you, a genie?"

"I suppose, owned by the hand that holds me."

"This is just a dream, right?"

He nodded. "Just a dream."

Selena stared at the vision he still played for her. "I want a lover. Not just any lover. One strong enough to stand next to me, to let me be me. I'm not good at following."

"That is a good wish."

After a moment, Selena turned to him. "What's your wish?"

"I want the same thing."

She turned on her side and put her hand on his chest. "Can genies take lovers?"

"I'm not a genie."

Selena nodded toward the beautiful star-scape he was playing. "You must be. Regular people don't do these things."

"I'm not a regular, either."

"Then what are you?"

"Your lover."

Selena smiled and shook her head. "No, my lover doesn't have so much hair."

Bastion turned onto his side, putting his hand on her waist, gently urging her toward him until their mouths were just a breath apart. "This one does."

Selena ran her hands over his chin and into his hair,

pulling him closer, closing the distance between their mouths.

An electric pulse coursed through Bastion at the contact. And when their tongues touched, heat slammed into his groin, hardening him. He hungered for her. For a moment, he let himself revel in his desire, something he'd not felt for a very long time, something he had been unable to pretend into existence since he'd been changed, though he'd tried like hell. The feeling was exquisite, as was its source. He could get drunk on the hum she made his body feel, and knew without a doubt the Matchmaker had found him his perfect mate.

Bastion slipped his hand behind Selena's ear, holding her to him as he took over the kiss, deepening it. The threat that the Matchmaker's curse might end this fierce, vibrant woman filled him with rage. He tried to roll over her, but she resisted.

That fear again. She didn't want to be under a man.

Who had dared hurt her?

Selena straddled him, laying her body over his. She wasn't a small female. No, she was a bundle of taut muscles and honed reflexes. Perfection.

He kissed her soft cheek, the hard line of her jaw, the warm stretch of her neck, all while she rocked her hips against his. He spread his legs wider, opening hers, hating the layers of clothes that separated their bodies.

"Selena," Bastion said as he rubbed his cheek against her throat, "tell me about the Omnis."

Her body tightened. She drew back from him and

frowned, withdrawing completely from their warm intimacy.

"This isn't a dream," she said.

"Of course it is."

"How did you get in here?"

"I am just a dream."

Selena scooted back from him, in full retreat. Bastion sighed as he stared up at the starry sky illusion he still kept in place, hating that she owed her loyalty to a team other than his.

"We are on the same side of this war, you know," Bastion said. They had to be. The Matchmaker wouldn't have selected her for him otherwise.

Or would he?

"Get out of my bed. And out of my room." She was crouched at the head of her bed, a cold and hostile stance for a warrior who'd just been like melted caramel in his arms.

Bastion got off the bed. He retrieved her knife and set it on her nightstand. He wished he could read minds as easily as Liege could. Instead, Bastion could only read energy and catch thoughts that were clearly broadcast, but that didn't preclude him from imposing compulsions, which was what he did now. Facing her, he compelled her to remember only bits of their encounter and none of the details about him.

"Know this: I am yours and you are mine. I'm coming for you."

2

In the hallway, Bastion paused to take stock of what had just happened. His body thrummed with excitement. He'd found his woman, his one and only. His light.

And it was entirely possible she belonged to his enemies—the Omnis.

He forced himself to get his shit together and get on with his mission. He became aware of the hallway he was in, of the rooms he'd passed on his way to hers, rooms where other mutants had once been or were now. The War Bringer, whose energy he and Liege had encountered in the Omni subterranean stronghold, was here. The War Bringer had fought his way out of an Omni torture chamber, but did the fighter's conflict with the Omnis signify a schism in their ranks rather than a direct hit from an Omni enemy?

There was much to see and understand yet. Bastion had been observing from the outside for a couple of weeks, but he needed to know more before he could report back to Liege.

At the moment, the mansion's occupants slept, oblivious to the threat walking among them. They had robust technical protections in place around the house and grounds against wicked humans, but nothing secured them from Bastion or his kind.

The house was filled with fighters—and their families. They lived here openly, with no attempt to hide their whereabouts from the locals or the Omnis. Bastion knew, from surveilling the household, that some of the women who were not fighters operated businesses, both in town and from the compound itself. People—regulars—were in and out of this place all the time.

Was this group hiding in plain sight? Were they under the Omnis' protection? Or were they just dangerously ignorant of the fight they'd entered?

He could feel the energy of more than one mutant around this place. If these fighters had mutants among them, then they should know what his kind were capable of...unless the mutants here had not shown their true selves.

So many questions.

Earlier, while he'd been on his way to Selena's room, several of the other rooms had caught his attention. Two had recently housed mutants. Bastion went into the first of those rooms. A male mutant had stayed here recently.

Did the other residents here know they'd had a mutant for a guest? If so, did that make a checkmark in the column for these people being Omni affiliates or enemies? Bastion put it in the pro-Omni column he was mentally tallying.

He went down a few doors to another room recently occupied by two mutants. A bonded couple had been here. He'd felt the presence of a mutant female from his patrolling outside the house. Was this who he'd been sensing? Both of these mutants had the stink of Omnis all over them. Who were they? Why had they been here? Was this couple the Ratcliffs—the scientists Liege had sent him to find?

He should have come inside when he first arrived rather than observing from a distance for so long, but he hadn't wanted to tip off his enemy, Brett Flynn. If Bastion had found this band of fighters, it was only a matter of time before Flynn did so as well. With his energy all over the place, Flynn would know it held importance for the Legion.

So far, Flynn was nowhere in sight, so Bastion couldn't put off this exploration. And now that the Matchmaker had connected him to his light, he'd had to come inside and find her.

Did the fighters who lived here know they'd been infiltrated by mutants? Perhaps that was why they could exist here with impunity; they'd struck a deal with the devil.

Definitely a tick in the pro-Omni column.

Bastion continued down the hallway into the main section of the house. He held his hands up near each door, letting himself sample the energies that used the room.

When he came to the room the War Bringer used, he felt a little thrill of anticipation. This man had survived Omni torture. Bastion wanted the whole story, but he couldn't expect to learn it tonight. He slipped inside the room. A man and woman were asleep in the bed. The woman was a petite blond. She fit the Omnis' white supremacist ideal of a perfect woman.

Another tick in the column of these people potentially being Omnis.

His gaze moved to the War Bringer. Bastion had been leaning toward the theory that this man had fought a fellow Omni warrior for the rights to the woman, but that theory crashed and burned when he got a good look at the War Bringer.

Olive skin, black hair, tribal symbols seared into the soft under-skin of his forearms. For the millionth time, Bastion wished he had Liege's skill for reading minds. The War Bringer's leather wrist cuffs were lying on the dresser. Bastion picked them up.

Guerre, I need you, Bastion said, summoning his team's healer. Guerre was hypersensitive to energies and could often read detailed events from objects. His psychometry worked even through a mental connection with any of the guys on the team.

Go, Bastion, Guerre said.

Can you get a read on the cuffs I'm holding?

Hang on.

A long stretch of silence chewed up the minutes. Bastion stayed quiet. Guerre could work miracles, but he needed complete focus.

What is it you want to know? Guerre asked.

Tell me about the man who owns them.

He's from an American Indian tribe. Lakota. I'm not sure which subgroup.

Huh. A tick in the column for Omni enemies.

Is he an Omni? Bastion asked. Might as well get Guerre's take on the guy's situation.

Again there was a long pause. *It's unclear. He's entangled with them, for sure, Guerre said.*

Thanks. Go back to sleep.

Bastion stared at the big leather cuffs. The Omnis would not admit a Native American into their wretched ranks, except perhaps as a servant, slave, or human experiment. Brett Flynn would love to turn the War Bringer into a ghoul.

Bastion looked at the couple sleeping on the bed. They had an extraordinary energy binding them. Pure, almost tangible, it was what the energy of love felt like. He set the cuffs down, suddenly feeling as if he'd overstepped. He left the War Bringer's room, more confused than ever about the loyalties held by this group of fighters.

The bedrooms in the rest of the upper floor were of no interest to him. Bastion went downstairs. A short hallway led to the southern bedroom suite on the first floor. The first bedroom was empty. Well, empty of current occupants, anyway. It was packed with the energies of many people, almost as if it were a passageway.

In the next bedroom, a couple slept. Bastion kept himself invisible, but even with such protections in place, his presence woke the man. He got up and looked around the room, then went out into the living room shared by the three bedrooms in that suite.

His absence gave Bastion a chance to focus on the blond female that shared the man's bed. She was a mutant.

Another female mutant. Maybe this was the one he'd felt from outside.

Bastion wondered what change had happened in the core Omni ethics, thin as they were, that they were now modifying female humans?

The man came back into the room and slipped under the covers. As he pulled his woman close, energy arced between them, like two halves of an electrical device that only sparked when the pieces were close to each other.

Bastion stumbled back and banged into a chair. His careless movement startled the man, who cursed and turned the light on. Bastion held still, confident he couldn't be seen. The man threw the covers off and stomped to the door again. Of course, there was nothing to be seen in the suite's living room.

When he returned to his bed and his woman, that energy arced again. This time, Bastion was prepared for it. Outside of this house, he'd only seen that electrical bond when Liege and Summer were near each other.

These two people were in love. Desperately. Beautifully. Completely. Like the War Bringer and his woman.

But that didn't mean they weren't Omnis.

Bastion tended to believe that Omnis were born

without souls—the most evil of psychopaths—but perhaps even the soulless could fall in love.

Given that the woman was a mutant, and the only mutants Bastion had ever met were ones created by Omnis, then it meant another tick in the pro-Omni column.

It was curious, though, that this woman didn't sense him. He'd been able to sense her from way out in the woods surrounding the property. Her man was more woke than she.

Bastion pondered that as he left their room and went into the next one. Two boys were fast asleep inside it.

He hated the fact that children lived here. It muddied the waters, making this place seem more of a familial retreat than a stronghold. The Legion couldn't strike against the compound without significant collateral damage. Perhaps that explained the presence of the children. Omnis would hide behind any shield they found useful.

Bastion had just stepped into the small living room shared by the bedrooms in that wing when a realization hit him. Human energy had many identifiers, but two aspects were most prominent. The first were biological markers shared by families of the same blood. The second came from a human's personality. An individual might share biological markers and have diametrically opposed personality markers, but you could always sense who was related to whom.

One of the boys in the room Bastion just left was a biological son to both the man and woman sleeping in the next room, and the other was biologically related to only the female. And there was another family bond from the man — he was a biological relative of the mutant male who'd had a room upstairs, the one who'd slept alone.

These people weren't just Omni allies; they were family.

What was going on here?

Bastion resumed his discovery of the house and its occupants. He walked down a short hallway, through two glass doors, and into another wing at that end of the house — a large gym building. The first room was a basketball court, or had been before it had been repurposed. Now it served as a classroom, a living room, and a bunkroom. About a dozen and a half bunks were stacked in rows at the far end.

Bastion stepped into the dark room. The only illumination came from the ambient light in the hallway, but he could see almost as well in low-light conditions as in daylight. He crossed the long space and wandered among the bunks. Most of them held sleeping boys. A few contained young adults — or older teens, at least.

More children.

Why were they there? Why did these people keep some children close but banished others to this huge gym wing?

The Omnis did things like that, use children in any way they wished — as servants, test subjects, sex slaves.

These kids had a vibe of abuse. Definitely a tick in the pro-Omni column.

The rest of the rooms in that wing were standard for a gym—a pool room, locker rooms, and a weight room. No one was in any of them.

He returned to the main house and went through the rest of the rooms, finding nothing of great interest. He didn't want these people to be Omni supporters, but the mental balance sheet he'd been tallying was leaning heavily in that direction.

And what did that mean for his Selena?

If she was in deep with Omnis, he was going to have to crack her brainwashing.

Or terminate her.

3

A knock sounded on Selena's door. She didn't get up. The door wasn't locked. If she were needed badly enough, whoever was knocking would come in. She still had ten minutes before needing to dress, so she lingered in bed, trying to hold on to the fading threads of last night's dream.

"Sel?" Ace asked.

"Yeah."

She came into her room. "What are you doing? You missed our workout."

Selena stared at the ceiling, remembering the stars that had been there in her dream. "You ever have a dream that felt so real that you actually miss the world it showed you?"

"No." Ace plopped down in one of Selena's armchairs near the window.

"I did last night." Selena looked at Ace then back at

the ceiling. "I don't want to move. I don't want to wake up and lose it."

"What was it about?"

Selena shook her head. "I don't really remember. There was a man. God, he was gorgeous. Big. Hairy. Obnoxious. Not at all my type."

Ace laughed. "But he was gorgeous."

Selena blinked. "There was something about him. Something addictive. In the dream, I think I loved him. You know, the real kind of love. Not a wannabe kind. Not the fill-in-the-gaps-for-a-while kind. We watched stars from my bed. But I think it almost turned into a nightmare. It's all fuzzy now."

"Shit, Sel. That sounds like a helluva trip."

Selena sighed. "Yeah. I guess it was." She sat up. "I just wish it had been real."

Ace bent her knees and braced her heels on the chair as she folded her arms around her shins. "I've had dreams I didn't want to let go of."

"Yeah?"

"Val's one. And you and the team. Having a place I belong. A family."

"We are your family." Selena gave her a sad smile. "I guess I have to let it go." Truthfully, it was already gone, burned by the daylight. "Sorry about missing our work-out. I'm going take a shower. I'll be down in a few."

Ace got up. "See you downstairs. Glad you're okay."

Selena turned the shower on after Ace left. She grabbed a thick towel, set it near the shower, then turned the light off and got undressed. Another wave of yearning ripped through her. She missed him…a guy who was a figment of her imagination. How could she long for something she'd never had, for someone who didn't exist?

The answer hit her as she stepped into the water.

Yearning was safer than having.

BASTION WAITED for Selena in the hallway, frustrated that his sense of decency consigned her to showering alone. After a few minutes, she came out of her room, dressed for the day, outwardly composed but inwardly still rioting—because of him. Her energy ripped through him like a rush of white water.

She was beautiful—the perfect image of a female and a warrior. Eyes that were a rich green. Lips that were soft when she smiled and hard when she threatened. Her neck was long and slim, her shoulders broad and straight. Her breasts were generous enough that a man could spend hours loving them. Her ribs and waist were slim, her hips nicely rounded. And those long legs of hers could make a man lose track of time.

This morning, her thick brown hair was drawn back in a severe ponytail. But her eyes showed how he'd affected her—the same as she'd affected him. He wondered if she'd seen the Matchmaker herself. The fiend had made an appearance to both Liege and Summer. Was it that way with all the couples he paired?

She leaned against the wall outside her room.

Bastion observed energy like a physical experience—he could see or hear or smell it. Sometimes all three. Right now, Selena's energy sounded like a rock band's jangled warmup session, each instrument being tuned independently of the others around it.

She seemed lost. She stared across the space at him. He kept himself hidden from her, but it was as if some part of her knew he was there.

He closed the distance between them, bracing his hands on either side of her head as he let his energy surround hers, encapsulating it, calming her. He bent his face toward hers, letting his mouth hover over hers as he whispered, "I feel as you do—shocked at the chemistry we share. Know that you are not alone. Whether I'm near or far, you have only to summon me, and I will be there for you. Go in peace today. I will visit you again tonight, if you'll allow it."

Pulling away from her was physically and emotionally difficult, but it had to be done. He had his mission and she had hers. She sighed as he put space between them.

He didn't yet know if they were working toward the same end in their dealings with the Omnis. Though all of his instincts said they had to be, he needed to find proof for Liege and for himself.

Could he do what had to be done if he discovered they were enemies? Did the Matchmaker ever make a mistake? Did he ever unite enemies?

Bastion watched Selena move down the hallway, briefly considering revealing he was the Matchmaker's latest project to Liege. He wasn't sure how his team lead would take the news. Perhaps Liege would take him off this assignment.

That would kill him. He'd only just found his mate; he couldn't leave her now.

The pull to follow Selena was irresistible. Almost a compulsion. Was this how Liege had felt? Was it a compulsion, or just perfect chemistry? Biology he could trust. Psychic manipulation he could not.

So which was at play here?

Bastion followed her downstairs and into the long dining room. He kept his presence hidden by jamming cameras and setting an illusion that caused anyone who might look at him to see the space he was in as it was before he was there.

A buffet was set up on one side of the room. The table accommodated at least two dozen, more if he counted the extra chairs pressed against the wall. There must be more leaves for it stored somewhere. When there was a break in the chow line, he filled a plate, then sat in one of the extra chairs in the far corner of the room, a spot that gave him the perfect opportunity to watch the house's residents interact with each other and Selena.

The mansion was as crowded as an apartment complex. Dozens of children and fighters and their families all lived in this big home. Were they a cult? Could Selena leave if she wanted? The Omnis were a cult. Of necessity, they forced cult-like behaviors on those who opposed them: secrecy, extreme loyalty, devotion to the cause. It was a sad statement when you became a mirror of the very thing you fought, but Bastion knew of no other way for the resistance to be effective. Perhaps it was the same for his Legion as it was for this team of fighters.

Or perhaps these fighters *were* Omnis—that was still an unanswered question.

Selena kept to herself. Though she laughed and joked in response to others, she never started conversations. Was that her norm? Why was she with—but not of—these people?

The other fighters and their families came and went for breakfast. Some filled plates and left with them; some only came for coffee; others sat and ate at the table. Two men appeared responsible for kitchen duty. They ate with the others, but checked the dishes on the buffet often, refilling them when needed. Everyone carried their own dirty dishes to the kitchen.

The meal was chaos, but seemed to work for the residents.

After a little while, Selena took her dishes to the kitchen. Bastion left his on the table and waited for her in the hallway. She walked down the long hallway to the southern staircase and went up to her room.

When she came out of her room, she went across the main stairs at the bridge between the two main bedroom wings of the mansion and took the north stairs down. She went into the den, then into a big closet and through a hidden door that Bastion hadn't noticed before.

Interesting. What was downstairs? He kept himself

hidden as he followed her down several flights of stairs. They came out in a large subterranean conference room.

The place was huge.

Some of her peers were already seated at the conference table. No spouses or children were with them—or so he thought until a couple came in: a tall blond male with a broken leg and a petite female with pink hair and a broken arm. The man pulled a chair out for the woman, who rolled her eyes and shook her head at the gesture, even as she sank into the seat he offered.

A hallway was at the opposite end of the room. Bastion strolled in that direction. More rooms opened off that short hallway: a bathroom, kitchen, and bunkroom. A set of steel doors opened to somewhere. He made a mental note to come back and explore the area more. At the end of the hall was an ops room with a bank of computers. A weapons room was just beyond it. He meandered around the glass cases in there, impressed with the range of weaponry the team kept. He reached out to Acier, wanting his friend to see he was seeing. *Look at this, Acier. They are well prepared.*

Fuck. Howdy. Not a custom blade in the place, Acier responded. *Make nice with these guys, Bastion. I could use new clients.*

An elevator landed and the doors opened. Two men walked out of it, both blond, one with eyes like arctic ice, the other with blue eyes and a military flattop haircut.

Bastion smiled, recognizing the team's leaders by their posture and attitude. The one with the cold eyes had been with the mutant woman on Bastion's tour last night. Bastion followed them into the main room and stood off to one side so he could observe Selena.

Silence settled in the room. Bastion was looking forward to the nuggets of info the top guys were going to drop—something that would let him know which side of the Omni war they were on. To his surprise, the news of the day was about one of the guy's wedding plans.

Merde. Were these hard-nosed men wedding planners and not fighters?

The man with the shaggy, dark hair was apparently the groom-to-be. They were talking about a cabin way out on the edge of the property where he was going to propose to his girl.

Bastion knew the girl—he'd seen them together several times while he was monitoring the grounds. She was the team's mechanic.

This couldn't be an Omni wedding. Top Omni echelon never married lowly mechanics—they always chose brides from Omni bloodlines, usually from society's glitterati.

Selena looked bored with the discussion. He grinned at her. She looked his way. Was she remembering pieces of their night together? Would she hate him when he returned those memories to her?

The team was assigned posts. Most of the guys were to head out to the cabin to finish up its renovations. Others had guard duty in various areas of the property. Selena had been tasked with some paperwork. Bastion could see she chafed at the assignment, but she didn't complain.

"One more piece of business," the flattop team lead told the room as his gaze settled on the pink-haired chick. "The FBI finished processing your grandfather's body."

"I know," the girl said. "Greer, Val, and I are going to Denver to pick him up today. We bought a plot for him in Cheyenne."

"Well, you'll have to put a hold on those plans. They've misplaced Santo's body."

Bastion's wandering mind screeched back to the present. Santo? This team of regulars knew about Santo? And Pink Hair was Santo's granddaughter?

That was definitely a mark in the column of "maybe Omni."

Her blond boyfriend scoffed at the news. "How does the FBI misplace a body?"

The team lead shook his head. "Dunno, Val. Lobo said he'd retraced all the paperwork at each hand-off. Everything was in order, until they reached Denver and were one coffin short. He's looking into it for us."

The pink-haired fighter gave her team lead one of the coldest glares Bastion had ever seen. She got up and left the room, rushing up the stairwell that let out in the den.

Val left as well, using the opposite exit with the hidden elevator. His leg was in a cast, and the several flights of stairs weren't manageable. Bastion followed him into the elevator car, wondering how he'd injured himself. Not having Liege's ability to read minds, Bastion had to ponder the energy surrounding the man's leg. It seemed it had happened in a fight recently. Definitely a fight rather than an accident. His girl was injured as well, but hers had happened in a different fight.

Evidently, this crew wasn't full-time wedding planners, unless planning weddings was a lot more dangerous than Bastion knew.

They caught up to the girl on the long patio that stretched the back of the house. The December air was freezing, but she didn't appear to feel it.

"Ace..." Val began—and stopped, apparently not knowing what to say.

"They didn't lose Santo," she said, turning angry eyes on him. "They never shipped him out. They must have found something in their autopsy."

"It's possible. Lobo was always making sure the bodies we racked up in our fights were sent to the FBI. I think they were looking for something—possibly human modifications."

Ace stopped and faced Val. "Do you think he was modified?"

Bastion nodded, then remembered he was invisible to these two and wasn't part of the convo. He knew for a fact that Santo had been one of the first regulars modified. His mods didn't take like later generations of the mutations. His did not reverse his age. Nor did they help him with rapid wound healing. But they did give him certain physiological and neurological enhancements—extreme memory skills, the ability to sense and manipulate energies, heightened instincts, increased strength, agility, and endless stamina.

Santo was single-handedly responsible for the Legion's survival in the training camps. He was who originally reached out to Liege and taught him about his new enhancements. It was because of Santo that the Legion existed.

This little fighter, a regular, thought she'd killed Santo? Bastion chuckled at her hubris.

Liege, Bastion said, opening a mental channel with his team lead, *Santo's in the wind.*

He is, but how did you know? Liege asked.

One of the fighters here is his granddaughter. She thinks she killed him.

Why would she fight him? Her own grandfather?

I'll see what I can learn.

He's not dead, Liege said. *I still feel his energy. There are reports that he's been seen in South America again.*

More training camps? Bastion asked.

Maybe. When I have solid intel, I'll be sending Merc down to check it out.

You think Santo picked a fight with his granddaughter so he could make an exit?

Yeah, Liege said, *that's more like it. Is she one of Owen Tremaine's fighters?*

She is.

Maybe Santo was letting her end their relationship—on her terms. Keep me posted.

Also, this team has a contact in the FBI who's been working with them. Seems he may know about the human modifications.

Find out who he is. We'll reach out to him.

He goes by the name Lobo. I'll get more info on him.

Bastion left the couple and went back to the hidden bunker area, where Selena was working alone. Stacks of documents sat on the conference table. She had set up two scanners—a tabletop one for regular-sized docs and a floor model for oversized ones.

What was she scanning?

Bastion examined a couple of the docs she'd completed. They were in a mix of languages, varying sizes, ages, and types of paper. The ones he could read talked about Omni issues: origin stories, histories, inventories, membership rosters, inventions, correspondence between members.

The oldest were in Latin, written by hand on parchment paper. Small, brilliantly colored letters and decorations made the page seem cheery, until he realized the illustrations were about people being murdered.

Liege, Bastion said via their mental link.

Go.

Did you realize the Omnis are an ancient organization?

Santo mentioned something about that, Liege said, *but he never elaborated. I always thought they called themselves Omnis because of their extensive association with international crime orgs. How did you learn this?*

The team here has an archive of documents, some dating back hundreds of years.

Good. I expect a complete analysis.

I can read French and English, even old French and English, but not Latin or many of the other languages represented in these docs.

Do what you can. Bring back a summary—and the digital archive.

Copy that.

One of the guys who'd been at the morning meeting came back into the conference hall with a stack of books.

"What are you doing, Rocco?" Selena asked him. "Max let you off love shack duty?"

Rocco chuckled. "I took a pass. There's too much here that still needs to be translated. Might as well jump on it while things are quiet."

The documents were in German, French, English, Spanish, Arabic, Portuguese, Latin, and other languages. The books he'd brought down were English translation dictionaries. Was this guy a polyglot? Yet another useful connection for the Legion...and for the Omnis.

Bastion stood behind the man's chair and read over his shoulder as he worked. His progress was slow with some docs and fast with others, probably because he was more fluent with some of the languages than others.

Selena and her teammate had a ton of work to do before the archive would be ready for Bastion to snag. There was nothing in these papers that indicated her team's stance on the Omnis; it was historical info—interesting, but not as pressing as examining the rest of the house.

Hiding his movements from any observers or recording devices, he opened one of the big steel doors in the bunker's hallway and stepped out onto a raised loading dock. He took the steps down and walked into the wide, cavelike tunnel. It ran a long way before opening out into a much larger cave with a high ceiling. Some motorcycles and extra cars were parked in that portion of the hidden access tunnel. Leaving the big cave, he saw a narrow stream that trickled past the front of it. Cottonwoods, willows, cedars, and some scrub pines obscured the entrance while still allowing vehicles access via a narrow dirt road that branched off from the track encircling the house and grounds. This bunker entrance was hard to see unless you were nearly upon it — Bastion had missed it in his surveillance.

He went back into the bunker tunnel and slipped inside, returning to the ops room and the armory beyond it, where he summoned the elevator. It only went to one floor. Which floor would that be? The basement, the main floor, or the second floor?

Bastion stepped out of the elevator into a bedroom — the one in the southern bedroom wing that had the energy of a bus station. That mystery was explained, at least — it was a frequently used corridor.

It was interesting to know the bunker could be accessed by three hidden entrances. The bunkroom down there would be a good place to stash the civilians if the Legion's enemy, Brett Flynn, ever brought the fight here. His mutant ghouls could break into this sprawling mansion with no trouble — there were windows everywhere, and dozens of French doors that opened onto the back patio. That hidden bunkroom was far more secure than the house itself.

Either the people here were sitting ducks, or they were safe from attack because they were in cahoots with the new breed of Omnis. Which was it? They weren't ignorant of mutants. They had one living in the house, and others had recently visited.

Bastion pondered that conundrum as he observed the household during the rest of the day. By suppertime, he was no closer to an answer.

4

Supper at the Red Team headquarters was a plated meal, more formal than breakfast or lunch. The mob of children was fed first. Bastion noticed that there were two older boys who seemed to be leaders of the wild bunch. Bastion learned their names from the group. Lion was a broad-shouldered blond with a lanky build and wavy hair, and Hawk was tall and dark-haired with haunted blue eyes. A troubled kid, Hawk could laugh at a joke one of the kids cracked and still look like he was drowning.

Something about those two reminded Bastion of himself and his brother. His brother had had the same dark spirit as Hawk and followed Bastion everywhere, even into the Army.

Only one female kid was among the group. An adolescent, she had the same bio signature as the flattop team lead who'd been at the morning meeting in the bunker. Casey was her name.

The kids were given plenty of food and a long hour for the meal. The girl's mom came by and visited with the group. She was pregnant. Bastion stared at her, feeling the energy of the baby intertwined with her own, a connection so raw that it robbed him of words. The woman was excited for her new child. Same with another pregnant lady who sat with the youngest in the group. Then the mutant female came in. One of her sons was friends with the youngest boy. Her older son was across the table, more connected to the wild boys than his brother.

Despite the odd mix of social and familial dynamics, Bastion could tell that there was a lot of love for these kids. Though some of them lived out in the gym, they weren't lesser members of the group.

The kids looked up to both Hawk and Lion. And the teenage female clearly had a crush on Lion, which didn't seem to be reciprocated, for he teased her like a sibling.

Tomorrow, Bastion would follow the boys to see how they spent their days. Maybe he could get a couple of them to talk about where they came from and how they'd ended up with this group.

When the meal was finished, the kids cleared the table. One of the cooks reset it with fresh linens and plates for the next round of diners. Some of the adults disappeared with the kids, apparently to get them settled before the grownups ate. Others gathered in the living room to have a drink. One of the ops guys was opening beers and setting them on the bar top. Bastion took one then moved off to the side so he could see everyone and watch their interactions.

The living room was large—big enough for two suites of furniture—but everyone crowded into the area between the dining room and the bar, some females sitting on their male's laps, men perched on arms of the wide armchairs beside their women, others standing by the bar. The couples were openly affectionate. This was nothing like the cold and structured Omni gatherings Bastion had observed, where everyone was trying to get an angle on everyone else.

No. This was like family.

Selena joined the group. Her beautiful brown hair was loose about her shoulders. Dark lashes framed sultry green eyes that perfectly complemented her dusky skin tone. Her height let her move with an effortless grace.

She grabbed a beer, then turned to face the room. She was a single female in a sea of bonded couples. A square peg on a deck of round holes. Her otherness sliced into him.

You are not alone. I am with you. You are mine and I am yours. Bastion knew his words registered in her mind, but not as something that came from him. No, they landed like something her imagination had conjured up to keep her from shattering. She smiled a little sadly as she stared at her beer.

"What's on your mind, Sel?" Val, the big blond, asked.

"Nothing. Just hungry, I guess."

I am hungry for you, Bastion whispered into her mind.

Still, she thought this was more of her imagination. Soon, she would know the truth.

"The beer warm?" Greer asked.

"No. Why?"

"You're frowning at it."

"Huh."

Bastion grinned. He had the irresistible need to freeze everyone so he could go over and kiss her. After all, when a mutant found his mate, it was stupid to waste even a minute of time they could have together.

Before he could act on his impulse, the cooks called everyone in to supper, sparing him a continued battle with himself.

Bastion stayed in the living room as everyone ate. He would eat later, when the house was asleep. After supper, the household continued with their normal routine. Some helped with cleanup; some went off in their own directions; those with children—or who were responsible for the wild boys—went to take care of them.

When Selena went down the hallway, Bastion followed her. He thought she was heading up to her room, but she went into the billiards room. Others from the group were already in there.

Dark paneling on the walls made the space look like a masculine clubroom. A pool table took up the front section. A massive antique bar on one wall was a focal point. Across from it was a large sitting area with two couches and several armchairs. Beyond that were a couple of gaming tables.

Selena picked up a cue stick and chalked the tip. Ace, the pink-haired female, smiled competitively as she took up another stick. The hulking blond fighter Bastion had seen with Ace in the bunker room stayed with her, and though he was entirely focused on Ace, Bastion sensed a strange energy in Selena whenever the giant was near.

That energy made him anxious. Something had transpired between them. Was that what had caused her to be so distrustful of intimacy with men? Had the blond hurt her? Selena and the petite female seemed at ease with each other. There was no jealousy or animosity between them. Maybe Bastion was just reading the energy wrong, though he didn't usually—he'd learned long ago to trust his instincts.

He watched as the girls laughed through the game, throwing friendly insults at each other. A couple of the other guys on the team came up to watch the game and play the winner.

Bastion wandered around the room, listening to conversations. Interestingly, no one talked about the upcoming wedding. Was it a secret? The groom-to-be didn't look particularly happy as he sat at the bar, frowning at the women sitting near his female.

Such weird dynamics. Now that Bastion knew a little more about these humans and the energy they emitted, he understood even less about them.

He went to stand in the corner beside the card table. The bosses were seated at the table, along with one of the ops guys and his female, and two other guys from the team. Bastion tried Liege's trick of slipping into each person's mind. He couldn't get a clear reading, other than the feel of their energy. They were all relaxed with each other. It was definitely a table full of friends.

There was another way to achieve his objective — urge them to talk about the Omnis. Bastion pushed that compulsion to the group, then followed up with a question: *What is most disconcerting to you about the Omnis?*

The cold-eyed blond opened the convo. "How they distort reality."

The flattop blond frowned. "What?"

"The Omnis," the first man said. "What I hate most about them is how they lie, cheat, and manipulate without regard to the lives they ruin."

Oh. Bastion liked that answer.

"I hate how they abuse women," the flattop guy said.

"They've invented a rich mythology that supports their every crime," the only woman at the table said.

Bastion was so involved in the revelations they made that he didn't see Selena until she was standing next to the table. She looked pissed.

"What are you doing?" she asked the group.

"Talking about what bugs us most about the Omnis," one of the guys at the table said.

"Don't. Just shut up. Don't say another word."

Well, *merde*. She was onto him.

"Sel, what's up?" the flattop guy asked.

"He wants you to talk about the Omnis," Selena said.

Blond brows rose over cold blue eyes. "Who?"

Selena opened her mouth and shot a glance around the table, then shut it. She shook her head; she didn't say because she couldn't remember. Bastion had stolen that from her.

"Never mind. I just… I don't know. I don't think we should talk about it here."

"No one's here but those who already know about the Omnis and all we've been through fighting them," the top boss said.

"Right. So why are you talking about them?" Selena asked. Her question cut through Bastion's compulsion. Irritated, she walked over to the bar and stood there, watching the group rationalize what had just happened.

"She's right," one of the guys said. "Why were we talking about them? It's not like it's news to any of us."

"Blade —" the flattop started, but Bastion didn't hear him finish it. Instead, he went over to stand in front of Selena, still keeping himself hidden from humans and tech alike. *I needed to know. Your instincts are phenomenal.*

Selena's anger wrapped around him, needling his sense of honor. He'd done what he had to do, what he was made to do.

"Sel — you breaking this rack or what?" Val asked.

Selena jumped. "Yeah. I'm coming."

Bastion was tired of this charade. He wanted Selena to himself, in her room. He followed her to the pool table. She took the shot, and he sent the solids down various pockets, leaving the eightball and the striped ones on the table.

Val looked dumbfounded.

Selena studied the table, then called her pocket and sent the eightball right into it. The game was won in less than two minutes.

"Shit. I've never seen that before," the blond said. "We need a plaque to commemorate that." He laughed and gave her a high five.

"Look, guys, I'm tired," Selena said. "Gotta call it quits."

The blond shook his head. "Nooo, you can't play like that then bail. Let's go two outta three."

She smiled at Val. Bastion's hackles went straight up. "I'm good for a rematch—tomorrow."

Bastion followed Selena up to her room. She was tired, but not exhausted. Why was she running off to be alone?

And then it hit him—she wanted to go to sleep so that she could see him again. Dumbfounded, he stood in the hallway and waited until her light went out, then waited some more. She was fighting sleep, wanting to be awake when he joined her, wanting to see if he was real.

SELENA STARED up at the ceiling. She'd tried all day to hold on to last night's dream, but the details of it had evaporated before she woke, leaving only a vague yearning. For what? Or whom? And what had she meant a few minutes ago, when she snapped at her bosses for talking about the Omnis? There was no one listening in on their convos; Max and Greer regularly swept the house for bugs.

She was confused. She lived by her instincts—they'd kept her alive to this point in her life—but right now she felt disjointed, filled with equal parts dread and excitement. Both emotions were discordant with the reality of her life.

She shut her eyes, willing herself to sleep, hoping last night's dream made a repeat visit.

IF BASTION WERE A SMARTER MAN, he'd stay away, let Selena struggle to find sleep and never see her again. He shoved his hands in his pockets, regretting being weak, but he was hooked on the Matchmaker's selection. He sent Selena into a light trance, her eyes closed. He didn't want her to see him come into her room. Leaning against the wall parallel with the bed, he cast an illusion across her ceiling. This one was of a nightscape over the Grand Canyon, with stars and clouds and a distant moon lighting the canyon rim.

Selena, open your eyes.

She did and gasped, then jackknifed into a sitting position, looking around for him. He smiled at her as he remained leaning against the wall.

"You're here." Throwing the covers off, she stomped over to him and poked him with her fingertips. They bounced off his hard chest. "You're real."

She sent a judgmental glance over his outfit. Tonight, he wore a long-sleeved wool and linen blend tunic beneath a moss-green over-tunic. His trousers were made from earth-toned suede, soft and flexible. He was a big buy and had had to hire a costumer to custom-tailor his clothes. He had several pairs of suede and leather pants, but these were his favorite. They were crisscrossed with stitched scars from old fights with ghouls. He liked that the suede was quieter than leather.

He never knew when he was going to have to engage Flynn's ghouls, so he always wore his sai weapons. And because those needed a belt to hold them, layers of long woolen and leather tunics worked better than parkas and jackets. Besides the two sai crossed at his back, and the third he wore in front, he also had a long Bowie knife. Acier had made all of his weapons. They fit Bastion's grip perfectly and were like extensions of himself.

The heavy suede pants he wore were another tactical choice that put a protective layer between him and the razor-sharp ghoul nails. His tall boots were military-grade black leather and nylon that gave him the flexibility he needed in a fight situation.

He looked like a Viking re-enactor, but the clothes worked for him. He supposed he should have cast an illusion over himself so that he appeared in regular civilian clothes. He just hadn't wanted to hide from her.

This was what he was, and she should know the real him.

"How'd you get in here?" she asked.

"This is just a dream."

"No. I'm not sleeping. I barely went to bed." She looked at the clock, but he compelled her to see it as if several hours had passed instead of the mere minutes since she came into her room. "Oh. Maybe I am."

"You are."

Bastion straightened and reached over to touch the tips of his fingers to the slim column of her neck. He leaned in, close enough to feel the heat of her lips near his before she pulled away.

"Why did you come back?" she asked.

"I couldn't stay away."

"But why here—why come to me?"

"Because I'm your lover. Your only lover, for the rest of your life—and mine."

Selena scoffed. "Yeah. No thanks. Pick another victim."

"I cannot. We are fated."

"You are so full of shit."

He nodded. "I am, but on this, I'm not lying."

Her eyes narrowed, putting him on notice. "For real, why me?"

"I crave you."

"You don't know me at all if you think that baloney works for me."

"I want to breathe the air you breathe. I want to see

the world the way you see it. I want to be the one to make you laugh."

"And curse."

"*Mais, oui.* All of it."

"If you want me, then come to the front door and knock, like a civilized guy."

"What makes you think I'm civilized?"

She sent a look over him, her gaze catching on his odd weapons. "What makes you think I want a barbarian?"

Bastion let loose a hearty laugh. "I will be glad when we can be together finally."

"Don't hold your breath. It was you in the game room tonight, getting the guys to talk, wasn't it?"

She'd put some air between their bodies. How he wanted to hold her against his heart, a hug for both of them to get them through the next few days. But he couldn't pressure her. And he couldn't even stay with her very long. She was already putting the pieces together.

"*Oui*, it was I."

"Why?"

"I needed to know if you're with the Omnis or against them."

"Why?"

"I was sent to find out." Bastion tilted his head as he filtered through the thoughts of her that were top of her mind. "You hate the Omnis."

"I do."

"But that doesn't mean they are your enemies."

"I want you to leave."

Bastion nodded. She locked her thoughts down, blocking him. She was strong, even though she didn't yet know what she was dealing with.

"Selena, you won't remember this dream either. It is the nature of dreams that we forget them." Bastion felt sad as he sent her back to sleep, stealing this memory as well. His compulsion had an instant effect on her. He caught her as she collapsed. Holding her against his body, he pressed his face against the soft skin of her neck, wondering if she'd ever forgo her dominance for his — in bed, anyway.

Getting her to yield would be a major event. Perhaps that was why he was so jealous of two of the men on her team that seemed to favor — she always softened around them.

"You won't remember me, but I won't forget you," he whispered, compelling those words, at least, to stay with her. *Sleep now.*

He settled her in her bed, covered her with her blankets, then stepped away until his back hit the wall. He hadn't lied when he'd said he craved her. He could spend the night in her room, watching her, waiting for another wakeful moment to visit with her.

He swallowed hard. No. He would not be reduced to stealing time from his fated mate. That fucking sucked.

Pivoting, he shielded himself as he left her room. He'd found the attics during his explorations earlier that day. There were two, one on each side of the bridge between the original wings of the house. One of the attics had an old mattress. The forgotten space would make the perfect temporary digs for him.

5

B rett paused at the temporary gate set up on what had been the White Kingdom Brotherhood's western headquarters as he compelled the gatekeeper to let him through. Thanks to his special skills, no one and no equipment saw him drive past the guard.

The biker gang who had called this compound their headquarters were long gone, thanks to the interference of the Red Team. Now the place was crawling with Feds.

The structures scattered around the surface acreage hadn't improved the property much. There were old farmhouses, barns, and some steel buildings of varying sizes. The ramshackle nature of the compound had hidden the valuable real estate in the silos below ground.

The bikers of the White Kingdom Brotherhood were valued allies in the Omnis' recent growth. The government raid on this property had sent most of them to ground.

Brett parked outside one of the larger steel buildings. Inside, he took the elevator down to the bottom of the structure. Only a small portion of the missile silo had been renovated. The genetic scientists of the Syadne Corp, the Omnis' research division, had been working here right up until the raid, an incursion driven by the Red Team, whose compound was just an hour's drive down the road.

The Omnis had planned to overhaul the entire Titan missile silo structure, but instead had lost it and some important data in the Feds' raid on the compound. And for whatever reason, the Omni powers-that-be had decided not to retaliate against the Red Team.

That was where he came in. The trick to success in life was always to find a need and fill it.

The Omnis needed the Red Team terminated; Brett was happy to oblige. And since the big dogs in Omni World Order had decided to let the furor die down over the two subterranean complexes recently confiscated by the FBI, Brett had the time he needed to find a way into the Red Team's hallowed headquarters.

Of course, Bastion had made things more difficult than they needed to be, with the site protection he put in place. The Legion was gifted with extraordinary powers of protection—the energetic dome Bastion put over the property kept Brett from physically entering the property.

Fortunately, there was always more than one way to skin a cat…he just had to find another way in.

Back above ground, Brett continued his exploration. He nudged aside the tattered Jewish flag that the bikers had used to wipe their boots before entering the clubhouse. The WKB had made no attempt to camouflage their hatred; that weakness had blinded them to the enemy they let infiltrate their nirvana. Brett didn't know the specifics, but someone had obviously broken the sanctity of the brotherhood from the inside out. This site had been a thriving Omni outpost for decades without issues, which meant even if the Feds had known about it, they couldn't have hit it without insider info.

For sure, the Red Team was going down.

The steel building of the clubhouse was now just a shed full of unused dinettes cluttered with empty bottles. The rest of the buildings on campus fared little better.

He walked around, kicking tumbleweed out of doorways. The scattered buildings looked as if they'd seen no maintenance since they were built—all except for one little farmhouse that sported a fresh coat of paint and fairly clean windows. There was a motorcycle workshop attached to it, full of tools that had been scattered around the floor and counters.

Brett continued moving around the grounds, checking out each building, looking for a human somewhere, anywhere. The whole campus was a ghost town, which was why the sound of two boys over by a Quonset hut was surprising.

The ancient steel building was on the very far edge

of the WKB compound, out of sight and hearing from the main entrance that was guarded by the FBI. Brett jogged over to see what they were up to. The boys were clearly civilians—they were too young to be agents and weren't dressed with agency identifiers. Folded moving boxes were stacked in bunches around the hut. The squeal of tape reels being pulled over closed boxes was loud.

The kids were boxing up the hut's contents—books, personal effects, papers, tools. The dorm looked to have been quickly evacuated, leaving much behind. But now the boys were there, taking what mattered.

Who were they? Keeping himself hidden from them, Brett moved about the long, two-room steel building. The clothes they packed were for children. The books were all primers and historical works, mostly concerning military studies. It was then that Brett realized what he had stumbled upon—a pocket of watchers. He grinned. They belonged to the Omnis. Groups of kids such as these had been used by the Omni World Order for centuries as spies and first-line defenders of OWO properties.

Brett took a closer look at the boys, wondering whose offspring they were. Watchers were almost always selected from top echelon families—they were the tithe that the top Omni families paid in exchange for the privileges granted to them by the Order. The Omnis used their sacrifice as a means of controlling their membership; they couldn't rat out the Omnis without also revealing their own complicity.

The boys looked to be in their early twenties or late teens. Both were tall and lanky, but they were the exact opposite in coloring. One was dark-haired, the other blond. Both had blue eyes.

Who was their Omni handler? He had to be powerful, if the boys were allowed to be on the WKB campus while it was infected with FBI rats.

Brett slipped into the blond's mind, availing himself of one of his super skills as a mutant human—his ability to read minds. It was troubling in there. Fear, worry, fierce loyalty. Interesting. That loyalty had nothing to do with the Omnis and everything to do with his collection of watchers, ragtag urchins though they were.

The second boy's mind was even darker. His energy was beautiful—a tall drink of anger, hatred, regret, and mourning. Brett lingered longer in the dark one's mind, sucking in the turmoil. He could use this one, grow him into his next host. The Legion had recently destroyed Brett's last host, leaving Brett full of hunger with no outlet.

The boys spoke little while they worked. When they were down to the last two boxes, the dark one looked around. Hawk was his name, Brett had discovered.

"Time to go," the blond one said. Lion. He called the watchers under his command his "pride." Hawk was his second-in-command.

Hawk's haunted eyes swung toward Lion. "We spent most of our lives here. I hated it every single day, but I feel odd leaving it."

Lion nodded as his gaze swept the room. "We're

leaving it for new and better times. New adventures. Nothing stays the same."

Brett followed them to the truck they'd stashed up the hill, on a Forest Service road. He didn't know where they were headed, but he climbed in the truck's crowded bed after its load had been secured. Where would a couple of former watchers hang out? Kids like these weren't equipped to join normal society. They needed to exist inside a structured framework, one that would support them—and use their special talents. If their being on the WKB compound while the Feds were here told Brett anything, it was that they'd burned their relationship with the Omnis and had been taken in by another group.

But who?

The Red Team, a group of fighters, wouldn't likely burden themselves with a bunch of abandoned boys. Had the state or the Feds taken them in?

Brett didn't have long to discover the answer. About an hour after they left the WKB compound, the kids turned off onto the Red Team property. Brett immediately felt the pain of his attempt to pass through Bastion's dome of protection. It hit all of his senses at once, making his body feel as if it were being crushed and burned at the same time. The boys hadn't fully left the road before the effects of the protection could be felt. Brett made them stop so he could hop out of the back and cross the street to the other side.

As soon as the aftershocks of the pain wore off, Brett laughed and danced around like a fool, knowing no one could see him. He'd found his way into the Red Team. The boy with the dark mind, Hawk, would be the perfect host.

Brett summoned a car that was heading into town. Taking the driver under his control, he ordered the man to take him to the WKB compound. Brett needed to fetch his car. The driver would never remember the ride out to the compound—he would awaken from his trance having lost two hours of time with no explanation at all.

BASTION WAS in the gym building when the boys' alarm went off the next morning. The room was still dark. Groans followed the wake-up call. Lion rolled out of his bunk and started slapping the boys' mattresses. Kids spilled from their bunks. The younger ones went to their trunks to dress. The older ones walked past Bastion on their way to the locker room.

The next few minutes passed in ordered chaos. Boys got dressed and made their bunks, then roughhoused unsupervised for a bit. Bastion followed the older boys to the locker room. Lion, the leader of the group, was shaving. Bastion leaned in to get a closer look at his reflection. There were tattoos beneath his brows. Reading backward in the mirror, Bastion made out three words in the elaborate script of his ink: "Fear the" on one brow, and "Lion" on the other.

What did that mean? Why would he ink his brows?

Bastion backed away and watched the older boys

shaving. Every one of them had those hollow eyes that young trauma survivors had, like their souls had been pried from their bodies, leaving behind the empty hulls. These males would be prime targets for the Omnis.

While the older boys were busy, Bastion went back into the gym. He compelled the younger boys to line up at the door in two rows, then ordered them to face him —all while keeping himself invisible and holding the boys in a trance.

"Who are you?" Bastion asked them.

"We're watchers," they answered—in unison, as if it were a practiced response.

"What do watchers watch?"

Several answers came at once. "King's gold."

"The woods."

"Whatever we're told to watch. People, sometimes."

Interesting. They were a group of baby spies. And what was that about King's gold? "Why are you here? What are you watching here?" Bastion continued.

"Nothing. We're not watching anything anymore."

"We used to be wild, but now we're caged."

Those answers took Bastion aback. The blond kid came into the gym, his fast stride slowing when he noticed the boys lined up and vacant-eyed. Bastion released them from the trance he'd imposed.

"What's going on?" the inked boy asked.

"Nothing, Lion. Why?" one of the older kids answered.

"Because you're all lined up and acting weird," Lion said.

"No we aren't," one of the boys said. "We're just waiting to go to breakfast."

Lion and Hawk exchanged looks. The boys finished dressing and made their beds. When Lion led them out of the gym, Bastion followed. Three more boys and the teenaged female were waiting for them in the living room. A young, heavy-set, dark-haired woman came into the room. There was an air of authority around her. She smiled at the boys with genuine affection, then ushered them into the dining room. Bastion soon discovered she was the kids' teacher. The cooks already had the buffet set up. One of the fighters came in and gave the teacher a hug.

The meal went much as the one yesterday morning went. The kids ate, cleared the table, then rushed off to play for a few minutes before classes started.

The energy in the room shifted from the kids' fast, unfocused, and explosive buzz to the more moderate, intense, and contained hum of the adults. Perhaps the fighters here were between battles, but they hadn't let their guards down.

Bastion lingered a little longer, waiting for Selena to come down. She did after almost everyone else had finished. She was sitting a few seats away from the last few people when the cold-eyed owner of the group walked in. Energy flashed from Selena to Owen, instantly raising Bastion's hackles. Who was this man to her? How dare he think to have two women, one of whom belonged to Bastion?

Bastion's eyes narrowed to slits as he mentally

squeezed Owen's skull. The bossman slammed his empty mug on the buffet table and pressed the heel of his hand against his temple.

"You okay, Owen?" Selena asked, frowning.

"Yeah. Weather must be changing. I need to go take something for this headache."

Bastion eased up on the pressure he'd imposed as Owen left the room and turned his attention back to Selena, who was entirely focused on her breakfast and showed no concern at all for her boss. What had he just seen pass from Selena to Owen if not interest? Maybe it was the same with Owen as it was with Val, the other blond giant. Maybe she had history with both men. Maybe whatever she'd felt hadn't been reciprocated. Maybe the yearning was still there.

Bastion squeezed his eyes shut, hoping that yearning was all she'd been feeling. He'd never in his life felt jealousy. Nor had he ever felt so violently possessive. What had the Matchmaker done to him?

Disgusted with his lack of control, Bastion forced himself to spend the day away from Selena. He drove his Jeep around the side of the house, following the track that the team took up to the love shack. The rough dirt road went deep into the hills behind the mansion. After a few miles, it became even rougher, passable only with off-road vehicles. Bastion got as close as he could, then parked and continued on foot. At the end of the trail was an old hunting cabin.

Judging from the debris scattered around, it looked like the cabin had been in sorry shape but was coming alive again. Max and Greer were working on the balusters for the railing out front. They'd selected various branches to make a rough, rustic look. Bastion went inside the cabin, where women were hanging linens on the windows and around the built-in bed. There was no electricity in the house, so the stove was an old-fashioned wood-burning cooktop. There was a fireplace that was the only source of heat in the one-room space.

None of the furnishings were what Bastion would have selected, but what fascinated him most was that the whole group was here participating on various aspects of the cabin's renovation.

Like a family.

It made him less hostile toward them — or less suspicious of them, anyway. No Omni of any ranking would put effort into something like this — they had servants for that. That thought should have been reassuring, but it wasn't.

He still couldn't explain why they were here.

Bastion went outside again and saw Max heading down a narrow forestry road on a motorcycle.

Bastion followed him, curious where he was headed and what else was hidden up here. It was close to a mile before he got to the point where Max stood overlooking a mountain ravine. It was a mild day for December in the Medicine Bow Mountains. But with the sun setting earlier than usual, a chill was creeping in. Bastion wondered what deep thoughts Max was contemplating as he stood at the edge of the bluff, staring into the ravine below. Bastion kept himself hidden as he watched the fighter. After a while, Max went back to the cabin.

Bastion wandered around the ridge for a bit, trying to understand why it was important to the fighter. All he saw was the rough terrain and the rugged hills of the mountains. He headed back to the cabin, but by the time he got there, everyone was gone. Tools were stowed. He took a last look at the cabin, wondering why it was important to the team.

He might never understand some things about these people.

AT LAST, the boy Brett had seen at the WKB compound was leaving the Red Team headquarters. Brett had positioned himself across the compound, waiting for the kid. He felt energy zing through him and sucked in a deep, delicious breath of it.

A different man was with the boy this time. He was the main housekeeper, though he also had the vibe of a fighter. Brett followed them into town. They parked in the grocery store. Brett entered the store behind them, keeping himself hidden. Finding a new host was never easy. He always needed to select someone who was capable of being in sync with him, usually someone with deep emotional wounds, someone in desperate straits, someone who was a beautiful wreck.

Like his Hawk.

Hawk's friend, Lion, didn't have a mind that was

easily penetrated. But Hawk's mind and his whole soul were screaming. Such delightful pain.

All the elements seemed to be in place for Brett to make Hawk his next host. Today, Brett would test how well he and Hawk could work together—after all, Brett wanted it to be a pleasant experience, since they would both benefit from their symbiosis. For a while, anyway, until Hawk's usefulness expired.

Brett took up residence in Hawk's mind as the boy helped the housekeeper shop. There were many times that Hawk wanted something but passed by it without putting it in the cart.

Why do you deny yourself? Brett asked via their new mental link.

I don't have my own money to spend.

That first communication was easy. Brett felt no resistance from Hawk. And the boy's answer was important; it revealed that Hawk wanted his own income—and his independence. Both were things Brett could offer him.

Those things and so much more. Hawk's joining with Brett would be his death, but he would enjoy his last weeks or months far more than was the norm for a nothing child like him.

Hawk went past a column of different beef jerkies. Brett felt the boy's rise of desire.

Get it. Take what you want. You deserve it, Brett urged him. Still, Hawk's innate self-control kept him from following Brett's compulsion. Brett stopped the cart before Hawk had left that section.

It's time you thought about yourself, Brett said, taking a gentler tack.

Hawk grabbed two big packs of jerky and dropped them in the cart. The housekeeper looked at the packs, then at Hawk, then moved on without commenting.

See? Nothing is forbidden to you. Whatever you want is yours.

Brett almost regretted taking Hawk as his host. Their time together would be exquisite, but sadly, he knew it would end. And when it did, Brett knew he'd never find another host who suited him quite as well.

6

Selena and Ace were in the gym working out on the machines. Selena had just finished a five-mile run. Usually, their morning exercise routine included some sparring time with bo staffs, but Ace's arm was still in a cast.

"Okay," Ace snapped. "What's up with you? You haven't heard a thing I've said."

Selena wiped her face with a towel. "Sorry. I don't know. I'm just not myself."

"Getting a cold?"

"No."

"More weird dreams?"

"Maybe. Nothing that I remember. But that's the thing. I keep feeling as if I've forgotten something that I should know."

"I hate that. Maybe you're just tired."

"Maybe. But I've been stuck in the bunker scanning docs for the last few days. That's not exactly tiring."

"Why not take some personal time? Go see your parents. We all just came through a rough time. Go home for Christmas."

"I guess I could, but I don't want to miss Max and Hope's wedding. Maybe after."

"Think about it, anyway."

BRETT FOLDED his hands behind his head as he lay on the bed in his hotel room. He could do his remote viewing from the comfort and safety of his own home, but it was a couple of hours south of Wolf Creek Bend, and he wanted to be nearby in case things shook loose with the Red Team.

He closed his eyes, listened to the sound of his breath, taking a few moments to relax himself from head to toe. When he no longer felt an awareness of himself, he was free to go where he wanted, traveling into the astral realm...or into the body of his new host.

He did the latter.

How delicious the boy was. Such pure energy he had. Full of hopes and fears and the boundless power of youth. Brett let his consciousness stretch into the skin of Hawk's lanky body. It felt like he was coming home for the first time in years.

Brett's previous hosts had been older, more used up by life. He'd chosen them because they were already inclined toward the proclivities that Brett favored—they had just never taken the plunge into the dark side. It had been a joy pushing them over the edge, seeing them indulge their criminal fantasies.

But Hawk—he was entirely different. Innocent. Wholesome. And so angry at life. With him, the journey would grow from scratch. It could take a long time to bend the boy to Brett's will, but Hawk would be a masterpiece when Brett was finished with him. He wished their end would never come, for when it did, it would mean the last moments of the boy's life—and their lives together. The boy would reach the pinnacle as Brett's creation, a last burst of brilliance before Hawk's life flamed out.

Brett actually shivered inside Hawk's skin, causing gooseflesh to rise on the boy's arms. How beautifully in sync they were.

Of course, it wouldn't be Brett's use of his host that would terminate him. No, it would be Brett's enemies. The Legion. They always caught up to Brett's hosts. The Legion would destroy Brett's perfect pet.

He realized he would actually mourn the loss of this one, when that time came. But that was a long while from now. A long, long time. He had the present to enjoy molding his new host. Best to focus on the now and not the terrible future.

Before the fun could actually begin, Brett needed to follow Hawk around, experience his days and nights, learn his joys and frustrations. He had to become Hawk.

Brett was actually curious to see what was happening inside the Red Team headquarters. This miserable group of mercenaries had begun cutting into

Brett's family's organization. Though they were only regulars, the Red Team had done significant damage. The Omnis had pulled back, electing to take a low profile while there was so much heat surrounding the Red Team's discoveries of two of the Omnis' subterranean fortresses.

That position was a weakness, to Brett's thinking. The Omnis should have struck hard and fast, throwing a shadow over the Red Team and all like them, sending a message to any other groups who thought they were equal to the task of bringing down the Omni World Order.

But Brett was not the one running the show. And as an Omni outcast, his opinion couldn't even be heard. No matter. There were always multiple ways to skin a cat.

Crushing the Red Team would be a significant blow to the Legion. With enough successful forays like this, Brett would earn a seat at the Omni table and would no longer be ignored. They'd have to acknowledge him. Scars and all.

Who are you?

A frisson slipped into Brett's astral body at Hawk's sweet voice. *Nobody,* Brett answered.

But why do I hear you?

Because I'm your spirit guide.

Have you always been there?

Not always. Your needs have changed, so your guides have changed. Don't worry. All will be well. I will help you. We'll have amazing adventures.

The boy left it at that, though Brett could tell his

mind was churning. Brett could simply conscript the boy's mind, but it would be ever so much more fun to feel the boy's observations of the new experiences Brett would bring to him.

∿

BASTION HAD an edgy feeling he couldn't ignore. After much preparation, Max had taken his girlfriend off to the love shack. They were alone in the remote back country. Bastion had set a protective dome of energy over the main campus of the team's ranch, but had neglected to shield the little cabin. An oversight he regretted now as the sensation buzzing in his chest became more alarming.

Another half-mile, and a strange chill crept over Bastion's skin, warning him. There was a predator in the woods, one not made by nature but by the Omnis. Evil and deadly, it was a direct threat to the couple.

Bastion parked his Jeep in a copse of evergreens. He tucked his sai into his belt, then stretched his arms wide and closed his eyes, letting his heightened senses fill in the blanks as he traced the energy he was feeling.

One of Flynn's ghouls was here. Bastion had been afraid of this—that the energy protection around the compound would attract Flynn and his monsters. Was this ghoul here because of him? Or had Flynn decided to hit the fighters he was surveilling?

The ghoul's energy led Bastion right to the little cabin. Warm light spilled out into the frosty night.

Standing a short distance from the front deck of the cabin, Bastion projected his energy into the tiny space, terrified of what he would find.

The table and chairs had been knocked over, and a ghoul was hunched over the stove, shoving food into its mouth. Bastion looked around the room. No one else was in the cabin. No blood spatter was on the walls.

He'd gotten there in time to stop this monster, but he didn't yet know if there were more in the woods, perhaps tracking the couple.

Sensing Bastion, the ghoul looked over its shoulder. It saw nothing, since he wasn't actually in the room. Bastion drew his energy back into himself as he stepped away from the house, slipping into the woods, drawing the monster out with him.

The beast made no attempt to move silently, as would most other large predators. No, this fiend stomped its way toward Bastion, breaking saplings and branches beneath its unnaturally large feet.

Bastion led it into a small clearing. Moonlight poured over the field like a spotlight. Bastion didn't need the illumination it provided; he could see in the dark almost as well as in the daylight. So could the ghoul coming toward him. It sniffed the air, scenting him, its doglike snout wrinkled in a snarl that bared powerful canines.

Bastion smiled and withdrew the two sai from the back of his belt. The monster had long, razor-like claws. Bastion couldn't take for granted that the coming fight would be an easy one. Another mutant like this one had delivered a payload of mutant enhancements to Summer, Liege's girlfriend, when it got close enough to slice her. No telling what other wicked deliveries Flynn had weaponized his pet monsters with.

Bastion sometimes played with the ghouls before destroying them. Perhaps it was cruel, but cruelty was a human concept, and neither he nor the ghoul was human. He did it to test the boundaries of the beast's lizard brain. Could it learn, adapt? Had it retained some of its human host's intellect? Was Flynn evolving his monsters as he made new generations of them?

Thought stopped and instinct kicked in as the ghoul prowled in a circle around him, looking for the best spot to attack. Bastion crouched, his sai held against his forearms. The beast lunged toward him, claws ready to rake Bastion, who blocked the thrust with his crossed sai then swept the ghoul's clawed hand away in a downward parry. He dug the curved edge of the sai along the inside of the beast's arm, slicing a trench in its flesh.

First blood was always a trigger. The monster got faster and more aggressive. Bastion moved ever quicker, hitting pressure points, advancing and retreating, before shoving the hooked handle of one of his sai into the ghoul's throat, ripping into it, releasing a rush of blood.

Ghouls ran on adrenaline for a few minutes after the deathblow, so Bastion knew the fight wasn't quite over. He kicked the ghoul backward. Caught off balance, it fell to the ground, gurgling and choking. Bastion flipped it to its stomach. He knelt on its back, and lifted its head, ready to slice its throat. A long moment passed where Bastion stared into the eye looking up at him. He could have sworn he saw emotion there. Peace, perhaps. Maybe gratitude.

Neither were emotions that he expected to see, given what was left of the ghoul's brain. Unfortunately, he didn't have time for further thought. He could hear the snowmobiles returning. He slashed the ghoul's throat and released his hold on its head.

Broadcasting his awareness into the woods around him, Bastion tested for the presence of more ghouls or other enemies. None were there.

Liege, aidez-moi.

Sometimes Bastion and the rest of the guys on the team spoke verbally via their telepathic link and sometimes they spoke in simple knowings. Words were often imprecise and took longer to communicate than pure thought. When time wasn't a luxury available to them, they simply shared their thoughts in their raw form. That was what he did now when he asked Liege to expand this search to a wider area and into town, looking for more ghouls or perhaps even Flynn himself.

The ghoul you killed was the only one around, Liege responded seconds later. Bring the body here.

I'm not leaving now—more could be on their way. Send Merc to fetch it.

Bastion remembered he'd hadn't covered the ghoul's tracks, nor had he cleaned the cabin. Too late. Max had stopped to take a look at the ghoul's tracks. Bastion quickly cast an illusion that covered the tracks, making them appear like a big cat's. He watched through the woods as Max frowned at the prints, then hurried over to his girlfriend, who was staring at the cabin's open door. Had they come back just a few minutes earlier, tonight's outcome would have been much worse.

Why just one ghoul? Bastion asked his team. One alone doesn't make sense.

Unless Flynn is spreading his flying monkeys out as far and wide as he can, Acier said, *having them check out possible targets. The Red Team isn't the only group fighting the Omnis.*

That answer didn't fit. *Perhaps,* Bastion countered, *but it becomes infinitely harder to control the beasts the more of them that are widely distributed.*

Maybe it was there because of you, Liege said. *Flynn's watching all of us closely.*

Or maybe it's there because of the other mutants who live with the team or have visited recently, Guerre suggested.

Find the scientists and get back here, Liege said. *Let's not bring more attention to this group than we already have.*

Oui, mon capitaine.

Bastion blocked his next few thoughts from Liege and the team. No one on his team was allowed to see his light. Not yet, not while she was still so new to him.

Selena.

He silently spoke her name, letting his tongue wrap around its decadent letters. She belonged to him, and he to her.

He'd said yes to Liege, but he'd meant no. There was no way he could leave here without her.

He made a slow circuit around the cabin, checking for shifts in energy, hints of other threats. He'd just settled in for a long, cold night when Merc showed up with a thermos of hot coffee and a foot-long sub with triple meat.

"*Merci*," Bastion said, setting both aside so he could help Merc pack up the dead mutant.

"Don't thank me," Merc said. "Thank Summer. She thought you might be hungry. I think she's getting used to living with meat eaters." He grinned at Bastion. "She put a shit-ton of it on your sub."

Bastion's breathing came to an abrupt, though brief, stop. Summer. Liege's woman, his light, his soul. She was proof that life mates were real. Liege had found his; it was possible the rest of them could find—and have— theirs without the Matchmaker's curse shredding their lives.

Merc sensed something was off with him. Bastion tried to hide the energy spike he'd just experienced, but his friend had felt it.

"Right, mate. What gives?" Merc asked.

"Nothing."

"Bullshit. You've been up here far longer than you should have been with nothing to show for it. What's keeping you here? And more to the point, what're you hiding from us?"

"Nothing."

"Then why keep yourself locked down? It's not like we haven't all noticed your retreat from us."

Bastion took the body bag from Merc and laid it out next to the monster. "Sometimes it's good to mind your own business."

"You are my business."

Bastion ignored him as he unzipped the heavy black bag.

"Who is she?" Merc asked.

Bastion stopped fidgeting and kept still. Slowly, he got to his feet. "What makes you think it's a woman?"

"It always is with you, isn't it?"

Anger tightened Bastion's body. He didn't want the woman who was the light of his life spoken about like that, so he didn't dignify Merc's probing with an answer. Perhaps that in itself was an answer.

"Are you going to help me with this or not?" Bastion asked as he bent down to grab the monster's ankles. They got the ghoul zipped up. For a moment, Bastion stared down at the body bag, remembering the look the ghoul had given him before Bastion had delivered the fatal wound. "This one seemed relieved that he was being killed."

"Not possible. They have no intellect and little cognitive function. The mutation process destroys the host."

Bastion looked at Merc. "What if it doesn't? What if more of the host remains than we think? What if the Omnis have changed their engineering?"

"Yet another reason to locate the scientists. We need them to help us unravel what the Omnis are up to." Merc hoisted the dead ghoul over his shoulder.

"I saw the Matchmaker," Bastion blurted out.

Merc dropped the body bag. "Bugger off. You did not."

"She's here. I can't…I can't leave her."

"Shit." Merc put his hands on his hips. "Tell Liege."

"*Non*. He will pull me out of here."

"He won't. He brought his light to the fort. I should think we all can, if we're lucky enough to find ours. Bring her back with you."

"She's one of the fighters here. She won't leave her team easily."

"Summer didn't leave her life easily either, but she's at the fort now, with Liege."

"I need time."

Merc gave Bastion a hard stare, then nodded. "Right, mate. I'll do what I can. You need help up here? Guerre doesn't think this team is loyal to the Omnis."

"Nor do I, but I cannot explain the presence of mutants here."

"Maybe the mutant female who lives here was changed against her will, like Summer?"

"Maybe, but then what explains the mutant male who's visited here whose DNA connects him to the team's leader? Or the couple whose DNA connects them to one of the civilian females? There are things I must explore further."

Merc nodded. "Not to mention your missus thinks you're a wanker."

Bastion sighed heavily. "I haven't actually met her yet. I mean, not for real. Not that I've let her remember."

"Well, to be honest, you aren't that memorable, mate." Merc grinned.

"*Ferme ta gueule*," Bastion growled.

Merc laughed as he hoisted the body bag over his shoulder again. "Seriously, mate, it's time to wrap this up. Show yourself to her." A question occurred to him. "Do you think she's seen the Matchmaker?"

"I don't know."

"Right, then. I'm outta here. Keep it together, bro."

7

The silence was as complete and deep as the shadows covering Bastion where he slept in the attic. He'd come back late the previous night after hanging out near the cabin, waiting for more ghouls to show up. None had. He'd extended the energetic protection he'd placed on the team's compound all the way up to and around the cabin.

Sooner or later, Flynn was going to realize he had one less ghoul on his team. That was only going to make him send more out here. Bastion's window of opportunity was closing fast. Time to break things open.

He'd hadn't gotten enough sleep. He folded his arms behind his head and gave himself the luxury of waking slowly. He liked it here at the Red Team's headquarters. He liked these people. There was no stink of desperation, no vicious whispers from anyone huddled in corners. It was clean and bright and busy. Children were happy. Women smiled often.

Everything here was normal—normal, that was, for fighters participating in a secret war. Most here were regulars. The couple that were mutants and the male mutant hadn't been back since Bastion had come inside the house. And the female mutant who was bonded to the leader here...Bastion wasn't certain she was still changed. The mutant energy signature she was emitting had weakened. It wasn't unheard of for human modifications to not take, or to exist only temporarily to perform a specific function. Perhaps that was her situation.

But Selena, she was all human. What did that mean for the two of them? Could they have a future as a mixed mutant and human couple? If they were destined to be together, as the Matchmaker's curse implied, then everything that was normal in her world would have to be left behind.

Was she up to that?

Was he prepared to rip her world apart?

Bastion sighed. He had no more answers now than when he'd gone to sleep hours earlier, not for himself, not for Liege. He'd been prowling around inside the house now for weeks. He knew so much more about these people, but it was still too little to draw firm conclusions.

Children lived here, with and without their parents. Women lived here, with their men. But one was alone, the one the Matchmaker intended for him. Selena. *She* wasn't why he was here, he reminded himself. He shouldn't let himself be preoccupied with her, but the pull to see her grew stronger every day.

He dressed, then went downstairs to her room.

After the first couple of nights he went to her, he'd kept himself from repeat visits. Until he knew more about the relationship between her team of fighters and the Omnis, he couldn't risk approaching her.

Flattening his hand on her door now, he tested the energy that lingered, curious who had come through this door since his last visit. Selena's was the only energy he felt. He tamped down the rage swelling inside him at the thought that she might not be alone. Sometimes, there was a man who went into her room—the housekeeper. Bastion knew she felt only friendship toward him. Besides, she was rarely in the room when he was.

Selena was alone, as she always was when Bastion visited. Did she feel him near her? Waiting to make her his was torture. He leaned his head against her door, thinking of the lore that surrounded the Matchmaker's curse: if Bastion denied the match, he would die, and if he accepted it, his mate would die.

Maybe neither of those outcomes were truly preordained. Maybe they were just two of an infinite number of possibilities.

Maybe, but fighting the match was killing him.

Things were going to change tonight. Bastion had to get Selena's team to recall the couple from the cabin in the woods.

It was time the team here knew he'd been watching them. He went down to the kitchen. A small vase of flowers sat on the table. He knew this room was being recorded on the security cameras—he was currently jamming them. The whole lower floor of the mansion was monitored, with all the French doors that were so easily breached. Upstairs, only the hallways and stairs were monitored.

He would get the ops guy, Greer, to review their security videos today. He was sharp; he would absolutely catch the fact that a flower had jumped out of the vase in the before-and-after feeds of the room. He'd see all the static from Bastion's interference and know something was up.

LATER THAT MORNING, Greer was in the ops room, sitting in front of a panel of computers. Bastion joined him there. Staying invisible to him, Bastion turned a chair around and straddled it. *Time to check the security cameras*, mon ami.

Greer didn't get the message. He had strong mental boundaries that were hard for Bastion to penetrate.

Bastion put all of his focus into sending Greer a sensation of anxiety, chasing that with a prompt to make sure the site was safe.

After a few minutes, Greer switched his screens to the files recorded by the security cameras around the estate. It was a slow and tedious process. One by one, he moved the files over to a separate storage device.

It took hours before he became concerned with all the static-filled images. And then he hit the video of

Bastion in the kitchen and saw the flower in the vase, the static, the flower on the table. He replayed that a few times.

Bastion could finally feel the alarm that Greer was feeling. Things began to move more quickly then.

Bastion spent hours whispering prompts to Greer. Find the patterns, Greer. They are there. You can see my movements across the campus just by tracing the order of the videos that become static-filled. Look for it. Your friends are in danger. I can't stay here with you, but you must summon the team.

Either his guard slowly lowered or Bastion's persistence paid off—Greer was at last feeling the urgency of the situation.

Someone called Greer up to supper.

Don't go. Finish this. Max and his girl are in danger.

Greer continued his work, now sorting the images by their time stamp. At last he'd found the pattern. He was going back through all the feeds, catching the last few minutes before the static appeared, then right after.

Greer shot to his feet, then started pacing around the ops room as he glared at the computer.

Once again, Bastion wished to have Liege's ability to read minds. He knew his messages had finally gotten through, and he knew that Greer had found the right pattern, but he still hadn't put the pieces together.

So much was at stake. Lives of everyone here. Bastion could have forced Greer's compliance, but he didn't—he needed Greer to make his own determination, come to his own understanding. Bastion followed

Greer up the stairs and through the house to the dining room, where supper was already underway. Greer's girlfriend had filled his plate. Bastion stood in the corner of the dining room and glared at Greer, pumping dark emotions his way, urging him to gather the team and head out to the cabin.

The team all saw something was off with Greer. They ribbed him for it. And then, at last, Greer took the action Bastion had wanted him to hours earlier: he locked the house down. Everyone headed downstairs to have a meeting about Greer's concerns—except Selena. She was left to guard the civilians.

Bastion slipped outside through the kitchen doors, which he locked again behind him. As he walked down the long patio that ran the length of the house, he saw Selena close the curtains in the dining room. He paused outside one of the sets of French doors in the big living room. She closed those curtains as well.

His heart beat fast. Tonight could be the night, the first time he let her see and remember him. He knew she could feel the pull between them—her energy was rich and heady, full of yearning. He let that energy loop between them, summoning her to come outside. A beckoning, not a compulsion.

She didn't. Time was passing quickly, and night had come. The couple at the cabin was in ever-deepening danger, as were all of the people around Selena.

Bastion could feel Selena's tension. He was standing outside the same pair of French doors that she was, only a curtain and some wood-framed glass panels separating them.

Selena moved the curtain and looked outside, then cracked the door open. Bastion sucked in a cold draft of air. He was about to reveal himself to her when the door was slammed shut and the curtain dropped back in place, leaving him alone in the cold night.

He put all of his attention into calling her to him. She was resisting him too well. He paced a stretch of the long patio, impatient with himself and with her. He let his consciousness separate from his body as he trolled the edge of the woods, looking for a branch. There were plenty to choose from. Instantly back in his body, he levitated the heavy branch from the far side of the lawn. It flew to his hand. Turning to the house, he threw the branch against the house near the window where Selena stood guard.

It worked. She pushed the curtain aside, sending an alarmed look around the portion of the patio that she could see.

Bastion stood frozen. He held his illusion in place, keeping his presence hidden from her. But when she put her hand against the glass, he hurried over and covered it with his, sending heat through the glass to warm her hand.

She blew on the pane, fogging it. He smiled. His woman felt him near — subconsciously, at least. He blew on the section above hers, near where her forehead was.

Message sent...and received.

And then Selena pulled back from him, returning to

the people in the room with her. He couldn't stay longer. Night had come an hour ago—it was prime hunting time for the ghouls. He fully expected Flynn to send more of his monsters out. At least Greer had finally roused the troops. Max and his girlfriend wouldn't be left exposed for long.

Bastion drove out to the rough Forest Service road that led to the cabin. He wanted to get into position before Max's team came to fetch them. He cast his energy out like a net, checking for enemies in the woods. None were out yet.

As he drove, he continued to monitor Selena's energy. He felt her excitement and courage. And then her energy rolled into that of the big blond. Jealousy spiked through Bastion. He forced the blond away from Selena, locked him behind a field of energy that kept him from moving or speaking or in any way interacting with his environment. Bastion held him in that frozen state until he felt Selena move away from him.

He reached the road that led behind the cabin and parked off to one side, hidden in a stand of cedars, covering his tracks with a mental illusion. He crossed the narrow road and walked into the woods. Max was out here with his woman. He was closer to them than to the cabin, near enough that he could shield them should a ghoul show up. The read he got off the woods indicated no monsters were yet prowling. Hopefully, Selena's team could get the couple to return to the main house. It was easier to defend his woman and her people if he weren't spread across such a large physical area.

Time ticked past, slowly, steadily, and then Selena was there, walking toward where he hid in the woods.

Come, Selena. Come to me, he urged.

She looked straight at him. An expression of ease came over her face. She might not be hearing his exact words just yet, but he knew she was sensing what he was saying.

Come. I will shield you from all of them.

And then the War Bringer stopped her. Anger flooded Bastion's body as he watched them discussing the footprints. Of course, Bastion hadn't hidden them from Selena, but Kelan only saw them in their illusory state—as deer prints.

My tracks. That's all, Bastion said to her, speaking directly into her mind so none of the others heard him. When Kelan touched her arm to pull her away from the woods and from Bastion, Bastion sent a wave of pain to the War Bringer, as he had all night when any of the guys had gotten too close to her. Unfortunately, the pain hit her and not the man, like she'd intercepted it to spare him.

That shook Bastion up. He'd was an expert in dealing out pain. He never sent it to the wrong recipient, so what was going on? Had his jealousy made him sloppy? Or was his woman strong enough to intercept an energy signal meant for another?

Or was this the Matchmaker's doing?

Bastion had no answers, so he just compelled the two of them to step apart as he withdrew the pressure he'd sent their way.

Dieu, he'd hurt Selena.

He'd never seen a regular take an energetic hit for another regular. If that was what had happened, her senses must be more developed than usual.

Selena and her people loaded on to the snowmobiles and started back for the cabin. She looked back and saw him step out of the woods. She told herself she had to be mistaken about what she was seeing. Her thought came through so clearly. He rarely could hear human thoughts, unless they were broadcast clearly, as hers had been. She followed that thought up with the belief that what she'd seen had been a bull elk not a person.

Think that if you wish, he said, pleased they seemed to be mentally communicating with such ease.

I don't know what to think, she said.

At last, they were tuned to the same energetic channel and could communicate with ease. That realization filled him with joy.

I understand. You will too, soon, he said. *Stay at the cabin.*

No. In her thoughts, she referred to him as a being, not a man. He was sad that he hadn't been able to leave memories of their prior meetings in her mind. Talking to her now was like starting all over.

I am a man.

No man I know can do what you can do.

That is true.

Stay away from me. And stay away from my friends.

I cannot.

He knew she wondered what that meant—that he couldn't leave her alone or couldn't leave her team alone.

The channel she'd opened between them was wonderful. He loved being able to talk to her mentally with such ease.

Both, he said, answering her unspoken question.

BASTION RETURNED to the cabin to make sure it had been properly secured before the team left the area. It was locked down. He drove back to the house and parked in the bunker cave, where he hid his Jeep behind an illusion.

He walked down the long tunnel to the loading dock and entered the secret conference room. Most of the team were there...except Selena and Max. He kept himself hidden from those in the room and any tech that might have identified him. It was weird to observe the group of fighters having a convo about him while he was standing there. In truth, he wasn't what they should be worried about. They needed to prepare themselves for war with Brett Flynn and his ghouls, not the Legion.

At least they were starting to recognize their enemy had access to tactics they'd never seen.

He left them to their meeting and went up to Selena's room. He still felt awful about the pain she was feeling. He'd have to find other ways of keeping the men of her team from her without using pain inducement. That was the only way he would know if her suffering was coming from him or her reaction to him or if it was something else entirely, like something the Matchmaker was doing.

Selena was lying on her bed with a cold cloth over her eyes and forehead. He wasn't sending out pain at all at the moment. The fact that she was still feeling it worried him. Had he harmed her earlier? Or was the pain coming from another source? *Merde*. He wished he could talk freely with his team to better understand what was happening to her.

Was the Matchmaker doing something to her? Motherfucker. The demon had better not be harming Selena.

A knock sounded on her door. Selena went to open it. Instantly, Bastion felt her pain expand. She backed out of the short hallway, bumping up against her dresser. The big blond tried to get her to move over to a chair, but she just shrank away. It was Ace who was able to get her to take a seat.

Send them away, he said to Selena. Without the others looking on, he could send her to sleep. He wasn't able to shield her from pain the way Liege and Guerre could; sleep was her only escape.

Ace sat next to her. "Sel, you don't look like yourself." She pressed her palm to Selena's forehead. "Maybe you should lie down."

"I can't. You have to leave. All of you. You have to go. Right now." Selena cupped her hands around her forehead. "My head is about to crack open."

"Just tell us what happened to you tonight," Max said.

Selena was silent. Bastion knew she was thinking about the night's activities. She didn't understand much of it, and how could she while he was keeping himself hidden from her?

Maybe the pain she was feeling was a stress response.

If so, that was on him.

"I just don't feel well, that's all. Nothing happened to me."

"Kelan thought you saw something out there," Kit said.

Selena looked from him to Kelan. "I saw deer tracks. The low light tricked me into thinking they were human footprints. My mistake."

She'd just lied, and to her team, no less. Of course she couldn't tell them something that ran counter to their understanding of reality.

Val stepped in front of the team and held his arms out to his sides, ushering everyone to move out of her room. "Let's just let her get some rest. We'll see how she feels when her migraine's gone."

Ace lingered behind everyone else. When the room was empty, she gave Selena a worried look. "I can stay with you tonight. You shouldn't be alone when you feel like this."

Selena shook her head. "Nothing's wrong with me that a good night's sleep won't fix. Really, I'm fine."

"All right. Come get me if you need me."

"Thanks, Ace. I will."

At last the room was empty. Bastion knew that

Selena was questioning her sanity. This needed to end soon. The longer he kept his reality hidden from her and her team, the more damage he might be doing to her. She was the only one he let see his actual tracks, so she and her team would never have been able to come to a consensus anyway.

He knew it was sometimes better to ease into radical shifts of reality slowly. He wished they didn't have to enter his reality at all, but they were already fighters in the Omni war—there was no escape for them. Perhaps, if the evil that the Omnis were spreading could be stopped, then at least civilians everywhere might be spared.

But probably not, despite the work his Legion was doing—and this team's every effort.

Bastion allowed himself to be visible to Selena as he opened her mind to their shared moments. She looked at him with her pain-hazed eyes. "No. God, no. Not you. I can't—"

Bastion knelt in front of her. "Shh. I'll help you." He touched her hand. "This is happening because of me. I don't know why, but I will figure it out."

Tears pooled in his mate's eyes.

"Close your eyes. I'll send you to sleep. It's your only escape right now."

She did as he asked, spilling a stream of moisture over her tense cheeks. Instantly, she was out. He carried her over to her bed, removed her boots, then covered her up.

Bastion straightened and stared at her, relieved to

see the frown ease from her brow. Pain inducement was one of the first skills he and all of the Legion had learned in the training camps. They were all experts at it. It was as first-nature as breathing. So why had his aim been so sloppy, harming Selena?

8

———

Selena jerked awake, then kept still as she took stock of her surroundings. There was daylight in her room, but she felt as if she'd just shut her eyes. She rolled over and looked at the clock. It was already nine a.m.

Someone was knocking on her door. She smiled, thinking the team had come to check in on her. She threw the covers off and stood, then stretched. Man, she felt great. Better than she had in a long time.

She opened the door. Ace was there, frowning. "So, um, you taking a sick day or what?"

Selena stood back and let Ace in. "No. I just overslept. Guess I needed it. I was out like the dead."

"Huh." Ace walked in and faced her. "You feel better?"

"Like a new person. I think Owen should have rolling days for each of us to sleep in." Selena smiled at her friend.

Ace pulled out a chair at the little table in the corner. "So, you missed the meeting this morning. Owen's going to be sending Lion and Hawk to college."

"Wow. Everyone cool with that? I thought Hope wanted some time with her brother."

"She did, but she sees this as a good thing for him. And for Hawk. But that's not all. The rest of the cubs are going to schools here in town."

"Wow. Owen's not worried about their security?"

Ace shook her head. "Looks like he's not. He thinks the Omnis have gone to ground. For a little while, anyway."

"Well, good. I think those are great things for the boys."

"Yeah." Ace gave her an appraising look. "You sure you're okay?"

"Much better. Don't know what happened yesterday. I swear I was hallucinating."

"How so?"

"I don't know. I just felt like someone was there. I saw footprints that looked human but weren't." Selena wondered if it was safe to say this next bit. "I blew on a pane of glass in one of the living room's French doors—you know how you do when it's cold outside?"

"Yeah?"

"I thought I saw someone's breath on another pane in response. From the outside."

"When was this?"

"When you all went downstairs during dinner. Before my headache got bad."

"That's weird."

Selena nodded. All of that was gone today. She felt normal. No pressure in her head. No paranoia. No extra voices. Maybe she really was losing it. "Ace, like I said, I feel good right now. But if I go crazy, will you tell me?"

Ace didn't laugh—and that scared Selena. "I've seen people lose their shit, Sel. I don't think you are."

"But if I do, you'll tell me, right?"

"Better than that: I'll take you to the doctor and hold your hand through your tests."

"Okay. Let's just hope it was the migraine that worked me over."

"Yeah. I'm down with that. Could have been fatigue, too, the way you slept so long."

"I hope so. Look, I'm going to shower. Ask Russ to keep a bit of breakfast aside for me." Selena walked to the door and held it open for Ace.

"You bet."

THE ENTIRE HOUSEHOLD was in a state of chaos that morning. Moving trucks were delivering furniture. The wild boys' hangout in the basketball court was being relocated down to the basement now that the construction was finished.

Bastion made his rounds over the compound, keeping himself out of the way. When he returned to the attic, he found a young boy asleep on his mattress. Ever since the household had decided to decorate for Christmas, Bastion had had to share his secret space with the household kids, who favored it as a playroom.

Sometimes he'd banish them with a compulsion. Sometimes he'd just keep himself hidden and watch them. Their antics reminded him of his childhood with his younger brother. Only a year separated them—they were more friends than siblings. He tried to hold on to memories of their time together, but he had to admit, those were fading. He was becoming more of an outsider to human society with every day that passed as a mutant. And while the sweet memories became hazy, the bad ones never lost their edge.

The sleeping kid shared the same bloodline as the leader's woman—but not the leader himself. And yet Bastion had seen Owen interact with the boy as if he were his own. The boy was younger than his brother, who did share the same blood as both Owen and his woman.

There were dynamics at play there that Bastion hadn't yet unraveled.

Bastion kicked the mattress, but the boy didn't wake. He poked the kid's shoulder—that worked. The kid sat up and blinked sleepily. Bastion frowned at him from the foot of the bed.

"Who are you?" the boy asked.

"No one. Why are you up here?"

"We play up here some. They said we could."

"Mmm. Are you the leader's son?"

"Yeah. One of them. Why are you up here?" the boy asked.

"I like it up here."

"I do too."

"They're looking for you downstairs."

"Oh." The boy rubbed his eyes. "I fell asleep."

"You'd better go to them. Your *maman* weeps for you." Bastion, whose hearing was far better than a regular's, shared with the boy the sound of his mother's crying.

He looked worried. "Mom?" he called out.

"She's downstairs."

It confused the boy that he could hear his mother two floors above where she was, but he stood and looked back at Bastion, who also came to his feet. "Okay. I'll go. Are you coming with me?"

"*Non.*" Bastion took that moment to hide himself from the kid, hoping it would startle him into staying out of the attic. The boy screamed and ran down the dark attic stairs. Bastion turned the stairway lights on. The boy pulled on the door, pulled and pulled, thinking it was locked. Bastion pushed the door open with his telekinetic skills, then sat on the top step.

He realized he should have thought that interaction through a little better. Truth was, he was tired of being on the fringes of life, an invisible bystander. With all the clues he'd given the team, he would have thought they'd pick up on the fact that something bizarre was going on. The Legion certainly would have, but then, they were trained to see the bizarre.

∼

"MERRY CHRISTMAS, MOM," Selena said. She'd called her parents after the kids had opened their presents. And after the huge breakfast spread that Jim and Russ had put out for the team. "I'm sorry I couldn't come home this year."

That was a lie, and she felt a little guilty saying it. She could have, but she would have had to miss Max and Hope's wedding.

"That's all right, sweetheart. We're disappointed too, but we do understand. I know you'll have fun at your friends' wedding. Did you get the care package I sent?"

"I did. The cookies were the best ever. And I loved the sweater, too. Thank you."

They made small talk for a little while and spent some time catching up on what the aunts, uncles, and distant cousins were up to. Selena was trying to keep things light, but the whole time she was a hairsbreadth from crying.

She wanted to go home, wanted the hole in her heart to heal so that she could quit feeling this awful aloneness.

"Is everything okay, honey?" her mom asked.

Selena drew a deep breath, forcing herself to sound composed. "Yeah. Great."

"Are you enjoying your work there?" her dad asked. She supposed he'd been listening in on speaker the whole time.

"Always."

"Good. That's great. I worry about you."

"No need to. Look, I have to go. I'll call again in a

few more days. Things here will be quiet for a while after the wedding."

"I look forward to that, honey. Love you."

She hung up shortly afterward, feeling worse than ever.

Seriously, something was not right with her, like her mind was out of step with her heart, and she didn't know how to sync them back up.

9

Today was a big day at the Red Team's headquarters. It was finally time to celebrate Max and Hope's wedding. Bastion had been at the house almost a month; his time there was running out. Liege wanted him back at the fort. And Bastion didn't know how much more Selena could take of their secret life that he kept her from remembering. Ever since their night in the woods, Bastion had tried staying away from her.

That seemed to be having the desired outcome. There was less stress in her face.

Now that the kids had vacated the gym, the big room was available for today's wedding. The austere room had been completely transformed with sprawling screens and flowers and lights, making it look magical, putting him in mind of all the things that could be possible in life and in love, if two people just fought hard enough for what they wanted.

Bastion watched the ceremony and the following celebration. Selena was sitting at a table with her friends, yet somehow alone in the midst of so much joy. He felt what she was feeling, and it cut deep. If he were truthful with himself, he would admit he'd felt a similar loneliness all the years since he'd been changed. At least he had his team, who'd been subject to the same restrictions and experiences, so he had friends to commiserate with. And they had always let him indulge in his human rituals of dating and charming and seducing human females, though none of that had meant to him what he'd hoped it would.

He'd been pretending to be a human for almost a quarter of his life. The irony was that the more he pretended, the less human he felt. Now, having met his female, everything, all the lies he'd fed himself all those years, felt hollow and lacking.

Selena, come to me. He could feel her response to him, her desire to answer his summons. He could also feel her fear and confusion. Something outside of herself was driving her emotions and behavior, and she hated that.

She was exceptionally sensitive. He wished he'd been able to show himself to her before this.

He left the gymnasium building, returning to the main part of the house. He took the back stairs up to the hidden attic access door on this side of the house. The kids had cleared a large area in the middle of the room. He smiled as he remembered the games they played. It had been an eternity since he was a kid. Like the boys who lived here, his own childhood had been rife with challenges, but he'd always tried to shield his brother from the worst of it all.

He missed that punk terribly.

SELENA SAT in the basketball court with the rest of the team and their families. The cubs were lined up in two rows facing the tables, dressed in their khaki pants and blue blazers, which they'd somehow kept clean all through dinner. Wynn had worked with them to learn a few holiday songs and some folk wedding songs as a gift to Max and Hope. Greer played their background music. Angel videoed their performance, and Ace took photos of both the boys performing and everyone watching them.

It was something to hear the boys sing together. They played off each other flawlessly, making their harmonies ethereal. Most of them still had feminine pitches, as their voices hadn't yet deepened. The others had rich male voices.

Hope was wiping her eyes. Max looked stoic. Selena felt the music deep inside her, playing with her emotions, haunting her mind. When the cubs finished their recital, Greer switched into DJ mode, lining up songs for the team to dance to. The first was a slow one, giving Max and Hope the chance to have a dance. Others soon joined them. Selena was keenly aware, as she watched couples move to the dance floor, that all the adults present had partners...except for her and the two oldest boys in the pride.

How was she ever going to find her significant other while she worked with the team in this isolated location of Nowhere, Wyoming? Her mood had darkened in a way that clashed with the joy of the evening. She quietly left the room and exited the gym building, desperately needing some space to compose herself.

She went down the hall toward the back stairs in the south bedroom wing, seeking a quiet place to gather herself. How could so much joy make her feel the hard edge of her emptiness?

She ached to belong somewhere...to someone. She felt the strange pressure of tears behind her eyes, which pissed her off. She wasn't by nature a crybaby. Tears accomplished nothing. The holidays had made her feel a little raw, as if she'd been peeled open. She heard someone coming down the hall from the gym. Not feeling like being social, she went up the back stairs, hoping to avoid whoever it was.

Outside the door to her room, she leaned against the wall. She didn't want to hide in her room. God, she was tired of being alone, even in a big crowd of friends.

After a minute, she realized she was standing opposite the hidden attic door, which was just slightly ajar. Was someone up there? She went through the door, flipped on the lights, and went up the stairs. The lighting was meager. One of the bulbs was out. Strange that she'd felt drawn to go up there, but it was a good place to be by herself. It took coming all the way up to the attic for the happy wedding music to fade. She stood in the middle of the room and shut her eyes.

Being still like this, she could almost feel *him*. Who was he? And why did he feel so much more real than just an imaginary person?

SHE WAS THERE, at last, his beautiful, statuesque warrior. Liege imposed on his team a firm rule about not messing with regulars, but Selena wasn't just any regular. She was Bastion's light. His hope. His future.

Bastion drew her into a trance that only the two of them shared. He would wipe this memory from her mind along with all of their interactions, at least until it was safe for him to give them back to her. He felt as if they were building a relationship, though he knew in truth it was only one-sided.

But damn it all, it was a fantasy he needed right now. And so did she.

The loneliness that ached within her grew like a cancer. Loner or not, this woman was not meant to be alone. Nor was he. The tension eased from her face the closer she came to him. If only this were real—she would feed his soul, and he hers.

Christmas lights strung across the rafters gave the cavernous space a sense of romance. The kids had made use of extra strands left over from the holiday decorations used elsewhere in the house. Bastion lit them with just a thought. They cast a soft, multicolored glow over the forgotten space around him and her.

Bastion waited for her to come close. Though Selena was acting under his compulsion, the moment still felt magical. She studied his face, her gaze moving from his eyes to his nose to his mouth and then his beard. He was wearing a beige wool sweater and a pair of black jeans, not the layered tunics he normally wore. He wished he had a tux as glamorous as her beautiful outfit. Even with her heels on he was taller than her by several inches. He liked the difference in their sizes. His woman was powerful and could be a force to be reckoned with, but at the moment she seemed slight and feminine in comparison to his bulk. In truth, her size made her more agile than his human self would have been.

"*Bon nuit*," he said.

She licked her lips; the motion her tongue made tightened his entire body. Even though she was entranced, she was still in possession of all of her habitual boundaries. "You again," she said.

He smiled. "*Oui. C'est moi.* Again," he said, smiling just slightly. "I wished to have a dance with you, but feared the sight of you dancing in my arms, when you alone could see me, might frighten your friends."

"It would."

He held his arms open and made just the slightest of bows. "Will you dance with me?"

For a moment, he held his breath. He didn't compel her response, so however she reacted, he would have to accept. But, to his everlasting delight, she stepped into his arms. Their stance was formal, with a generous space between their bodies. They couldn't hear the music up there, but Bastion had found an antique record player during his early exploration of the attic. In preparation for tonight, he'd cleaned it off and plugged it in, playing some of the old records that were dumped in the attic with all the other forgotten things.

He used his telekinetic skills to start one of those records playing. The sound it produced seemed to hang in the air without any real substance.

Dancing with Selena was heaven. She moved like an extension of him. Bastion lost himself looking into her eyes. They moved across the entire bare space of the attic, their eyes never losing contact. Everything about her was heaven.

How had the Matchmaker known she was perfect for him? Instead of finding and killing him, perhaps Bastion should thank him.

Of course, there was still the matter of the curse they had to contend with, but his woman was strong. Together, he knew they could beat whatever challenges the curse brought them.

Bastian still hadn't told his team about Selena—except for Merc. This was too new, too rare, too tenuous for him to expose it to the glaring inspection of his team. *Merde alors*, even Selena, the object of his fate, didn't fully know about him. At least not consciously. Bastion sighed. This was all so elusive; it could be swept away at any moment. And perhaps it should. Hooking up with a mutant couldn't be good for a human female.

As they moved around the room, Selena's hard eyes softened. What he would give to have her look at him consciously the way she was while in this trance. When the music ended, there was a click from the turntable as the next record dropped. Bastion slowed his steps, bringing Selena closer to him, his arms around her waist, hers around his neck. Each step they took moved their bodies in gentle swaying motions against each other. Bastion bent his head toward her neck and let his lips graze her skin. Her reaction skittered along her skin, raising gooseflesh on his as well.

She reached up to touch his cheeks, just above his beard, with the cool tips of her fingers. Their dancing slowed even further. He kept his arms around her waist, but he spread his fingers over her lower back, fighting the urge to explore her as she did him. He tried to smile to lighten the mood, but he couldn't. Her green eyes were so intense that he could do nothing but stare into them. She leaned forward and he leaned down, and then their lips were touching. She slipped her fingers into his hair pulling him even closer as she ground her mouth against his.

The kiss lasted seconds, minutes, or an eternity— Bastion lost track of time as they shared themselves with each other. Her body fit against his in ways he never imagined possible. In a flash of insight, he could picture what their future lives might be like. They would fight the Omnis, two warriors in sync with each other, so much more devastating together than apart. The possibilities were intense and exciting.

And they filled him with dread.

What if they did share their lives for some period, be it short or long, only to lose each other? It would kill him. And if the Matchmaker's curse was a guaranteed outcome, what he was feeling for her now, before they'd really even begun, meant his death would come soon after hers.

The hedonistic part of him wanted to set all of his fears aside and be here in the moment with her, storing all of their seconds together so that he would never forget her. If he survived losing her, she would be the ideal against which he would forever measure other women. He knew without a doubt that none would make the cut.

She leaned her temple against his jaw, no longer trying to direct their movements in the dance as she had since the beginning tonight. But then they weren't moving anywhere except against each other. He kissed the crown of her head and breathed in her scent. The music had stopped a while ago, but Bastion couldn't bring himself to separate from her long enough to reset it.

In the midst of this heaven, Bastion became aware of someone coming up the stairs. It was one of her team. Owen, the blond guy the team belonged to and for whom she had a special affection.

Bastion turned her so she was facing the stairway, but kept his arms around hers, holding her close, wishing their time together hadn't ended. Connected to her as he was, Bastion realized that the affection he'd been sensing that she held for Owen was the same as she felt for everyone else on her team. There was something more, too. A longing, an emptiness, but not for Owen specifically, nor the other big blond on the team. It was more that she wished to experience a love of her own, something neither Owen nor any of the men here could have given her.

She yearned for the very things that Bastion wanted.

Bastion kept himself hidden from her and Owen as she left his trance, leaving behind all memory of the time they'd spent together here in the attic.

SELENA WRAPPED her arms around herself, and in her mind, it was as if he, her make-believe lover, wrapped his arms over hers. She pretended to feel the warmth of his body against her back. He was tall. Her height did nothing to intimidate him.

She let her mind dwell in the fantasy of her daydream. Briefly, for the space of a breath or two, she felt less alone, but that respite made the persistent ache of her longing all the more acute.

Someone was coming up the stairs — had to be one of the guys, given the heavy footsteps she was hearing. Owen cleared the stairs.

"Sel." He nodded toward the stairs as he came toward her. "I'm trying to discourage Troy from using the attics alone. Saw the door open and wondered who was up here." He frowned as he looked around.

"Just me." And the phantom lover she'd conjured in her mind.

"Troy's run-in with Captain Hook a few days ago was odd," Owen said.

"How so?"

"He said the man he saw asked if he was the leader's son."

The warmth of her daydream vanished, leaving a chill behind. "Wow. That's not something Troy would have made up, is it?"

"No." Owen prowled around the space, looking behind large pieces of furniture and stacks of junk.

"Maybe Eddie should bring Tank up here," Selena suggested, feeling embarrassed for having been caught with her imaginary man.

"Whatever it was," Owen said, "if it was anything, is long gone. Greer checked for electronic surveillance — and ghosts — but didn't find anything." He opened an old wardrobe. "Maybe there's some new kind of tech we don't know about yet, something that piped in the questions Troy said he answered."

"What...something like telepathy?" As soon as she said it, Selena felt humor from her imaginary friend.

So warm, almost hot, in that guess. You will soon know the truth.

Owen frowned. He straightened and focused on her. "What is it?"

"What do you mean?"

"I don't know. You looked off there for a minute. You okay?"

"Yeah. Fine."

"Well, not telepathy," Owen continued. "I was thinking something like an untethered hologram."

Ah. A shame—he is cold again.

Owen's pale eyes studied her. She refused to squirm. "What are you doing up here?" he asked. "You've been up here for a while. They've already cut the cake and moved to the game room to relax. The kids are in the theater room watching a movie Greer put on for them."

Selena looked at her watch. She'd been gone more than an hour. How was that possible?

"Guess I just needed some space." She turned and looked behind her, still feeling the presence she'd conjured up a few minutes ago. Nothing was there. She needed to talk to Greer. Maybe he'd felt something too but hadn't been comfortable telling the team they had a ghost.

She sighed. Whatever had just happened, her solace was broken—she might as well go downstairs and rejoin the festivities. As she moved toward Owen, she felt a pressure in her head, like the beginnings of a headache. Owen looked like he was suffering one too. He rubbed his forehead. Maybe a storm was coming through the area. At the altitude where Blade's house was situated, it was easy to feel shifts in barometric pressure—they often triggered headaches.

She followed Owen down the stairs.

"You coming back to the party?" he asked as he shut the lights off and secured the door.

"In a bit." She moved toward her room, but stopped. "Owen, was Troy frightened of what he saw up there?"

Owen considered that a moment. "I don't think so. At least, he wasn't until he saw the man disappear. That's what made him run out of the attic."

Selena went into her room, hoping to restore her composure before returning to the party. She sat on the end of her bed. What she'd thought had only been minutes in the attic had been more than an hour. How had she lost so much time like that?

Come back, that warm, buttery voice said in her head.

No, she answered. God, her imaginary lover had taken on a consciousness all his own. He said things she would never have thought up herself—including using a persistent French accent.

I'm real. Flesh and bone.

Did you speak to Troy? she asked.

Yes.

Fuck. She jumped to her feet and rushed out of her room. Her mind was obviously splintering into multiple personalities that were now communicating with each other. She imagined she heard laughter.

Greer was still with everyone in the game room. She watched him, hoping to catch him alone, and lucked out when he went to the bar to get a drink for Remi.

"Hey," Selena said as she sat at the bar.

Greer nodded at her. "You having fun tonight?"

"Sure. Listen, just between you and me, what did you find in the attic when you went up there?"

Greer looked at her, then swept the room with a glance before answering. "Nothing. Absolutely nothing."

"Greer, this me you're talking to. I need the truth. No ghosts?"

He slowly grinned. "No ghosts. Why?"

"Owen said Troy told him the man he'd seen up there asked if Troy was the leader's son. That's not something a kid would make up."

"Well, Zavi calls Owen the chief. Maybe Troy was just curious about the team structure. He's still new here. Who knows what weird things kids come up with?" Greer took the drink he'd made over to Remi.

Selena looked around the group, seeing the happy faces of her friends and coworkers—friends who would turn to enemies when they learned she was suffering a mental breakdown. Not only would Owen return her to her regular Army post, but she'd be run out of there on a Section Eight.

She'd better shut up and act like nothing was the fuck wrong. She walked out of the game room and went up to her bedroom. Digging through her dresser, she frantically searched for a pair of earbuds she knew she had somewhere. She found them at the back of her makeup drawer in the bathroom. Her hands were shaking as she plugged them in to her phone and flipped to a playlist of hard rock. She changed into her gym clothes then hurried down to the weight room. She needed to put in a workout, see if she could chase out the crazy and get back to having only one voice her head.

Halfway through a fast jog, the lights flickered in the gym. What the hell was wrong with the electrics in this old house? The gym building was one of the newer additions—it should have dependable wiring. Her treadmill had come to quick stop when the power blinked. Sweating and panting, she mopped her brow as she looked in the big mirror that ran the length of one wall. Someone was there, watching her. She just caught a glimpse of him before he vanished.

"Kelan?" she called out, turning to see who it was.

BASTION'S HEART banged like a jackhammer. He was going to do it, finally. He was going to reveal himself to his mate. His emotions made the lights surge then blink out. He let one light come back on. Like an animal sensing a predator nearby, Selena drew her earbuds down and stepped off the treadmill, keeping still and silent, listening, waiting. Fearing.

"Come out, you coward," she called out. "Show yourself."

Bastion smiled at her bravado. She was a warrior through and through, his woman. He stepped forward, moving into the dim light.

Selena sucked in a breath as her gaze slowly moved over his upper body and face. Bastion knew she liked what she saw—he could scent the pheromones coming from her heated skin.

Their eyes locked on each other as he walked toward

her, stopping just inches from her. She touched him tentatively, then let her hand linger just below his neck where his sweater was open.

He smiled, enjoying the effort she made to define his scent, something that was pleasing to her. Leather and sweet clover and a musk that was unique to him.

He leaned down, breathing in her scent as she had his. He lifted his head. Heat rose on her skin, moving up from her neck to her face.

Bastion. Je m'appelle Bastion.

She heard him quite clearly, though she tried to deny it. Bastion loved hearing her thoughts so easily. She wasn't blocking him at all.

"I am real." He caught her other hand and brought it to his chest. "You feel me." He tugged at the earbuds in her fist. "These won't keep me from you. Nothing will. And for the record, you smell sweeter than a clover field yourself." He smiled, his eyes filled with humor.

She stiffened, offended that he was laughing at her.

"Never. I would never laugh at you."

The moment of her sweet openness passed as quickly as it came. She poked her fingers at his chest. "Listen, motherfucker, I did not invite you in. You have to stay out of my head. How do you do that, anyway?"

"You wound me. But I will do as you wish." Bastion tensed and looked toward the hall. Someone was coming. When she looked away, he hid himself from her.

Her friends Kelan and Greer came into the room. "There you are," Kelan said. "We've been looking for you."

"Why?" Selena asked. She reached for her hand towel, but Bastion had taken it. He lifted it to his face and drew in her sweet scent.

Greer walked around the workout room. "You didn't have your comm unit in."

"I thought we had a few days off," Selena said.

"Your security necklace was malfunctioning, and we had a power surge down here," Greer said. "You alone?"

"No. Captain Hook was here with me."

Merde. Je suis *Bastion.*

Selena smiled. Bastion knew she'd felt his irritation. "He's French. And he's just as Troy described him."

Kelan exchanged loaded glances with Greer, then asked, "Uh, Sel, how much of Russ's spiced wine did you have?"

"I'm telling you, he was here. He's probably still here."

"Uh-huh." Kelan looked around. "And he's, what, invisible?"

"Sometimes."

Kelan shook his head. "You probably shouldn't be alone right now."

"I don't think he means us harm," Selena said. "If he did, we'd all be dead already."

I don't mean you harm. She thought of him as an intruder. He was that, but so much more. *Say my name. Bastion.*

Greer took her arm. "Okay. Say goodnight to your invisible friend now and come back to the game room with us."

Selena glared at him. "You're one to talk, you with your ghosts. I never mocked you about them."

"Because they're real. Why would you?" Greer shook his head.

"I'm telling you, he's real too. Two of us have seen him now."

Selena thought about taking a shower in the locker room, but worried he'd watch her, a thought that irritated Bastion.

I am not a monster. And see? I let you walk with them because you have no feelings for them. I have learned who I must keep away from you.

Selena gasped. Kelan and Greer frowned at her.

The others feel pain when they are near you. I punish them.

"You okay, Sel?" Greer asked.

"I'm telling you, he's here. We have an intruder. I'm not making this up."

Kelan nodded. "We're learning that anything is possible. Before we saw Nick and the Ratcliffs, with their reversed age, or Addy with her strange eyes, I wouldn't have believed you. Now, who knows? There's that odd static that keeps showing up. We'll look into it when we drop you off with the others."

"I'm going with you," she said.

Greer nixed that. "You're not, because you're not being rational right now."

Bastion felt Selena's anger. *What I am, what I think, and what I do are none of your business,* she told him.

Her words coming so clearly to him felt like a victory.

Ah. You are a natural mind talker, Selena. I knew you would be. And you are mistaken. You exist for me, and me alone.

SELENA DITCHED the rest of the evening's festivities, telling Kelan and Greer that she needed to shower first. Alone in her room, she leaned against her door...or at least she thought she was alone. She tested her senses, trying to see if she could tell if Bastion was with her or nearby somewhere. As far as she knew, he wasn't.

What was he? A stalker? She had curiously intense feelings about him, as if he was someone she'd known a long while, someone she craved. Was that part of his game? Was he somehow influencing her?

She locked her door and thought briefly about propping one of the chairs from the little table up against it. But he could probably just get through that. She had no idea who he was or how he was getting around their compound without anyone seeing him or any of their tech capturing him. Even all the dogs and Blade's old cat never seemed to pick up on his presence.

And yet he was real, not a ghost. He'd shown himself to her tonight. His real, physical self. God, he was big and smelled divine.

No. There was nothing delicious about him. He was an enemy, spying on them. An intruder.

Selena ripped off her workout clothes as she stepped into her bathroom. She turned the water on, then caught sight of herself in the mirror. She looked at her face, only that, not her body. There were shadows under her eyes, lines bracketing her mouth that weren't usually there.

It was the tension. This situation was out of control. All of it. Her. Him. Her team.

She shut her eyes, remembering his scent, remembering his intense and dark gaze as he stood before her.

Maybe this was a test of some sort, a qualification she had to meet before joining the team on a permanent basis, a last hurdle before she could separate from the Army. Maybe that was why she was the only one being affected by Bastion.

Her gaze lowered to her breasts. She shut her eyes fast, but touched the familiar scars on either side of them, tracing the shallow ridges.

She yanked a towel from a stack and hung it up next to the shower, then shut the lights off and stepped into the stall. When the hot water sluiced over her chest, she began counting backward from five to one, following the advice of one of the many counselors she'd been forced to visit over the years.

Five...four...three...two...one.

She didn't feel any better, but at least she was breathing.

10

The hour was late, but Hawk was edgy and restless. He paced around his bedroom, then went down the stairs to the living room. He'd lived with Lion and the cubs at the house where Lion's sister was for the past several months, but he still couldn't get used to existing inside so many walls. The Quonset hut on the biker compound where he and the pride had lived had those big walls that curved from one side to the other. And when they'd lived in the little cabins on the mountain, it had been easy to go outside and slip into the woods at any point.

Not so here, at Kelan and Fiona's penthouse apartment. He supposed that as college towns went, Fort Collins wasn't huge. But they were miles from the foothills.

He took the stairs up to the rooftop deck. There at least he could feel the fresh—and bitterly cold—air. He tilted his face up to see the stars, searching the sky for familiar constellations. If he narrowed his eyes, squeezing out everything but the sky, he could pretend he wasn't so far from the mountains, where his heart lived.

Maybe what he needed was to go for a walk. He slipped out of the apartment. Lion had been hovering over him like a controlling parent. Hawk had told Lion many times since they came to town to attend the local community college that he wanted to go back to the woods, to their wild, free days spent hunting and scavenging for food.

Lion wouldn't listen. Times had changed, he kept saying, and they both had to change too.

He's right.

There it was. That soft, firm, knowing voice that had been popping into his head a lot lately. Hawk hunched his shoulders as he walked into the cold January wind. At least he wasn't alone. At least someone understood him.

I don't want to be here, Hawk told himself. *I want to go back home.*

You don't have a home.

I have a huge home, full of trees and boulders and rivers.

You aren't an animal to live in the wild. You're a man. You know what you have here that isn't in the woods? Women.

This was a familiar conversation he'd been having with himself for the past week he and Lion had been here. Women were a nice benefit, but it wasn't like Hawk knew how to speak to them—or even approach them.

But I do. I'll help you.

Hawk felt warmth spear through him. Without his being aware of the change in direction, he soon found himself walking toward the bars on the main strip of road in Old Town. It was winter, so the doors were closed, but many of them were still full of people. The university was out of session for another couple of weeks, but kids were coming back to their old hangouts after the holiday break.

Hawk went up to one of the doors, but a burly guy out front demanded to see his driver's license before letting him inside. Hawk dug it out of his wallet. The guy stamped his hand and then opened the door. Noise spilled outside, along with the sight and sound of young females, heated from dancing.

"Going in or what?" the bouncer asked.

Hawk stepped inside. This was so not his normal behavior. He felt like was watching himself rather owning himself.

Get a beer.

I don't have money.

Check your pocket.

Hawk pulled out a fifty-dollar bill and frowned at it. Where had it come from? He went up to the bar and ordered something cheap. Wasn't like he knew the different beers. Lion and he hadn't done the bar scene yet, so they hadn't started their education in that arena yet. Val and Max had promised to come down and teach them, but that hadn't happened yet.

"Buy one for me?"

A girl stood by his elbow. Petite, dark-haired, her face painted with makeup that made her look more like a doll than a human.

See how easy it is? They come to you.

The bartender handed Hawk his second drink, which Hawk handed to the girl. He walked away, feeling a little spooked by her. The place was throbbing with loud music from a band everyone in the room but him seemed to know. They laughed and danced and screamed out the refrains. The room seemed to close in on him, faces spinning around, laughing at something he didn't understand.

He set his beer on a nearby table and left. Doll-face followed him out. The bouncer stopped her, making her hand off her bottle before running after him.

"Hey! Hey—where are you going?" the girl asked.

Hawk shoved his hands in his hoodie pockets and turned the corner. She scrambled after him.

Go in the alley. No one can see you there.

Hawk turned into the dark corridor, letting the girl catch up to him at last. In shadowy space between the brick walls, her face was even more terrible than in the bar. It was pale and fake and seemed distinctly inhuman. She smiled at him and slipped her arms around his neck. He closed his eyes so he didn't have to look at her. While her face terrified him, her body set his on fire.

Lift her and use the brick wall for support.

Hawk did just that, liking the way he fit between her legs.

The girl stiffened in his grip. "Wait. What are you doing? I just wanted you to come back to the bar."

You have her where you want her. No one will hear her scream. I'll see to that.

What did that even mean? He didn't want her at all. She was pushing against his shoulders now. He dropped her and stepped back, sickened by the track his thoughts had taken.

You idiot. You could have had her. We could have had her.

Hawk stumbled away, watching her rush out of the alleyway. He hated this night and himself and everything about this town.

When would Lion let them go home?

LION WAS in the living room when Hawk returned. "Hey, where'd you go?" he asked.

Hawk shrugged and slumped into one of the armchairs. "For a walk."

"What's got you so restless?"

Hawk tugged at the sleeves of his hoodie. He had been taken into the pride a few months before Lion joined them, so he'd been able to show his friend how to exist. They'd grown up together, survived together, knew everything there was to know about each other. Hawk just wished he didn't feel like a stranger to himself.

"Do you have a spirit guide, Lion?"

Lion took a moment before answering. "I think so."

"Do you talk to it?"

"It's a 'him.' Yeah. Sorta. Not out loud, just in my mind."

"Does he tell you to do things?"

"He gives me advice. Not always in words, kind of just in knowings. Why?"

"I think I have one too."

"That's good. You could use one with the changes happening in our lives. Going to school and living away from the cubs and all."

"Yeah. Do you trust your guide?"

Lion nodded. "He hasn't steered me wrong yet."

"I'm not sure I trust mine."

Lion chuckled and slapped Hawk on the back. "You don't trust anyone or anything right now. Just chill and go with it for a while. See how it all works out. We'll be going back to Blade's house this weekend. Maybe being with the pride will help settle you."

"Maybe."

11

Brett Flynn set an illusion about himself that would cause anyone looking at him to see him as a short, stout, middle-aged farmer, clothed in flannels, plaids, and coveralls—the typical garb of the diner's patrons. This town belonged to Owen Tremaine's mercenaries, and Brett didn't want anyone to know it had hit his radar.

The mercenaries were enemies of the Omnis. They'd been trained and groomed for the fight in the Army's Red Team. He'd had one of his flunkies check them out after King's Warren fell to the Feds. The subterranean castle was built in the footprint of an old missile silo. Losing it was a big hit to the Omnis.

Brett's intelligence had indicated that the group of fighters here were simple regulars who didn't pose a threat to the Omnis—not where the OWO was headed, at least.

Brett didn't agree with that assessment. It felt too

easy, like they were ignoring an obvious threat. They ignored him too. They shut him out of the Omnis' business, patted him on the head and told him to not worry. He'd been shut out most of his adult life. Passed over by others less flawed than he.

His family was blind to all he had to offer. He'd been honing himself into a brutally effective weapon, all while behaving in a self-effacing manner toward his parents' peers in the Omni ruling class, as he tried to make a spot for himself.

Truth was, he was a festering wound among his own people, who underestimated his potential for violence. Always. Always. His parents had paid him off and cut him loose, seeing no use for him, finding nothing redeemable in their own son.

Because of *her*. One stupid female.

Selena Irving.

She'd joined the Red Team for a time, then followed several soldiers out of the Army and into Tremaine's service. Brett stroked part of thick scar on his cheek. It started at his cheekbone and continued down to his mouth, shredding the symmetry of his lips.

Oh, yes, he was not finished with the estimable Ms. Irving. His plans for her were long and terrible. Brett sipped his steaming coffee. Patience was an art, one rarely practiced anymore. His lengthy stalking of his enemy was enjoyable, giving him the opportunity to consider at his leisure the myriad ways he could destroy her.

He'd ruined her parents' lives, breaking them down

a little more every time they ran from him. They didn't have a lot of fight left in them, but still they lingered, like a dying person taken off life support. He wanted them to experience his *coup de grâce* — Selena's capture and torture would be their undoing.

Or perhaps he would do the opposite: have Selena watch him end her parents.

Either option gave him delicious shivers.

The object of his fury came out of the grocery store, walking next to a man pushing a cart.

Brett hissed a victory sigh. Patience always won the day.

Brett tried to slip into her mind to see where they were headed next, but Bastion had set a protection around her, blocking her from such invasions. The man she was with, however, was still wide open to his mental probing. Brett urged him to go for a coffee at the shop next to the grocery store.

Bastion's meddling didn't surprise Brett — after all, he was protecting the forces on his side of their war. What did surprise Brett was that Bastion hadn't put a protection on the man with Selena, or on all of those who worked for Tremaine.

Brett smiled, feeling the victory that would soon be his. Bastion had a thing for Selena. Taking her would be like sinking a knife in the Legion's breast.

Everything Brett wanted would soon be his. All it would cost was a little patience.

The man with Selena announced they were going for

a coffee after they stowed their groceries. Ever alert, Selena looked around them before agreeing.

Brett went into the café, keeping the two in his line of sight. When Selena walked past him, he drew the scent of her into his nose, testing her scent, reacquainting himself with the nuances of her energy. She wasn't afraid at the moment, but when he had control of her, God, how delectable it would be to taste the way fear tempered her essence.

He kept himself invisible to the regulars. Selena and her friend were standing at the counter. Bastion's damned protection meant he couldn't get physically close to Selena, but it didn't prohibit him from projecting his astral body into her energy.

Brett stood a few feet behind Selena as his astral body leaned close to her, bending near her shoulder, inhaling her scent—the smell of her skin and blood and bones, all of which Brett would soon sample. His physical body swallowed the saliva that filled his mouth, soaking him with anticipation. Of course, she would be alive when he did what he was planning. Alive and screaming. Oh, how delicious her agony would be, like all of his pain over the years, condensed into a much shorter, more intense period of time.

She was a regular, so she wouldn't heal rapidly. He could take his time drawing out her agony. He rubbed his palm over himself at that thought.

Brett wrapped his astral arms around her waist, letting his energy infuse hers. He felt her body tighten with alarm. She looked over her shoulder, but there was nothing for her to see. He bent his astral head low, letting the ghost of his face drag along Selena's shoulder.

She jumped and turned to face the room, her eyes darting about as her mind tried to meet the rest of her senses halfway. Brett smiled as he watched her struggle. Humans never trusted their instincts.

She reached over to her companion, grabbing his sleeve. "Jim, we have to go."

Jim took the change the cashier handed him. He looked at her, then turned and sent a look around them. Brett wasn't certain what Jim's role in her life was, but the man had a warrior's essence. He was, therefore, an enemy of the Omnis.

"Why?" Jim asked.

"Because we do."

"We haven't gotten our coffee."

"I don't care. Let's go."

Jim frowned. "Selena—what happened?"

"I don't know."

Brett let his astral hands touch her cheeks. Selena gasped and stepped back, backing into the counter.

"Sel?"

Selena folded her arms in front of her.

"Go outside," Jim ordered her quietly. "I'll get our drinks."

Selena shifted her attention to Jim, and then Brett felt it, that first hint of fear. God, it was delicious. He clenched his teeth and sucked in a long draw of her energy.

"I'll wait," Selena said.

Jim stepped nearer, providing her cover from the rest of the shop. "What happened?"

Selena shrugged. "Someone touched me."

Jim looked around again. "I'm the only one near you, and I sure as hell didn't. Russ would kill me," he said, chuckling.

"It wasn't you."

"Oh." Jim frowned. He leaned close to ask, "So what are we talking about, then? A ghost? You sure are spooked."

Selena shivered. "I felt... I thought... Never mind. Forget it. Let's just get out of here."

THE OPS GUYS had reconfigured triggers for the different security sensors, making them more sensitive to energetic interruptions. Bastion had been forced to switch his shields from emitting sweeping electromagnetic pulses to more mechanical tweaks, like simply pausing any recording devices while he was in range of them. It was something that required more concentration.

Bastion gave it no more thought. His time here was ending. The team was already looking for him. And his presence seemed to be causing Selena extreme discomfort. Never in his life had Bastion harmed a woman—he sure as hell didn't want to start a new trend now, with his own light.

Bastion gathered his shower kit and headed out to

the gym building. It was the middle of the night. The team didn't begin straggling into the gym until a couple of hours before dawn. He figured this was a safe time to hit the showers, since he had at least an hour before the first fighter would be in the locker room.

He set up his shaving mirror and got his shampoo, soap, and shaving gear out. Then he got into the water and stood under its hard streams, letting it hit his back and neck for long, luxurious moments before washing up.

The stall showers were all individual booths with blue polyester curtains in the front. Each had a small anteroom with wall hooks and a bench. There were no cameras in the locker room, but Bastion wasn't taking any chances—he'd set an illusion over his stuff so that, in the unlikely event one of the team came in early, it wouldn't be seen.

That habit saved his hide.

Greer came in while Bastion was shaving. "Hey," Greer called out. "Who else's guilty conscience is keeping him up tonight?"

Bastion supposed Greer was talking to him, but of course he didn't answer.

"Yo. I'm talking to you," Greer said.

Still, Bastion didn't answer.

"Shit." Greer ripped the curtain aside.

Bastion had his razor poised for another stroke on his neck when the cold air hit him. Greer reached in and shut off the water.

"Motherfucker. I will find you and kill you for using all the hot water," Greer grumbled under his breath.

Bastion gave Greer a compulsion to leave the locker room and get on with his workout. Pushing a compulsion over Greer wasn't as easy as it was with some regulars. He'd clearly had training—and significant practice—shielding himself from psychic intrusions. The fighter left the shower area and went over to the toilet stalls, slamming each door open before he was satisfied that no one was hiding in the room. He finally left, still in a high funk.

Bastion finished his shave, then dried off and dressed. He gathered up his gear and left the locker room, his shields in place because the team had cameras in all the public places in the house and across the compound.

A kid was coming into the gym wing—one of the older wild boys. Hawk was his name. It was still dark outside, but Bastion could see perfectly well in the low light. The kid looked right at him, right into his eyes. Bastion stopped. There was no way a regular human could see him, not through his illusion.

What had just happened?

Bastion dropped his shower bag and hurried back to the kid, but whatever he'd just experienced was over; the kid now showed no sign he was aware of Bastion, though he shouted at him, walked backward in front of him, tried in every different way to get his attention again.

Bastion stepped back when the kid went into the

workout room. He stared at the closed door, trying to make sense of what had just happened. Had he imagined it? The kid was a regular. No doubt about that.

He collected his bag and returned to his attic hideout. He slumped into a creaky old rocking chair, rocking while he puzzled over the issue. He definitely needed a closer look at Hawk.

SELENA SEEMED ODD THAT EVENING, Bastion thought. She didn't want to socialize with the others in the billiards room. Instead, she took herself off to her room, preferring some alone time.

Bastion hid in the attic, away from cameras, and waited until Selena's lights were out before visiting her in her dreams. This was always tricky to do with humans. When he'd visited her before, she'd always been awake, though he'd convinced her she was sleeping, and later, he'd compelled her to sleep.

Now his astral self reached out to her sleeping mind. He couldn't enter her sleeping mind, not like Liege could. Her shields were too strong against him. But he could tap on her consciousness, like an awake person could physically tap another person's shoulder.

Selena. Talk to me.

He wasn't expecting what came next—Selena sat up. Well, her astral body sat up while her physical body stayed in repose. *Mon Dieu*, she was stunning. She had a purple glow about her. This was the first time he'd ever seen color around someone, and the sight was breathtaking. Best of all, in her current state, she could see his astral projection too.

She got off the bed and came toward him with narrowed eyes.

My love, why are you angry? he asked, speaking psychically.

There was another of you in the coffee shop this afternoon, she said.

Bastion frowned. *What do you mean? There is only one of me.*

Another one like you. Another mutant. He touched me. Did you send him?

Selena, you know I can't tolerate male regulars near you. Why would I send a mutant male to you? I would not.

Then who was it?

Bastion shook his head. *I don't know. I've been feeling another's energy here lately, but the energy signature is weak. I can't get a read on it.*

It wasn't weak this afternoon.

You think it was a "he"?

She nodded and folded her arms in front of her.

I have a protection on you. Nothing should have come near you.

I don't need your protection.

You do. You don't know what you're up against.

I do know. Things like you. Things that can act like ghosts.

Oui, but I'm not a thing. I'm a man.

Are there many like you? Mutants?

Bastion nodded. *Far more than there should be. The Omnis are building their mutant forces.*

Selena held up her astral hand. She didn't notice at first that she was pure energy—not until she touched her hand to his and they merged into an amorphous shape. She gasped and looked up at him, but before he could explain what was happening, her astral body was instantly reunited with her physical self.

She jerked awake. Bastion did not reveal himself to her. She turned on the light and looked around the room, then got up and checked her closet and the bathroom—looking for him, he was sure.

He hated this, hated only being able to connect with her spirit self or in situations where he would have to wipe her memories of him. How were they to have a future if they couldn't be together?

Bastion pulled his astral projection back into his body in the attic. Keeping his eyes shut, he focused on surrounding Selena with an energy field that would block physical and psychic attacks.

He was not successful. She had set her own boundaries and he was not allowed to break them.

She was strong. He admired that. She would make a good candidate for taking the human modifications. All of her natural talent could be channeled and trained, honed into pure power.

Still, Bastion had to find a way to protect her.

It wouldn't surprise him at all if Flynn had found a way into the house, despite the protection Bastion had on it. Perhaps Flynn was using one of his minions to infiltrate the compound and stalk Selena. Perhaps others from the household were likewise in jeopardy.

He should talk to Liege. It was past time to blow this open. The fighters here were used to secrecy—it was why they lived together: less exposure to the outside world, and much easier to protect each other. The Legion could trust them with their awful secret.

12

Barely two weeks after Max and Hope's wedding, the team was again celebrating nuptials. This time it was Owen and Addy's wedding. Bastion crashed Addy's bachelorette party—in his astral form. Owen's fiancée was the exact opposite of Selena. Addy was gentle, sweet, almost meek, and yet Bastion sensed a core of steel within her. Tonight, the women had spent the evening helping her plan a sex fest with the boss.

Bastion hadn't laughed so hard in his life.

He tried to tamp down the hunger the party had aroused in him. Selena felt it too. She went behind the bar to begin cleanup as the night wound down. Her body was on fire. She was inches away from driving over to the local bar to find a hookup.

Don't do it, Bastion said, insulted that his light thought to find relief with a stranger. *It isn't a stranger you crave.*

Ignoring him, she continued cleaning up. He felt a wave of her loneliness as the door to the game room opened and the women began pairing up with their men as they left for the night. Selena wiped the granite counter of the bar.

You aren't alone, Bastion told her. *You have me.*

She squeezed her eyes shut, rejecting that. She still thought he was a figment of her own mind.

You've seen me, touched me. I am real.

Ivy commented to Kelan that he was a lucky man. The look he sent his girlfriend should have incinerated her. He pulled her close and kissed her.

"Yes, I am." His growly answer came long after Ivy had already left. He wrapped an arm around Fee.

"You sure I can't help, Sel?" Fee asked.

"Nope. Got it under control." Selena forced a smile. "Go show Kelan what you learned tonight."

Kelan frowned. "What did you learn?"

Fee giggled and took his hand, leading him from the room.

Show me what you learned tonight.

Selena gritted her teeth, fighting her own desire. She loaded the dishwasher with the dishes the women had brought over to the bar.

Come upstairs. I will be with you in the way that I can. I will not leave you alone when you are in need.

Selena's pulse sped up. Bastion could almost feel its drum. She swept the room with a glance, looking for something that needed straightening, something—

anything—that would let her delay the inevitable, but there was nothing more to do.

She crossed the room and switched the lights off as she left. Her heart was pounding. She hungered for what she knew was coming. She stepped inside her room and locked her door. Bastion turned on the lamp on her bedside table so she would know he was there. She walked deeper into her room, searching for him.

"Bastion? Are you here?" Selena asked, seeing no one in her room.

I'm with you. Heavy arms encircled her. But she was alone, so it was only the impression of him there, holding her. How could that be? She opened her eyes and looked around, flooded by a sense of emptiness when she realized this was all in her head. All of it. The crushing sense of aloneness made her want to vomit. She covered her mouth and headed toward her bathroom.

Stop.

As if she'd hit a wall, she was absolutely blocked from moving forward.

You are not alone.

A hand under her chin turned her face toward the floor-length mirror that leaned against the wall. He was there, behind her. Nude, though her body blocked her full vision of him.

You are my woman, and I will not leave you in need. Give yourself to me and I will give myself to you.

He was gorgeous. Wild. Tall and broad-shouldered. His thick brown hair was in that man-bun he favored. He moved his arm around her waist and nuzzled her neck. Shivers rippled over her skin like an electrical frisson.

She stared at her reflection as she touched his forearm. She could even feel the coarse, dark hair under her palm as she stroked him. But all of that disappeared when she looked down at herself and saw her hand hovering over empty air.

Her gaze cut to his reflection. He closed his eyes as he pressed his face to the side of hers. He was a beautiful man, in the same way that a craggy cliff is beautiful, and he wasn't in any way real.

I am not beautiful, he said—to her ears or through her mind, she didn't know; it was all blending now.

You are to my soul, she answered. Truth, those words, but how had she found them? Something about Bastion stripped her to her essence.

He covered her eyes with his big hand, blocking her vision. Don't look too closely. You'll see knots of scars and the terrible things I've done that make me me.

I have scars too.

He kissed her temple. I know. But yours make you strong.

She pulled his phantom hand from her face. *Bastion, what are we doing?* She kissed his palm. His skin was warm against her lips. Her body quivered. How she needed him.

I will give you release. His hand trailed down her neck, down her chest to the buttons on her shirt. One opened, then the next.

She pulled her eyes from the image of him standing

behind her in the mirror and watched as the third button released itself, controlled by some unseen force.

It was a cruel reminder that he wasn't really there with her. She jerked herself away from him, backing up to the wall. Her eyes darted around the room, madly searching for him. How was this happening? How could she feel him if he wasn't physically there?

She looked into the mirror, but it was now empty. She covered her eyes and slumped to the floor. What was she doing, indulging in this? Letting this being into her mind was potentially dangerous. What if he took over? What if he said and did everything he needed to in order to gain control over her?

What if he used her against the team?

She could feel Bastion's soft efforts to reach her, but she blocked him from her mind. She couldn't continue with this. She knew nothing about him.

And there it was, yet another reality-defying thought.

He wasn't anything. He didn't exist. He was merely a figment of her imagination. Maybe she never did actually see or touch him in the gym after Max's wedding. Kelan and Greer never found evidence of him when they searched the house that night.

But if that was true, how had he turned on her light or unbuttoned her shirt? She hadn't touched those things—had she? How was any of this happening? And why her? Was she the weakest link on the team? Had her loneliness been an open invitation to him?

She fisted her hands and squeezed her head,

reminding herself that he wasn't real. None of this was really happening. Someone was slipping her psychedelics. That had to be the answer. But who? The Omnis had used them on both Fee and Addy. Maybe Ace too.

But no Omnis were in the house.

Had she consumed something no one else had? She'd run errands today with Mandy. They'd stopped for lunch at Ivy's diner. Maybe someone there had slipped her something. Maybe there were Omnis all over town.

God, she was so fucking paranoid. But why was she the only one this was happening to? Had to be because she was the weak link.

The Omnis had somehow hacked her.

She was so fucked. And because of her, so was the team.

She crossed her arms around her ribs, holding herself in a bruising grip as she fought the shaking that was overtaking her, an addict jonesing for a fix. She tried to steady her breathing, slow it—end it, even—but that only made the craving worse. There was one thing she could do to break herself out of this spiral.

She closed her eyes, feeling the darkness swallow her, starting with her feet, as it always did. She stamped them, trying to shove it back down. It wouldn't go away. It slipped up her calves. She choked on a sob. She hadn't let it get higher than her waist for a long, long time, but up, up it went, eating her, inches at a time.

"No, no. Nonononono—" she murmured, terrified of the numbness it brought.

BASTION'S astral body sat next to Selena as she kept herself folded tightly against the wall. Her face was flushed, her eyes wide and dark—not with passion but terror. This was his fault. He'd scared the hell out of her.

He tried to surround her energy with his, hoping to calm her rising panic, but it had no effect. He was about to hurry down from his attic retreat, but she got up and rushed into the bathroom. Was she ill?

She yanked drawers open and rifled through them, madly searching for something that she wasn't finding. He stepped close to her, trying again to send her soothing energy.

She grabbed a travel kit and dumped its contents on the counter, then stared hard at the empty toiletries bag. Her breathing calmed. Maybe his energy surges were getting through to her. He was about to summon his astral body back to himself so that he could come down and be with her in person, when she reached into the bag and pulled something out.

He leaned over to see what it was. A box cutter. Why would she be so frantically searching for that? Or maybe that wasn't what she'd been searching for at all. *Dieu*, he wished she hadn't blocked him from her mind.

She set it down on the counter, staring at it as if she expected it to come alive. She backed away from it, never taking her eyes off it. Maybe it was what she'd been searching for. Why did it hold so much power over her?

She turned the shower on, still staring at the steel tool while steam began to spill over the top of the shower stall. After a minute, she tore her clothes off, stripping down to her bra and panties. Still she stared at the box cutter. She moved closer to the mirror now, then reached behind her to unhook her bra. As much as Bastion had yearned to see her nude body, this felt waaaay too close to voyeurism. He was just about to slip out of the bathroom, when Selena dropped her bra to the floor. Her breasts were luscious mounds with small, dark nipples. Even his astral body tightened in arousal —which in itself almost made him pop back into his physical body.

Selena cupped those gorgeous mounds and held one off to the side, looking at herself critically. And then he understood the connection between her panic, the box cutter, and her breasts. Judging from the messy criss-crossing of raised scars he saw, she was headed some-place dark.

Right now.

It would take him three minutes to rush down from the attic and get into her room, three minutes that would be too long to stop her from what she was about to do.

She made the same examination on the side of her other breast, which was similarly scarred. Bastion stepped behind her and caught her wrists in his astral hands. *Don't do this. I beg you. Don't. Do. This.* He was so panicked that he lost the ability to manipulate the phys-ical world. She reached down and picked up the box cutter.

No. No. Selena. Please. I will do anything for you, anything, just stop this now. Tears slipped down his astral cheeks. He briefly wondered how that was possible without yanking him back into his body, but he pushed that question aside. Three minutes for him to get here. He couldn't risk that delay when he might yet be able to stop this.

Selena stepped into the steaming shower, still wearing her panties. She adjusted the temperature of the water, then let it bead down over her open palm, where the box cutter sat.

She slowly slumped down, sitting so just her feet were in the water. Her hand tightened on the steel tool. Bastion sat in front of her, his astral legs bent on either side of hers. He tried to get a hold of her wrists again, but his phantasmal fingers just moved through her flesh.

Normally, he could still interact with physical material while in astral form, but not tonight. He was too panicked.

Please. Selena. Stop. Look at me. Look at me.

He pushed a compulsion at her, but it just slipped over her head, blocked by her powerful mind. He tried and tried to grab her hands, to block their upward movement.

And then the blade nicked her soft flesh, drawing a new, thin line through the mat of tangled white scars. She sucked in a sharp breath and her eyes rolled back as her eyelids lowered over them in painful, exquisite relief.

Bastion was instantly back in his body. The three-minute countdown began as he leaped down the attic stairs, slammed through the door to the hall, crossed the hall, mentally unlocked her door, then did the same with the bathroom door.

It took him two minutes.

She looked up at him, but her eyes were unfocused. He would wipe her memory of this whole event later. Now, he just put her in a trance as he stepped barefoot into the shower. The hot water pelted his bare back as he crouched in front of her. She'd made a second cut under the first. Neither was deep, but both flowed freely, the thick red of her blood thinning out from the water splashing off his shoulders.

Relaxed in the trance he'd imposed, Selena let her hands drop to her thighs. Bastion freed the box cutter from her grip and tossed it out the open shower door, where it skittered across the floor.

He caught her hands and kissed her knuckles. Why, Selena? Why? You could have come to me. I would help you—always.

Rape bait.

The term clearly came to him from her mind, but he didn't understand its implications. His tears fell freely as he observed his woman, sitting in some hell her mind had conjured, bleeding, slumped against the side of the shower in the grips of his trance.

He shut the water off and stepped out of the stall to retrieve a washcloth. He blotted her cuts dry. Part of him wanted to reach out to Guerre so his friend could heal her, his light, but he didn't, coward that he was. He still wasn't ready to come clean with his team. Not yet. Not that they could undo what the Matchmaker had done. But they both needed time — her more than he. And if time was the only gift he could give her now, then he damned sure would.

Seeing that her wounds were superficial and had already stopped bleeding, Bastion finally drew a calming breath.

He carried her out of the bathroom, then set her on her bed and pulled the covers over her. He went back into the bathroom and fished through the drawers for a medical kit. From it, he took some gauze pads, tape, and antiseptic ointment.

Selena was still lying in the bed where he'd put her. He sat beside her and leaned over her to tend her wounds. This was not how he'd imagined first touching her breasts. He kept himself focused on the task at hand — getting her patched up quickly. When he finished that, he leaned back and studied her. The scars were on the sides of both breasts.

Mon amour, I need to see the rest of your wounds. Please stand for me.

It wasn't fair, what he asked, taking from her rather than waiting for her to show him. He needed to know what he was dealing with — not that he had any idea how to help her heal, but at least foreknowledge would help him hide his shock when she did ultimately reveal herself to him.

Taking her hand, he helped her to her feet. The only thing she wore was a pair of beige boy briefs. Trimmed with elastic lace, they matched the bra she'd worn earlier.

He sat in front of her. He wanted to pull her body against his—as much to absorb the feel of her against himself as to reassure both of them that this would pass...whatever this was. He didn't though. He knew this memory would return to her, as all those he'd hidden from her would one day. She might hate him for it later, but that wasn't going to stop him from helping her now. He slipped his hands inside the waistband of her panties to push them down—but stopped when his fingertips encountered more spiderwebbing scars, on either hip. He squeezed his eyes shut and swallowed hard, afraid of what he would see when she was bared.

She obviously was aware that cutting herself wasn't okay, because she'd picked places hidden from the eyes of others. Secret places, secret like her sexuality.

Motherfucking hell. What had happened to her?

When they'd stood and talked about scars, he'd been talking about the thin one on her face and the one on her hand. Not these.

He pushed her panties off, helping her step out of them. A white patch of thin, raised scars marred her hip. Her upper front thighs had no marks. He turned her around, terrified of what he would find, but the only other scars he found were the mirroring ones on her other hip.

Dieu, how he wished to hold her. But that wasn't necessary to her care and wasn't a privilege she'd granted him—yet. He tilted her head up. Her green eyes were open but unfocused, just the blank stare of a tranced regular. He bent close and whispered, "We will figure this out. Or, at least, I will stand beside you as you figure it out. You aren't in this alone anymore, Selena. I am yours to command, to use, to hold, to consume."

He lifted the covers and urged her to get into bed. He had a bathroom to straighten and a dry pair of jeans to change into before settling in bed with her. Tonight of all nights was not a good one for her to be alone.

WHEN SELENA WOKE the next morning, before moving, before even opening her eyes, she knew something was wrong. She took stock of herself and her situation. It was early yet—well before sunup. She was in her room, in her bed, wearing a T-shirt she usually reserved for working out in...and her underwear was missing.

She sat up fast and sent a look around her room, uncertain what—or whom—she was expecting to see. No, that wasn't true. She was expecting *him*. Bastion.

She fisted the sides of her head as she tried to remember what had happened last night. Addy had had her bachelorette party. Bastion had spoken to her at the end of it, telepathically, summoning her up here.

Selena tried to clear the fuzz in her head, tried to remember details, but they kept just out of range, like a word you knew and used often but suddenly couldn't remember. The harder she tried, the less she remembered.

The underwear she'd had on last night was on the floor beside her bed. She got up and grabbed it, surprised that it was wet. She looked over to the mirror. A memory flashed of her and a naked Bastion standing behind her.

As soon as it came, it left, leaving her dazed. Had it been a dream? Had he been here? Why couldn't she remember what happened? There had only been the wives and girlfriends of the team at Addy's party last night. No one would have slipped her a Mickey.

She went into her bathroom, trying to understand the confusion she felt. Something was sticking to the side of her breast. She pulled her shirt off and looked down to see a long, narrow bandage taped to her skin. Her lungs locked up. She couldn't breathe—in or out. She stumbled over to the tub and sat on the edge.

This was bad.

She removed the bandage and looked at the thin scratches, recognizing them as something typical of her cuts. She'd done this to herself. No one else. But...had Bastion been there? Did he see her do this?

No one knew about her secret. She hadn't even told Ace, and if anyone here would understand, it was Ace.

This was not good. She hadn't cut herself in over a year. Until a few weeks ago, she thought she'd made progress away from using her go-to relief valve. Sure, she'd come close recently, but she hadn't given in those times.

Selena stepped into the shower and turned the water on, letting it pelt her face and shoulders, then lifted her arm to rinse the thin red lines she'd cut across the snaggle of white scars.

She was clearly losing her mind. She wasn't sure how much more she could take. If this were some fucked-up test Owen and Kit were running to build a psychological profile on her, then she didn't want any part of what they were up to.

SELENA WENT INTO THE DEN. This was not a good day to confront Owen. With his wedding just a few days away, he was wound tight...and shit always rolled downhill.

He looked up from where he was sitting at the desk. "Need something?"

"I need to talk to both you and Kit."

"Can it wait until after the wedding? I have a stack of things I'm trying to wrap up before then."

"No."

Owen's cold blue eyes studied hers, then he texted Kit. He leaned back in his seat, keeping his eyes on her while they waited for Kit to join them.

Selena closed the door when he did.

"'Sup, Owen?" Kit asked, his gaze moving between both of them.

Owen nodded toward her. "Selena's show."

"Just exactly what is it you guys are doing to me?"

she asked. The question caught them off guard. Not the reaction she was expecting.

"'Doin' to you?" Kit asked.

"You're making me lose my mind. Why?"

Kit and Owen exchanged confused glances. Owen got up from behind his desk and came around to lean on it. "Where's this coming from, Sel?"

"Is it a test? Another qual I have to pass?" she asked.

Owen frowned. "I'm not following you."

"I'm still active duty in the Red Team, here by arrangement with the Army. You're paying my salary, Owen, but I'm not a permanent member of your team. I want to know—are you trying to find my breaking point to see if I'm worth bringing on board for good?"

Owen rubbed his forehead, buying a few seconds before answering. "First, I'm already working on your separation papers. Second, you have nothing to do to prove yourself worthy or capable. You did that when you saved Kit's daughter. Third, I consider you a permanent member of my team. And fourth, what the actual fuck are you talking about?"

Tears watered Selena's eyes. She almost wished it was some screwed-up test he wanted her to pass. She waved her hand. "All the crazy stuff that's been happening."

"Like?" Kit asked.

"Like the voices, and partial memories, and—"

"Voices?" Owen asked.

"Well, the one voice. His voice."

"Whose voice?" Kit asked.

"Bastion."

Again, Kit and Owen exchanged looks. "This is worse than I thought," Owen said.

"What is it?" Selena asked.

"I don't know for sure," Owen answered. "I do know you aren't going crazy. And I do know we are not fucking with your head. My dad and Jax are on their way here for the wedding. We're going to have a phone conference with the Ratcliffs. Let's hear what they have to say about all of this." He studied her a long moment. "We'll help you, Selena. Whatever it is."

Selena hated that she was reduced to near-constant tears. She blinked them away and swiped at her face with her upper arm. "I hope you do it fast. I can't take much more."

Two new men arrived at the house, probably coming for the second wedding that was about to happen, Bastion supposed. These men were connected to Owen and his fiancée. Jax was Owen's soon-to-be brother-in-law. And Nick was Owen's mutant father.

This was interesting. Another modified human in the family. Although, to be honest, Owen's fiancée's mutant energy signature was continuing to fade—it wasn't as strong as it had been just a month ago.

Bastion wondered who had changed them, when and why. The Ratcliffs hadn't visited the house in the time since Bastion had been inside. Had they sensed him from his patrols around the grounds? Was Bastion why they were staying away?

And why were fighters in the Omni resistance modifying humans? Beyond that, there was a strange lingering energy between Owen and these two men. Residual threads of resentment, abandonment, and betrayal. It surprised Bastion that they had overcome their past to have a relationship now. Perhaps, in time, Bastion would learn what had happened.

Whatever it was, they'd put it behind them for the wedding.

13

———

Bastion's senses tingled. Trouble was prowling near the edge of the compound, just outside the area covered by the protection he had set. Whether it was Flynn or the ghouls, Bastion couldn't tell.

It had been dark for hours. Most of those living in the house had already retired. Bastion dressed in his tunics, wool and leather, then stepped into his suede pants. He slipped his sai into his belt, two in the back, one in the front.

He hurried from the attic, through the house, and out one of the French doors in the living room without running into anyone. In the open lawn area, he kept himself hidden from the team's security devices as he spread his arms and shut his eyes, opening his mind to the energies he felt, trying to get a read on how many ghouls there were. He could fight some, even several, but if this were a multipronged attack, the people he was protecting would be better served if he waited for backup before engaging. Were he to take a lethal blow, the protection he had in place would be jeopardized.

He read the energies of only three of the monsters, just beyond the woods at the side of the house, on BLM land. Bastion opened his mind to Liege, making him aware of the situation. If Bastion faltered, Liege would take up the protection.

He went across the lawn, through the woods, and walked out the other side. The tall, desiccated winter grass crunched beneath his boots. Across the narrow dirt road, at the edge of his protection, stood three ghouls.

Flynn definitely had it in for the Red Team. Not surprising, really, considering their fight against the Omnis.

One of the ghouls was standing up straight, sniffing the air. The protection Bastion had in place shielded him from being seen or heard, but it didn't entirely mute his energy signature. The beasts could feel him near. Bastion jogged a little farther down the dirt road, staying inside his dome of protection. The ghouls ran on all fours, keeping pace with him. They would know the instant he stepped away from his area of protection.

Liege, are there other ghouls around the property, or are these the only ones?

Liege took a moment to answer. Only those. Acier is on his way up.

Don't need him. I'll burn these three when I'm done.

Bastion projected an image of himself punching

through his protective energy and running down the dirt road away from where the real him stood. The simple feint worked. The ghouls chased that mirage and ignored Bastion's presence. He stepped across the dirt road onto the open pasture. The property wasn't owned by the Red Team and so wasn't under Bastion's protection. Frozen grass and patches of crispy snow crunched beneath his feet, catching the attention of the monsters.

They bumped into each other as they turned their attention to him, trying to determine whether he was another mirage or their actual target. Their minds weren't capable of complex strategic thought—they were engineered to kill, not think, a shortcoming that kept them from charging toward him again.

Bastion moved his sai from his back to his sides, ready for quick access. He withdrew the front sai, then charged toward the ghouls. As the distance between them closed, he threw it toward the first monster, which was running on all fours, pinning its front paw to the ground.

Bastion palmed his other two sai as he reached the first ghoul. He swept the monster's slashing claws to one side with his left sai as he shoved the long spike of his right sai up through its throat and into its brain.

The other two were immediately on him.

He used the flat head of one sai for a chest punch against the nearest ghoul, knocking the wind from the beast. There was no time to finish that one off before having to face the last monster.

Bastion battered it with blows from both sai,

breaking an arm, some ribs, a collarbone before shoving the long spike through the ghoul's eye and into its brain. By then, the second monster was on its feet again, crazed by the sight and smell of blood. When it slashed at him, Bastion snagged its arm in the sai and cut down-ward, slicing its forearm open. That barely stunned the beast, as hopped up on adrenaline as it was.

Bastion had long ago learned to read the rhythm of a fight. Each ghoul, each fight, had its own flow. This beast had switched to pure fury. Lashing out maniacally —but without strategy—it still managed to land some wicked cuts on Bastion's chest and legs.

Bastion held his sai against his forearms, then used the beast's own forward motion to hit its clawed hands with punches that broke its wrists. After that, it was easy to flip his sai forward and slash the arteries in its thighs, then rip out its throat.

When the fight was done, Bastion stood over the three corpses, panting hard. He finally became aware of the many cuts he'd sustained in the fight. He was covered in blood, his and theirs. *Are there more, Liege?*

No. You're clear.

Bastion used his telekinetic skills to draw twigs and branches and dried leaves out of the woods on the Red Team property and into a pile on the pasture. Lighting the pile on fire was a simple matter of focusing a spiral of energy on certain spots. In no time, fire danced over the dried slash pile. He found cut logs by the edge of the woods and added them to the bonfire.

When the flames were strong, Bastion dragged the

bodies over to the fire and loaded them on top. He controlled the pyre's fury, containing the sparks and ash in a narrow column high into the air until they'd flamed out. He hid the fire from any regulars that might be near enough to see or smell it. The ghouls stank like putrid flesh as they burned.

As Bastion looked around, he saw blood spread across the field. With a wave of his hand, he drew it up out of the snow and poured it over the fire, making the funeral pyre hiss. He did the same to the blood covering himself, sending it into the flames. He used his telekinetic skills to clean his weapons, then tucked them back into his belt. He leaned over to spit out the foul taste of ghoul blood and wiped the back of his wrist against his mouth.

Though the ghoul blood was gone from his skin and clothes, his own blood continued to seep through his clothing. Were he a regular, he'd need a trip to the emergency room to stitch up his many wounds. Being a mutant, Bastion knew his cuts would be closed by the time he took a shower, so he barely spared them a thought.

He stood there a long time, watching the corpses turn to ash. Liege had said he was in the clear, but those ghouls should never have been there to begin with. Were they there because of him? Or had they been sent for the other mutant—Owen's dad—who'd come in for the wedding? Or for the leader's mate, even though her mutant energy was faint now?

Liege, these people are in danger from Flynn. He's testing the waters, seeing what resources we've devoted to protecting these fighters. I can't hold him at bay for long. We need a plan.

Agreed, Liege said. *The Omnis didn't seem too concerned with the Red Team until now. Either they've sent Flynn to close that window, or he's acting on his own initiative.*

There was a short pause. Bastion stared into the fire. It wouldn't be a surprising strategy for Flynn to make a decoy situation that forced Bastion and his team to focus their attention away from whatever Flynn was really up to.

How is the woman handling all of this? Liege asked.

Bastion choked on a breath. He'd been keeping Selena away from the connection he shared with the guys, but Liege had sensed her anyway.

Which one? There are several here.

Neither of us is an idiot, Bastion. You would have finished this assignment a long time ago if not for her.

She suffers because she tries to block me.

No means no, my friend. Even for us.

It isn't no for her and me, it's no for her fear of what I will do to her team.

Are they candidates? Liege asked.

I believe so. They already have changed beings among them, so the concept isn't a foreign one to them. One is the leader's wife, though the energy signature of her mutations has been weakening. I believe her changes weren't permanent. The leader's father, however, has been changed, and permanently so. Then there was a married couple who were in the house before I went inside. They were both changed. I suspect they're the scientists we're after. We've heard that they changed themselves.

What's your evaluation of these people? Liege asked. *You've watched them for months. Are they Omni sympathizers?*

Non. *They have been fighting the Omnis since last year, maybe longer, though in an unorganized way until recently. They are strong. They are honorable. It is possible that we could recruit them. Or some of them. They also have connections with another group of Omni fighters. Friends, not relatives, I think — but close enough that they share holidays and weddings with this group — who might also be contenders to join our fight.*

Changing them will take them out of the fight for a while — and at a critical juncture, Guerre said, joining the convo.

And leaving them unchanged will as well. The Omnis will swat them as flies. Bastion pressed his lips against his teeth, then huffed a sigh. *But they are not only fighters — they are husbands, papas. It becomes complicated to use them.*

I don't want anyone else changed, but we may not have a choice in the matter, Liege said. *We're losing this fight. I'm hearing rumblings of more mutants surfacing not far from the jungle where our training camp was. It's unclear whose side of this fight they're on. When I know more, we'll collect them — or terminate them — as the situation demands. Until then, we'll continue disrupting Flynn's activities.*

I don't think we're disrupting his plans — I think he's disrupting ours, Bastion said. *He's up to something. He's hiding behind the escalation he's causing up here.*

A clapping sound broke Bastion from his conversation. Brett Flynn stood on the opposite side of the fire, his pale face lit by the dancing flames into something far warmer than his devilish soul. "Congratulations on your kills tonight. I thought they'd get your attention."

"Why are you here, Flynn?" Bastion nodded over his shoulder to the compound behind him. "These people are just regulars, blind to our world. They are no threat to the Omnis."

"Aren't they? Have you no memory of the fire ants in our jungle camps? So little compared to the size of us, but still able to make us miserable. I don't feel like suffering your friends any longer."

"Then walk away."

"I might, except then I wouldn't know why you're here, protecting these nothing regulars."

"We protect all regulars."

"But why the intense interest in these? Hmm?"

Bastion started walking around the circle of fire to get to Flynn, curious whether he was here in the flesh or merely an astral projection. Flynn moved away as he approached, stepping backward as he continued his torment.

"Did you know the town here dislikes this group? They'd love to see them destroyed and disbanded. You've put all of your weak defenses into protecting them, and none at all into the innocent civilians in town."

Bastion didn't take the bait. "Are you ready for that step, Flynn? Exposing yourself to the world of regulars—and to your enemies within the Omni World Order—is a bold step. If everything isn't perfectly in place when you make that leap, you will have both the Legion and the Omnis to contend with."

Flynn's smile was like a jack-o'-lantern, wide and

haunting. He stopped walking. So did Bastion. "I came to propose a détente."

"So propose it."

"You leave, and I leave these people alone."

"What do you gain in the bargain?" Bastion asked.

"I can simplify my portfolio. If I don't have to be here overseeing you, I can put my focus elsewhere."

"And what do we get for complying?"

Flynn's smile was chilling. "I'm into negative inducements these days. If you stay, you'll need reinforcements up here, because my pets need to eat."

"Bring it. I can deal with that."

"Perhaps you can, but when you're all up here fighting for these nothing regulars, who will be in Fort Collins protecting Liege's sweet daughter?"

Bastion heard Liege's hiss through their mental link.

"Of course, Liege could force her to go to the fort, but then there's still his woman's friends, and all the innocent women Liege's daughter has been fighting to protect." Flynn tilted his head as he stared at Bastion. "It's your war. Pick your hell. I'll know your answer if you're still here tomorrow."

Wind cut across the field, lifting the flames into a tower inferno. When it settled down, Flynn was gone.

Come back to the fort, Bastion, Liege said. *We need to regroup.*

My woman is here. I cannot leave her.

She is under your protection. She'll be safe while we make a plan.

Bastion listened to the still woods behind him. This

batch of monsters had been dispatched, but what if more were on their way? If these had gotten through his protection and reached the house... He didn't let himself finish that thought.

And now Flynn had found a way to get him to abandon his post.

Bastion went to the edge of the woods, staying deep enough in the shadows to keep from triggering the security cameras.

Selena was standing on the patio outside the kitchen, looking his way. Damn, but her instincts were strong. She wasn't wearing a coat, but didn't seem affected by the cold.

Unable to stop himself, Bastion crossed the lawn, approaching her in long strides. He ached to speak to her, craved letting her see him. He could only imagine a smile from her lips, a look of gentle welcome in her eyes. If she saw him right then, he would just be a nightmare, covered in his own blood, his eyes still glowing orange with rage from his talk with Flynn.

Her dark hair was up in a ponytail. He telekinetically sliced the band holding it, freeing her dark mane to spill around her shoulders, leaving it to the whim of the wind. Some locks streamed across her neck, others across her mouth and forehead.

It seemed she didn't notice, so intense was her focus on something behind him. Bastion paused just a foot from her. Nothing was behind him, he knew, but she didn't—her senses weren't as acute as his, and she had a regular's poor vision in the dark. He wondered if she'd heard some of the fight a little while ago or sensed the energy that lingered from it.

He imagined stroking his fingers down her cheek, smoothing an errant lock of hair behind her ear. As if she felt his yearning, she touched her knuckles to her cheek, stroking herself as he craved to do. She closed her eyes.

Rage danced with hunger inside him. *Mon Dieu*, how he wished he weren't invisible to her.

Why are you out here in the cold? he asked. *And alone?*

Her lips parted on a sharp pull of air. She looked around, searching the empty space for him. *Bastion?*

Mon amour?

I heard something.

It was just me. I was running in the woods.

Show yourself.

I cannot. He could hide the blood from her, but he still couldn't touch her because it would soil her. No, better to stay out of sight.

There was something else in the woods. I felt it.

I don't sense anything, but I will check it out. Go back inside. You'll freeze standing out here much longer.

I want to see you again. For real. In the flesh.

Bastion shook his head, even though she couldn't see him. *It is not possible tonight. Go inside. I will keep you safe.*

Sooner or later, she was going to find herself confronting the ghouls. He wouldn't be able to protect her forever.

Movement at the window behind her caught Bastion's attention. A face hovered there. One of the wild boys—a tall one. Hawk. His pale face seemed to float in the dark room behind him. His eyes once again looked directly at Bastion. Maybe it was a fluke. Bastion moved over to the other side of Selena, but Hawk's eyes kept pace with him. He only pulled away when Selena looked back at the house.

I have to go, Selena said.

Stay away from Hawk. Something's off with him. Bastion stood at the edge of the patio, watching her go inside, hiding this memory from her, like all the others.

This was wrong, all the secrets and stolen memories. Nothing was really gone from her mind; at some deep subconscious level, it was all still there, festering, causing her stress that she couldn't find the source of.

It had gone on so long now that he may have destroyed their shot at a life together.

And now it would have to go on longer while Bastion gave Flynn a chance to lose interest in these people.

He hated giving that bastard anything, but there was much more at stake than Bastion's own dreams and hopes.

THE NIGHT WAS WELL PROGRESSED by the time Bastion made it to Grumpy's Beer Haul, the college bar in Fort Collins he and the guys preferred. His friends had a table already. It was good to see all of them together.

They wouldn't have that opportunity once Merc left for South America.

Two women ran up to him and tried to lead him over to the table. Instead, he caught their hands. "I have news to tell you."

The girls giggled and shimmied closer to him. He had no hunger for them—hadn't ever hungered for them. Their frequent *ménage à trois* encounters had let him pretend he was still normal, still human.

All of that was in the past, now that he'd found Selena.

"Our time together is over. I have found the woman I love." He wanted to break up the mutant way, saving himself and them drama, but he felt he owed them the opportunity to process their feelings in their own way, so he did it with words instead of compulsions.

Surprisingly, both girls hugged him and wished him well. When they left, Bastion sat at the table. The guys were staring at him as if he'd sprouted a second head.

"'Sup, assholes?" Bastion said.

"So it's true." Acier spoke first, looking at the two coeds Bastion had just fired.

"I didn't tell them about her." Merc held up his hands.

"As if we wouldn't know," Guerre said. "You never keep yourself so separate from us."

Merc laughed. "It has been nice not having Bastion live-stream his every thought."

"Where is she?" Acier asked.

Bastion looked at Liege then Acier. "It's complicated."

Acier didn't buy that. "Is she your light or not?"

"She is. But I have not—we have not—actually spoken in person. Much. Not in a way I've let her remember, anyway."

"So you're shit at being someone's light, is what you're saying, mate," Merc said, still grinning.

"She's a warrior and is a package deal with her team. To come out to her, I'd have to come out to them. And doing that means they'd have to step into our reality. So, *oui*, I'm shit at it." Worse than just being bad at it, he'd likely killed any shot they'd had at a future.

"Given Flynn's interest in her team," Liege said, "bringing them into our reality is going to happen sooner rather than later. I'd like you to stay at the fort for a few days, let things cool down with Flynn."

"I'm not finished my reconnaissance up there. And I don't know how long I can be away from Selena."

"Selena, is it?" Merc asked. "I like that name."

Bastion ignored that. "Owen Tremaine, your equivalent on her team, is getting married this weekend. His father is a mutant. I should be up there right now."

Guerre looked at Liege. "Someone in the resistance is modifying humans too?"

Bastion nodded. "This is part of what we need to understand."

"Maybe it is time you brought them in, Liege," Merc said.

Bastion looked to see if Acier shared that opinion. "You don't agree, Acier?"

Acier's hard blue eyes shifted to Bastion. "I suppose it was only a matter of time."

Bastion tried to drill into that cryptic comment, but Acier wasn't letting anyone dig through his mind, which, of course, made Bastion all the more curious.

Guerre broke the awkward silence. "Wait until you see the fort, Bastion. Summer is nearly finished working on the greenhouse in the pool room. It looks like a jungle. And she put in a kitchen garden with all the herbs you'll ever want."

"Liege's missus has a soft spot for you, mate," Merc said. "But enough about Bastion. Let's talk about me."

Bastion frowned. "I'm suffering, Merc. I could use a little more focus."

"Mm-mm. I'll be leaving soon."

"Already?" Bastion's gaze shot from Merc to Liege and back.

"There have been Santo sightings in Colombia. I've got to fetch him back."

"Oh." His departure would thin the team here considerably. And with Flynn going ape shit, it wasn't a good time to be down a man.

Maybe it was time they brought Selena and her team in.

14

Bastion sat next to Selena on her bed, stretching his legs out to cross them at the ankles. He hated to wake her—she'd been sleeping so restlessly. It was all his fault, he knew.

He put her into a trance. What he'd come to say could wait.

He wanted to check in with her before the wedding, which he wouldn't be able to attend after all. Flynn had summoned him and Liege for a meetup. Bastion wasn't going to mention it because he didn't know when he could be back. And besides, he could always visit her like this, as his astral self. Given that he was appearing inside the dome of protection he'd put on the compound, visits like these shouldn't cause an energy flux detectable to Flynn.

Bastion sat next to her for hours. When dawn neared, he lifted his sleep compulsion so they could talk.

She gasped when she saw him, then scrambled out of bed, instantly alert.

"You are extraordinarily stubborn," he said.

Selena's gaze darted around the room. She grabbed her phone, checking first for alerts. Bastion zapped it with an EMF pulse. She reached for the security necklace that she always wore, but Bastion hid it from her.

She tossed her phone to the ground and pressed her wrists against her temples as terrible thoughts slammed through her mind.

It hurt that she still thought him a monster, but given all these stolen moments, he supposed he'd earned that. Her eyes darted over to her nightstand where her pistol lay.

Bastion flipped the light on. "Go ahead, shoot your bed." He disappeared then reappeared in the same place. "I'm not here, so you won't be shooting me."

Selena rubbed her forehead. "I asked you to leave me alone."

"I tried. It would seem I have a weakness I did not anticipate."

"Oh? What would that be?"

"You. Come back to bed. We need to talk. I don't like it when you block me from your mind."

"Too bad. My mind, my rules."

"I would honor that were so much not at stake."

"Where are you? I mean the physical you."

"I am not far. Just a few hours away." He gestured to the half of the bed he wasn't occupying. "Please, let us talk. I will not touch you."

"Get out of my bed first."

He disappeared, then reappeared next to her. "Is this better?"

Selena's eyes moved up his chest, neck, and beard. When their eyes met, his gaze held hers captive. Her nostrils flared as she scented him. That, more than anything else, turned him on.

Her thoughts were easy to read tonight, probably because she'd been so abruptly roused from sleep. She thought he smelled delicious, then wished he didn't. She was furious with herself for thinking something pleasing about him.

Bastion laughed. "It is my own scent you are enjoying. My pheromones trigger a chemical response in you, as yours do in me. It is distinctive, addictive."

"Except you aren't here, so I can't smell you at all."

"You have a clear memory of my scent." He gave her a half-grin. "I wish you could know what you smell like to me. In a sea of a thousand sweet-smelling women, I would find you with my eyes covered and hands bound."

"Just what I wanted. My very own bloodhound."

He laughed again. She couldn't pull her eyes from his smile. He gestured again toward her bed. "Please. I have said I won't touch you."

"And you always keep your word."

He sighed. "Not always. I've failed more times than I'd like to admit. I won't fail you, however."

Selena adjusted her pillows then sat on her bed. When she looked up, Bastion wasn't where she'd left him.

"I'm here." He was now sitting on her dresser, across from the foot of her bed.

"Since we're having this awesome convo, let's start with your real name," Selena said.

"I've had many names over many years. I shed them like a snake sheds his skin, having grown out of what he was. So call me what I am. I am the walls that protect you. I am your fortress. I am your Bastion."

"I don't need protecting."

"You do, but you don't know it yet. All of you here need protection."

"Someone purporting to be my *bastion* would not harm those I love."

"Have I harmed your team? I could have, at any point, eliminated them, killed them gently in their sleep, leaving their women to wake next to dead partners. They are as defenseless as infants to me. Your men are not my enemies, that much I've learned."

"So what do you want?"

Her. The two of them together. He wanted the life the Matchmaker had given them, for as long as he could have it before the curse separated them.

But that wasn't an answer she was ready for, so he gave her another, also true, answer. "The Ratcliffs."

Selena shrugged. "I don't know where they are."

"Find out and tell me."

"So you can kill them?"

"No."

"Why, then?"

He flickered out. *Bastion! Damn you. I will not let you use me.*

Bastion hadn't gone anywhere at all, except to disappear from her sight. He'd tried to keep things light—and fast-moving—hoping to just check in on her before going with Liege to meet Flynn's mysterious summons. He lingered now to make sure she was all right. He was only in astral form, so if his visit triggered her, he'd need to find Ace and compel her to check on Selena.

He watched as she did a check of all the nooks and crannies in her room, looking for him. When she didn't find him, she shut off all the lights and climbed back into bed. Folded up tight against the headboard, she was anything but relaxed. At least she wasn't so worked up that she returned to her hell in the bathroom.

OWEN AND ADDY were having their wedding rehearsal tonight, so the whole day, really the whole weekend, would be a festive one.

Selena was happy for them, but so not in a joy-joy place herself. How could she be? Bastion had stolen everything from her. Her team. Her future. Her sanity.

Selena swiped the heel of her hand across her eyes. They were angry tears, born of frustration. She was cornered and she knew it, something she'd promised herself she'd never let happen again.

Someone knocked on her door. She didn't answer it, but they came in anyway—Owen and Ace.

Selena ignored them as she continued shoving things into her duffel bag. Owen leaned against her dresser, next to a column of empty, opened drawers. Ace moved about the room, probably checking for Bastion.

"Talk to us," Owen said, folding his arms.

"I'm leaving. I'm done," Selena said.

"Where are you going?" he asked.

Selena straightened. She looked at him then at the wall behind him, no ready answer coming to mind.

"This is because of Bastion, isn't it?" Ace asked.

Selena glared at her.

"Is he here?" Owen asked.

She resumed packing. "He's not here. He's somewhere three hours or so from here."

"How do you know?" Owen asked.

"He told me." Selena stared at her open duffel bag. "He was here, this morning." She shook her head. "Not exactly here, but"—she waved her hands around the room—"here." She didn't think Bastion was in the room with them—physically or otherwise—but then, how would she really know?

Owen started toward her, then began rubbing his temple. Selena backed away from him, holding a hand out. "Get away from me."

He stood his ground, wincing from what had to be pain blazing in his brain. "Selena, you have to stop. You're not going anywhere."

"No." She shook her head. "I mean get back. Go back over there." She pointed to where he'd just been leaning against her dresser.

He did back up a step, and another, and as he did so, the pain in his head must have eased—more with each step. "What the hell's going on?"

"It's Bastion. He's doing that."

"So he is here." Owen looked around the room. Ace shook her head.

"No. He's not in here." Selena waved her arms around again, indicating the room, then poked at her head. "He's in here." Selena covered her mouth with her hand, fighting back a ragged sob. "I have to go. He can get to us through me. He doesn't have to be here to attack us."

"You're saying he caused the pain I just felt?"

"Yes."

"Why?"

Selena sent Ace an embarrassed glance. "Because you and I— Because I had feelings for you once. Sort of."

"Is he hurting you?" Owen's eyes narrowed.

Selena shook her head then gave Owen a terrified look. "How do I know that he's real? What if this is some psychedelic-induced craze? Or a full-on mental breakdown? How do I know?"

"*I* know. You aren't crazy."

"And Bastion's real," Ace said. "We just had a debrief on him with the Ratcliffs."

"You aren't off the team, Sel," Owen said.

"My being here endangers all of you," Selena said. "I have to go."

Owen sighed. "Maybe that is best. For now. Finish packing. I'm going to send you someplace safe."

"Where?"

"Away from us. I can't tell you specifics. Just know that it's only until this blows over—or until we know how to deal with him. You'll leave after the wedding."

"I should go now."

"I don't have arrangements made yet." Owen started to leave, but paused. "Please avoid the bunker for now, but other than that, there are no restrictions on your movements in the house. You aren't going to reveal anything Bastion hasn't already seen. Don't leave the property."

ACE CONFRONTED Owen in the hallway. "She's not going alone."

Owen was heading toward the back stairs, forcing her to keep pace with him. "She won't be alone."

"I'm going with her. I told her I had her back."

Owen sent Ace a glare. "We all have each other's back. You're staying here."

Ace stopped walking. Owen stopped too. She gave him a wounded look, then pivoted and went back to Selena's room.

ACE SLAMMED THE DOOR OPEN, making Selena jump.

Selena sat on the edge of her bed as Ace paced angrily. "Owen won't let me go with you."

"It's for the best. Bastion is ruthless. He'll use anyone or anything to get back into this house. I wouldn't let you go either."

Ace stopped. "I promised to have your back."

Selena reached up and took Ace's hand, dragging her over to sit on the bed. "I have to tell you something, something I should have said long ago." She hadn't wanted to say anything before and still didn't want to now, but on the off chance Bastion might think to use it to blackmail her, she had to unload.

"What?"

"I had a crush on Val. Well, sort of a crush. Nothing happened."

Ace busted out laughing. "Of course you did. Have you *seen* Val?"

Selena chuckled. "I had one on Owen too. Nothing happened there either."

"I get it. Owen does nothing for me, but I can see that he might for you."

Selena looked at Ace, still feeling worried. "You forgive me?"

"Fuck yeah. I figure crushes are like trying samples at Costco—they give a little taste of a bigger dish you may or may not want to commit to."

"How many crushes have you had?" Selena asked.

"One." Ace grinned. They both knew it was on Val.

"I'm glad you two are together. And I'm glad Owen and Addy are getting married. You all faced some pretty long odds and made it anyway. I'm going to miss you."

"I guess communications with you will be frozen."

Selena nodded. "I don't know what Bastion's fully capable of. I don't want to take any chances."

Ace got up and started toward the door. "Fine. We'll do this for a while. But if you need me, then fuck Owen. I'm there—wherever there is."

THE FIELD FLYNN had picked for their meeting was a section of open grazing land. The only witnesses were the giant power lines and the surrounding wind turbines. The land that far east of the mountains was basically flat, but this had a slight hill that let them see in all directions for miles.

Bastion and Liege had both scanned the area for ghouls or other Omnis hidden behind Flynn's illusions.

None were there.

Flynn parked and came over to join them. He held his arms wide, gloved hands palms up, greeting them as if they were long-lost family members. No one had ever been fooled by his twisted brand of charm, not now, not in the camps.

"Look how we can meet and negotiate like civilized partners," Flynn said, steam from his breath rising into the crisp night.

"If we were civilized, we'd have been able to meet at a library or bar, somewhere warm and busy," Liege said.

"Aw, my friend. I am sorry to disappoint. I thought meeting here would give you comfort in being able to see around us for such a great distance. Not a ghoul in sight." Flynn laughed. "Shall we get started with our negotiations? I have what you want. You have what I want…"

"I'm listening," Liege said.

"You want your daughter and her social endeavors off-limits."

"Both are off-limits."

"Not tonight. No, everything's on the table. It always was."

"Then we have nothing more to talk about." Liege started to turn away, but Flynn stopped him.

"I want Owen Tremaine's team."

Say nothing about Selena, Liege warned Bastion. *Knowing she's your light will make him want her to get back at you.*

"And we get?" Bastion asked.

"The Ratcliffs."

"What's your interest in the fighters?" Liege asked.

"That's my concern. Do we have a deal?"

"Forget it, Liege. He doesn't know where the Ratcliffs are," Bastion said. "He can't barter with something he doesn't own."

"I'll have them within a month."

Liege laughed. "No deal."

"Laughing at my offer is a huge mistake."

"Offering a trade of no value is a worse one," Liege said. He and Bastion started walking way.

"I've given you warning, Liege."

Liege looked back at Flynn. "Give me something of substance, then. The factory where you're creating your ghouls. Tell me where you're taking the women you've been snagging off the streets. Give me something that I value."

Flynn held firm. "I'll have the Ratcliffs in a month."

"Then in a month, we'll talk again."

WHEN BASTION and Liege got back to the fort, they went into the kitchen. Merc and Guerre joined them. Acier was at his place in Fort Collins but joined the quick conference via his telepathic link.

I don't know why Flynn's so interested in the Red Team, Liege said. *Maybe because taking them down would remove a thorn in the OWO's side. They may be a team of regulars, but they're a force to be dealt with.*

We can expect Flynn to step up his attacks, Bastion said, *both here in Colorado and in Wyoming around the Red Team headquarters. He'll have to save face from his failed negotiations.*

Do you think he really does have a bead on the Ratcliffs? Guerre asked.

That's anyone's guess, Liege said. *He's full of bullshit and bluster. He's also sneaky as hell. We can't let him know Bastion's light is with Owen Tremaine's team.*

I need to get Selena out of there, Bastion said. *I want to bring her here where she'll be safe while we work with Tremaine's team to bring in the Ratcliffs.*

Liege nodded. *Then it's time to bring them up to speed. Get back up there, Bastion. Let's get things rolling. We have at most a month before Flynn does something drastic.*

Why do you suppose he warned you? Merc asked. *What's he really up to?*

If you figure that one out, Liege said, *clue us in. Right now, our primary objective is to secure Selena and her team, then find and secure the Ratcliffs.*

15

Selena had had many new starts in life. Too many. But none had begun with her blindfolded and rushed under the cover of night to a safe house, hours away from the work she'd been doing and the team of mercenaries she'd begun to think of as family.

She had a bad feeling about this.

Of the two guys who had volunteered to join her in exile, only Jax was still human. Owen's dad, Nick, was a mutant like Bastion. His modifications had happened much more recently, however. It was still unknown if he would have the same or similar superpowers that Bastion had.

She knew little about either man other than the surface stuff. Jax was Addy's brother and Owen's childhood-best-friend-turned enemy-turned bestie again.

And Nick was a piece of work. He'd disappeared into the shadow world of the Omni resistance when Owen was a teenager and had only recently resurfaced.

He was a man in his sixties whose age was reversing. Thanks to the modifications he'd taken, he now looked more like Owen's brother than his father.

The knot in her stomach got tighter. Neither man's history instilled much confidence in her, but Owen trusted them, so she had to as well. She should have just gone AWOL. Everyone would have been safer then, away from her and the mutant stalking her.

She squeezed her eyes shut behind the blindfold, blocking Bastion from her mind. Instinctively, she understood that any thoughts about the mutant opened some kind of a link from her to him. Beyond that, her team didn't understand much at all about the changed humans—not their abilities, their objectives, or how to fight them.

The effort of keeping her mind empty was exhausting. No one spoke on the helicopter ride over, but even if they had, she wore sound-deadening headphones, ensuring she wouldn't hear anything the pilot might have had to say. A blindfold covered her eyes.

She couldn't hear or see—it was like volunteering to live in a soundproof room with no external stimuli. Her mind was already screaming, yet her exile had only just begun.

Selena breathed through a wave of panic. Strong emotion was another cord that somehow tied her to Bastion. He seemed to feel what she felt when her emotions were high.

No emotion. No thoughts. No visual or audio input. She should just be dead.

Lives depended on her surviving this period of hell. Her team needed as much time as she could give them to unscramble the mystery she'd somehow gotten wrapped up in. She intended for them to have every minute they needed.

The helicopter landed. Without the ability to see or hear, time had become distorted in the long ride here. Minutes had seemed like hours. Selena wasn't sure how long they'd been in the air or how far they'd actually traveled. The pilot had made several turns during the flight, perhaps to throw off her sense of direction. That was probably a smart decision. The less she knew about where she was, the better she'd be able to thwart Bastion's attempts to locate her.

She could feel him with her, pushing in at the edges of her mind, trying to get inside. He was desperate to get to her—she could feel that in him, almost to the point of pain. But was that because of her, or because her leaving had shut off his access to the team? The harder he pushed, the harder she forced her mind to focus only on her own breathing and the mind-numbing rhythms of the music on her playlist.

She and Bastion were practically different species. She had no future with a man like him. He had to know that, which then made her realize that he wanted what he was after—and that wasn't her. She'd just been his tool.

Fuck. It. All. She was tired of being used by men.

Jax tapped her arm. She removed her headphones. "We're here," he said.

She didn't ask where "here" was. She couldn't know.

"Hang tight," Nick said. "We'll guide you to the house."

She was about to remove the blindfold, but Jax stopped her. "Leave it on, Sel," he said as he leaned close to speak over the roar of the helicopter. "The less Bastion can see of where we are, the better."

"I'm not staying blindfolded the whole time I'm here."

"No, of course not. Not inside, anyway. But for a few days, let's limit your exposure to the property. Maybe he'll give up and quit using you. One week, max."

Jax and Nick helped her out of the chopper, into brutally cold weather and wind that raked her exposed skin. Someone handed her bag to her. She tossed the strap over her head. The guys each took an arm and quickly led her down a hill. They crossed a long, flat stretch of snow-covered ground.

"Some steps now," Jax said, then they climbed about a dozen stairs. Selena heard a heavy door creak as it opened.

"Good evening, sir," a man said as they went inside.

The door closed behind them, making a heavy echo. Selena reached up for her blindfold and removed it.

A middle-aged man she didn't know greeted her with a slight bow and a warm smile. "I'm Spencer Hudson, butler here and part of Mr. Jacobs' security staff. I'll show you to your room, if you're ready."

Selena nodded at Jax and Nick, refusing to let them

see how unsettled she was. She forced that—and all—emotion from her mind as she went for full-on neutral and followed the butler up a wide set of marble stairs.

This had to be Addy's house. She recognized it from the things she'd said about it.

They turned to the right and entered a long wing. Though Selena wanted to explore the house, discovering for herself all the entry points, hiding places, and anything else that would let her take up a defensive position, she had to curtail her curiosity for a few days. A week, maybe, as Jax had requested.

She could do this. It certainly wasn't the hardest duty she'd ever been assigned. She just hated having to depend on others. She didn't like being the weakest link.

"There are four bedrooms in this wing," Spencer said. "You're free to select the one you like. They all have an en suite bathroom."

Selena looked down to the other end of the hall. It terminated in another tower. "Where does that door lead?"

"To some stairs," Spencer said.

Selena walked to the end of the hallway and selected the last bedroom, knowing that a close exit was of strategic importance.

"Very well." Spencer made a slight nod. "Is there anything else I can do for you this evening? Something from the kitchen—a sandwich, perhaps?"

Selena dropped her bag on the floor and turned to the butler. "Thank you, no."

"We have a landline here, since cell service is spotty.

The numbers you'll need to reach me, Jax, or Nick are next to the phone. Should you need either of them, Nick's taking a room on this floor in the other wing, and Jax's room is downstairs in the tower. The internet has been turned off, for obvious reasons. If there's something you need to access, the terminal in the library is properly encrypted. As far as I know, you have free rein to explore the house, but Jax has asked that you stay inside for a few days. The solarium between the two wings is lovely and has recently been restored. You might enjoy spending time there."

"Got it. Thanks, Spencer."

The butler nodded and left the room. Jax's crew was a ton more formal than Owen's. She wondered how many people Jax had on his "security staff," what their specialties were…and how any of them would manage in a fight with Bastion.

Maybe they'd do better in sheer numbers against the mutant, but maybe not. Bastion had been able to put at least one of her teammates into a trance. Maybe he'd be able to do that to multiple people simultaneously.

Maybe she should still find a way to go off on her own, away from anyone connected to her. Then, in the privacy of full isolation, she could open herself to him, find out who he was and what he was really up to.

IT WAS night when Bastion returned to Selena's compound. Lights were on all over the house. He'd missed the wedding by several hours, but seeing the house lit up gave him hope that he hadn't missed all the festivities.

He parked his Jeep on the grassy area next to the driveway in an area that wasn't likely to get much traffic, then covered it with an illusion that made it invisible to regulars. He wanted to use the front door, as Selena had requested, but it was not yet the time. He needed to first speak to her and make a plan for revealing himself.

It was the least that he could after taking so much from her.

He walked around toward the garage entry. As he neared the house, a bad feeling began to grow in the pit of his stomach. Something was not right here. The house and its residents had nothing of a festive vibe. It was heavy and dark.

What happened? He entered the garage through a locked side door, then went into the house through the garage door, all the while shielding himself.

He passed the den, the kitchen, the wine cellar, the living room, and went down the hall to the billiards room. No one was in any of those rooms. As he walked up the back stairs to Selena's room, the lights shut off in most of the house, leaving it as dark as if everyone had packed up and left.

Maybe the whole group had gone on Owen and Addy's honeymoon.

Not something he would let happen on his honeymoon, but this group was weird.

The dark feeling he'd had outside deepened as he got

to Selena's room. Before even opening her door, he knew she was gone.

His body went cold.

He stepped into her room, seeing her open dresser drawers first. Her bed was made but unused. The drawers were empty. He went into her bathroom. Her things were missing from there as well. His heart beat hard as he searched for her toiletry bag. It was gone.

She was gone.

He went back into her room and quieted himself, trying to hear or feel or know or see the last trails of her energy. Had she been afraid? Happy? Did she know where she was going?

Nothing. He got nothing.

He pivoted and slammed out of her room, then stalked down to Owen's bedroom. He had no idea what time it was. Maybe it was really late and the ops guys were only just shutting down the house. He walked into the southern bedroom wing and went straight into Owen's room.

The team's boss was asleep in bed with his woman. His new wife. *Merde.* Bastion remembered too late what had happened earlier that day.

Where is she? he shouted, but couldn't remember whether he'd spoken audibly or telepathically.

Owen sat up and looked around his room. Then he rose, nude, and pulled on a pair of jeans. *Not in here,* he said.

Son of a bitch. The bastard was a mind talker too.

Bastion followed him out into the sitting area outside the suite of bedrooms in that wing.

"She's gone, Bastion. You have to let her go." Owen clearly didn't know where Bastion was or even if he was still nearby. He addressed Bastion looking in the wrong direction.

I will not.

You have no choice.

Rage boiled up like a dormant volcano suddenly blowing. Bastion glared at Owen, squeezing his brain until his nose bled.

A quiet reminder slipped through his mind that this was Owen's wedding night. Fuck it all, he'd been about to crush the man's brain.

As soon as he released Owen, the man bent over, grasping his knees as he struggled to breathe through the fading pain.

Helpless, hopeless, Bastion let loose a sonic scream that boomed through the entire property like a plane breaking the sound barrier.

Addy and the boys rushed into the sitting room. Owen straightened and told his wife to stay with the boys.

"Owen—you're bleeding," Addy said, horrified.

Owen swiped his nose with the back of his hand. "Take the boys into their room. Now, Addy."

He went into his room. Bastion watched as he retrieved his earpiece from the dresser and issued a warning to his entire team.

"Bastion's here. Say nothing to him or to each other. Do not speak or think of Selena. Block her from your mind so that he cannot harvest info on her. Do you copy?"

Bastion's rage flared again, breaking every piece of furniture in the sitting room. He was about to step into Owen's room and continue his destruction, but he found himself frozen, encapsulated by Liege's energy.

Calm yourself, Liege ordered him.

Energy, of course, cannot disappear. It can only dissipate. Liege was Bastion's lightning rod, taking all of his rage and impotent fury, funneling it away from Owen, his home, his family, his fighters.

When it was gone, Bastion was left empty. There was nothing. There was no him, no Selena, no past, and no future.

Only numbness remained. And breathing.

I'm coming for you, Liege said.

Bastion didn't answer. He couldn't.

Liege released Bastion. He wandered out of the house to the lawn. He looked back at the sprawling mansion and realized he had a skill he hadn't known he possessed. He could level a building with a sonic roar.

He'd almost killed everyone inside. Because of his rage. He'd almost killed everything that Selena cared about. Thank God for Liege.

Bastion lost track of time, but then he saw Liege come out of the house straight for him. His team lead and friend stared into his eyes. He set his hand on Bastion's shoulder and said, "Only two people on Selena's team know where she went, and both are somehow blocking me. I don't know where she was taken, but I do feel that she's safe."

"She's not. Flynn will find her before we do. And when he does, he'll kill her."

"He doesn't even know she left."

"He will have sensed my explosive energy and will come to investigate," Bastion said. "He'll soon know she's outside the wire and will send ghouls for her. All because I lost it."

"I would have lost it too if Summer somehow disappeared. Stay here and watch for her."

"She won't come back while I'm here."

"No, but regulars have short attention spans. One of them will falter, sooner or later. I don't think you'll have to worry about Flynn. He's preoccupied with scrounging up the Ratcliffs. He won't even notice that Selena has slipped away."

"How are they blocking us, Liege? They're only regulars."

"They're mentally strong. Not surprising, given their backgrounds in special operations. It's all part of their training." Liege looked back at the house. "Makes me want to work with them that much more."

"I need to find out what they did with Selena before we come out to them."

"Agreed. But the clock is ticking. Remember Flynn's deadline."

THE DARKNESS WAS ABSOLUTE. Selena ignored the knocking on her bedroom door. The closet she was in was the only place she felt she could relax. She still had to fight to keep Bastion from slipping into her conscious mind. She could feel him there, trying to crack her resolve.

How pitiful was it that she wanted to let him in? They'd only spoken a handful of times when she was back at the Red Team headquarters. She'd seen him physically one time. The other times he'd been a mere projection of himself, and her memory of those times was spotty at best.

It was uncanny what he could do. He'd infiltrated her team's compound, slipping inside their home, unseen, unheard. Whenever she was lonely, he reached out to her, offering Selena her every dream, like a genie. He was as dangerous as any addiction. He pushed himself to the front of her mind. He was the why of every decision, which was how she found herself here, in her boss's wife's remote home somewhere in the Rocky Mountains.

Selena was a mere mortal human—unequal to the challenge of controlling Bastion. She didn't know if he would leave her team alone now that she'd left—that meant believing he'd come for her, not her team. Time would tell who his real target was.

She considered opening her mind to him, just to get it all over with, but the truth was that she, her new handlers, and her team were not individually nor collectively capable of fighting Bastion with any hope of success.

She had to stay strong.

Owen was playing for time, working some angle that he refused to reveal to her. She wondered if Jax or Nick knew what he was up to.

Worse, she wondered if she'd ever be accepted back into her team.

Selena stood up and started pacing around her closet. The space was bigger than many master bedrooms. Thankfully, it had no windows, so she wasn't tempted to peek outside. Three days she'd been in there. Sit-ups, planking, pacing...none of it helped. The sensory deprivation was taking a toll on her mental health. She had no television, no reading materials. Only her music and headphones offered respite here and there. The constant effort of keeping her mind closed to Bastion was giving her a low-grade migraine.

A knock sounded on the door to her room again. It was Spencer. He would leave her supper tray just inside her room, as he had with each meal.

She didn't rush out to get her food. Anxiety had robbed her of an appetite. Or maybe it was her persistent headache.

Another knock sounded on her door. That wasn't the pattern of the last few days. She was still operating under the belief that the fewer people she spoke to and the less she saw of the house and the world around her, the better off everyone would be.

The knocking stopped. Good. She didn't want to

deal with anyone yet. Time was the only thing she cared about. Her team needed as much of it as possible. She heard the door to her bedroom open and close. The floors creaked as someone approached the closet. Damn it. Probably Jax. Her closet door opened. Sure enough, Jax stood there with Nick by his side.

"You guys just bust into any old bedroom you want?" she asked.

"You didn't answer the door," Jax said.

"I didn't want to."

"What are you doing in here?" Nick asked.

"Hiding."

"Selena, you can't exist like this, in the dark," Nick said as he stepped into her closet. "Come out. Your body needs sunlight and your soul needs people."

"And my heart needs my team to survive."

"Come out and eat your breakfast," Jax said. "We can figure this out."

"Not much into food right now," Selena said.

"Are you sick?" Nick asked.

"Or pregnant?" Jax asked.

Selena gasped. Was that even a possibility? Had Bastion tricked her into something she couldn't remember? "Last I knew, a person had to have sex to get pregnant. Of course, the laws of nature as we know them may not work as they used to."

"Do you want to see a doctor?" Jax asked.

"Fuck no. I'm not pregnant. I'm not sick. I'm *hiding*."

"Could you maybe hide with us?" Nick asked.

Selena shook her head. "It takes all of my concentration to keep him out of my mind. If you distract me…"

"We'll fight Bastion with you," Jax said.

Selena scoffed. "You can't even see him. How can you fight him?"

"Fine. Whatever." Jax glared at her. "We'll die with you if Bastion comes for you, since you've pointed out how useless we are. You can't exist like this. Come work out with us. That'll at least help your appetite. Are you sleeping?"

"I have drugs for that." Selena had to admit that a hard workout would feel fantastic. "What's the word from Owen? Any news from the Ratcliffs on how to handle Bastion?"

"Not yet," Jax said.

Selena looked at Nick. "What about your trainer? When's he getting here? He might know something."

"There's been a snafu with that," Nick said. "He found out about you and Bastion and decided to take a different assignment."

Selena hadn't expected that blow. "Can he do that? Just cherry-pick his assignments?"

Jax folded his arms. "Guess he doesn't have a death wish."

I would not hurt you or yours. Bastion's voice came through Selena's mind like a clear radio signal.

You said you would not hurt me, but didn't provide that same guarantee to my team and friends before now.

I will not hurt them. Tell me where you are.

Selena wanted to believe him. His assurance

promised her the peace she craved. But she had to see his words for the strategy they were; of course he would tell her the very thing she most needed to hear. And of course he would know exactly what that was.

But damn, his voice was seductive, his promise compelling.

"Is he talking to you now?" Nick asked.

Selena nodded. "I told you I can't be around both of you and fight him, too. You need to leave."

"Come with us," Nick said.

"No."

Jax took a step toward the closet's door but stopped to give her a shake of his head. "Your choice, but Spencer isn't going to be delivering your meals anymore. You want to eat, you'll come downstairs."

Selena returned his hostile stare. "Works for me," she said, wishing she could feed Jax to Bastion.

A wave of humor came from the monster in her mind. *I am no cannibal. Although I want to eat you.*

Selena sucked in a sharp gasp and looked at her closet door, grateful the guys had already left.

Tell me where you are, Bastion said. *I will get you out of there. And I will feed you.*

No. She wanted to ask him about that night after Addy's party, the night she cut herself, but she also didn't want to open a can of worms. Maybe she'd just imagined him in her room. It wasn't that unusual that she'd grabbed the first T-shirt in her drawer or ditched her wet underwear. Her memory was spotty, but it often was after an episode.

Your boss's dad is a new mutant and needs a trainer. I volunteer.

No. This has to stop. You and me…whatever this is.

It won't. Ever. We are bigger than you and me. We were chosen, me for you and you for me.

Who chose us?

Tell me where you are. I will come and tell you the whole story.

You should know where I am. You're in my mind.

I am merely speaking with you. I can't read minds. I can only read energy. Sometimes I can pick up on thoughts that are clearly broadcast, but you are very good at controlling our connection.

Selena scoffed. *If that were true, we wouldn't now be talking.*

I'm glad we are.

Bastion, Selena said with sigh, *what is it that you want?*

You.

16

Exile didn't sit well with Selena. The house she'd been stashed in was a luxurious mansion, but a gilded cage was still a cage. She didn't like being confined. She didn't like hiding. And she didn't like being in a situation that had a beginning but no end.

She'd lost track of how many days she'd been hiding in her closet. More than a week. It was night now, time to crawl out and go find some food.

She went into her bathroom, intending to take a shower. So as long as she kept the window covers pulled, she couldn't give too much away if Bastion were able to see what she saw.

Her toiletries bag was on the counter. She stared at it a long minute, trying to resist everything it represented. Her past, her present, even her future. And the sickening relief she craved.

She hadn't cut herself since she been at Addy's. She'd thought isolating herself in the quiet retreat of her closet would help her manage her stress. And maybe it would have, if Jax and Nick hadn't broken into her sanctuary a few days ago.

Are you pregnant? Jax's question still haunted her. Was she? Could she be?

She had so many missing and incomplete memories, thanks to Bastion, including the night she'd cut herself after Addy's bachelorette party. He'd been in her room with her. But it had only been a projection of him. He hadn't physically been there, so they couldn't have had sex.

She slipped down the wall next to the sink to crouch on the floor. A cold sweat blanketed her skin as she thought of the day her hell started, twelve years ago. Awful memories blew like a gale through her mind, breaking through the blocks she'd had in place all the years since it happened.

She reached up and grabbed her kit, tucking it between her body and legs as she wrapped her arms around her knees. She was going to need it tonight. She rocked back and forth, tucked in a ball around her bag as she surrendered to the pull of her devils.

The empty halls of her school. The broken mirror and its shards that sliced into her. The blood, everywhere.

Selena opened her hand and looked at the thin scar between her thumb and forefinger, then bent her head to her knees and cried.

How little she'd understood about the world in those days, about human males, about power and justice, about how little control anyone had in their lives.

It was why she'd started cutting herself.

Cutting was wrong. All the shrinks had said so—all but one. He'd said it was an outlet, not a healthy one, but an outlet nonetheless. He'd worked with her to find other healthier outlets, but time and again, she'd gone back to cutting herself.

It was the one thing, the only thing, she could control.

But she wondered now if she really did have control over her urges to slice into herself. If it was an urge, was any control involved at all?

She shoved the bag away from herself, but still stared at it, craving the release it offered. She could cut herself. No one here would know. One small bar. And as long as she kept Bastion out of her head, he wouldn't know either.

Only she decided if and when to cut. She controlled that. Maybe only that, but it was entirely, and only, up to her.

She'd used different instruments over the years, but once she joined the Army, she hadn't wanted her secret habit to be mixed with any of her service weapons. Whenever she saw her cutting tool, she'd start yearning for the relief it promised, and she didn't want her head clogged with craving when her mind needed focus at work. That was when she bought her first box cutter, a tool she never used on the job.

She stood and set the bag on the counter, then

stripped in front of the mirror. She shut her eyes and put all of her attention on insulating herself from Bastion's incursions. When she felt as if she'd adequately blocked him, she turned the lights on and glanced at her body, hating the curves of her breasts and their tight, upturned nipples. Her frequent workouts made her midsection taut, her waist thin, all of which made her hips too wide.

While on active duty in the Army, she'd had to time her secret habit so that her wounds were healed by the time she went for her annual physicals, which, of course, had defeated the purpose anyway.

The Army had taken control of her body from her.

But it was hers now. She was free to give herself the relief she needed; even if it only lasted a few spare minutes, it was relief. Pure, beautiful relief.

A tear slipped down her cheek. The cuts on the side of her left breast were still scabbed. She shouldn't cut herself again so soon.

Control. That was what this was about. She knew it. She'd joined a support group her senior year in high school. It had been fully anonymous, so no one knew her name or where she went to school. They weren't allowed to talk about personally identifying details. They'd even had to anonymize relationships or assault details so they could be discussed freely without fear of being outed.

It had helped. For a time.

Her assault had been twelve years ago, when she was fourteen. She hadn't told anyone she'd been raped by two guys, not that support group, not Ace, not even

Greer, when he found out about her connection to the Omnis. Her parents knew—those details had been discovered when she underwent a physical examination that day.

She looked at her disgusting body. Men wanted it. They'd wanted it when she was only fourteen. She should have cleaned herself up that day, explained away all the broken glass in the girls' bathroom with a lie like she'd had a seizure and had fallen into the mirror then onto the glass. That would have explained all the blood.

But it wouldn't have explained the physical evidence the boys had left on and in her body.

Her schoolmates had taunted her after that. Not knowing the facts of what happened to her, they'd called her Carrie, from the horror flick. She'd been bleeding all over, where her face had been smashed into the mirror, from the small nicks that seeped through her tee, from between her legs, from her sliced-up hand. They spray-painted "Carrie" all over her locker.

Her parents had filed suits against her attackers, their families, and the school. Somehow, that glob of flesh she'd cut from one of the boys and had handed over had gone missing. And then the DNA evidence from her rape kit had been mishandled in its processing.

It had devolved into a he said/she said. The judge dismissed the case.

The principal asked her parents to send her to a different school. But it didn't matter. Not at that point, anyway, not when so much else was crumbling in their lives. Her father had lost his job by then, and the whole town seemed to turn on all of them. They'd made the decision to move to a new state and start over — the first of many such changes.

She'd ruined her parents' lives. Her life.

She should have died that day.

She wished she had.

And now she might be facing that same horror all over again. So what had happened that night she cut herself? Had Bastion raped her? She touched her stomach, wondering if she was pregnant. Could a mutant impregnate a human?

No way to know yet, at least not without a trip to a doctor. That wasn't going to happen.

She shoved her toiletries bag into a drawer, then turned on the shower and stepped into the water, not waiting for it to warm up. She bent her head and closed her eyes, wishing she didn't have to keep revisiting the same nightmare.

It was terrible that something she hated had framed her entire life.

17

Selena was sick to death of hiding in her room, only venturing out at night to snag something to eat when she thought no one else would be around.

Tonight, she'd showered and dressed in a fresh pair of jeans and a sweater. Even though Spencer was forbidden from bringing her food, he still took her laundry away...and brought her a snack every afternoon with her wash neatly folded, both of which he left outside her door.

If anything, it was he who kept her feeling somewhat sane in this weird limbo state she was in.

There'd been no word on any progress toward fighting Bastion and his Legion. For all Selena knew, this was the new normal of her life—Nick had been right. She couldn't hide in the closet forever.

She started down the wide stone staircase in the main tower. Halfway down, she sat on a step. As much as she could tell, the mansion was shaped like a V, with towers at all three end points, the biggest of which being the one she was in. Paintings covered the walls, going up two oversized floors. Here and there, peeking out from behind some of the art, were darker patches of paint, as if the art had recently been rearranged.

She wondered what was missing.

Jax came into the big foyer. He was wearing a slim blue suit, a pale blue dress shirt, a patterned blue silk tie, and a complementary pocket square. He looked up at her and tugged his cuffs. His broad shoulders made the suit. The man was a tailor's dream.

"Selena," he said, nodding at her.

"Jax."

"Are you coming down?"

"I don't know. Thought I'd sit here for a while."

"There are more comfortable places to sit in the salon."

"Maybe I don't feel like committing."

Jax grinned as he leaned against the wall. "Committing to comfort?"

"To anything. You're dressed for dinner."

"It's what civilized people do, no?"

"We didn't at Blade's place. I don't have anything to wear"—she pulled at her sweater—"that's not like this. I had to pack fast."

"Would you like me to order some outfits for you?"

"Do you shop where Val shops?" Selena asked, thinking of her teammate back at their headquarters who seemed to know every haute couture boutique in the U.S. Maybe the world. If he ever stopped being a sniper, he'd have a lucrative career shopping for wealthy women.

"I don't shop," Jax said. "I have shoppers."

Of course. "Well, thanks, but no thanks."

"Too much of a commitment?"

"Way too much." She propped her elbows on her knees and rested her chin on her hands. "I don't plan on staying here long, so you'll just have to put up with my civvies."

"The length of your stay hasn't been determined."

"Shit, now you sound like Owen." Selena's boss had a cold and determined way about him that few dared run afoul of.

"Need I remind you that there's a mutant stalking you?" Jax asked. "Where were you thinking of heading?"

"When I figure it out, I'll let you know."

"When your mutant's been contained, we'll let you know what happens next."

Nick, Selena's other handler, popped his head out of the blue salon. "Having supper on the stairs, are we?"

"No," Selena and Jax said simultaneously.

Nick held up a glass with an amber-colored liquid. "My daughter-in-law stocks Balcones." He smiled, pleased with that discovery. "Want a glass?"

Jax nodded.

"Run along, you two," Selena said. "I'm not done thinking."

"Spencer is expecting you for supper," Jax said.

"He's been setting a place at the table every night since I told him you'll no longer be dining in your room."

"Uh-huh. Why don't they eat with us?" Selena asked.

"The staff?" Jax looked taken aback.

"They're your fucking crew, Jax."

"They have their jobs and we have ours," Jax said.

"Addy must hate it at our house," Selena said, thinking of her boss's wife—Jax's sister—who owned the gilded cage they were in.

"She loves it there," Jax said.

"We're a lot more casual. Russ and Jim eat with us. We wear civvies to dinner. Hell, we have dinner instead of supper."

"Addy hated dressing for her husband, but not doing so netted her a beating—or worse, one for the boys. Her bastard ex had cameras all over the house. He knew when she was noncompliant. So no—she loves her new digs and the freedoms she has."

Selena blinked and lowered her gaze to the bottom step. The wind outside got louder. Being here, in this remote and hostile location, she wondered how Addy had survived as well as she had, alone except for her cruel husband until her divorce a couple of years ago.

"Selena," Nick said into the thick quiet, "Balcones will warm your soul."

Selena looked from Nick to Jax. "I'll take a beer." She went down the rest of the long staircase and into the blue salon.

Nick fetched a beer from the bar, took the cap off,

then handed it to her. "Does this drink choice mean you like your soul cold?" He grinned at her.

Selena ignored the humor in Nick's eyes as she took a long swallow. He was so different from his uptight son. She settled on the blue sofa. "I'm getting used to it, with everything that's going on." In this room, too, there were spaces on the walls where artwork didn't fit the discolored spaces on the wall.

"Did something change recently in Addy's art collection?" Selena asked.

Jax looked at the walls around them. "Spencer is mixing things up, trying to keep the collection fresh. We need to repaint, but that's been low on the priority list."

Selena doubted that was the whole story, but Jax, like Owen and everyone else she'd met in this Omni war, held his secrets close to his chest.

She should have stayed in her room. She felt rangy and quarrelsome, not fit for human company. But she wasn't exactly in the company of humans, was she? Nick, her bosses' dad, was a mutant, just like her stalker.

She looked at Nick. "What's it like being changed?"

Nick sat in an armchair next to the sofa. "Different." He waved a hand over his body, which had reversed its age to the point where he and Owen looked more like brothers than parent and child. "It's odd getting your youth back, rewinding from my sixties to my forties."

"Do you think you're finished growing younger?" Selena couldn't suppress a sideways grin as a thought hit her. "What if it doesn't stop?"

"What if I regress to nothing? An infant, maybe?" He took a deep swallow of his Balcones. "If that's the case, I hope my caretakers use cloth diapers on me."

Selena laughed.

"I don't know the answer to your question, honestly," Nick continued. "I can't tell you how many times in my regular life that I'd thought about what I would do if I were young again and could bring with me the lessons I'd already learned. That's exactly what happened. Except I'm a better me than I ever was, mentally and emotionally. Physically, too. My vision is stronger than a regular human's. I can see details and distances like a machine. I can hear to the point of sensory overload. I can distinguish between thousands of similar scents in infinitesimally small amounts. And there are other things, things that I sense but don't understand. I'm stronger than I ever was. I have more endurance. My memory is nearly perfect. It's a lot to take in."

"Would you do it again, knowing what you know now?" Selena asked. "Even knowing you might outlive your son and grandkids?"

"Yes." Nick nodded. That certainty in his eyes reminded her of Owen. "We need more fighters highly tuned to the challenges we're facing. We have to be able to fight the Omnis on their level."

Selena asked Jax, "What about you? Are you going to take the changes?"

Jax plopped into the armchair opposite Nick and glared at the glass in his hand. "Probably. Nick's right that we need more enhanced fighters. I'm neck-deep in this fight already. My only family—Addy, the boys, and Owen—are in this dark fight as well. I'm not married. I have no kids. I'm a good candidate for the modifications. The only thing that would miss me, if the changes destroy me, is the war itself." He sipped his whisky. "What about you, Sel?"

She shook her head. "I don't know. I'm not sure I want to live forever."

"The upper limit of a mutant life span hasn't been established," Nick said. "We may just live out our hundred-year lifetime as forty-year-olds, then croak as usual. Who knows?"

"That's what gets me," Selena said. "We understand so little of how these modifications work. We already saw what can happen when the mods are used against the modified—Addy's modifications nearly killed her. Changing oneself requires a level of trust in the science and the practitioners that I don't have. At least not yet."

Nick swirled the ice in his glass. "I wished my trainer hadn't backed out. I'm anxious to get started."

Selena felt a little whirl of excitement as she thought about Bastion's volunteering to help with that. "Bastion said he would train you."

Nick's brows went up. "I thought you weren't talking to him."

"He got through when you guys were in the closet with me."

"That's a hell no," Jax said. "We know nothing about him and little about his abilities. Nick's mind is fragile."

Nick choked on a sip of Balcones. "Thanks, bro. So's your dick."

Forget sixty reverting to forty—Nick had the mind of a twelve-year-old.

Jax brushed that off. "Your neurological pathways are, at this moment, being rewired. You're like a molting crab. My point—"

"Yes, what is it again?" Nick said.

"—is that who knows what Bastion might do to you? Download some hidden instructions. Reconfigure your new wiring. Who knows? No. We are not having Bastion here."

SELENA MADE the mistake of sleeping deeply that night —a luxury she'd resisted since she'd been here. She dreamed about a wedding. Hers. But for some reason, she was late to the ceremony. When she tried to get into the venue, all the doors were locked. She knocked and knocked, but no one came to let her in. She went around the side of the building and looked in a window. There was Bastion, dancing with another woman.

She woke abruptly, angry and sad and shaking.

The thing she feared the most had come to pass—she was alone, because of *him.*

Where are you? Bastion whispered through her mind. He sounded angry.

She was tired of blocking him, tired of the pain it caused. *I don't know*, she answered.

Talk to me. I will find you.

I don't want you to. But she did want that. Terribly. In part so that she could stop fighting herself. And in part because she'd missed having him just a thought away.

Yes, you do. I can feel your pain.

Can you feel everyone's pain?

Only yours...and my brothers'.

Do you have a lot of them?

Yes. Please, let me come to you.

You can't use me anymore, Selena said.

I never did use you.

You asked me to get info on the Ratcliffs.

A favor. For a friend. They have information we desperately need, but I don't care about any of that. Tell me where you are.

I don't know. It hurts, Bastion, keeping you out.

It's because we are carved from the same soul, and having found our other half, we cannot exist apart.

I don't believe in souls.

I do.

Selena tried to block a sob, but it broke free. She covered her face with a pillow, but it was no match for Bastion, since he was already in her head...and maybe in her heart. *I wish you were here.*

Don't block me. I will find you.

How sick was it to crave her stalker?

This wasn't going to end well.

18

_____

One evening, a few days later, Selena walked into the blue salon and came to an abrupt stop. The Ratcliffs were there, sitting on the long blue sofa.

Noooo. Not them. She had to get out of there before Bastion felt them near her. She sent a look over her shoulder, wishing she could just backtrack to her room.

"Selena," Jax said, "you remember the Ratcliffs— Joyce and Nathan."

She nodded. "You shouldn't be here. It's dangerous for you. Bastion could find you through me."

"We wanted to come," Joyce said. "We've been doing some research on the Legion. We want to meet Liege and Bastion. They may be able to help us."

A chill slipped through Selena. "Or they could kill you."

"Possibly, but we've learned a few defensive tricks

along the ways through our own modifications," Nathan said.

"Bastion does want to meet you," Selena said, "but I don't know why. I don't know any of the whys about him at all. I think someone so powerful has to be dangerous. I've been waiting for Owen to figure out a plan of attack, but nothing's happened yet." She looked at Jax. "If the Ratcliffs want a meetup with Bastion, you need to run that past Owen."

"Agreed." Jax nodded.

Nick handed her a beer. She moved back a few steps, then a few more. She should leave. It wasn't safe for anyone in the room if she was there.

Before she could make her escape, something outside caught her attention. An orange glow. It was well past sunset, so it wasn't sunlight reflecting off a boulder. It looked like there might be a fire out there. She held the gauzy curtain aside as she turned to Jax and Nick. "You guys see that orange glow over there? What is that?"

Jax came over to the window. He narrowed his eyes, then leaned closer to the window. "What orange glow?"

Selena looked again. "It's gone. It was right over that ridge."

She stood at the window another minute, trying not to feel like a fool for pointing out some phantom light. Maybe there was a hiker over there, someone doing some winter camping. It was out on National Forest land, not on Addy's property. But it was only fifteen degrees Fahrenheit outside. No one in their right mind would be out on a night like this, except maybe hunters, but what game was in season at the moment?

Maybe tomorrow she'd go out to look for footprints or other signs that someone was camping so near Addy's house.

Another thought struck her. Bastion had been able to camouflage his footprints as those of random animals common in the area. Was he here? Had he found them?

Selena dropped the curtain and folded her arms. Was it someone other than Bastion? An Omni mutant? Was she certain Bastion wasn't an Omni?

"Sel, you okay?" Nick asked.

She nodded. Joyce smiled at her, catching her attention. "What did you see out there?"

"I'm not sure," Selena said. "Jax didn't see it. I guess it was nothing."

"But what did *you* see?" Nathan asked. "You mustn't doubt yourself."

"I saw an orange glow. I thought it might be a bonfire or something, but it disappeared."

"Orange?" Nathan and his wife exchanged intense glances. Selena wondered if they were communicating mentally, as she and Bastion could do.

"We've heard stories of a mutant being called the Matchmaker," Joyce said. "He stalks mutants and pairs them with their one true mate."

"It's just an urban legend, as far as we know," Nathan said.

"That could be said of everything about mutants," Nick replied.

"True." Joyce came over to look out the window. "Like a campfire horror story, the legend says that if the mutant refuses the Matchmaker's match, he'll die. And if he accepts it, his human mate will be the one to die."

"That's absolutely horrible." Selena wondered if Bastion knew about the legend. Of course it wasn't real. And anyway, how could a mutant and a human hook up? Well, Owen and Addy had, she reminded herself. Joyce and Nathan were mutants and were married. Neither of them had perished as a result of their union, but perhaps it had skipped them because they'd been married before their change.

Selena shut down that line of thinking. It was merely an urban legend, like the wendigo that the kids liked to make up stories about back at the team's house.

"What's the purpose of that legend?" Selena wondered aloud. "To keep mutants and humans apart? Can they be together?"

"They can," Joyce said. "However, a side effect of most of the modifications is a complication in the mutant's libido. They lose it, almost entirely. So while they can have intimate encounters, they are, let's just say, less than satisfying to the mutant."

"That modification, we believe, was an intentional outcome," Nathan said. "Operatives who aren't distracted by the needs of their sex drive would naturally be more focused on their mission objectives."

Selena's gaze moved between both scientists as she considered that. "You think the Matchmaker is real?"

"Legends and myths generally have a kernel of truth in them," Joyce said.

Nathan added, "Or maybe it's just something to keep hope alive in the modified warriors—a path to love or death. Either, I think, would be an acceptable outcome to the changed."

"We've heard rumors that some mutants only regain their libido when they find the human who is their perfect match." Joyce's gaze softened in a way that showed she felt sorry for Selena, as if she knew Selena was being targeted.

Selena looked at Nick and Jax, checking their reaction to all of this. Everyone seemed to have already arrived at the conclusion she just getting to herself. "And the humans chosen in these matches? Have they no say in the matter?"

Joyce looked saddened. "It appears not."

"Then it's death or surrender, and if the human surrenders, they die. So it's death or death. Great options." Everyone's gaze stuck to her in a silent moment that stretched awkwardly into seconds. "I don't care for those options. I refuse. No one is going to force me to love someone." She sipped her beer, trying to break the room's tension.

She was going to need a lot more beer.

Selena slept restlessly that night. She'd left her curtain open, wanting to see if that strange glow would show up again. It couldn't have been a fire—fires don't extinguish themselves as they jumped around from hotspot to hotspot. Nor was there ever any scent of woodsmoke. Maybe it was a reconnaissance drone—or one with more lethal intent, like the armed one that had sliced into Addy's house when Owen was here.

The light was out there now, on the hill, bright enough to cast a warm glow in her room. She sighed and threw the covers off, unable to sleep now until she put her worries to rest. She'd bundled up in her warmest gear, then made a quick pass through the main level of the house. No one else was up, so she didn't tell anyone where she was going.

Stepping outside of the main door into the cool winter moonlight, she could absolutely make out the orange-red glow on the first hill to the west. It wasn't far, maybe a fifteen-minute jog. The moon lit her way. She kept alternating her focus between the bright light and loose rocks scattered across the hill.

When she was about twenty feet from the top, the glow moved beyond the ridge, down the other side of the hill. Damn, but she wished she'd brought a pair of night vision-goggles or binoculars, something—anything—that would let her get a better look at what she was chasing.

She felt certain it was aware of her. It had to be. It had only been appearing to her, and now it moved in response to her presence. That thought brought her up short. Was this some new Omni technology? Were they trying to lure her far enough from the house to kidnap her?

The word "matchmaker" flitted through her mind, but she dismissed it. She was a firm believer in science, logic, and rational thinking, not glowing specters delivering a curse. Or a promise of love. Or whatever the hell the urban legend was.

Selena made it to the top of the ridge, but the glowing orb had jumped to the top of the next hill over. No way a human could move that fast. Had to be something technological—which in itself was as terrifying as a forest fire.

Someone or something was observing Addy's house and its occupants. Selena knew it wasn't from her team. It had to be the Omnis. This was not good. And she'd had no luck convincing Jax or Nick what she'd been seeing.

Who would believe it, anyway, if they hadn't seen it themselves?

Flynn was near. Bastion could feel his energy beating a summons. He got in his Jeep and drove into town, following Flynn's sticky feel. It led him right to the coffee shop by the diner.

Selena said she'd had an experience there. She'd asked if there was another mutant like him nearby. *Dieu*, he hadn't put the two things together until just now. Had it been Flynn touching her that day? Bastion had a protection on her, but it might not have stopped an astral projection from getting through, which would have freaked the hell out of her, as she wouldn't have known who or what was attacking her.

Bastion went into the shop and sat at Flynn's booth. The guy was looking as ghastly as ever. He presented a smooth persona to the regulars, but Bastion and the rest of the Legion could always see beneath it.

"Ah. You came," Flynn said in a cheerful voice.

"Why am I here?" Bastion asked.

"In honor of our recent partnership, I wanted to give you fair warning that I know you've violated the terms of our agreement."

"We never had an agreement."

"One of Owen Tremaine's team is missing. Selena Irving. Bring her back."

Bastion considered going a few rounds of playing an innocent. He didn't, though—he didn't like any amount of Flynn's focus to be on Selena. Besides, how had Flynn known she was gone?

"I don't know where she is. I can't bring her back."

Flynn leaned back in his seat, his blue eyes trying to slice their way into Bastion's head. He was unsuccessful. "Our agreement was that in exchange for me bringing you the Ratcliffs, you leave Tremaine's team alone."

"As I recall, we walked away from your little détente, so I don't really give a fuck what you think your takeaway was from that meeting."

"Don't you? Do you no longer care about all your beloved regulars?" The doors to the café opened then slammed shut, startling everyone. One person turned from the counter and dropped her cup of hot coffee to grab her head. Pain jumped from her to others in the room. Everyone became alarmed.

Bastion blanketed the shop and those in it with a protective energy, calming them, blocking Flynn's psychic incursions.

"You used to be trustworthy," Flynn complained. "You were the one whose moral compass could not be corrupted. I expected you to keep our agreement."

That statement was a distortion of reality; there wasn't a man in the Legion whose moral compass was corruptible. "What's your interest in the girl?"

Flynn's smile was like a skull's grin. "She's a female and a warrior. Such an unusual combination. I want her."

Bastion had to focus on keeping himself under tight control, something he'd been working on since Selena disappeared. There were other females at the Red Team compound. Yes, they were all spoken for, but that had never stopped Flynn before. One of them, the little pink-haired one, was even a warrior. Why had he chosen Selena? When the hell had he ever even seen her?

Unless that time here at the café…

Bastion leaned back in his seat. "This is the trouble with you taking so long to round up the Ratcliffs. Things change. The team now is one fewer. Take two more weeks and more may vacate the team compound. It's their business, not mine. I'm not in charge of their staff."

Rage shot through Flynn's eyes, an emotion he

quickly stamped down. "I do have a lead on her where-abouts. And I will find the Ratcliffs. And I will kill all of them. Our détente is off."

It was hell for Bastion sitting across from the bastard and having to act civilized while his light was being threatened. He and Flynn both had their own personal protections in place. They could fight, but neither would even get a punch in on the other. Only innocent bystanders would be hurt in a clash between them. Bastion got up and walked away, knowing more—and less—than when he came in.

Flynn still didn't have a handle on the Ratcliffs. And he wanted Selena with an unwavering lust that made no sense to Bastion. The Matchmaker had selected her for Bastion. So why was Flynn fired up about her?

Had the Matchmaker given her to two mutants?

19

The woman on Merc's lap wiggled suggestively. The invitation didn't tempt him. Acier and his female of the night were already occupying the family restroom — not that such a nicety was needed. A mutant could have sex in the middle of a crowded room and no one would even know, if their shields were up.

The woman Merc was holding leaned forward to tongue-fuck his mouth. He tried to pretend it was as pleasurable to him as her deep-throated moans indicated it was for her, a pretense that was more for his own benefit than hers. Acier still enjoyed sex, but Merc didn't — hadn't since he was changed. He wanted to believe, as Bastion claimed, that pretending to feel lust was three-quarters of the way to achieving it.

But it wasn't. Not for Merc. Not now. Not with this female. He slipped a hand behind her head, bringing her mouth to his again. Trying, trying to like it.

Acier came back to the table alone, his energy completely altered from the oppressive hunger he'd been experiencing when he and his female of the moment had left the table.

"My beer's warm," Acier growled as he dropped into his seat.

"Well, you were gone longer than usual," Merc said, gratefully using the convo with Acier to interrupt the woman who kept vying for his complete attention.

Acier gave him a half-grin. "We had a lot of ground to cover."

Merc grunted something unintelligible. Fortunately, Liege broke into the moment with a mission order.

Acier, Merc, get over to the airfield, Liege said via their mental link. *Bastion's in trouble up at the Tremaine headquarters in Wyoming. The pilot's already warming up the helicopter.*

Copy that, Merc responded. Both men stood and downed their beers. "Apologies," Merc said to the female whom he'd just set down. "We have an appointment we have to keep."

Acier paid their tab. As they walked down the block to their SUV, Merc looked at Acier, taking in his super-relaxed vibe. "I envy you."

Acier flashed at grin. "Why?"

"'Cause fucking still feels like something for you."

Acier's grin widened. "Yes, it does."

"I wonder what's different between your mods and mine?"

Acier pulled up the open cuff of his leather jacket,

exposing the lower part of his arm. "You're welcome to open a vein and find out."

Merc sighed. "Maybe when we find the researchers we've been looking for, I will—though I doubt learning the secret to your sex drive will be tops on their list."

They reached the SUV. Merc got behind the wheel.

"Truth is," Acier said, "I'm more jealous of you than you are of me."

"Why's that?"

"You and the others were changed in the same mutant camp. You guys have a bond I'll never really be part of."

Merc paused, his hands on the wheel. "Bullshit. Liege has accepted you as one of us." He looked at his friend, whose illusion of pale skin and dark hair made him appear like a black-and-white photo—except for those piercing blue eyes. They held their color even in the heavy night shadows. "Once he takes you in, you're as good as blood with him."

Acier leaned against the headrest. "But I feel separate."

"Yeah. Well, I *feel* like I could use a royal fuckfest. *Feeling's* a bitch, so don't do it, mate." He pulled into traffic. "Let's go save Bastion's ass."

HURRY, Bastion, Liege said. *Ghouls are inside your protective boundaries at the Tremaine compound.*

Bastion floored his Jeep's accelerator and made a

fast turn onto the property. He'd only just left Flynn in town. Now he understood what Flynn had meant by giving him fair warning.

Bastion drove into one of the ghouls, tossing its body twenty feet off the drive, though probably not delivering a lethal blow to it. He parked in a grassy area in front of the main house and camouflaged his car and himself. He had no idea how many of the beasts were here, but better they come at him than at the regulars who lived inside the mansion.

Fucking Flynn.

I guess he wasn't happy with my answers just now, Bastion said to Liege.

What's his interest in your light? Liege asked. *He didn't care about any of the team's other women.*

They're all taken.

So's Selena.

But he may not know that, Bastion said. *Not that he ever cared about a female's relationship status before.*

Merc and Acier are on their way up there.

Bien. *Don't let the regulars go after the ghouls. I'll keep the ghouls from going inside.*

Done.

The ghouls came at Bastion one by one and three by three. He used his sai to dispatch them. A pause in the onslaught gave him a chance to breathe…and think.

Liege, what if Flynn's found Selena and he's pinning us down here so he can get to her?

It's possible. Anything is possible. But we still don't know where she is. There are only two people at the compound who do —Owen and Greer. Find them and press them for answers.

Bastion had to put two more ghouls down before he got to the bunker entrance on the far southern side of the house. He kept himself and his energy hidden as best he could from the ghouls as he disappeared into the shrubs covering the bunker entrance.

Inside, he paused, mentally preparing himself. How had the fiends gotten through his protection to venture so close to the house? Normally only those who had been approved could come and go as they pleased. Obviously, Bastion had never approved Flynn or his ghouls to cross his protections.

How they did it, he didn't know, but discoveries like this new behavior weren't unheard of. They were all developing new traits and skills—Flynn too, Bastion supposed. Somehow, he'd figured out a way in.

Bastion still didn't know what Flynn's interest in Selena was about. Or maybe it was just that Flynn wanted to destroy something Bastion cared about. Maybe this onslaught tonight was revenge against the human fighters who were slowly dismantling the Omni World Order? The warriors quartered in the mansion were strong, disciplined, and capable fighters, but they were still only regulars. No regular could win against a mutant, much less a pack of bloodthirsty fiends like Flynn's creatures.

Maybe Bastion was to blame for their change in behavior tonight; his desperation to find and secure Selena had doubtless been broadcast far and wide, energy that was easy for any mutant to pick up. It was his own fault for losing his self-control when she first went missing. He knew better than to do that. Flynn loved strong emotion, especially fear, which had seeped from Bastion's every pore in that moment—not for his own welfare, but for Selena's.

Twigs snapped close to Bastion. A ghoul was near. He could smell it. Flynn's monsters were an unholy blend of human and animal DNA. The human host was destroyed in the mutation process, leaving only a primal lizard brain, one easily controlled by a master manipulator like Flynn, who had developed these fiends for one purpose—harvesting his enemies.

This one smelled like hell—woods, mud, rotting flesh and blood. It came into sight, climbing on all fours over the boulders at the bunker entrance. It had the height of a grizzly and the frame of a man, but with long forearms and powerful thighs. Its hands and feet were weaponized with bearlike claws. Its face was distorted with its long snout. Thick canines pressed against the skin covering its lower jaw. There was nothing natural in its eyes, not human, not animal.

It sensed Bastion's presence and came closer, poking the air near where he stood with its snout, sniffing for him. Not being able to see or hear him, the mutant beast left him alone and continued his prowl.

Bastion wondered if Flynn was shielding his monsters from the tech that monitored the property. Had they been detected, the fighters inside the mansion would have mobilized—and been slaughtered.

Flynn's new boldness made Bastion even more panicked about finding Selena. Was she facing the same surge of ghouls?

Bastion turned and stepped into the wide cave entrance of the bunker. Team vehicles were parked in the big space here in the front. A wide tunnel led from the cave to the entrance to the team's bunker below the mansion.

Motion lights came on as Bastion moved deeper into the tunnel. He saw two fighters standing a few yards ahead. Bastion didn't try to hide himself. He was done being invisible. It was time to deal with the Red Team in person.

He recognized the men in front of him—Greer and Max were their names, the team's tech nerds.

Bastion stopped only feet from them. "Where is she?" he asked. He knew they knew exactly who he was asking about; Selena was the only fighter missing from the premises.

"She's gone," Greer said.

"Where?"

"She's not your concern," Max said.

Bastion's eyes changed to a glowing orange, the color of his anger, as he turned his attention to Max. "I will end you and everyone in this house, soul by soul, until I learn where she's gone."

"Not true." Greer waved that off. "You're a soldier, like us. You follow orders. If you'd been ordered to kill us, we'd already be dead, given your abilities. So what's your interest in her?"

Bastion's burning eyes turned to Greer, the energy of his anger emitting a dangerous pulse. Greer winced and looked over at Max. Bastion could feel their pain as the energy he was creating became a deep, terrible sound, like something just at the edges of a sonic boom.

Max hit his knees.

"Enough!" Greer shouted as he bent over. "Enough!"

Bastion severed his connection with them, breaking the pulsing pain he'd been sending their way.

Greer gasped at the reprieve. Still holding his knees, he looked up at Bastion. "If there's something you want, meet with us. Let's talk about it."

"You took my woman," Bastion said through clenched teeth.

Max shook his head and slowly straightened. "She's ours, not yours." He and Greer moved back a step.

Bastion stepped forward. Something with knifelike teeth clamped onto his leg mid-shin. The pain was worse than what he'd just pushed on the two men. He looked down to see the steel teeth of a bear trap digging into his leg. He staggered forward, slipping into the jagged teeth of a second trap.

A howl ripped from him. The sound merged with his telekinetic abilities, sending a sonic punch into the two men in front of him, knocking them off their feet. They landed several yards back and lay unmoving.

He didn't know if they were alive or dead.

He didn't care.

Pain coursed through him in waves of hot and cold, stealing his breath.

Bastion. What is it? What's happened? Liege asked via their mental link.

Pain stole Bastion's ability to answer. *Merde*, he couldn't even breathe yet. He slumped to the ground and pressed the sides of the trap on his right leg, releasing it, gasping as another wave of pain ripped through him.

Movement of any kind made the lower part of his shins feel as if they were being ripped from his body. A scream cut its way up his throat. He clenched his teeth, but it spilled from his mouth anyway. The pain was draining his strength.

Talk to us, Bastion, Liege ordered him.

The bones in his right leg had been shattered. He bent his left knee and brought that trap close enough that he could release it. Both legs were bleeding profusely. His left leg didn't feel broken, but it couldn't support his weight.

He had to get out of the bunker's tunnel; the ghouls were coming. He didn't want to fight them here, so close to the house.

He had to pause and breathe slowly. The pain was nauseating. He didn't respond to his team lead—he couldn't put a coherent thought together.

On the heels of that thought came an easing of the pain as a warm calmness slipped inside him. Guerre, the team's healer, was helping him. His efforts slowed the bleeding and intercepted the pain—the abrupt lack of which was nearly as stunning as its sudden onset. Bastion collapsed on his back in the loose dirt. The only thing he could console himself with was the knowledge that *she* wasn't here. Hopefully that meant she was safe from the ghouls, wherever she was.

You must move, Liege said. *They are near.*

Bastion rolled to his stomach. *Protect Selena's team, Liege. They cannot fight the ghouls and win. They don't know how.*

Done. Get out of there. Merc and Acier are almost there.

Going on instinct alone, Bastion rolled to his stomach then got to his hands and knees and began crawling down the wide dirt tunnel, something he could not have done without Guerre's assistance with the pain.

With each inch toward the bunker entrance, the exit seemed even farther away. Time and space became distorted.

He paused, head hanging low, to draw a few fortifying breaths, then looked back at the men he'd blasted. He could see them lying prone in the dirt. Maybe they were dead. He hoped not.

He crawled a few more feet, wanting to put as much distance between himself and the other fighters before the ghouls came. The rest of Selena's team would shortly come looking for them. Bastion had to get as far as he could before that happened.

He tried setting an illusion to cover his tracks, but he was too weak to sustain it.

Liege, Bastion said, connecting with his team lead, aidez-moi!

We got you, Liege said. *I've hidden your trail and shielded you. Keep making your way to the end of the tunnel. When you get to the parking area ahead, hole up there and wait for us. The guys will be onsite soon.*

Bastion didn't have the strength to respond, but he knew Liege was in his mind and didn't need a response. He resumed crawling out of the dark space. It was slow going. He was tired. He leaned against the dirt wall of the tunnel and shut his eyes, slowly slumping to the dirt floor of the tunnel.

Something warm was dripping onto his face. Bastion slowly opened his eyes and looked up—into the gaping maw of a ghoul. It couldn't see him, but it smelled him.

Bastion pulled his sai from his waist. Holding the long spike against his forearm, he pounded the flat end of the handle against the corner of the ghoul's open jaw, then flipped the sai forward and shoved the long spike into its ear, through its head and out the other side.

He yanked it free.

Rolling onto his stomach, he forced himself to keep heading toward the entrance. What little mental reserves he had left, he spent keeping himself hidden from the perception of the ghouls and the Red Team. His tracks were there, but no one had the ability to see through the slug trail of energy Liege was using to obscure them.

The Red Team. They weren't enhanced. They were just regulars. They were supposed to be as helpless as infants against his kind. And yet they'd gotten the drop on him.

Bitterly cold night air spilled over him as he neared

the end of the tunnel. He dragged himself between two of the vehicles parked there. Cold sweat stuck to his face from his exertion. If he passed out, he'd not be able to maintain the energetic cover that hid him.

Liege. Aidez-moi. His mind was too foggy for him to remember to speak English.

Just let go, Liege said. *I've got you covered. Hole up where you are. The guys are almost there.*

Bastion looked back at the shadowy tunnel. He couldn't see where he'd just been. If Selena's team brought out their search dog, they'd find him fast.

I said *we have you. You are hidden from all threats.* Liege sounded irritated as hell. Bastion would have laughed, but his blood loss was making him sick.

Thank God for friends. Bastion leaned against one of the vehicles and shut his eyes.

MERC ROLLED HIM OVER. Bastion looked up at the man he loved to hate. Merc had to be everyone's conscience. Fucking sucked that it was he who'd saved him. "Oh, it's you."

Merc smirked. "Sure, don't thank me for saving your life, mate." He looked at Acier. "We need to stabilize him and send him back, then deal with the ghouls."

Through Merc, Guerre sent Bastion a wave of energy, warm and fortifying. Bastion let it roll through him. He couldn't help the tears that came to his eyes as his friend eased his deepening shock.

Merc checked Bastion's legs. Bastion barely felt his not-so-tender ministrations, thanks to the pain block Guerre provided.

He's lost a lot of blood, Merc said to Guerre. *Get his transfusions ready.* Merc gave Bastion a narrow-eyed glare. "If you hadn't been following your dick around, this wouldn't have happened and no one would need to save you. Where's your Jeep?"

Bastion let his eyes roll shut. Merc was at his bitchiest when he was scared, which was a little unnerving right now. "I was following my heart, not chasing my dick."

"You're always chasing your dick."

"*Non.* It is not true. I was searching for my heart. I have found it here. I told you, she is my light."

"The fucking Jeep, Bastion," Acier said.

Bastion sent him and Merc a mental image showing his vehicle's location. Merc stood, then grabbed Bastion's arm and hoisted him up over his shoulder. Catching an arm through his leg, he lifted him and jogged over the lawn to the helicopter that was still running.

20

Selena was standing at her window when excruciating pain ripped into her lower legs, dropping her to the floor. She cried out in agony. What was happening? She dragged herself over to her nightstand and flipped the light on, yanking up the cuffs of her yoga pants to check her legs.

Nothing was there. No injury. No bruising or blood. Her legs weren't sensitive to touch, and yet the pain was throbbing and terrible.

And then it stopped.

Bastion was hurt. The pain had been his—somehow she just knew it, like she knew his humor and his anger. What was happening? God, was Bastion okay? Who could have hurt him, mutant that he was? Another wave of pain cut through her shins, this one so intense that she wanted to vomit. A cold sweat broke out across her face and neck. She had to pant her way through the torture.

God, what was happening? Bastion was suffering.

She reached up to her nightstand and fumbled around for the phone. She punched in Jax's number.

He answered fast. "Sel, 'sup?"

"My legs are broken."

"Fuck." The line went dead. Barely seconds later, she could hear him charging down the hall. He slammed into her room. "Sel! Selena! Where the fuck are you?"

The pain had her tucked into a tight ball, making it impossible to respond. He came around the bed and saw her, then dropped to his knees beside her. He brushed her sweat-dampened hair from her face. She looked up at him, but was unable to stop her controlled breathing long enough to get any words out.

And then it stopped again. She went limp. It was going to come again, she knew it. Jax was checking her legs out, feeling from her hip down to her ankles, watching her the whole while. When she didn't flinch, he pushed her pants up past her knees and ran his thumb down her shin.

"Sel, your legs aren't broken."

"I know that. I was just standing there and then I couldn't stand. I feel like they've been cut in two."

Jax reached for the phone and dialed Nick's number, then the Ratcliffs', ordering them both to Selena's room.

"I think it's Bastion," Selena said.

"That bastard's hurting you?" Jax was furious.

"No. I think he's been hurt. The pain keeps coming and going...like...maybe he's going in and out of consciousness. Call the guys. I need to know what they're doing to him."

Jax lifted her to her bed. Nick rushed in. "What's going on?"

"Bastion's hurting her."

"No. *Bastion* is hurting," Selena corrected Jax, not that either man listened to her.

The Ratcliffs were the last in. Selena wished she'd just suffered in silence. There was nothing any of them could do. Except maybe Jax could get her team to stop whatever it was they were doing to Bastion.

Jax was on the phone with them now. Nick was getting the Ratcliffs up to speed. Joyce sat beside her on the bed just as another wave of pain bit into her legs. She folded her legs and wrapped her arms around her knees, unable to stop herself from crying.

Joyce rubbed her back.

"Where does it hurt?" Nathan asked.

Selena showed them where on her shins the pain was. Nathan pushed her yoga pants up and, of course, saw nothing. "It's not me. It's him."

Nathan and his wife exchanged glances. "I can give you a sedative," Joyce suggested.

God, that sounded good. Except Bastion was hurt and needed Selena. She had to go to him and couldn't do that drugged out of her mind. "No." She threw the covers off and pushed her way through the crowd beside her bed.

"Whoa, whoa, whoa—where do you think you're going?" Jax asked.

"I have to go help Bastion."

"The fuck you do."

"Jax"—Selena glared at him—"if you don't get out of my way this instant, I will relocate your balls into your throat."

Jax didn't move. "No. That bastard has found a new way to get to you. He's sneaky as hell. The team at the house can deal with him just fine."

"Do they know what happened? Do they have him? Are they helping him?"

"No, no, and no. They're looking for him. They think he got away."

"Then I'm going."

"It'll take the helicopter an hour to get here, then an hour and a half or more to get you there. By that time, who knows what the situation will be. You're staying here."

"Take the sedative," Nick said. "If you're asleep, he can't keep doing this to you."

"So you think," Selena said. She got back into bed— reluctantly. Jax was right. In a couple of hours, anything could happen. She'd be no more help to Bastion there than she was here, if he'd found a way to escape her team—something a normal man wouldn't be able to do, but he wasn't a normal man. She just wished she knew what had happened to him.

She looked around at the crowd in her room. "I think it stopped. It hasn't hit me in a few minutes."

"Nathan's gone for the sedative," Joyce said.

"I'm not having a shot."

"It's a pill," Nathan said, rejoining them. "I'll leave it with you in case you change your mind."

Selena was suddenly exhausted. She nodded. "Thank you. I think I'm going to sleep now."

Everyone left. Jax looked back before stepping into the hallway. "Don't fall for this new game, Sel. Don't reach out to him."

"Night, Jax."

"Call if you need me." He stepped back into her room. "I can stay if you want."

"No need. I'm just going to sleep."

"Right." He shut the door behind him.

When she could no longer hear anyone in the hall outside her room, she reached out to Bastion.

Can you hear me? Where are you? Tell me so I can help you.

Those were the same things he'd said to her while she was here. Maybe the pain had been a ruse, as Jax feared. But maybe it hadn't been. She was so torn.

Bastion, talk to me.

No response. She sat up in bed, glad to not be in pain any longer but disliking her inability to reach him. Did her lack of pain mean he wasn't in pain either? What the hell had happened tonight?

She reached for her cell phone and called Greer. The sound of wind came over the line before Greer spoke. "Yo. Sel. 'Sup?"

"You tell me. What's going on over there?"

"Who told you anything was happening?"

"Greer. I swear, I'ma fuck you up, feel me? Where's Bastion?"

Greer's sigh was loud. "We lost him. We had him, and we lost him." He paused. Selena waited for the rest of the news. "Aaand it looks like the search was just called off. Shit, Eden just got the dogs here, too."

"Tell me. Please. What's happening?"

"For real, how did you know anything was happening?"

"I had an inkling."

"Did Bastion ask you to call us?"

"No. Bastion's not talking at all. I had the weirdest pain in my legs. I mean, a crippling pain."

"Christ. We caught him in a bear trap."

Selena choked on a huge wave of emotion. "Greer. God. How could you?"

"He's an enemy, remember, Sel? He still managed to knock us back. When we came around, he was gone, no sign of how he got out or where he went."

"You've got to find him, Greer. Promise me. Get back out there and find him. He can't be alone wounded as he was."

"We're done. We didn't find him. It's over. Gotta go." Greer hung up.

Selena pressed the cool screen of her phone against her jaw. It wasn't over. Bastion was out there somewhere, terribly injured. She dropped the phone and leaned over her lap, covering her face with her hands.

A memory slipped into her mind of the night Greer had sent them out to fetch Max and Hope. She'd breathed on the glass of the French door. Bastion had been there, outside. She saw him now, saw the warm breath he blew on the pane by hers. His dark eyes were so sad, so intent that night.

Quick on the heels of that memory came another. Bastion was in her room, lying crosswise on her bed… kissing her. He'd made her ceiling come alive with an illusion of a summer evening. She'd thought that was just a dream.

He was who she'd been hungering for all those months when she'd felt him nearby but didn't know who or what was the source of her yearning.

Now she did.

Another memory crashed into her. She'd thought she was alone in the attic during Max's wedding, but she hadn't been. Bastion had been there, holding her, humming to the tune coming from the old record player while they danced.

Memory after memory poured through her mind, unordered and fast, a lifetime flashing through her consciousness.

Bastion was standing in front of her, cut up and bloodied. He made the wind stroke her face. She'd asked him to show himself. He refused. What the hell? Who had he killed to be covered in blood like that?

She lifted her knees and dropped her head to her hands, fisting her face between her wrists. A whole slice of life she'd been missing had just unpacked itself in her mind. How was that possible? How had he stolen her memories? How had he returned them?

They kept coming, each shoving the previous aside

as all the details of every encounter filled her mind, hours of them in mere seconds.

And then she came to the worst of all—the night he'd come to visit after Addy's bachelor party. He'd been with her in her room, naked, starting to make love to her, until she'd stopped him. She'd sunk against the wall, feeling more broken and isolated than ever before…and he'd sat next to her. But he hadn't stayed there. No, he'd followed her into the bathroom…he'd seen what she'd done to herself.

Selena covered her face and cried, remembering everything about that horrible night. She saw him, in his astral form, straining to stop her from cutting herself, his ghost hands like smoke against her physical self. He couldn't stop her. And then he was gone. Gone. He didn't watch her draw blood, but he was there seconds later. It was him, his physical self. Where had he come from?

He put her in a trance. That was the piece of the night she thought she'd forgotten, the bit that led her to wonder if he'd taken advantage of her that night.

How wrong she'd been. He hadn't. Her underwear was on the floor because he'd taken them off her to search for more scars. He'd kissed the ones he found on her hips, on the sides of her breasts, all the spots she hid from everyone.

Bastion. Talk to me. The man, the mutant, knew her secrets. All of them. And still he'd wanted to be with her.

He'd covered her with a T-shirt that night, then sat

up with her in the shadows of her room, crying. When morning neared, he'd written something. He'd torn the page from her notebook. Odd; she'd never found a note from him.

And then she knew exactly what he'd done. He'd put his note with her box cutter. She hadn't looked in that pocket since that night. In fact, everything in her bathroom had been tidied—she assumed she'd picked up after herself and had blocked out the memory, as she often did after an episode. But that night it was Bastion who'd straightened everything.

She scrambled out of bed and rushed into her bathroom, swiping her tears from her cheeks as she flipped on the lights. Her hands were shaking as she opened her toiletries bag. There was one pocket she hadn't unpacked yet—the one she reserved for her box cutter.

She unzipped it. The box cutter was gone. In its place was a folded piece of paper, white fringe still lining one edge. She took it out and opened it up. His handwriting was neat, small, and all in caps.

IF YOU WERE WIND, I'D BE LEAVES TO FEEL YOU
BRUSH AGAINST ME.

IF YOU WERE WATER, I'D SINK MY FINGERS INTO
YOUR COOL DEPTHS TO SEE YOU CURL
AROUND ME.

IF YOU WERE THE STARS, I'D BE THE NIGHT TO
SHOW YOU HOW YOU SHINE.

IF YOU WERE A SOUL, I'D BE YOUR SHADOW SO
YOU'D KNOW YOU WERE NEVER ALONE.

IF YOU WERE MINE, I WOULD LOVE YOU
FOREVER.

Selena read it twice, three times, then stumbled from the bathroom and sat on the foot of her bed. This was the truth of what she'd felt about Bastion. He might have been the one for her, but she'd never know because he'd stolen her memories of their time together.

And now it was too late.

Bastion! Please!

Nothing.

It couldn't be too late. He had to be at the house somewhere. What was it that the Ratcliffs had said about Bastion belonging to a legion of mutant fighters like him?

Selena. Her name was spoken by a different voice. A rumbling baritone that wasn't Bastion's. Strange how she could know that even through a telepathic link.

Who are you? she asked.

I am Liege.

Bastion's hurt.

I know. We have him. He's healing.

I need to see him.

He needs to heal. I'll send for you when you can come.

But he's all right. He's safe?

He is.

Okay. Selena sucked in a breath, hoping her sob didn't go across their telepathic link.

Tell me, are you safe? Liege asked.

She nodded. Then realized he couldn't see her. *I am.*

Good. Watch for a sign. You will know when to come to us.

21

Bastion squinted at the bright sunlight streaming in through his bedroom window. The first thought that came to his mind was Selena. The second was his total lack of pain. He sent a look around the room and saw Liege lounging in his armchair, staring at him. Acier and Guerre were there, too.

How long had he been out?

Yeah, I'm here too, Merc chimed in telepathically.

"Why were you hiding her from us?" Acier asked before Bastion could say anything.

Bastion pushed himself up into a sitting position. "I told you before—it was complicated. I thought I could take some time to let her warm up to the idea of us."

Merc laughed. *Stalking's more like it, mate.*

"Was the Matchmaker involved in this?" Guerre asked.

Bastion nodded. He caught the looks the guys

shared. "She wouldn't yield to the Matchmaker either. She is a stubborn woman. She suffered for it."

"How so?" Guerre asked.

Bastion tapped his forehead. "Migraines. She had them when I wasn't sending out pain signals. It had to have been him."

Liege looked at Acier. "Bring her here." He mentally provided the lat and long of her location. He didn't have a magic skill that let him divine those instantly, but once he felt an energy signature, he could always locate that on a map.

"How did you find her?" Bastion asked. "I could not."

"While you were out," Liege said, "she opened herself to you. I followed that link from you to her."

"*Merde.*" Bastion leaned into his pillows. "How long have I been here like this?"

"Ten days," Guerre said. "If you're up to a shower, I can help you. You have to keep your walking boots dry."

"How bad was the damage?" Bastion asked.

Guerre reached out to help him up. "Your tibia and fibula were crushed on your right leg, only bruised on your left."

Bastion moved to sit on the edge of the bed. "And Selena's team? Did I—did I harm them?"

"Shook them, for sure," Acier said.

"What has become of them? The ghouls were swarming that night."

Liege came over to help Guerre with Bastion. They hoisted him to his feet, then let him settle a minute.

"Nothing. I was able to keep them inside while Merc and Acier took out the ghouls. After that, her team went looking for you but never found you. But because they've now come to Flynn's attention, they'll have to be briefed on the danger he poses."

"I'll return with your light, Bastion," Acier said, grinning. "We'll have a nice, long convo about you on the way over."

Bastion stopped walking and turned toward the door. "I should go for her, not him."

Liege urged him toward the bathroom. "You should shower before you see your light. Trust me. You smell like a pigsty."

IT WAS MIDMORNING when Liege's messenger came for Selena. He stood on the hill just below the helo deck. The helicopter behind him was still running. Selena stared out her window, wondering when Jax's team would sound the alarm and all hell would break loose. The man was tall and wide-shouldered. He had shaggy black hair.

I've come to take you home, the man said.

Home. That sucked the air out of her. Did she have a home? It wasn't here, in exile. She wasn't sure it was at Blade's house with the team. *I don't know where that is.*

Bastion is your home.

Yeah, that was fucked on more levels than she could

count. Instead of accepting that, she changed the subject. *Is he well?*

Yes. Do you need a hand with your things?

No. Where is everyone?

They are in a pleasant state of suspended animation. Once we're in the air, they will be returned to normal.

Where are we going?

You'll see when we get there.

She grabbed her phone to text her team, but her phone was dead. *I need to let my team know.*

Not yet.

Selena moved away from the window, toward the duffel bag that sat next to her door. She'd been packed ever since Liege said he'd send for her. Going with Bastion's friend was a huge leap of faith. What if he wasn't Bastion's friend at all? How did she know she could trust him?

Her door opened, startling her. The man from outside stood there, filling her doorway. He had blue eyes—almost electric-blue eyes. And pale white skin with a mustache and goatee. He grabbed her bag and gave her a smile. "The chopper's gonna run out of fuel while you stand here ruminating. You'll be safe where I'm taking you. We're all safe and can be trusted."

And just like that, she followed him out of her room, down the stairs, and out of the house. She wasn't moving on her own volition—who takes the word of a bad guy when he says he's safe? No, this was more like she was forced to go with him.

When they were settled and on their way, she

worried again about Jax and Nick. The household at Addy's were used to Selena hiding out in her room. No one would even think to go looking for her until dinner —they'd be beside themselves then. "What's your name?"

"Acier."

Acier. That wasn't a name she remembered hearing in any of the convos she'd had with her team about Bastion and Legion. A frisson slipped down her spine. What if she'd been coerced into going with him?

"Be at peace, Selena. Bastion did send me."

That did nothing to calm her nerves. "Do you know what's going on?"

"Yes." Humor made crinkles appear next to his eyes. "I have all the answers, but they aren't mine to give. You'll have to ask Bastion your questions."

After that, Acier quit talking. Selena settled for watching outside as the helicopter flew over spiky mountain ridges.

A WHILE LATER, the helicopter landed on a field out on the plains, near an adobe fort. The whole northern horizon was shrouded in a black cloud. Rather forbidding, if you took that sort of thing as an omen.

She grabbed her bag and got out. The chopper blades were kicking up dirt and bitterly cold air that burned her cheeks and nose.

Ducking, she jogged away from it, toward the

massive building—the only dwelling in sight. She wasn't quite to the covered parking area when the helicopter took off. The silence it left in its wake was loud. She looked at Acier, who gestured toward a huge blue gate —the only entrance on this side of the fort. The big doors opened outward as she approached, though she couldn't see anyone operating them. Inside, a short tunnel opened onto a wide courtyard. No one was there. The gate closed behind her with a thunderous rumble. She looked back, but Acier was gone.

What was this place? Bastion was here. She could feel him. A door on her right opened. She went through it to a kitchen—a cavernous thing that made the big kitchen at her team's headquarters seem tiny.

In the middle of the room, near a table and a kiva fireplace, a man stood alone. Bastion. He had on a white tee and jeans that were cut open from his ankles to his knees, baring the two black walking boots he wore. He leaned on a pair of long crutches. His thick, wild dark brown hair hung in rough waves to his shoulders. His beard was long and bushy, his mustache trimmed around his lips.

Their gazes met. His dark irises were small in his big eyes, giving him a soulful look. She felt the tremor that slipped through him. Was he real? Was this just another projection of him? Would he disappear if she touched him?

Selena dropped her bag and lingered near the door as waves of emotions trampled through her mind. They'd had months of time together, but he'd stolen all of her memories of that time. She doubted he would have ever released them had he not been injured.

"That is true," he said. "I would not have—at least, not without being with you when they came back."

He knew everything about her, even the secret things that she didn't share with anyone.

"We all carry our own shame. It was not my intent to overstep, but I couldn't leave you alone in your hell that night."

"You stole my privacy, my freedom. You helped yourself to everything about me. You took my team away. Probably my job as well. I have nothing, because of you."

Selena glared at him, angry and scared, relieved and hopeful—a contentious mix of emotions that had been brewing for months. She crossed the room, stopping a couple of feet from him, close enough to breathe in his scent, that strange mix of soap and clover and his own sweet musk.

"Your poem was sweet, but not sweet enough to undo all you've done."

"I merely wished to replace a negative with a positive. I'm sorry for how we began."

"We haven't begun. *We* are nothing."

Her heart beat hard. She tore her gaze from his as she moved around him in a wide circle. He held still, letting her look him over. When she stood in front of him again, she poked him. He was solid. Her memories were still so scrambled, but she could only think of the one time that he'd let her see him physically. It was that night after Max's wedding. He disappeared then. He might now.

She reached a hand out, flattening it on his chest. He didn't move away, didn't speak, didn't reach for her. He waited, yielding to her, giving her all the moves.

The rumble of his heart matched the rhythm of hers. She met his eyes again, then stepped closer, closer, touching her body to his. How many times had she done this in her daydreams? She moved her hand up his wide chest to slip around the back of his neck. His dense mane warmed her cold fingers. A muscle bunched in the corner of his jaw. His eyes never left hers, but he leaned close, bending down to meet her halfway.

Selena blinked. He was real. He was here. She wanted to kiss him, which was unfathomable to her. How could she desire a man who didn't respect her?

"I do respect you," he said. "I did what is now my nature to do."

"To destroy?"

"To observe. Do you hate the sun for the cancer it causes or love it for the life it provides?" he asked.

"I don't love you."

He nodded. "I don't love myself, either."

"Tell me something." She pinned him with her eyes, watching for a tell that would give away his lies. "Were you using me?"

"Yes."

"So none of this was about us?" They were an "us," despite her denying it earlier. They'd shared…something…even if she didn't quite know what it was.

"All of it was about us. Every moment. I offer myself for you to use as well."

"I don't use people. Where do you get these notions?"

He tapped his head. "It's all scrambled in here. I only know that I need you like I need air, that if the only way we could be together was for me to keep hiding myself from you, I would still be doing it."

"My needs be damned?"

He shut his eyes. Miles and miles separated their stances on everything, but still she craved him. She stood on tiptoes, touching her mouth to his. His eyes shot open, but he didn't disappear.

The only sound he made was a low growl as he wrapped his arms around her, crushing her to him, taking over the kiss. She felt the wiry fur of his beard and mustache, liking and disliking it. His lips brushed hers. Any time she tried to drive the kiss, he broke contact, only to make it again, moving his focus from her whole mouth to the corner, then opening his mouth so their tongues could touch.

She didn't care who owned the kiss; she just wanted more of him. Later, she could teach him that she wasn't a passive lover.

After a minute, he smiled against her mouth, still keeping their bodies tight as he eased her back to the ground. She hadn't been aware he'd lifted her past her tiptoes. She wasn't a short woman; most men weren't able to sweep her off her feet.

He leaned his face against hers. "You think to teach me how to love you?"

"Maybe. Depends on how teachable you are."

"Come upstairs. We'll get a baseline."

Selena pulled away, then stepped back—and saw his crutches standing next to him, all on their own. This new reality—his reality—was something she'd never get used to.

"What happened?" She nodded at the boots he wore. "I felt your pain. And then I didn't. I tried to reach you, but I couldn't."

Bastion's lips thinned. "I lost my head and forgot my training. Your team set an excellent trap. Bear traps, to be specific."

Selena hissed as her memory of his pain hit her again.

He winced. "I'm sorry I caused you pain."

"But you're okay."

"I am. I'll be back to running in no time."

"And the guys? You didn't hurt them?"

"*Non*, I did not hurt your friends. Well, not much, anyway."

Selena rubbed her chest, soothing the tightness that had been there for so long. Bastion moved her hand aside and set his hand on her chest. Heat and an odd sense of ease moved from his palm, slipping inside her body. She covered his hand with hers.

"Be calm, Selena. We do not mean you or your team harm."

"What is this place?"

"It's our fort."

"Where are we?"

"Northeastern Colorado."

She took her phone out of her pocket, forgetting it was out of juice. "I really need to call my team."

"Your phone will not work until we allow it."

Selena's eyes narrowed. "My first loyalty is to my team."

"Not anymore. Your first loyalty is to me."

Selena shook her head. "Yeah, your lessons are going to take some time."

"Selena," a man said from the kitchen door.

She turned to face him. He was tall, black, and had an air of authority. "I can show you to your room, if you like. Once you're settled, we can decide what's next. It's time our teams met in person."

"So you're done spying on us?" Selena asked, but Liege was already leaving the room and did not respond.

She picked up her bag. Bastion stopped her. "Selena —tell him you want my room." He grinned at her.

"Not happening, Bastion."

"But you just kissed me."

"Did I?" She frowned and shook her head. "I can't remember. I have a hard time keeping any memories, it seems." She followed Liege across the short entry tunnel, into a glass corridor and up a set of stairs.

Liege turned the corner to the right and opened a door. "Make yourself comfortable. Bastion's room is just there." He pointed to the last room on the north hallway to the left.

Selena looked inside, but stayed where she was. "I haven't decided if I'm staying."

"Do as you wish. At least you have a room of your own while you're here."

"You aren't going to make me stay here?"

"Why would I?"

Selena was unconvinced. She was a captured pawn. They both knew it.

"Get yourself settled, then come back down to the kitchen. We need to talk." Liege left her alone outside her room.

22

She went inside and dropped her bag on the king-sized bed. The room was austere. The walls were the same peachy-beige stucco as the rest of the fort. A white-linen duvet cover was spread over the bed with a beige wool throw folded at the foot of the bed. Three rows of different-sized pillows in more white linen were lined up like soldiers at the head of the bed. A set of antique wooden doors, brown and weathered, framed the end of the bed. Really, the headboard was the only decoration in the bland room. Hotel rooms had more sense of style. Two nightstands with lamps flanked the bed. A set of single-paned double French doors let light in and opened to a terrace.

Selena walked into the closet, then into the big bathroom. Not much to see in either space, except for the fact that both rooms were obviously designed for large humans, given the height of the ceilings and fixtures. She made use of the restroom, then washed her hands and face. For a moment, she stared at the water slipping through her fingers. This day had not gone as she'd expected.

Nor had her life, for that matter.

She plugged her phone in. Hopefully after the coming convo in the kitchen, it would have enough power to make a call. She shoved her hands into her jeans, unsure what to do with herself. No point hiding. She'd better get down to the kitchen to hear them out. Kit and the rest of her team would go bonkers once they discovered she was missing, so hopefully she could reach them first.

She paused with her hand on her doorknob, remembering her visceral reaction to Bastion just a few minutes ago. She'd had no control over herself. She'd had to touch him. Kissing him seemed the only thing she could have done at just that moment, after seeing he was alive and healing. She needed to get her head on straight and get a lock on her emotions. She was alone in unknown territory—best make the most of it so she could bring good intel back to her team.

Her composure resolved, she left her room and went around the bend in the hallway. As she reached the stairs, Bastion's door opened and a wheelchair came out. By itself. Moving on its own locomotion, it turned down the hallway but didn't take the stairs—because what self-running wheelchair did that? As far as Selena could tell, it wasn't motorized, so she had no idea how it was moving. But after seeing all the tricks Bastion had pulled while she was at her team's headquarters, this didn't surprise her. Much.

She followed it past the stairs, down a short hallway, down another hallway, and into a vestibule with an elevator. The smell of laundry detergent was strong. She could hear machines running in an area behind a door.

Such a human activity in a house of altered reality.

The elevator opened. The chair entered. Selena followed it. A button lit up. A moment later, the doors opened and the chair went out of the vestibule and into the kitchen.

Four men sat around the kitchen table. A fire was lit in the kiva fireplace, giving that area of the cavernous room a cozy feel. She wanted to make a joke about the pet wheelchair, but their serious expressions nixed that idea.

Selena made eye contact with each of the men, sizing them up, searching them for signs of malice—toward her or her team—especially after Bastion's injuries.

She found no ill will in them, which was terribly confusing. The men stood as she approached the table. A seat was open at the opposite end of the table from Liege, kitty-corner to Bastion.

He smiled at her. "You followed my chair."

"It seemed the thing to do," Selena said.

"We are going to show you our silo," Bastion told her. "Guerre said I still need to rest my legs, so it appears I must use the chair on our tour."

Selena met his dark gaze, wondering if she should apologize for what her team did to him.

"No apology is needed," Bastion said. "I behaved as an enemy. Their strategy was magnificent. Makes me admire them all the more."

"Selena," Liege said, "you are among friends here. You cannot shield yourself from us, so there's no point trying."

"This is my team," Bastion said. "They are pretty, *non*? One is not here, but he is not pretty."

Pretty wasn't the word she would have used. Lethal would have better described them. They were like fallen angels—broad shoulders, strong hands, taut judgment hardening their eyes.

"There is *mon capitain*, Liege. Next to me is Guerre. He's our healer. There is Acier, whom you met. He's our weapons maker. *Mes amis*, this is Selena, my light," he told the group.

"Back up, Bastion. I'm no one's light, whatever the hell that is."

His smile was tinged with sorrow. "It is what it is, Selena."

Liege cleared his throat, drawing their attention to him. "As you may be aware, we've been monitoring your team for months. It's time we meet to share what we know about our common enemy, the Omni World Order."

"Okay," Selena said, not as convinced as he was.

"I understand you have access to two scientists, Nathan and Joyce Ratcliff, who are themselves modified," Liege said.

"I don't, but some on my team do."

Liege nodded. "We have secure facilities for them here, which you'll see in a few minutes. You may be aware that the Omnis are taking their scientists off grid, possibly terminating them."

"We are aware of that," Selena said. "I need to check in with my team."

"You do," Liege said. "But first, we need to show you our labs. And some of the new challenges your team may not have encountered yet."

Bastion got up from the table. He leaned heavily on his crutches as he moved to his wheelchair, which was parked behind him. Selena could feel the pain he tried to hide from her. He met her gaze, chasing the pain away with other thoughts that made her mouth go dry.

Before they could leave the room, a blond woman came into the kitchen, a sketchpad tucked under her arm. She was pulling off dirty gardening gloves. She smiled at Liege and went straight over to kiss him, then looked at Selena curiously.

"Summer, this is Selena," Bastion said. "She is a warrior—and she is my light."

The woman's eyes went wide before she gave Selena a big smile. "See?" she said to Liege. "They do exist."

"So it would appear," Liege replied. "We're going to give her a tour of the labs. Want to come?"

"No." Summer shook her head. "No, thank you." She shivered. "I just came to get a glass of water."

Summer came over to Selena and held her hand out. "It's nice to meet you. I told Liege there were women like you—fighters. I'm glad he got to meet you too."

Selena was unsure what to make of that, so she just smiled and shook the woman's hand. The guys started to file out of the kitchen.

Selena looked at Bastion. "Shall I push your chair for you?"

He smiled and shook his head. "There is no need."

Right. Because this was some parallel universe where the laws of physics were easily manipulated. She followed him out of the kitchen, across the entry tunnel, and into the glass hallway.

At the end of the hallway, they went down another set of short hallways to another elevator. The cab on this one was large enough for all of them to fit, even with Bastion's chair and its extended leg supports. It was hard to tell how many floors they descended, since the buttons were labeled with text, not numbers.

So these guys had a bunker too. And a lab. What were they up to? She looked at Bastion, wishing she had his ability to read minds. She was blindly following them into an unknown lair. If she'd mistaken their intentions, her team might never find her again.

By now, if they'd discovered she was missing, they had to be either worried sick for her or were doubting her trustworthiness, going AWOL as she had. Maybe both. She couldn't blame them. So much was at stake right now—it was a bad time to go missing.

We'll take you back to them after this, Bastion said via their mental link. *They will soon know, through you, more about us.*

The elevator stopped and the doors opened. The

area they walked into didn't look like the silos Selena had seen from the compounds owned by the White Kingdom Brotherhood or the Omni World Order.

There were two hallways, one in front of the elevator and one that went to the right. They took the one that led off from the elevator. The corridor was wide and sterile. The walls were white. Industrial linoleum tiles covered the floor like in a hospital ward. Big windows looked into long labs—one of which appeared to be a morgue.

Acier opened the door to the morgue and held it for her and Bastion.

Be calm, my warrior, Bastion warned her. *What you are about to see is the stuff of nightmares.*

I'm not your anything, Selena snapped, glaring at him.

My warning stands, Bastion said.

"We, as you know, have been changed," Liege said. "I know you've encountered other mutants. Your leader's woman, his father, and the scientists. The Omnis are proceeding at a reckless pace with their experiments. They aren't just enhancing humans— they're making monsters. Whether this is by intent or by error, the fact remains that they are setting loose the deviants they're creating." He nodded toward Guerre, who clicked open a slide show on the large glass pane.

Selena gasped as the images covered the screen. The monsters were just that: disfigured, gargoyle-like beings come to life.

"What are these things?" she asked.

"Omni lab creations," Bastion said. "We fight them several times a week."

"It may only be a matter of time before they come for you and your team," Acier said. "You guys need to learn how to fight them."

"This is why we need to connect with the scientists your team is hiding," Liege said. "If we can find and destroy the labs creating these monsters, everyone will be safer."

Selena sent a look around the room. "Makes sense. So why all the skulking around our place? Why not just ask for a meetup?"

"Because your team hadn't yet caught the attention of those we're hunting," Liege said.

"The fuck we haven't. There's a reason we live together on a compound."

Liege silently regarded her. "The Omnis are a diverse group."

Selena's brows rose. "Yeah. About as diverse as all shades of white."

"Skin tone isn't what I'm talking about," Liege said. "Focus is. The Omni World Order is comprised of dozens of petty autocrats, each holding his own sort of power, each with his own objectives, each seeking to control powerful sectors of science and technology. Beyond that, the OWO contains dissidents, like us, like your team. The scientists we're after fall in both camps."

"We've learned that."

"So far it hasn't been the changed Omnis coming after you. Their focus has been on eradicating other changed beings and building their forces. How long that will be the case, I don't know."

"So patch my team in," Selena said. "You're wasting your time having this convo with me. I don't have the authority to sign us up to join forces with you."

Liege glanced at Bastion, then at Guerre. The looks they exchanged were lengthy, as if they were having a private discussion, which they probably were, given how Bastion had been able to talk to her mentally.

"Out loud, Liege," Bastion said. "My woman cannot hear you."

Selena narrowed her eyes at him. "I'm not your woman."

"Yet."

Guerre walked to one of the freezer drawers. He rustled through a body bag, then pulled out something that looked like a ball wrapped in clear freezer bags. "When we take you back to your team, you'll take this." He put the frozen ball in a small cooler.

What the hell was that?

Liege handed the cooler to Selena. "Take this to anchor your conversation with your team."

"What is it?" Selena asked.

"Show and tell," Acier said, then grinned. "The mic-drop kind."

She set the cooler on one of the steel gurneys and looked inside. Staring up at her, through layers of plastic wrap and tape, was the frozen head of one of the monsters they'd just shown her images of.

Jesus, Mary, and Joseph.

The disfigured thing looked like a prop from a horror flick. Selena slammed the cooler lid down.

It was cruel. I am sorry for that, Bastion said. *But words cannot make real the danger your team faces the way this artifact does. That is all we meant by giving this to you. Perhaps it is something that will entice your scientists to come forward.*

Selena felt tired suddenly. She'd spent the last several weeks in a holding pattern, always conscious of her thoughts, always worried of revealing something sensitive to Bastion and his hidden forces.

Always missing him—a man she neither knew nor trusted.

"Guerre and Bastion will take you back to your compound," Liege said. "I'm open to meeting with your team, here, there, or any other place, any time. Sooner the better."

He nodded at his men, then left the lab.

23

The black cloud that had darkened the northern sky when Selena arrived had now rolled south, bringing with it a snow squall. It was hard to see anything heading straight into the storm as they were.

Guerre was driving. Bastion was in the back, resting his leg across bench seat. The monster head was all the way in the back cargo area of the Escalade they drove.

She looked out the front passenger window, worried about what she was bringing to her team. Truthfully, she wasn't bringing anything new. Bastion and his guys had already found them. Thank God he hadn't hurt anyone.

I would only hurt an enemy, he said via their mental link. *And do not spare a thought for me. My pain does not matter.*

You invaded our space, she said.

To find you. I was out of my mind with worry.

Selena looked at him in the back. *Why?*

It is the nature of things. Mutants like me rarely make a connection with regulars, but when we do, we cannot undo it.

Selena stared into the snow slashing toward them. It would be dark before they arrived.

A long while later, she checked her watch as they pulled off the highway and drove around the outskirts of Wolf Creek Bend. It was almost time for dinner. The families at her team's compound would be gathering in the living room. She didn't want any of the civilians to see what—and whom—she'd brought home.

Guerre pulled up on the side of the house where the garage was. Wind was whipping the snow into a frenzy as it whistled around the corner of the house. Selena stood outside the closed garage doors, waiting for her team to be alerted. Guerre helped Bastion out of the SUV and into his wheelchair. He set the cooler on Bastion's lap, then drove off. Selena watched him turn down the driveway. His headlights disappeared. "Did he go? Or is he still here somewhere?"

"He is nearby," Bastion said.

She took the cooler from him and set it on the ground between them. She knew the motion sensors would alert the team that they were standing there. Unless...Bastion had jammed them again.

"I have not."

One of the doors opened. Bastion got to his feet and moved slightly in front of Selena, leaning on his crutches.

"Don't do that," Selena said. "These are my people."

"The least I can do is shield you."

"I don't need shielding," she said, stepping out from behind him.

Max, Greer, and Kit came out of the house, but stopped as they noticed Selena's strange behavior.

"Get Tank," she said. A moment later, Eddie came out with the dog on a leash. "Send him alone."

Eddie released her dog. He rushed over and sniffed Bastion, her, the cooler, and its contents, then Bastion's chair. Selena wondered if he'd scent Guerre in the SUV that was somewhere nearby, but he didn't. Tank made another circle around them, then hurried back to Eddie.

Selena breathed a sigh of relief. At least she knew there wasn't a bomb hidden in the gruesome head.

Bastion returned to his wheelchair. Snow was still swirling about them, sending cold and wet flakes inside her collar.

Kit walked in front of Max and Greer, glaring at Bastion. For his part, Bastion gave him a big grin as he said, "Hello."

"Bastion?" Kit asked.

"*Oui*. It is I."

Kit looked from him to Selena. "What's going on? Jax said you left."

"I did." Selena nodded. "We have a lot to talk about. And none of it is fit for civilians."

Kit looked from her to Bastion. "You want me to invite him in?"

"I believe him when he says he's not an enemy. I've met the rest of his team. Like I said, we have a lot to talk about."

Kit nodded toward the cooler. "What's in there?"

Selena couldn't stop the sigh that broke free. Now came the hard part. "The head of a monster."

"Fuck. Me." Max stepped next to Kit. "Since when do we take trophies?"

"It is not a trophy," Bastion said. "It is a sample we've preserved from a mutant. It's proof of what we've come to say."

Kit glared at Bastion. "And what would that be?"

Owen came out to join them. "In the den. Now." He nodded at her to go with the others. She stopped on the steps at the garage door and looked back. Owen and Bastion were having a stare-down. Bastion was again on his feet, grasping his crutches. He was a little taller than Owen, but height didn't seem an issue between the men.

"No tricks," Owen said. "No headaches. No trances. No fucked-up electronics. No games."

"The time for games is over," Bastion said. "But I cannot shield you from what you are about to learn." He squared his shoulders. "I wish to apologize for the damage I did to your sitting room."

Owen's expression didn't soften. "You think I buy your crap? That you could undo what you did with just an apology? You were a fucking tornado, Bastion. Around my wife and kids, no less."

Bastion nodded. Selena knew his regret was real. She wondered what had happened. "I lost my control. I'm afraid the damage would have been far worse had Liege not stopped me."

"And now you think I can ever trust you?"

"I have never felt such rage. Or fear. You took my woman, Owen. Should any harm befall her, I cannot promise that I won't lose my control again."

Wow. What had happened? Selena was going to get the scoop as soon as it was safe to do so. "I am my own woman, Bastion—not yours."

Her comment brought Owen's attention to her. He stared at her a long and uncomfortable moment. Was he testing Bastion's promise of good behavior? She hoped he wasn't getting a headache being so near her, as he had before.

"Are you hurt?" Owen asked.

"No," she said.

"Under his influence?"

Selena glared at Owen. "I wouldn't have brought him here if it wasn't the right thing to do."

Owen nodded, gave Bastion a warning glare, then went inside.

She looked at Bastion, relieved they'd gotten over the first hurdle. He grinned at her and spread his arms, leaving his crutches to stand on their own. "See? They love me already."

Selena shook her head. "What was that all about?"

"The day you left, I went a little crazy. I confronted Owen. He is a good mind talker too. When he refused to tell me where you were—and blocked my compulsion to do so—I blew up his sitting room. I've never done anything like that. I didn't even know that I could, but then I've never felt such anguish either."

Oh, man. Today was going to be harder than she'd

expected. Bastion walked toward her, leaving his chair to follow. She carried it up the few steps from the garage into the house, then fetched the cooler. Ace was in the hall waiting for her. Her friend reached out to hug her, a gesture Selena happily accepted.

Ace stepped back, gripping Selena by her arms as she checked her over. "You look good."

"You too." Selena nodded at Ace's aqua ombre. "I like it." Ace was forever changing something about her hair.

Ace looked behind Selena and narrowed her eyes at Bastion. He smiled at her in a friendly way. "I am Bastion."

"I've heard about you," Ace said.

"Of course. I am famous."

Selena grabbed Bastion's wheelchair, giving him a warning glance. It was best not to let the thing move on its own here—not for a while, anyway. Maybe never. She rolled the chair into the den and parked it near the big mahogany desk.

The whole team was gathered in the room. She looked around at their familiar faces, glad to be back. There were ten on the team, counting Ace. Twelve if she included the two former Red Teamers, Russ and Jim, who now ran the household. Thirteen if she counted herself, but the truth was that she didn't know where she fit anymore. If Bastion continued to use her, her place on the team was gone.

She took the cooler from the wheelchair and set it on the big desk that Owen was leaning against. Her boss watched her with those icy eyes of his, waiting for her to get the party started.

She looked around at everyone. "I don't know where to start—"

"So I'll start," Max said, glaring at Bastion.

"*Non*. It is only polite to give the floor to your guest. *Moi*." Bastion settled himself in his wheelchair, then looked at Max then Greer. "It was a brilliant trap you set. Brilliant. I apologize for my abrupt behavior that day. I was out of bounds. You were right to stop me."

"You're sure doing a lot of apologizing," Kit said.

Bastion met his hard eyes. "I regret my loss of control, but I regret even more having to bring to you the information I'm about to share. If I could have kept it from you, shielded you from the danger you're facing, I would have. Forever."

"You didn't just overstep that day, Bastion," Kit said. "You overstepped the whole time you were spying on us."

Bastion shrugged. "That is a matter of perspective. In bounds or out, I have learned what I needed to. You are not working with the Omnis. That is all I care about."

"You still have some explaining to do," Kit said.

"*Oui*." Bastion exchanged glances with Selena. "I have been watching all of you for some time."

"We know that," Max said.

"It is because the war we fight with the Omnis must remain hidden. And until I'd gotten to know you, I couldn't feel I trusted you."

"You're after the scientists," Angel said. Angel's girl-friend was the daughter of the two scientists, so Selena wasn't surprised at his protectiveness.

Kit crossed his arms and spread his legs. "Let's hear him out, Angel."

"You have had modified people here." Bastion looked at Owen. "The scientists, your woman, and your father. I did not know at first if you understood what they were, if they were friends or foes. However, my due diligence is finished. I am confident that you stand on the same side of this Omni war as my team. I have come to request a meeting of our teams."

Owen sent Kit a hard glance.

"There will be no tricks," Bastion said. "It is neces-sary that we share some information we have with you. You need protection from a new threat the Omnis have devised, a tool of terror they are using. And we need help finding and securing Omni scientists. I think there is something we can do for each other."

"What is this new threat?" Owen asked.

Bastion made a disgusted face. "Monsters." Selena opened the cooler, but Bastion stopped her before she could lift the head out. "*Non*. Do not touch it. Hand the cooler to me."

Bastion hoisted himself to his feet. He leaned his crutches on his wheelchair, then lifted out the head. Limping around the room with one crutch, he showed it to each fighter then set it on the coffee table.

"What the living hell is that?" Kit asked.

"It is the head of a monster. We fight these things all

the time. Liege has a Legion of fighters spread around the world, and all of them are seeing more and more of these things."

"But what is it?" Ace asked.

"It is a mutant, like me. But its engineering resulted in a different outcome. These were once human. Their genes have been crossed with various animals, resulting in this *méli-mélo* of biologics."

Bastion returned to his seat, then projected an image of a deviant into the center of the room. It was transparent—an illusion only, but the effect was ghastly. The thing slowly moved in a circle.

"They sometimes look like this. Sometimes a little different, sometimes a lot different. We've been collecting samples from them—their heads, their blood. We need to find the scientists in the Omni program who know what's going on with these, where they are being made, who is driving that program. It has to be stopped. They are vicious killing machines. They have no capacity to think for themselves. Instead, they are assigned a handler who runs them like puppets."

Bastion ended the illusion and looked around the room. Selena knew each of her team was as stricken as she'd been when Liege first showed the monsters to her.

"If we cannot keep these things hidden, then we will not be able to keep our own mutations hidden. And if they become known, then all human systems that exist now, all law and order, all societal norms, will end." Bastion looked at Owen. "This is why I had to take my time and be certain that you could be trusted."

"You want us to get into bed with you after showing us a hologram and a movie prop." Kit chuckled. "Good one."

Selena couldn't blame him. Rejecting this version of reality was so much easier than accepting that it might be true. But not for her—she'd been living it for the last few months. She'd experienced firsthand things that made no sense, like Bastion's appearing and disappearing, trances, and telepathic communications.

"We've seen what the mutations have done to Addy," Owen said. The fact that his wife had almost died from the changes forced on her still haunted him and the team.

"But those changes seem to be going away," Kit said.

Bastion nodded. "They are ending. What was done to her is leaving her system. My team lead believes her mutations were temporary. They were an attempt to terminate her. There is much we don't know. We must have access to the researchers who do." He nodded at the wrapped head defrosting on the coffee table. "These beings changed Liege's woman."

Summer was changed? "In what way?" Selena asked.

"They delivered some type of nanos into a wound they carved on her arm," Bastion said. "The Omnis may be on the verge of using these creatures for widespread damage to human populations."

Owen looked at Kit. "We've seen some of what these mutations can do. The Ratcliffs have reversed their age. My dad too. There is something real going on. I don't know that I believe in monsters, but if one thing is possible, then the other may be as well."

"But how do we know this Legion is on our side of this conflict?" Blade asked. "He wants a meeting that we all attend. Great way to wipe us out."

Kit and Owen appeared to have the same concern. "Bastion, we'll consider your request," Kit said. "But we need some time to discuss it."

"I understand," Bastion said.

"We'll let you know our answer," Owen said.

"I'm sure you will."

"Time to go, bro," Max said, starting toward him. He managed to take two steps before he was locked in place.

"I am not leaving until I have your answer," Bastion said. "And you should know, acquiescence is your only option. You do not want Liege to come here to resolve this."

"I said no tricks," Owen said quietly.

"Ensuring your safety is not a trick."

Owen's cold eyes went a shade cooler. "Threatening us is."

"Oh, for God's sakes," Selena said. "Enough with the chest thumping. We have no choice but to accept. I've met his team. I trust them."

"And yet he threatens us with Liege," Owen said.

Selena met his angry eyes. "There's a pressing need to make this meeting happen. I've seen what he wants to show you. You need to see it too."

"Selena," Val said, "I mean no disrespect when I ask

—how do we know you haven't been compromised? You've been connected to Bastion for months."

"You don't know." Selena shrugged. "You have to take it on blind faith. Take the head to Doc Beck, if you want. Have him check it out. Or hold it here for the Ratcliffs. Jax and Nick should be informed about these things too."

"They can join our meeting," Bastion offered. "If you refuse to trust me, we can split the meeting into two sessions, half of you at each. Jax and Nick can have a third meeting with us, when they are in town." Bastion used his crutch to hoist himself to his feet. "I only care that you meet with us. Soon. Like yesterday."

Kit and Owen swapped looks. "When?" Kit asked.

"Now. Tonight. Tomorrow. Selena and I will wait outside while you discuss this."

"Selena stays here," Owen said.

Bastion faced him. "Then I also stay here. I will not be separated from her again."

"You holding her hostage?" Owen asked. The room stilled.

"No. He is not holding me hostage. Geez, Owen," Selena said. "Get a grip." She couldn't explain what was happening between her and Bastion. Maybe Bastion couldn't either. She just knew that when she was away from him, she had extreme anxiety. She wished Owen wouldn't make a big deal of it.

"So are you with them?" Owen asked. "Or us?"

"Why is it either/or?" Selena answered. Owen didn't move or speak, so she added, "My priorities haven't changed." The guys were sure edgy. There was no way she could calm their nerves. They needed to see what she'd seen so they could quit questioning her loyalty. "Look, we've delayed dinner. And I'm starving. I'll eat in here with Bastion. Any chance someone could bring us a couple of plates?"

"I gotcha covered," Ace said.

"I have a favor to ask," Bastion said to Owen. "My friend is waiting for us. Could you make that three plates?"

"Where is he?" Greer asked, flipping through screens on his phone.

"I'm here," Guerre said, revealing himself.

"Ah. *Bien*," Bastion said calmly, as if a man appearing out of nowhere was a common thing.

The expressions of the team were unwelcoming. "How many more of you are here?" Kit asked Bastion.

"No others. Only the two of us. This is my friend, Guerre." Bastion introduced him, calling off the names of all the fighters in the room. "They are Selena's people. They answer to Kit, and he to Owen. Guerre is our healer."

Guerre nodded. His eyes were somber. For some reason, perhaps because Bastion had broken the ice, the guys didn't seem threatened by him. Or maybe Bastion was just too in-your-face for the team, and Guerre gave off a different vibe.

"This is a lot to take in," Owen said. He looked at Bastion. "How imminent is the threat you're here to tell us about?"

"It is not something that's happening now, but it could come at any moment." Bastion nodded at the monster head. "They have already been here. I've fought them three times while I was observing you. The night I confronted you was the worst. They were swarming the compound. It's why I pushed so hard to find Selena."

"We've seen no evidence of these beings on the property," Kit said. "No blood. No torn-up ground. Nothing on our cameras."

"Because my team and I shielded you from them and removed the evidence. I'd hoped that I would not need to expose you to this threat, but after the last encounter, I think my enemy has you in his sights. You will not be safe for long without us."

Owen nodded. "Then you two stay here tonight. In the morning, we'll meet your team. Selena, bring them to dinner. No talk of monsters. I want to keep this from our families, if we can."

"Copy that," she said.

"What are we doing with that head?" Kit asked, staring at the melting blob.

"Save it for the Ratcliffs," Bastion said. "Or if the doctor you mentioned earlier is trusted, give it to him. We have dozens more. Sacrificing this one specimen won't impact our research. But it can't get out to civilians."

"Angel—put the head in the freezer in the kitchen downstairs," Kit said. "I don't want the kids to see it."

"Roger that," Angel said. He picked up the head and

put it back in the cooler, then disappeared into the hidden entrance to the bunker.

Bastion released the freeze he had on Max as people started leaving. Max finished moving into Bastion's space. They were similar in height and build. Before Max could escalate the situation, Selena wedged her shoulder between them.

"Don't poke the bear," she said to Max.

His angry eyes turned on her. "I *am* the bear."

She put her hand on his chest. "Not anymore." Bastion drew her hand away. She pulled free, but quickly realized there was about a foot of space between her and Max that she didn't remember putting there. She sent Bastion a warning glare. She hated being manipulated.

Bastion shrugged the tense posturing off. "I'm not a bear either. I'm not even a man."

"No," Max said. "You're just a fly on the wall."

Bastion nodded. "This is true."

Max's eyes narrowed. "How are the legs?"

"Healing. How's your head?"

"Healing."

"Good."

Greer, who had stayed behind with Max, asked, "How did you get out of there? We looked for you, but you disappeared."

"*Oui*. My team and I made it appear that way to you while I dragged myself out of there."

"That's a long way to crawl," Greer said.

"It was."

"How do you do what you do?" Max asked.

Bastion tapped a finger to his forehead. "It is all mind games. Liege will tell you in the meeting tomorrow. There are things you must learn if you're to fight in a world with mutants like us." He looked at Greer. "I believe you had the same trainer we did: Santo."

Greer shut his eyes. Selena could tell he was shocked by that news. "How did you know?"

"You and Ace share his DNA. He would not have left you untrained."

"Wait." Greer said. "Was Santo changed?"

"He was. It was early, early days for the technology. It did not work on him quite as he wished. It did not reverse his age."

"But it stopped his aging," Greer said.

"*Oui.*"

"He's dead, you know," Greer said.

Bastion's brows rose. He didn't hide the humor that washed through his face. "Is he?"

Greer and Max exchanged glances, but said nothing more.

Selena pivoted to follow everyone, but Bastion caught her. He wrapped an arm around her waist, spreading his fingers wide, making his big hand span the space between her hip and lower rib as he drew her back against him. He bent close to say, "You think I am the bear?"

She could hear his smile in his voice. "I was trying to stop things from escalating. Max has no fear of battering a brick wall with his head. He's not one to back down."

Bastion let out a low growl, clearly displeased that her concern was for Max, not him. "There is no competition between me or any on your team. I have you. I have won."

Selena shook her head. "You have *not* won me." She pulled free and faced him. "Who says stuff like that, anyway?" Her eyes moved back and forth between Bastion and Guerre. "No weird stuff. No disappearing. No trancing. No wandering."

Bastion looked affronted. "My love...am I allowed to breathe?"

Selena scoffed at that and put some space between her and him.

WHEN THE ROOM WAS EMPTY, Bastion smiled at Guerre. *It is a good day.*

Guerre shook his head. *She's not exactly falling at your feet.*

Her fate is sealed with mine.

Doesn't make her yours yet, Guerre said. *Perhaps you should find the way into her heart.*

Bastion nodded sagely. *It is a hard heart.*

No, it isn't. The way to it is through her people. Protect them.

Of course I will protect them. They are regulars.

Don't do it because it's what we do. Do it because it matters to her. Her people are her heart.

Selena popped her head back in the den. "Coming — or what?"

Bastion grinned at her. "*Bien sûr.*"

They stepped into the living room where everyone was gathered. Bastion faced Guerre, prepared to freeze everyone so they could finish their conversation.

Don't do it, Guerre warned him. *What did I just tell you?*

Bastion glared at Guerre. *I have never had to work at getting a woman before.*

That's because you never had a female you cared about before.

A boy came running across the room. "Captain Hook!"

"Hello, Troy," Bastion said, smiling as the kid took hold of his wrist.

"See, Dad? I told you Captain Hook was here!"

"*Non.* I am Bastion. Not *Capitain* Hook." Bastion held his crutches under his arms and showed his hands. "I have no hook."

"But you do have peg legs," Troy said.

Bastion laughed. "That I do. For a while more, anyway."

"Will you read a bedtime story to us after you eat?" Troy asked.

"No," Owen said, answering for Bastion.

"*Alors*, I cannot tonight," Bastion said. "Perhaps another time."

"Promise?" Troy looked up at him, his brown eyes earnest.

"I do."

Addy led the boy back over to stand with her and Owen. She gave Bastion a narrow-eyed glare, then sent the same look over to her husband.

Bastion may have won a tense truce with the team of fighters, but their women were a whole different story.

The two men who ran the household were adding three place settings to the far end of the table. Selena introduced Bastion and Guerre to her people. Even without all the children there, it was a large gathering... like a little village that all ate together. Bastion liked the familial feel of it.

One of the pregnant women came over to them. Bastion remembered her name was Mandy. Her husband, Rocco—the polyglot—was close on her heels. "So are you from another team like ours?" she asked.

"*Oui*. We are in Colorado. We wanted to meet up with your team and share what we've learned in our fight against the Omnis."

"Where in Colorado?" the other pregnant woman asked.

"Northeast. Not far from Sterling. We have a large compound like this."

Addy put her hands on Troy's shoulders. "But you were here, in the house."

"I was. A few times."

She sent Owen a worried look. "How did your systems not alert us?"

"I disabled them," Bastion said, taking the heat from Owen.

"Bastion and his friends are mutants, like you were, like my dad," Owen said.

Addy gasped, the wheels of fear spinning into overdrive in her mind.

"I'm surprised that we are just now hearing about you guys," Greer's woman, Remi, said.

"Teams like ours tend to specialize," Guerre said with a nod. "We naturally keep to ourselves."

Bastion could feel the warm vibe Guerre was emitting, easing everyone's nerves, squelching the rising wave of civilian panic by sending a sense of peace and harmony throughout the gathering. They were such opposites, he and Guerre. The Legion's healer was totally Zen, always seeking an even keel. Bastion, well, he would have loved a good fight before supper, then a few beers, then the feast that was already being set on the table. He looked at Selena, thinking that in a perfect world they'd end with a half-dozen rounds of fucking.

He smiled at her. She narrowed her eyes.

24

Selena helped their housekeeper, Jim, and cook, Russ, put food away and clean up after the meal.

Maybe she was hiding.

Okay, she was absolutely hiding.

It was overwhelming to think that Bastion was here, openly moving among them as he must have done every day during the long months he'd been spying on them.

Jim dropped a plastic container, and Selena about jumped out of her skin. "My bad," Jim said.

Russ put an arm around her shoulders. "You know there's an extra room at the guest house. You're welcome to it as long as you like."

Selena sighed and leaned into him a bit. "That would just make everything more awkward. And it would only postpone the inevitable. Owen thinks I'm a Benedict Arnold."

"No, he doesn't," Jim said. "He's just trying to get a

handle on what all of this means for the team and their families."

Selena nodded. "Bastion can't be kept out of anything. He slips in like the wind. He would follow me to your place."

Russ's face hardened. "We can deal with him."

Selena reached over and took Jim's hand. "I love you guys. I'm so glad you've joined us. But I don't need you or anyone to fight my battles, though a hug here or there sure wouldn't hurt."

Both men gave her that hug, then all three resumed their kitchen duties.

BASTION SIGHED. He'd hidden himself and stood off to one side. Selena's energy was screaming—with nerves, fear, and a sorrow he couldn't place. Though he'd observed her for many long weeks, he still knew so little about her. He closed his eyes and summoned a calming energy, filling himself with it before sending it her way, letting it wrap around her, fill her, soothe her.

When he looked at her next, she was standing in front of the opened refrigerator door. He saw her sigh, take a deep breath, then square her shoulders.

And not a moment too soon.

Owen came into the kitchen. "Selena, I'd like a word with you in the den."

She looked at Owen, then Jim and Russ, then nodded and followed her boss out of the kitchen.

I'm coming too, Bastion told her.

No. Dammit, Bastion. Were you in the kitchen just now?

He ignored her question. *This situation is because of me.*

No, it's not. It's because of the Omnis. I don't need you to fight my fights. I got this. And quit skulking around.

Merde alors. They were both fighters. Fighters didn't exist in a vacuum; there was always a hierarchy that had to be answered to, so of course she was going to have to face her boss. One thing Bastion knew about Selena was that she defined herself by her strength and her courage as a fighter. Take that away and she'd have a hard time understanding herself.

If they kick you off their team, you'll have a place in ours.

I'm not afraid. It's just Owen.

Your almost-lover.

My never-lover. And fine. Come along, but just keep the fuck quiet. I can't talk to you and him at the same time.

Kit caught up to Selena in the hallway. His face was tense. He looked as if there were something he wanted to say to her, but he didn't have a chance before they went into the den.

Bastion followed the three, keeping himself hidden.

Owen leaned against his desk. Clasping his hands together, one foot on the floor, one knee bent over the edge of the desk, he pinned Selena with a glare. "What happened? Why go AWOL?"

Kit leaned against the other end of the big mahogany desk and folded his arms.

Selena stood in front of them with her hands clasped behind her back, her legs slightly apart—the classic pose of a soldier facing her superiors. "I did what I had to do."

Owen's right brow lifted. "So you take orders from Bastion now?"

Selena's eyes lowered to Owen's chest, then to the surface of the desk. "No."

Kit shook his head as he came forward. Touching Selena's arm, he gestured toward the leather sofa and armchairs. "Sel, it's just us. Let's sit and talk this through."

"No. I prefer to stand. I don't want to feel at all comfortable with what's happening."

"Good," Owen said. "So tell us what did happen. Start at the beginning, because an AWOL stint doesn't come out of nowhere."

"It started here. You're aware of Bastion's attempts to communicate with me. Well, he did more than that. He came to me. In person. Sort of. Remember when I thought you guys were messing with my head?"

"Sonofabitch," Kit growled. "What did he do?"

"We just talked." She sent Owen a pained look. "I liked his visits, but he wiped my memories of them. I thought I was losing my mind. The day he was caught in the traps, all those hidden memories came flooding back."

"He used you to get to us," Owen said.

I did not, Bastion interjected.

Yes, you did.

"He listened to me. I—I liked that about him."

You did?

"We listen to you," Kit said.

Selena huffed a breath. "Not at all the same, Kit. You're my bosses. He was like a friend —"

I am a friend.

"—a secret friend, one who knows me and cares about me and puts me first."

"That's Spycraft 101, Sel," Owen said. "I can't believe you fell for that."

"I didn't. I resisted him."

"Did he ever ask you for information?" Kit asked.

Selena nodded. "He wanted the Ratcliffs."

"Motherfucker." Kit's eyes narrowed as he shot a look over to Owen. "It's good we sent Sel away."

"Not really. Bastion and I were —are —connected telepathically, so he was still able to communicate with me there. I learned that I can block him by shielding my thoughts. I did that as much as I could, but it's hard to maintain. Though I knew I was at Addy's house, I didn't know where her house was. So there was that, at least. It was obviously in the Rockies somewhere, but that covers a huge swath of territory."

"Jax said you spent days hiding in your closet," Owen said.

I hated that. You wouldn't let me help you.

Selena nodded. "The headaches I had here were even worse there. Sometimes, it was impossible to shield my thoughts, so I would hide in there or in my room, where I would keep the lights out so he couldn't see or hear anything through me."

Kit glared at Owen. "And this is the manipulative bastard you want to hook us up with, am I right?"

They have no choice. It's us or Brett Flynn and his ghouls.

I'm getting there. Keep it cool, Bastion.

Selena felt the press of tears gathering. She ground her teeth, forcing herself to keep her emotions at bay. There was just so much at stake, and breaking down in front of her bosses would totally undermine the message she was trying to communicate. Besides, Owen and Kit, with their powerful alpha protective instincts, could only react with the limited understanding they had.

"Bastion wasn't causing the headaches," she said.

"So he has you believing," Owen said.

Selena sighed. She was trying to choose her words so carefully, but the guys had their hackles up and were soon going to go for the pitchforks. Maybe she should have taken Kit's offer to sit down and talk this out.

She sat on the coffee table. "There are so many forces at play, and we don't even know the half of them. Not even a tenth of them. We thought we were fighting other humans in our battles with the Omnis. And perhaps we were, but even Lobo knew something was up with the human modifications. Didn't you ever wonder why he insisted on the FBI taking custody of all our kills?"

Owen and Kit were frowning at her.

"I'm just beginning to learn what's going on. I'm not the right person to speak about all of this. I will tell you that I trust Bastion. I've met his team. They are as fierce and protective as we are. We're on the same side of this fight—only they're about a hundred levels above us. They want to share their knowledge. They want to help us."

"In exchange for what?" Owen asked.

Selena shrugged. "Ask them. You can't resist them. Trust me, I've tried."

"So what made you leave Addy's?" Owen asked. "I still don't get that."

"The headaches were worsening into crippling migraines. I couldn't move or think or sleep or eat. I started to hallucinate."

I hate that you went through this. I tried to get them to tell me where you were. I failed you. The only job I had to do as your mate, and I couldn't help you.

It's okay. It's over now. I hope.

"What do you mean, 'hallucinate'?" Kit asked.

"I started to see an orange glow outside, in the distance. I thought it was a forest fire or a campfire, but it was bitterly cold outside, and no one was reporting a fire in the area. I noticed, though, that every time I looked at it, my headache eased, like it was summoning me."

That was the Matchmaker. So you did see that fiend.

"A couple of weeks into all of this, I felt the most terrible pain in my shins. It was crippling. I couldn't walk. I didn't know what was happening."

It was me. You were feeling my pain.

"The pain was Bastion's. I couldn't reach him for days. I think his team was keeping him in a coma or something. Then this morning, they sent one of their guys for me. As soon as I left with him, my headaches stopped. I haven't had one since. Acier, Bastion's friend, took me to the Legion's fort in Colorado. I met his team. His boss, Liege, showed me things that you need to see. And now, we are where we are."

"At the bottom of a deep pit," Kit said.

We will help them, my love. We are not their enemies.

Selena looked at Owen. "We need the Legion—if only to help us better understand how the Omnis are leveling up and where we fit in their new schemes. There may be no place for us, but if that's the case, we need to know that as well."

Owen nodded. He rubbed his chin as his eyes took on a faraway look. "We'll start with a meetup and go from there."

"She's right, O," Kit said. "None of us expected any of this, but the Ratcliffs did warn us."

"Yeah," Owen said. "They did. But who in his right mind would have believed that all of this could really be a thing?"

Selena knew who it was knocking on her door later that night. She'd showered and changed into a tank top and a pair of flannel pajama bottoms. After that, she'd spent a half-hour pacing, wondering if Bastion would come to her so they could finally face this thing happening to them.

What were they to each other—besides strangers? Or, at least, he was to her.

She opened her door. Geez, he was a big guy. She stepped back to let him into the short entry hallway, but didn't move deeper into her room, didn't want to give him the wrong idea about anything. Instead, she shut the door and backed up to the wall, waiting for him to speak first.

"Hi," he said.

"Hi."

"I wanted to say goodnight."

She nodded and pressed her hands behind her hips to keep herself from reaching for him. "Night."

"It was a big day today."

"It was."

"It's good to be out of hiding. I do not like being invisible."

Bastion was a vibrant, noisy man. Selena didn't know how he had ever survived being silent for as long as he had.

"It was the most difficult thing I've ever done," he said, responding to her thoughts.

"More so than becoming a mutant?"

He lifted a shoulder. "I was not given a choice in that, so it was just a matter of getting through it."

"Did you have a choice in your assignment here?"

"*Non*. But I did have a choice in whether to reveal myself to you."

"So why didn't you?"

"I was afraid. Of wrecking it. Of blowing my chance

with you. Of putting us ahead of our team obligations. I'm glad we are together now."

"We aren't together, Bastion."

"We are more so now than over the past several weeks. Or months."

"I can't get past the pain you imposed on me. The headaches, the fear, the paranoia."

"It was not I. I would not—could not—harm my light."

"You gave the guys headaches."

Again that brief shrug, this time accompanied by a slight grin. "I did not like them near you. But it was not always coming from me, their pain. And never yours."

"Then from whom?"

"I suspect it was the Matchmaker."

"I don't believe in that myth."

"It doesn't matter whether you do or not. He's real. He's who matched Liege and Summer. You saw his orange glow."

"She was a regular human, wasn't she, when they were first matched?"

"Yes. That's true."

Selena wondered what that said about her own future. Would it be as a human or a mutant?

"I think that's your choice. The change is risky. I don't want you modified."

And, of course, because he didn't want that for her, she wanted it for herself. How foolish was that? She didn't even know what it entailed. She was letting her arrogance lead her.

She moved away from the wall and went into her room. "You were here with me some nights."

"Some."

Selena looked up at the ceiling. "I had crazy dreams. Like the outside was inside my room."

"Like this?" Bastion cast an illusion of a summer sky, complete with a mild breeze and the sound of crickets. He shut off the lights, leaving only the soft glow of his illusion.

It was beautiful.

"Selena, could we sit down? This is the first day I've been up and around since the bear traps."

"Oh. Yes. I'm sorry." She gestured toward the armchairs that flanked a small table. Too late, she realized he'd rather sit with her on the bed. She wasn't ready for that intimacy, even if nothing happened between them. He was everything she'd wished for in a man—magical, entertaining, funny, kind, powerful. And terrifying.

She could lose herself in him, and that was very, very dangerous.

He sat at the small table and set his crutches to the side. "Why do I terrify you?"

Of course he'd heard that thought. She crawled to the middle of her bed and gathered herself into a tight ball against her headboard, her arms wrapped around her folded legs. "Because of everything. What you can do. What I can't do. There is no parity between us. I don't know where our boundaries are."

"Nor do I. I only know that being without you makes me crazy."

No man had ever put her first. Ever. She'd always been second—or last—in their lives.

"This scares me," she said.

He nodded. "Me too."

"I like you…I think."

His white teeth flashed at her. "This is good. It is a start."

"What if we do get together—"

"You mean *when* we get together."

"No. *If.* What then?"

"I don't know. We are both warriors. I guess we will do what we do."

"I don't know how to do this. The couple thing."

"You have never had a boyfriend?"

"Not really. Some dates, here and there. Nothing that lasted."

"You liked two of the blonds here."

Selena laughed. "Not exactly. I wanted to…I don't now…have someone who cared about me." She shrugged. "It didn't work out. For any of us. The chemistry was wrong."

"It is true. You and I have powerful chemistry. You would not have meshed with anyone but me."

"So you say."

"So I know."

"I don't want to rush into anything." She could feel the heat of his stare.

"I'm not sure I can do slow, Selena, having been near

—but not with—you for so long, and then surviving the time we were apart."

"Slow's the only option you've got, Bastion. Take it or leave it."

He grinned. "I will take it, and I will change your mind. Now, can we go to sleep?"

"Sure. Which room are you in?"

"Yours."

She choked out a disbelieving huff. "What did I just say about going slowly?"

"I said sleep, not fuck. You'll know when it's time for fucking. Tonight is not it."

"You don't get to decide that. Not unilaterally."

"I wouldn't have it any other way." He hoisted himself up and limped over to the bed, leaving her the side closest to the door. The mattress shifted as he settled next to her. She scooted close to the edge on her side, but she needn't have worried—he rolled to his side and seemed to forget all about her.

He had to be exhausted, this being his first day up and about after his injury. She had to admit that he'd dealt with her team like an expert in human relations, never taking umbrage at their blustering behavior.

She looked at his wide back. It wasn't the first time she'd had a man in her bed—but it was the first time in a long time.

Her relationships had been complicated things she'd never relaxed into. She had stringent rules that were mood killers—no nudity, no lights, no sleepovers.

She'd had sex but never a real boyfriend.

"I can work with rules." His voice was just a whisper. In fact, she wasn't sure if he'd spoken or if she'd heard his thought. Already, she didn't know where she ended and he began, so blended were their minds.

When the meaning of his words hit her, she realized he'd just lied. He and rules were like oil and water. "What happens tomorrow?" she asked.

"Tomorrow happens tomorrow."

"I mean with us." No answer from him. "I don't want to want you." She didn't…but she did.

Bastion rolled onto his back. He stared up at the illusion he'd set on her ceiling. "Is wanting me so terrible? You tried fighting it, but that caused you terrible pain."

"I hate being forced or coerced or tricked into anything."

"Then I will hunt the Matchmaker down and kill him to free you from his curse."

"And free you."

Bastion rolled over to his side again. "I don't want to be freed. I've wanted you my whole life."

Selena looked at the stars twinkling overhead. It was just like sleeping outside under a summer stars-cape. She had the strangest yearning to move nearer to Bastion, to feel his heat, to feel *him*. She fought the feeling for a long time, but when his breathing became soft and regular, she did move closer to him, close enough to feel the length of him all along her side.

She shut her eyes, soaking in the deliciousness of being near him. After a moment, she turned on her side, facing him. Keeping her hands fisted between their bodies, she rubbed her cheek against his back, breathing in the hint of clover that covered him.

BASTION SMILED, then clamped his jaw to tamp his emotions down. He stayed on his side, not daring to move. His light was full of fear, but he knew she was also capable of great love.

He couldn't wait until she knew it too.

25

Bastion was gone when Selena woke the next morning. She felt exactly as she had the mornings after those strange and wonderful dreams she'd had while he was stalking the team.

Empty.

Except there was one major difference. He hadn't wiped her memory. He'd been with her the whole night, near her, touching her, but never asking anything from her.

And for the first time in a long time, she woke without her perpetual headache.

A knock sounded on her door. She heard it open. "Just me," Ace said.

"Get in here!"

Ace hurried into her room and sat on her bed. Her pale green eyes moved all over Selena, but paused as she studied Selena's expression.

"I'm fine," Selena said, chuckling.

"He was with you last night, wasn't he?"

Selena smiled. "He was."

"And?"

"And nothing. We slept. That's it. I was out cold. And no headache this morning!"

"Are you in love with him?"

"No. Were you when you first met Val?"

"Yes."

Selena gave Ace a curious look. "I do feel weird around him."

"How so?"

"Like...he's a caramel macchiato triple-shot latte and I'm addicted to them."

"So it's a good feeling?"

Selena nodded. "But I don't know anything about him. I don't know how we can have a future together—we're practically different species. How can any of this work?"

Ace crawled up to sit next to Selena as she leaned against her headboard. "I think what you're afraid of is loving someone. The rest is just noise."

"I am scared of that."

"So go slowly. Don't commit. Leave your options open."

Selena sighed as she looked at her petite friend. "I'm glad you're here, Ace. You get me."

"That's 'cause you're as fucked up as I am." They both laughed. "For what it's worth, I like him. He charmed all the guys, even when exchanging insults. Val thinks he's a hoot."

"Val would. Probably because he fries Owen's sense of authority just by breathing."

Ace elbowed Selena's arm. "Get dressed. Today's going to be awesome."

Selena got up and began unpacking her duffel bag. Shoving things into her dresser drawers, she thought of something that happened yesterday when Ace and Val had left the room. "Hey—I have to tell you something." She turned to face her friend. "Bastion knows Santo."

"Knows? Not knew?"

"Yeah. Santo trained him and the guys on his team. I get the feeling that they don't believe he's dead."

Ace released a long and shaky breath. She rubbed her chest. "I was with him when he died, Sel. I saw him impaled on that steel spike. I heard his last breath. He can't be alive."

"Right. Right. Unless…it was all an illusion. Maybe you weren't even fighting him."

"How is that even possible?"

"I don't know. That's the thing. Bastion and all the mutants have special skills. He visited me here when he was stalking us, but he wasn't really here. It was just an astral projection of him. Or something. I don't know. I don't how any of this works. I just know that Bastion doesn't think Santo is dead."

Ace looked away, staring at the wall for a long minute, then left without saying anything more.

❧

SELENA STEPPED out of her room. As she often did after leaving her sanctuary, facing what might be a challenging day, she paused right outside her room, gathering her wits and her strength and her determination to make the day the best it could be.

Unlike any other morning, however, Bastion appeared across the hallway, his dark eyes studying her. He closed the distance between them. She kept still, caught between wanting to hurry away and her need to stare him down as she reclaimed her boundaries. He lifted his arms and braced his fists against the wall beside her head. That dominant posture should have fired off all sorts of alarms…but it didn't. It felt protective and caring.

She drew his delicious scent into her lungs, holding it there as long as she could.

This will be a good day, he said telepathically.

How do you know?

It's been a long time coming. What you and your team will learn is important. Things have changed in the Omni war you've been fighting. You need to know what's happening behind the scenes. He grinned. *And I will be with you the whole day, as I have been for much of the past few months, only today, I can be with you openly. So it is a good day.* His grin widened. *And if you've decided now is the time for fucking, I can freeze the whole household until you've had your fill of me.*

Selena actually gave that a moment's thought. "Another time. As you've said, too much is at stake. And your boss won't like the delay."

Bastion straightened. "Liege can go fuck himself."

Selena laughed. The sound was contagious, for he laughed too.

He was right. This was going to be a good day.

SELENA CHECKED the mood of the group as they waited in the bunker for Bastion's team to arrive. Owen asked Bastion and Guerre to make themselves absent so the team could have a private convo.

Bastion had easily obliged, saying they'd guide their team in via the tunnel.

Little did Owen know that Bastion was in her head, listening. She thought about blocking him, but at this point, what did it matter?

The group was eerily quiet. None of them was looking forward to the coming meeting, Selena included. It felt like a change was coming, and not the little kind of changes, like the team weddings they'd been celebrating. Or the babies that would soon be making an appearance.

This felt like Armageddon.

As that thought hit her, she looked at Owen. "This is it. The Armageddon we've been warned about all along."

"Shit," Blade said. "That's why the Omnis called their biologic research company Syadne—end days."

Kit nodded. "Even when we knew the meaning of their company name, we didn't have the context for it to make sense."

"It does now," Greer said. "The long list of little machinations—I just couldn't see where it was going."

They're here, Bastion told Selena.

"It's time. They're here," Selena told her team.

Greer and Max quickly flipped through several screens on their phones. Greer started to tell her nothing showed up in their security system, but one look at her and he went quiet.

They moved toward the end of the bunker conference room that opened to the hallway, where the steel doors were at the loading dock.

"Hey, guys," Blade said. "I just want to say, before all hell breaks loose—thank you. You've made this past year the best ever."

"I agree," Greer said. "We know so much more about ourselves than we ever would have if Owen hadn't pulled us together."

"Yep." Kit put his fist out in front of him. "Live or die, our families come first. And the pride. Whoever remains standing after all of this, know that we're relying on you to guard our own."

Blade nodded. "And also know this: I've signed this house over to a trust for the team. Whoever survives and wants to remain living here will always have a home."

Selena put her fist out with the others. God. These people were her family. She couldn't let anything happen to them. She had no dependents, only her aging parents. She already was the canary in the coal mine, so she'd finish out that path and take the first hit, if doing so would save any on her team.

The seconds were tense as the group waited silently for the rest of Bastion's team to arrive.

Val started snapping his fingers.

"What the fuck, dude?" Max asked.

Val gave him an innocent look. "What? C'mon don't tell me this doesn't have a *West Side Story* vibe. The Sharks and Jets. This is just like that. Their boy, our girl."

Selena sighed, but Val kept snapping.

LIEGE PARKED in the wide area at front end of the cave. Bastion and Guerre were waiting for them at the end of the tunnel, on the loading dock. Liege exchanged a long look with Bastion as he joined them. They didn't need words—or even thoughts—to communicate. Guerre had taught the whole team the power of nonverbal communication through the use of knowings. Knowings were universally understandable because they weren't tied to linguistics. They even crossed species lines.

Liege used those skills now to scan Bastion's wounds and catch up on the pulse of the team they were about to meet. The exchange of info took seconds, and when he was finished, he nodded at Bastion.

Bastion heard the finger snapping coming from the bunker behind the steel doors. His whole group heard it. Liege smiled, enjoying the joke. Then he did something that always terrified regulars...he spoke aloud to them before entering the room. Bastion didn't question Liege's approach—he never did anything without significant forethought. Bastion had no doubt Liege had taken a read of the group and felt the need to establish authority.

And given what the group was about to learn, some dramatics may well have been the right approach.

Bastion heard Liege's voice coming from the bunker, fully disassociated from the person who still stood outside the doors.

"We are not gangs. And we should celebrate two members of our groups finding love." Liege compelled the snapping to stop, then psychically opened both doors, making a grand entrance.

Bastion scanned the faces of Selena's team as his team moved inside the bunker.

Apologies, my love, Bastion said. *Liege likes setting the stage. I believe the American term for that is "shock and awe."*

You think?

Owen shook hands with Liege. A long, silent moment passed between them as they stared at each other. Selena waited tensely as the silence lengthened. To Bastion, she asked, *What's going on?*

Liege is reading Owen.

Can he do that? Selena asked.

Easily, Bastion said.

Acier gave her a small grin from where he stood behind Liege. *They are butting heads and thumping chests. But Liege will win.*

Maybe, but don't underestimate blue eyes. He has a core of steel, Bastion said.

Possibly, Acier said, *but Owen has never met a fully empowered mutant before.*

He's met Bastion, Selena said.

Acier shrugged. *Like I said…*

Selena checked to see if that insult had offended Bastion. He just gave a slight shake of his head. *Liege is stronger than any of us. He is a formidable leader. It's an honor to follow him.*

I feel that way about Owen, Selena said.

Bastion nodded. *Then it's good that our leaders are meeting. There is much work for our teams to do.*

The long moment between Owen and Liege finally broke loose. Owen seemed a little perturbed but quickly regained his composure as he introduced his team and Liege did the same.

Both groups took seats at the long conference table. Guerre and Bastion managed to sit on either side of Selena, something she didn't realize was probably a strategic move until she saw some of the guys from her team glaring at the mutants.

Oh, for fuck's sake. Selena leaned forward to try to shut them down, but Guerre caught her wrist and said, *Be calm. This is new to them. And it's overwhelming, as it shatters their reality.*

Selena frowned. *You can talk to me.*

We all have different skills, different abilities, Bastion said. *Guerre is our healer, so of course he can communicate.*

I have a lot of questions, Selena said.

And now that we're dealing with this openly, we'll answer all of them, Bastion said.

Owen, in his typical fashion, stood against the wall behind Selena. Liege, possibly because Owen stood, took up a position opposite him, arms folded. The two leaders stared at each other.

Owen nodded at Liege. "You have the floor."

"You and I have many things in common," Liege said. "Our teams are both fighting the Omnis. Our women have been modified. We're worried about keeping our teams and the civilians around us safe. The only civilian we have at the fort is my girlfriend. She was changed against her will, as all of us were. You have access to the researchers who could possibly reverse her modifications, or at least help us understand them. I need to talk to them. I want to bring them out to the fort, where we've built a secure lab and research facility. We can house them and guarantee their safety."

"My wife's modifications were temporary," Owen said. "It appears they're out of her system—she's no longer a modified human. We believe her modifications were intended to kill her. She was being used as pawn between two Omni leaders, one of them her father."

Liege nodded. "Something similar may well be the case with my girlfriend. But we'll need the researchers in order to determine that." He held Owen's gaze for a long moment. "Your wife wasn't the only one changed in your group, was she? Your father was also changed."

Owen sent Selena a sideways glance, which made her feel awful, but he wasn't off-base. Who knew how much Bastion and his team had pulled from her, even though she'd resisted their attempts? It was Liege, not Owen, who cut her a break.

"Bastion felt your father's mutant energy here at the house," Liege said.

"You've been spying on us for months. Now you want a truce. Why should we trust you?" Owen asked.

"Because you have no other option," Liege said. "If you weren't fighting the Omnis, things might be quite different. But you are and we are, and now they've constructed a new threat that you can't be blind to."

"And what threat is this?" Owen asked. "Monsters like the one belonging to the head Selena brought to us?"

"Yes." Liege nodded at his men. Seconds later, a hologram-like projection appeared in the middle of the room. It showed Bastion and his team fighting the monsters. The weird thing was that the hologram looked different depending on where the viewer was in relation to the replay—like it was showing the fight from several different perspectives.

"What I'm showing you," Liege said, "is an amalgamation of one of our confrontations with these deviant mutants, a 3-D image of our combined perspectives. These are lethal enemies, but they are not sentient. It's more like they are programmed for a mission that they will complete or die attempting. The good news is that if you prepare yourselves to fight them, you may not all die. The bad news is that the training will take time. There is no good way to approach this situation. The Omnis are making more and more of these ghouls.

Sooner or later, you are going to have to confront them. Bastion has already gone several rounds with these things right here on your compound.

"To be successful against them, you'll need to make physical modifications to your headquarters. And you'll need to train for these beasts. There is the option, since you have access to the researchers, to take the modifications yourselves, but then that opens up all-new ethical issues you should not have to be faced with."

Liege looked at Owen. "With your father having been changed, and your wife modified for the short time that she was, I'm sure you've given that option much thought. Perhaps your team has as well. Your choices, as I see them, are one—to stop fighting the Omnis, disband, and return to civilian lives so you don't bring interest to yourselves from the Omnis; two—continue fighting them, fortify your compound, and receive intensive training from us; or three—take the modifications, hope you survive them, and still fortify your compound and receive intensive training from us."

Owen shook his head. "I'm not loving those choices, except perhaps for option two. You and I both know the Omnis never forget and never forgive. We could disband, but they'll still come after us. We wouldn't be as strong on our own as we are together."

"That's true," Liege said. "So if you want to continue as you are, you have to strengthen your defenses. You have to train your team. And consider taking the changes to fully join the fight. These ghouls can inflict mortal wounds with their razor-sharp nails. You regulars don't heal as quickly as we mutants do. If you choose to fight the ghouls, you need to be damned sure of your skills, because if they get through you, they will get to your women and children."

"To be honest," Bastion said, "these monsters aren't what you should most fear—it's the mutants running them."

"These things are being run by Omni operatives, correct?" Owen asked.

"*Oui.*"

"With what objective in mind?" Owen asked.

"It's a power play, but isn't everything with the Omnis?" Liege said.

"So they further the objective of the Omni agenda," Owen said.

"No." Liege shook his head. "The world isn't what it was just a few years ago. You know the Omnis have spent the last several decades building their infrastructure, creating their own dark nation that exists globally. Perhaps you might think they were doing this for regular human ambitions, but it's much worse. Now that they have the technology to mutate humans at will into monsters, warriors, breeders, servants, and leaders, etc., they no longer have use for any human paradigms or social structures. Soon they will be able to impose their will over all of humanity. And then the world becomes theirs, because who could stop them? They alone hoard the technology that gives them the power they'll have."

The room was silent for a moment as that sank in.

"How do we know any of this is real?" Owen asked. "How do we know you're not manipulating our minds right now, convincing us we're seeing what we're seeing and that it's true?"

Liege sighed, then nodded. "Good question. I hate to say this, but you have to take it on faith for the moment. As you learn to work with energy, you'll discover ways of penetrating and altering perceptions of reality. All mutants have access to those skills. Omni mutants have no compunctions about using those skills against humans. Your training will show you how fluid reality is. Such knowledge alone can fracture the human capacity for reason. It is that very concern that's causing governments to keep all of this quiet."

"So the Feds know about these mutations?" Selena asked.

Liege shrugged. "Some in their ranks, I suppose. Of course, only those with the clearance to know it."

"We should ask Lobo about it," Kit said to Owen.

"I wonder if he even knows," Owen said.

"If you don't prepare for an encounter with these ghouls," Liege said, "if you aren't trained and ready, you'll die." Liege looked at Owen then Kit then Selena. "My men and I will train you. We'll equip you. We'll do everything we can to help you be successful in the fight, if you decide to continue fighting. You don't have time to waste. These things will be coming for you. It may well be the more we continue to interact with you, the more we endanger you. They've already tracked our energy trails to you."

"So for real," Greer said, "what are these things?"

"Yet another reason we need to get a hold of the scientists you are hiding," Liege said. "These mutants are lab-created beings made from human hosts. They can only be controlled by their assigned handlers, so they are not like wild beasts that can be contained. I don't know whether we can stop the spread of human mutations at this point, but I hope we can stop the creation of these deviants. I have teams like my men here all across the globe. We are fighting a losing battle. We need help. I don't want to cause mutations in order to stop mutations—I don't want to become what we are fighting, but we may have no other choice."

Greer looked at Owen and rocked back on the hind legs of his conference chair. "This is why Jax kept a tight lid on the Ratcliffs. It's why he got them away from here so quickly after Thanksgiving. He knows about all of this." Greer looked at Bastion. "The Ratcliffs must have sensed you around the house when they were here over Thanksgiving."

Bastion nodded. "It is possible. Depending on the type of mutations the doctors and Nick have, they may be extremely sensitive to energy. We in the Legion all are."

Owen frowned. "Jax did say that we should take the mutations or get out of Dodge." He looked at Liege and asked, "What exactly are you proposing for our teams?"

"I want us to work together. My team can create the simulations that will get your team ready to face these ghouls. Acier, our weapons master, can equip your team."

"We have all the weapons we need," Owen said.

"Maybe you do or maybe you don't," Liege said. "You won't know that until we begin training."

"Where do you want to do this training?" Kit asked.

"Ideally, at our fort," Liege said. "I know, from the reports Bastion has given me, that you have a household full of civilians and children. We can accommodate moving all of you down to the fort, but that may not be feasible, given you've become deeply invested in the town here. So, we can adapt. Some training at the fort, some here. We'll set energetic protections on your people. That will protect them to some degree, but it will also expose them to those hunting us. There's a fine balance between helping and hurting, but we'll have to find that balance."

"You want us to trust you after you've spent months infiltrating us?" Owen asked.

Selena worried he would decline Liege's offer. To be honest, this mutant stuff scared her. She'd been at the receiving end of their secret skills. But this shit was real, and ignoring it wasn't going to make it go away.

"You call yourselves the Red Team," Liege said. "A red team infiltrates, assesses weaknesses and failure points, then terminates an enemy. We are also a red team. If I could have kept all of this from you, I would have. I would have wiped your memories and shielded you from what's happening. But you're a team of warriors, and I need you. Our skills will get you into any physical location you need to access. Your team can give us access to databases and systems. You have an impressive collection of historical Omni data. All of that may be useful in piecing together their infrastructure and physical locations. Even residual patterns of behaviors might tell us something of what they're now doing." Liege sighed. "I need more fighters. I need your team. And you need us."

"So, wait," Blade said. "These ghouls aren't sentient. Bastion said they have handlers. Who's operating them?"

"The ones in this area are puppet beings run by a man named Brett Flynn. Flynn was changed when we were. He went through the same training we did." Liege changed out the hologram, bringing forward a waist-up image of Flynn.

He was a handsome man with harsh, Nordic features and blond hair, maybe early thirties. His blue eyes were as cold as Owen's.

"Where is he now?" Rocco asked. "If we kill him, then he can't run the beasts."

"You kill him, another Omni will just take over," Bastion said.

"He's perfected possessing regular humans," Liege said, "so getting anywhere near him is dangerous for you. All of this brings us to our current situation. Not only must we find and terminate the labs where these ghouls are being created, but Flynn's going on a free-for-all, collecting females for some unknown Omni program. We don't know what they're doing with these women. They may be modifying them, using them as test subjects. They may be looking for certain genetics for their modification programs. They may be populating new monsters we don't even know about yet. They could be practicing genetic modifications on pregnant women and their fetuses. My daughter runs a shelter for women. She and several other shelters in the area and across the country are all reporting anomalies in their current and former client lists. Some of these women have had their entire existences erased. We know that that can only happen through Omni machinations. Their families don't remember them. Their employers don't remember them. Their driver's licenses have been taken out of the system or edited to belong to other individuals. This is why we need your help." He looked at Greer and Max. "I understand some of you have extreme technical skills. We need your help. I also understand that you have several females living with you. You need our help protecting them. Your team must learn to fight the monsters and to block infiltration by Omni operatives like Flynn."

Owen heaved a deep sigh, then rubbed his face. He looked around at the group assembled at the table. "I need to talk to my team. I'm happy to share the historical info we've collected on the Omnis—we're working on digitizing and translating it at the moment. And I'm okay with offering you use of our technical capabilities. But as for the rest, what next steps we take, I can't make that decision for anyone."

"Sounds good," Liege said. "Why don't you come

down to tour our fort's facilities today? Then think things over tonight, so we can talk more tomorrow about our next steps."

Owen sent a look around the table at his team, his gaze stopping with Selena. She nodded.

Owen gave Liege a single nod. "Let's do that. Kit, Blade, and Max, hold things down here. The rest of us have a road trip."

26

Everything felt surreal to Selena as her team prepared to head over to Bastion's fort. Their world had shifted, only none of them understood what that change was. One thing she did know was that after the guys saw Bastion's fort, nothing would be the same.

Guerre's SUV pulled up in front of the team's mansion. Liege and Acier had already headed back to their fort. Addie hugged Owen goodbye. All the other wives and girlfriends were off-site at their jobs. Selena was torn as she watched their parting, half feeling that she should stay and guard the household here, the other half intensely curious about what would be said and how the guys would react to what they were about to be shown.

Bastion, who stood next to her, gave her a meaningful look. *There is no question in this. You are coming with us*. It was as if he knew she wanted to be in the thick of things, not relegated to guarding the civilians. It was a far different role than she'd had in her service in the Army or since coming here.

It is your rightful place. Whatever is coming, however it shakes out, you are going to be part of the solution. So, yes, you are with me.

She nodded.

"Owen, Greer, ride with us," Bastion said, the invitation sounding more like an order. Selena's team would fit in a second vehicle, but it wouldn't be a comfortable ride for all of them if some didn't go with Bastion and Guerre.

Bastion opened the back passenger door for Selena, then the front passenger door for Owen. Greer climbed into the third row. Selena hadn't heard him give the seating chart to the guys, but didn't doubt he'd influenced their decision about where to sit. She lifted a brow at him. He smiled innocently as he stowed his crutches then sat next to her on the middle bench. His wheelchair was already in the back.

Once they were on the highway heading south, Owen broke the tense silence. "Tell us what we're getting into."

"It's everything I discussed in the den," Selena said. "Unlike Blade's place, their fort was built for a defensive situation. The bunker beneath it is built on top of a missile silo they've retrofitted for their purposes. They have offices, labs, a morgue—a full research facility down there. I'm sure there's more, but that's all I saw of it before insisting on looping you in."

"The only thing we don't have are researchers to fill it," Bastion said.

Owen looked back at Selena with a long and hard glance. She felt the same tension. What if everything Bastion and his team had showed her was a ruse? What danger had she pulled her team into with all of this?

You wound me, my love. I don't know how to earn your trust.

Perhaps it's a time thing. Maybe it'll take me as long to begin trusting you as it took you to begin trusting us. Three months, was it, that you stalked us?

Two and half, maybe. Bastion folded his arms and spread his legs a little wider. *I don't like that answer.*

A WHILE LATER, Guerre pulled off the highway at Cheyenne.

"Where are we going?" Owen asked.

"We're taking a shortcut to the fort," Guerre said. He drove into the downtown area near the state government buildings, then pulled into a parking garage. He went up to the third level and parked in one of the last two remaining open spots in the row near the elevator. Greer parked next to him.

"How is this a shortcut?" Owen asked as everybody followed Guerre and Bastion to the elevator.

Guerre looked at Bastion and grinned. He hit the

down button, then faced Owen while they waited. "Much of what you'll see today requires an open mind and a lot of trust."

"Both of which I have a short supply."

"The adventure has already begun," Bastion said. "You can't get off the ride until it comes to a stop."

"Has it ever come to a stop, Bastion?" Guerre asked his friend.

"Not yet, it hasn't." He offered Owen a smile, but the gesture didn't have the intended effect.

Greer was wearing sunglasses with a camera, sending the video back to the team in real time. Selena tensed when Kit spoke into their comms, complaining that the video feed had some interference.

Greer sent a narrow-eyed glare at Bastion.

Bastion grinned. "Oh, fine. You can have your little camera. Liege agrees that seeing what you see will help the others who stayed back at your headquarters."

The elevator opened, forestalling further discussion as a man got off. He sent a worried look at the group standing there, then sidled out of the way. All ten of them got into the car. Someone came running toward them as the door closed, hollering to hold the elevator, which Guerre did. When the doors opened fully, the guy had second thoughts. Bastion stepped back and made a few inches of room for him.

"Please, join us," Bastion said.

It was too late to change his mind, so he did just that. He looked at the control panel and didn't see the first floor selected. Guerre punched that button for him. The car landed on the first floor. He rushed out, ahead of the herd of big guys, but when he looked back, the doors were closing again. The car descended again—but how far, Selena didn't know. Down, down, down it went. There were no buttons or indicators that where they were headed was even on the elevator's route.

Bastion reached over and squeezed her wrist. He didn't hold her hand, didn't do anything to indicate that he or anyone had noticed her nerves, but the gesture was enough to settle her.

After a moment, the elevator landed and the doors opened. They stepped out into a short, brightly lit hallway, then went through a fire door and exited onto an area that looked like a small subway station.

How could that be? There was no subway under the city of Cheyenne. So what was this place?

A puff of air burst through the depot and then a white pod stopped in front of them. No one else was on the depot platform, so when its door opened, she knew the ride was for them.

Her team exchanged glances but all stepped inside and took a seat. Owen sat up front with Guerre. She and Bastion were in the second row. Everyone else filled in around them and fastened their seatbelts.

Guerre leaned forward and punched some code into a control panel, then the pod left the depot.

"This goes to the fort?" Selena asked Bastion.

Bastion nodded. "It does."

"Your fort has its own train station?"

"*Oui*. There are many things we have not yet shown you. Remember, keep an open mind."

Not fifteen minutes later, the pod came to a stop in a different depot station. This one was even smaller. They all got out of the pod and walk through another fire door to an elevator. Guerre hit the button for a floor that had neither name nor number.

When the elevator doors opened, Selena recognized where they were—the labs in the silo below the fort. Liege greeted them in the hallway. He had an air of power. His brown eyes were not friendly or welcoming, just determined. Owen moved to the front. For a moment, they stared each other down. Then Liege held a hand out and Owen shook with him.

Though their teams had met earlier in the day, this still felt more like a meeting of Cold War enemies than one of potential allies. The whole thing set off alarms in Selena's mind.

It will be fine, you'll see, Bastion said.

It doesn't look fine, Selena replied.

Such is the way of new alliances.

Guerre and Liege led them down a few hallways, past what looked like offices and labs. They went straight to the morgue. Without any audible instruction, Guerre and Acier began pulling out long steel drawers and unzipping black body bags.

"These are ghouls that we've taken after our fights with them," Acier said. "We're running out of room, so we've switched to just taking heads. They have to be separated from the bodies anyway, else it's possible, if the Omnis put their beasts on life support quickly enough, they could resuscitate them."

Selena held back, dreading a closer look at the physical evidence in front of her. Bastion didn't try to protect her from it, which gave her the strength she needed to approach the wicked things.

Acier held up the clawed hand of one of them, bringing everyone's attention to their curved nails. He drew one across the back of his hand, leaving a thin line of blood—a wound that began healing before he'd even tucked the monster's hand back inside the body bag.

"We are *so* not in Kansas anymore," Val said.

Selena laughed nervously. Leave it to Val to break the tension. And how nice it was to hear words spoken audibly, when so much was communicated telepathically among Bastion and his team.

"Okay, given that this appears to be real," Owen said, "what's next?"

Liege nodded at Acier to close the drawers. "I'd like to have you bring the Ratcliffs here to continue their work. We need to know more about these monsters, more about the modifications that were forced on my girlfriend and are, perhaps, being forced on other innocent civilians. We need to stop the Omnis from taking more human women—we have no idea what they're doing with them or where they're holding them. We need to stop them from creating more of these monsters. The OWO has a wide distribution of functioning labs, here and in other countries. Basically, we need to shut them down."

"To do that," Bastion said, "we've got to get you up to speed and train you or hide you. These monsters aren't the only new threats you'll face. You also have to deal with Omni fighters who are enhanced like us. There is much we need to do."

"I think, friends, even if you decide to go into the wind," Guerre said, "you'll still be in danger. You're in too deep with the work you've already done. If you were my team, I'd take any help Liege offers."

"Tell me, does the government know about the train system we used to get here?" Owen asked.

"Some in the government know," Liege said. "The system connects every state capital, every military base, every transportation hub, every key research or industrial location across the U.S., Canada, Mexico, and into South America. There are systems like this in place in Europe, Asia, the Middle East, and parts of Africa."

That was stunning news. "With so much infrastructure already in place, how is it that you think we can put the cat back in the bag?" Selena asked.

"I don't," Liege said. "That won't ever happen. But we need time to push back against Omni expansion until better governance systems can catch up with the technology."

"And we must do it without exposing what's happening and risking collapse of systems now in place," Bastion said. "Total chaos would make what we have to do much harder, and it would give the Omnis something to hide behind while they continue to grow stronger."

"So, I'm guessing you have a plan?" Owen said.

Liege smiled. "Shield you. Train you. Use you. Recruit other groups like you. Gather the scientists who haven't been totally brainwashed by the Omnis, let them continue their work—but for us."

"Sure. Simple stuff," Val scoffed.

"I didn't hear anything in there about modifying us," Greer said.

Liege stared at him. "I don't want to change you. The outcomes are never guaranteed, and the death rate is too high. You are all too valuable to risk undergoing the human mutations. That said, we could really use more mutants."

"So if it's something we choose?" Greer asked.

Liege looked at his men, then Owen, before answering Greer. "I would leave that up to you and your team. As it stands now, I don't have a way of modifying anyone. We would need the researchers for that."

"I think you should take the changes," Acier said. He held up the hand he'd sliced open a moment ago. It was completely healed. "It isn't only the superior physical prowess you have to deal with from these ghouls, but the extreme neurological enhancements powering the rest of the mutants—something you'll see when we begin our training."

Selena studied the guys on Bastion's team. She had a good vibe from them—they seemed to be straight shooters, laying out the facts, both good and bad, so she and her team could come to their own conclusions.

"You don't have to make any decisions immediately," Liege said. "I'd like to give you a full tour of our facilities here and the fort above. We have space to house your team and families here, while you train."

Owen rubbed the back of his neck as he considered that offer. Selena could tell it wasn't one that sat well with him. "What's the probability that we'll actually ever see these ghouls of yours?" he asked.

"I've mentioned we've already fought them at your place," Bastion said, "so you've hit Flynn's radar."

"These monsters are only sent out after dark," Guerre said. "With the shielding we have on your premises, provided everyone is inside before sunset, you should be fairly safe."

"But we cannot guarantee that," Bastion added.

Selena didn't like the odds of being able to keep everyone bottled up at night. Eden had to care for her dogs in the kennels. Mandy had the stable to tend. Ivy had her diner to see to. Remi had university events and meetings some evenings. "What about Fiona and the boys at school in Fort Collins?" She looked at Owen. "How is this even doable, given the obligations we all have?"

Owen nodded. "How long are we looking at?"

Liege didn't answer quickly, which itself was an answer. "Forever. Or until the world catches up with what the Omnis have unleashed."

"Once modified," Rocco said, "can those modifications be altered? If we take friendly mods, could they later be overridden by enemy modifications?"

"They could," Bastion said. "The new battlefields aren't geographical anymore—they're inside of us."

"Once you break the seal that Mother Nature provides, you have to deal with the devil that comes out," Guerre said, "as at that point, there remain no natural checks and balances."

"Which is why we have to be better, faster, more strategic than our enemies, or we'll all become slaves to them," Acier said.

"And we know the Omnis are not altruistic," Liege said.

"Are you?" Selena asked the mutant leader. Silence filled the room.

"No," he said. "We have a single goal in mind, and that is to save humanity. I have no illusions that can be achieved without bloodshed and/or with only minimal destruction, which is why I built this fort."

Kelan looked at Owen. "Selena was right. This is the apocalypse that Lion was told about."

"If so, this has been in the works for generations," Rocco said.

Selena felt a chill wrap around her. She folded her arms and sent Bastion a worried glance. Unlike his usual jovial self, he didn't try to allay her fears.

"My team and I aren't ready to make permanent decisions," Owen said. "Let's begin with the training you've offered, then once we know more, we'll decide how much assistance we can provide."

Liege nodded. "We'll come up to your place to begin, as that's where you'll most likely be facing the ghouls and any other Omni challenges."

HOURS LATER, the team gathered for a debrief in the bunker. Owen looked at Bastion. Selena knew he was going to block him from joining them. Owen kept them aside as Ace and the rest of the guys filed past...as if she were no longer a welcome member of the team.

She thought that by this point in her life, she'd be used to being an outsider. Staring into Owen's icy blue eyes, she had a pressing urge to bolt, but this was something she couldn't escape.

"I didn't start this, Owen," she said. "I didn't ask for this. I don't want this. But we can't ignore what's happening. You've seen the evidence with your own eyes of what Bastion can do. He's one of who knows how many fighters like him. Liege told us he has teams around the world. We're lucky they're on the same side of this fight as we are. But there are others like them still deep in the Omni machinery who are not on our side."

"So you want us to get cozy with beings whose capabilities we don't even fully understand?" Owen asked.

"Your own father is one of those beings," Angel said.

Selena was so focused on Owen that she didn't realize a few of the guys had come back into the den.

"Yeah, I'm afraid this train has already left the

station, Owen," Blade said. "We have to deal with reality as it is, not as we'd like it to be."

"This isn't Selena's doing," Val said.

"You can't effectively keep Bastion out of the conversation we're about to have. You know that, right?" She tilted her head and gave her boss an impatient look. Both of them knew he couldn't really keep Bastion from attending—it was just a matter of whether his presence was seen or unseen.

I would not spy, if you wished me not to, Bastion said to Selena.

Bullshit. You were made to spy.

I was. But I will always try to honor your wishes.

"Fine," Owen said, then followed the group down the long flights of stairs to the bunker.

Owen stood by the end of the conference table, where the three team members who had not gone to the fort were. "Were you able to see much from Greer's feed?"

"Yes and no," Kit said. "When he was stationary, the resolution was good, but every time he moved, it got scrambled. Were you really in a secret transportation pod?"

Angel answered, "Yep. And it took us from Cheyenne to northeastern Colorado in about ten minutes—a trip that would usually take more than an hour."

"And no one knows about that train system?" Blade asked.

"Some must," Owen said. "It's a huge engineering

endeavor that didn't happen overnight. And it can be accessed by thousands of major transportation points across the U.S."

"We should see if Lobo knows about it," Angel said. "I'm sure he's been read in on more than we would expect, seeing as he's the FBI point man on the WKB and the Omnis."

"Hold off talking to Lobo," Owen said. "We don't want to tip our hand sooner than we have to."

Blade gave Owen a measuring look. "He's a friendly."

"He is," Owen agreed, "but we know nothing about his higher-ups."

"I want to see their fort," Max said. "And I think Nick and Jax need to be brought in, too."

"So you think those beings they had in the morgue were real? Or just movie props?" Kit asked.

"They are real," Bastion said. Selena didn't sense frustration in his voice, or resignation, or anything that indicated he was losing patience with the firm grip her team had on the world as it had been before mutants entered it. His patience surprised her.

I've had ten years to come to terms with this new reality, he told her. They aren't going to shift gears quickly. Patience is the only way forward, ma chérie.

"One way to find out," Kit said. "Get that head over to Doc Beck. See what he makes of it."

"I assume this Doc Beck is someone you trust?" Bastion asked.

"He's in the Omni resistance with us," Selena told him. "He's patched all of us up, at one time or another."

"Maybe none of this real." Blade glared at Bastion. "Maybe it's an elaborate hoax to trick us into handing over the Ratcliffs. We know how well they can manipulate us."

Bastion nodded. "Never doubt it—we mutants are capable of any ruse to get what we want. But in this case, those things are real. Tomorrow, you will learn more about our abilities, and then you will be better equipped to make the decisions you must."

Selena stared at Bastion. *That's what you've done to me, isn't it? Manipulated me.*

I have not.

No? What do you call wiping my memories if not manipulation?

I could have done much worse, Selena, than hide myself from you.

That is not reassuring, Bastion.

I know. That's why it took me so long to reveal myself. I was at war with Fate.

So you don't want what's happening between us?

My heart and my mind were yours the night I first saw you. But in making you mine, I had to bring you and your friends to the point we're at now. I did not want to shred your world.

Selena hated having her options ripped from her. Every decision she'd made since she was fourteen, had been to keep from being cornered, and yet here she was.

"You all know that I'm in the 'trust them' camp," Selena said.

"How do we know that you aren't being manipulated by him?" Owen asked. "How do we know your thoughts and opinions are your own?"

"Because we have to trust our instincts."

"And how do you know that what you believe is your instinctive reaction to all of us is really yours?" Blade asked. "I mean no disrespect, Sel, but given the circumstances…"

Selena accepted that as a valid question. She looked at her team, who also appeared to want the answer. "I'm not saying that we should follow Bastion or Liege or Nick or Owen or anyone without question. I think we must always understand the decisions we make and why we make them. I've been interacting with Bastion consciously and unconsciously for months now. I think I have a feel for when he is influencing or projecting and when I'm responding to my own instincts. Remember, I was able to block him. Yes, with extreme effort, but I've always been aware of the difference between us. Let's trust them until they fail us."

"And by the time they fail us, we'll all be dead." Owen said.

"But if we don't trust them, we may all be dead long before that," Selena said.

Owen gave her a stare-down, then did the same with Bastion. "Liege and others are coming up here in the morning. We'll see how that goes before deciding anything."

"That is a wise decision," Bastion said.

~

Doc Beck led Angel to his office. Angel closed the door, then took out his phone to do a security sweep.

"Cloak and dagger, much?" Beck said as he leaned against his desk.

"Had to be sure. Your office is open to everyone all day."

Beck folded his arms. "What's on your mind, Angel?"

"I need you to examine something and answer two questions: is it real, and what is it?"

"Okay."

Angel set the cooler on one of the guest chairs and lifted the lid. Beck looked inside, then reached in and took out the specimen.

"Shit."

"You don't sound surprised."

"I'm not. I've heard stories—urban legends, I'd hoped—about Omni werewolves."

"Please tell me this isn't a werewolf. I really don't want that word in my vocabulary."

"It's not. If werewolves existed, which they don't, they would live in one of two states—human or werewolf. These chimeras have only one state. They don't shift. They're a mix of human and one or many different animals." He looked at Angel. "No has ever captured one of these things. We have no known science describing them."

"So it's a big find?"

"Huge. Career-making."

"Right. Then I'm sorry to have to tell you that this is top secret. Word about this thing can't get out to the general public."

Beck sighed and put the head back in the cooler. "I expected as much. But I will need to consult with the Ratcliffs on it."

Angel nodded. "Agreed. When you have some specific info, give Owen a call."

27

Selena pushed herself to a sitting position on her bed. She'd almost fallen asleep several times, but kept waking up, her mind spinning over everything that was happening.

It had been a relief to have her team shown all the things—and more—that the Legion had shown her. Even better was the fact that they'd come to the same conclusion she had about the need for further dialog with the mutant mercenaries.

She looked over to the side of the bed that Bastion had occupied last night. She hadn't invited him over tonight—nor had he asked to join her. Maybe that was for the best. She needed time to adjust to everything.

A sea change had happened, and ninety-nine-point-nine percent of the human population had no idea it was already afoot.

I feel your distress, my love. Do you want me to come over? Bastion asked.

No. She did, but more importantly, she needed time to get her headspace right. *If we catch and kill Brett Flynn, we still won't be able to stop this thing, will we?*

Non, Bastion said. *The Omnis seem like a single megalithic entity, but really they are a consortium of petty despots, each building his own sphere of influence and power. Their structure is much like medieval kingdoms—fragmented and self-focused. Taking down any of the big players just makes the remaining ones stronger.*

So what could our strategy be to buy the time Liege said is needed to devise new governance structures?

The single best thing we can do is collect all the scientists we can find who are working on these human modifications for the Omnis. Without them, the Omnis lose their source of power.

That's huge, Selena said. *These scientists have to be hidden all over the place.*

This is true. And it will be easier for us to capture the researchers who want out of the Omni hell, but we'll hit a wall with those who see the power they hold and have the ambition to compete with us and the Omnis.

The more Selena learned, the worse it all seemed. She changed the subject. *Remember that night you came to my room after Addy's bachelorette party? How far would it have gone if I hadn't stopped you?*

You would have been very happy.

And you?

As frustrated as I was—as I am.

Why?

I can't complete an intimate encounter while in my astral body. It always rips me back to my body.

You've tried before?

Of course. Selena could sense his sigh. *Our libido was one of the first casualties of the modifications we underwent.*

Why?

Because those who designed the mods we took architected it that way. I believe they thought our sex drive was a major weakness that our enemies could exploit, so they edited it out of our psyches. Some of the guys who came through the same camps that we did thought it was temporary, that our natural needs would return once we healed. They did not.

But you could still have sex…

Yes, but in reality, it was like bingeing on a favorite food might be for a regular…after the first few bites of something delicious, you stop tasting it. Eating it just becomes something you do—habit even. Except for us, we no longer even had the initial pleasure of those first few bites. Sex was just blah, beginning to end.

But you tried to have it while in your astral state.

I did. Always with willing partners, I want you to know. I thought that if the act didn't involve my body, that I could experience pleasure differently. I didn't.

Would it be different with me?

It would be.

How do you know?

Because with you, all of my sensation is back…my anticipation, hunger, need. I crave you, Selena—in a way that I haven't since my modifications and even before them.

She smiled, wondering what astral sex would be like and if it would make her more—or less—panicky.

Why would you be panicky? Bastion asked.

She shut her eyes. Maybe he hadn't stolen all of her secrets. In this instance, she wished he had, because she wouldn't have to discuss it. *There was a time I wasn't as strong as I am now.*

I am not so cruel as to put my desires before yours.

He'd mentioned craving. God, she knew that feeling. She'd had it since he was first near her, when he was stalking them, before he'd ever come inside. *Show me, Bastion—show me what would have happened.*

Selena felt his big hand take hers and lead her from her bed. It was odd, in that it was—and wasn't—a touch. There was a distinct sensation of fingers and palm, and the pull as he tugged at her to stand in front of the long mirror. A thin line of light from the hall leaked from beneath her doorway, enough that she could see her reflection.

We stood here, as I recall, he said.

Her mouth was suddenly too dry to speak, so she only nodded. Not the mirror. She hated mirrors. He'd been behind her that night, naked. *The light was on then.*

That is true, but seeing me so clearly freaked you out, so I have not turned it on tonight.

That wasn't what freaked me out.

What was it the mirror itself?

Yes, and more. Me, you, other things I didn't want to share with you. And the realization that what I felt for you flew in the face of everything I knew about reality. I feared for my team—you were so powerful.

Her hair moved behind one shoulder as he lifted it away. His lips touched her neck in a phantom caress.

Mm-hmm. All of which is still the case tonight. Will you banish me again?

Maybe. I don't know. Blocking you hurt. I don't want that pain again.

A big hand slipped beneath her loose tank top, moving upward, lifting gooseflesh from his whisper-soft touch. She stiffened, dreading the moment when his hands would brush against her scars. Thankfully, he didn't go higher than her ribs.

I never sent you pain, he said. *I don't understand how there could have been pain between us, unless it had to do with the Matchmaker's curse. You cried that night. I sat next to you, but could do nothing to ease your worry. All I could do was bear witness to what you were going through.*

Selena leaned back against him, feeling the solid mass of a physical form that wasn't there. He moved her hair higher off her neck, kissing the soft skin there. She could feel his beard, his lips. In a way, this was more pleasant than a true physical encounter, as it was ephemeral and ethereal. His ghostlike hand gripped her chin and leaned her face to one side, giving him access to her jaw, which he caught between his teeth in a gentle grazing motion.

His hands shifted. Catching the hem of her tank top, he lifted it. She blocked him.

Easy, my love. I know this secret.

Tears filled her eyes. *Bastion.*

I told you that night your scars are what make you you.

My scars show my weakness.

He chuckled. She felt the air of it blow against her

neck. No. Your scars show your strength. They're the soldering that keeps the pieces of you together. You will know that one day.

In the shadowy light, she could barely make out her own outline—she couldn't see him at all. His hands spanned her ribs as he bent to kiss her shoulder.

Selena put her hands over his, pressing him tighter against herself. She could feel the bumps of his knuckles under her palms, but when she peeked into the mirror through the shadows, she saw nothing. For a moment, all sensations from him wavered, as if he existed only in her belief, not in her physical reality.

It was disorienting.

Move back to your bed, Bastion said.

She got back in bed, and as she turned to her side, she saw him stretched out next to her, a faint glow coming from him, letting her see him in the dark...and letting her see through him at the same time.

Bastion, come here. I mean in person.

No. You aren't ready to trust me yet.

You don't know that.

I read energy, remember? Maybe it isn't me you aren't ready to trust but your own self.

She squeezed her eyes shut. The shadows from the past and her reaction to them had formed the foundation of her adult life. Without them, she had no protection. *I can't yet.*

He must have seen the sadness in her eyes. Her reluctance had cost her many a relationship, some with great potential.

Maybe your soul knew that you were waiting for me, but your mind wasn't listening.

I didn't wait for you or anyone. I did what I wanted at the time.

Which was always give the least amount of yourself to your lovers as possible.

That's not true.

I see the truth of that in your eyes.

Could he see that? Was he right? Was that why none of her relationships had lasted more than a handful of weekends?

They scratched an itch, and scratching can only exist for a short duration before it causes pain. I, on the other hand, soothe your soul. He grinned at her, bracing his phantom head on his hand as he watched her.

He did seem to have that effect on her. He was noisy, boisterous, troublesome, and...peaceful. She'd never met someone who calmed the emotions raging inside her.

I give you all of my days and all of my nights for the rest of my life, Selena.

That won't work. You'll outlive me by some huge order of magnitude. Unless I take the modifications. Do you want me to do that?

His soulful eyes grew pensive. *Selfishly, yes. I want you with me forever. And it is also strategic, as you'll see in the training you'll do tomorrow. But realistically, it's too dangerous. I would die if you didn't survive the change. And putting you through it now will render you your weakest when we need you at your strongest, given the dangers we're facing. So no.*

Yes and no. She sighed. *We're all having to decide this. I have no idea what the guys will choose.*

You don't have to decide right now. He leaned over and kissed her forehead.

Bastion, I want you here. I mean your physical body. No sooner had she said that than his shimmering image vanished. She heard a door slam somewhere down the hall, then seconds later her door opened, closed, and locked.

Bastion walked in, already pulling off his T-shirt. He unzipped his jeans and kicked them off, leaving only his black boxer briefs. He hurried around the bed and settled on it on his side, just as his astral self had done moments earlier.

"Where are your boot casts?"

"Guerre has said it was safe to remove them."

Wow. That was really fast healing for the degree of injuries he'd had.

"I don't like being away from you," he said.

"Me either. Maybe you should just bunk in here."

"Agreed."

She regretted having shut her blinds and closed her curtains, for it was far too dark in the room to see much of Bastion's face. As if responding to her thoughts, both window coverings opened themselves.

"How do you do that?" she asked. The man really was magical.

Bastion set a hand on her ribs and leaned over to kiss her neck. "It is not a topic for discussion right now."

His body was warm next to her—and deliciously solid. "You can't be on top."

"*Bien*. But to the side is all right?"

She nodded. "Or under me."

"Good. We have options, then. You see I am not between you and the door."

Selena squeezed her eyes shut, hoping Bastion hadn't read all of her secrets. She pushed them from her mind. Perhaps if she didn't think about the terrible things, then he wouldn't know them. She reached up and threaded her fingers into his dark hair, feeling the thick, wavy strands. She pulled him close as she turned to her side. His arm went beneath her head. Their lips touched. She pressed her face tighter against his, suddenly loving his beard and mustache. This was Bastion. Dark and hairy and beautiful and magical Bastion.

She opened her eyes and caught him watching her. Silhouetted as he was against the faint light from outside, she couldn't read much of his expression, but she knew he was letting her set their pace, yielding so she could take what she wanted of him. She flattened her hand against his cheek. "Don't ever shave this off."

"Never."

"Even if facial hair goes out of style."

He seemed affronted. "I am Bastion. I set styles, not follow them."

A broken breath slipped from her chest, half laugh, half sob. This man had a beard. This man she would know in the dark as well as the light.

I smell different as well. And my energy is unique to me. You will always know me.

She leaned her face against his and nodded. He kissed her forehead, her cheek, then caught her mouth again. His tongue slipped inside her mouth, letting her taste the sweet essence of him. This she would always know too. This was what her man tasted like. She stroked his tongue with hers, wringing a moan from him.

"Did you bring any condoms?"

"*Non.* I do not need them. Because of the modifications, I cannot get or transmit any diseases. And I can shield you from becoming pregnant."

"Mmm. The perfect man," she said.

"I am the perfect man. For you."

She looked at him, still holding his beard. "Do you really believe in the Matchmaker? If we'd met somewhere else, would we have known we might be like this together?"

"Until the Matchmaker connected Liege and Summer, I did not believe. And even then, having not experienced it for myself, I was not convinced. But now I have seen the fiend, and because of him, I have you, so I do believe. Completely. But I think he may have only sped things up for us. I would have found you. My heart was screaming for you; I just did not recognize the pain it felt was loneliness."

That had been exactly what Selena felt when, one by one, she witnessed each of the guys on the team find their perfect partners. And as each had left the single life behind, she'd felt more like an outsider. She hated being jealous of her friends. Jealousy was a weakness, a belief that she couldn't have what her friends did.

Now she thought maybe that hadn't been the problem at all. Her heart was just pointing to what she most wanted: a love of her own.

Still, she had a lot of fear and doubt and worry.

I know. Bastion pulled her closer.

Maybe that was all behind her now. She was here, in her bed, with this very male mutant.

We are like fortune cookies—always add "in bed" to the end. Like this: Mutants put regulars to shame. In bed, he said.

Humility is a good thing, Bastion.

I will be humble for you. I am humble for my team. For the rest of the world, I am Bastion.

Selena tried fighting the chuckle his arrogance aroused, but she wasn't entirely successful. His humor made some of her anxiety recede. She found herself entirely focused on the feel of his big body lying next to her. He was heavier than she was, so gravity naturally pulled her toward him.

Or maybe that was more of his magic.

One of her arms was folded between them as they lay on their sides, but Selena explored his chest with her free hand. Running her fingers through the coarse texture, she was surprised, given how hairy his forearms were, and with all the hair on his head, that his chest was only lightly covered.

She pressed her face into his neck, burrowing beneath his beard to the soft skin there. She drew his delicious clover scent into her lungs with a long pull of air, which made her want to be even closer to him. Pushing her knee between his, she wrapped her arm around his ribs and stroked his wide, smooth back, then moved her hand lower to the small of his back, then his curved, muscled ass, then his heavy thigh.

"This is so much better than being intimate with the astral you," she said.

"*Oui.*" That single word seemed strained. She smiled to herself and kissed his neck, the side of his Adam's apple, the hollow between his shoulder and neck. When she teethed his collarbone, he sucked in a ragged breath.

Bastion threaded his fingers into her loose hair, fisting it gently but firmly as he said, "It is torture letting you explore me but not getting to do the same to you."

"In time, you can."

With his grip in her hair, he drew her head from his body and crushed her mouth with his. "In time for what?" he growled in the middle of the kiss. "While we both still live?" He kissed her again.

"When I'm ready for you."

"Better get ready." He caught her chin with his teeth. He kissed her neck, the corner of her jaw.

She took hold of his face and kissed him again. It was delicious to have his firm body next to hers, to feel his heat. She didn't complain when he wrapped his arms around her and rolled to his back, moving her on top of him. She straddled his hips and pushed up from his chest. She could feel the hard length of him against her core. When she looked into his eyes again, she realized they'd begun glowing a warm orange color.

He sat up and wrapped his arms around her, flattening her breasts against his chest, holding her as he arched beneath her, rubbing himself against her. Pulling back slightly, he caught her breasts in his hands. She looked down to see the orange glow in his eyes become hooded as he focused entirely on nuzzling, sucking, nipping her breasts.

His mouth moved over the scars on the side of her breast, making her tense. She shut her eyes at the butterfly-light touch there.

It was a decision point.

He knew about her scars. And he hadn't run for the hills or reviled her for them.

He'd accepted her. And that was magical.

Before she could think her way out of what was happening, he took a nipple into his mouth; she arched her back, shocked at sensations he was causing through her body. His beard and mustache on her skin lifted gooseflesh down her arms. All thoughts of ending this vanished. She wanted him to taste all of her, every inch.

"I will. In time." His breath was as hot as his lips.

"When? In our lifetime?" she asked, mocking his earlier complaint.

He leaned back, drawing her down over his chest. He ran his hands down her hips, slipping his fingers beneath the rim of her panties and pushing those down her hips, leaving them mid-thigh, where they sat like a soft binding, keeping her from spreading her thighs. He pushed his underwear down as well, freeing himself. He positioned himself to slide between her legs, against her sensitive core but not in her.

He kissed her mouth as he slipped his hand between their hips. He cupped her mound, then pressed one finger between her nether lips. Selena broke their kiss as she gasped at the sensations he was giving her, gently massaging her clit, his body rocking under hers, his cock sliding between her legs. His hand moved deeper between her legs, and he slipped two fingers into her. Thrusting gently, he used his thumb to work her clit.

An orgasm hit her, fast and violent. She cried out and dug her nails into his shoulders as she surrendered to the waves of ecstasy.

He reached down to push her panties to her knees so she could kick them off, then he held her hips as he lifted her up his chest then to his mouth. "I want to taste you as you come." He held her hips, moving her back and forth over his mouth, licking her from her clit to her opening, fucking her with his tongue.

Selena held on to her headboard, her long hair curtaining her face as she watched what he was doing to her. Too soon, she was orgasming again, her body rewarding him with the nectar he sought. He moaned against her wet core. Before the last throes of her orgasm settled, he moved her back to his hips and thrust his heavy penis deep inside her. That was all it took to send her deep into another orgasm. Bracing her hands on his pecs, she rocked and ground against him. He was pounding his hips up to meet hers, taking over their rhythm. He sat up and wrapped his arms around her body, moving her to meet his thrusts. She took his face in both of her hands and kissed him, then cried out as a long, endless orgasm exploded from between her legs, out through her whole body. She felt as if she'd been blown apart and put back together at the same time, shattered and whole.

Bastion must have reached his peak at the same time, for she felt him slowly relax beneath her. His eyes had changed from the burning orange to a glowing green. "You are mine and I am yours, Selena, so long as we both still live."

Forever.

She wasn't certain if that vow came from her or him, they were so deeply connected.

28

Bastion quietly shut Selena's door behind him using his telekinetic skills. Two men were approaching in the hallway, Val and Owen — the blonds he'd been most concerned about when observing this group. They moved toward him with intent, eyeing him distrustfully.

"Aaaah," Bastion said, smiling as if he'd just downed a cold beverage on a hot day. "*Bonjour, mes amis.*" He spoke in a hushed whisper so he wouldn't wake Selena. The men did not give him a warm greeting. In fact, it looked like he was about to get the third degree. Interesting. They'd left their own warm beds to roust him from his — except he hadn't been there, which must have been what alarmed them. "By what time must Selena awaken?"

"We meet at eight," Owen said.

"Wonderful." Bastion gripped their shoulders and turned them to walk with him as he led them away from

Selena's door. "I know she fired both of you. You are both losers. I have won the ultimate prize. Selena is mine."

Owen tossed his arm off.

"I'm surprised," Val said, leaning forward to look around Bastion at Owen. "I really thought she'd go for another blond."

Bastion laughed.

When they reached Bastion's door, Owen faced him. "I don't know you. I don't trust you. And I don't like that you've been manipulating one of our own."

"Ah. I see," Bastion said. This confrontation was long overdue, in his opinion. He clasped his hands behind his back and rocked back on his heels. "So where does that leave us?"

"Leave her alone," Owen said.

Bastion looked at Val to see if he was on the same page as his boss, but the big blond only continued assessing Bastion. "Well, I cannot. She is my light."

Owen scoffed. "Bullshit. She's just a tool to you."

Bastion felt rage explode within him. He let the first wave of it wash through him, then settled into the quiet that followed. "She is my woman. Mine. The one I have wanted my entire life. No one will take her from me."

"And what exactly are your intentions toward her?" Owen asked.

Bastion let that question hang in the air a long moment before answering. "I intend to feed her, fight beside her, and fuck the hell out of her for the rest of our lives."

Val laughed. "Just don't get in her way, Bastion. That's the one thing you won't survive."

"You're okay with this?" Owen asked Val.

"Sel deserves happiness, O," Val said. "When he stops making her happy, she'll eat him as she did all her other partners. While I don't trust him, I do trust her."

Bastion nodded as he gave them a look of pity. "I know that she fired both of you. Though you are losers in love, I do not wish us to be enemies because I won what you could not."

Owen looked like someone cut off the blood supply to his head.

Val fought to not laugh. "That's not how it went down. She knew we weren't a match, either of us. And she was right, because we both found our one-and-onlys. Sel has too, it seems."

Bastion gave him a nod. "I am happy for you. All is well then."

Owen gave Bastion a hard glare. "We may have started out merely a team, but we're family now."

"She has said this to me. Have no fear—I have told her I will love and protect you, her family."

"We don't have fear. And we don't need your protection," Owen said.

"Not yet, perhaps. But for what's coming, you do. I look forward to beginning your training this morning. But for now, I'm going to shower and then see if Russ will let me assist him in the kitchen."

SELENA WAS glad Ace was the only other person in the gym that morning. She was jogging on one of the treadmills. One look at Selena and she shut her machine off.

Selena used her phone to turn off the surveillance equipment monitoring the gym. She didn't want anyone watching or listening to the convo she was about to have with Ace. There were just some things she didn't want to share with the guys.

Ace peeked at her over the white hand towel she held to her face. Her eyes were alight with hope and joy.

Selena went over to lean on her treadmill. "Oh. My. God."

Ace shrieked and bent over the handlebars to hug Selena. "It was good?"

"Better than good. Better than ever before. We talked, we had sex, we talked, we had sex. All night long." Selena teared up. "What if I'd never met him? What if I'd never known he existed?"

Ace shrugged. "Sometimes I do believe in fate. I don't think you could have not been together." Ace took her hand and led her over to a bench. "Tell me everything."

"I thought I'd hate his beard and mustache, but you know what? I love them. They're a constant reminder of who I'm with. He made me feel safe and important." She waved her hand. "I know that's crazy. You and I, we make our own safety."

"But it's different when we're falling in love. We're vulnerable."

Selena stared at her. "You think I'm falling in love?"

"I know it." Ace grinned. "For the record, once I actually met him, I liked him a lot. He'll be good for you."

"Is it crazy that I just want to be near him? I love our morning workouts, but I don't want to be away from him. I crave touching him."

Ace laughed. "So go do that!"

"No. I don't want to seem weak and clingy."

"I cling to Val."

"More like he clings to you."

"True, which I love."

"No, I'm not going to dump my routine. I already feel as if he's turned everything upside down. I need some normalcy."

"Right. So let's get to it. I've already got ten minutes on you. You need to catch up."

SELENA SHOWERED AFTER HER WORKOUT. She considered drying her hair and putting on some makeup, but she resented anything that put time between now and when she could see Bastion again.

She sat on the edge of her bed, shocked at how far she'd lost her way since the night before. Bastion was in her every thought, either a memory from the night before or anticipation of when she'd see him again.

Never had she ever felt anything like this.

And even as she tried to suppress her feelings for him, her heart hammered nervously as she left her room.

She jogged down the back staircase. She wondered how she should greet him. Cautiously, as all her other teammates would? Joyfully, like a lover would? Were they ready to bring their relationship to the attention of all the others?

A movement in the shadows caught her attention; Hawk was coming out of the gym building. He looked preoccupied. She hadn't realized the boys were back at the house—they didn't come up every weekend. Maybe this was one of their long weekends. She almost wished they weren't here. Today was an important day for both teams. She wanted to protect their new alliance from any threats.

That thought brought her up short. Since when had she considered Hawk a threat? True, he'd been acting oddly of late, but did that make him a threat?

MOVING through his enemy's stronghold, hidden inside one of its beloved members, was a special kind of thrill for Brett. Possessing the kid had been easy. The poor thing had been so hollow inside that there was lots of room.

Brett knew that Hawk loved the people here but didn't especially like being in their house. Every shortcoming the kid focused on strengthened Brett's hold on him.

It was time for breakfast, a meal the kids typically— though not always, Brett had learned—ate separately from the adults. Brett was discovering so much about the household layout, the team's routines, how they all interacted.

Such sickening harmony. It would be a win just to fuck that all up.

An easy win.

Hawk looked up and saw a woman coming down the back stairs.

Everything inside Brett shrank inward, then exploded in a fireball of fury. He couldn't believe he was seeing what he was. It was *her*, Selena Irving, his prime enemy. Finally. She'd been gone from the premises for so long.

She was the hellspawn who'd wrecked his life. The woman who'd caused his fall from grace and cast him into a life of exile and hell.

"'Sup, Hawk?" she asked. "You look like you've never seen me before."

Brett, still reeling from his emotional reaction, kept Hawk from answering. Selena moved off the last step and came toward him, concern in her eyes, an emotion she might feel for Hawk but she'd never feel for Brett.

Nor he for her.

She had destroyed him.

Unmitigated rage poured through Brett's astral body and seeped into Hawk. Instinct alone drove Brett to grab Selena's neck and slam her against a wall.

Selena pushed her hands between Hawk's elbows and shoved them apart as she kicked the side of his knee, dropping him to the floor. She caught and bent his hand up behind him. Holding him facedown on the floor, she leaned over him and asked, "What's wrong with you?"

Brett forced Hawk to chuckle. The sound came out choked. "I thought I could take you."

"Well, you can't. You've been slacking in your training. Work harder. And never push me against a wall." Selena leaned closer and whispered in his ear, "A woman never forgets and rarely forgives, so don't do it again, no matter what wrongheaded notion you had."

Hawk tried to nod. "My bad, Sel. I won't."

Brett felt Selena release his pet. He made Hawk sit up so he could watch his enemy walk away. Selena had grown strong in the time since they'd first met, and yet he could tell what had happened haunted her still.

A woman never forgets and rarely forgives.

That had to mean she hadn't forgotten him. He certainly hadn't forgiven her. While she apparently had had a life of quality despite their history, Brett had not.

Hawk's first task as Brett's pet would be to even that score.

Selena felt oddly rattled after leaving Hawk behind. He'd never behaved like that before. Maybe school life was changing him. Maybe he wasn't adjusting well to being away from the pride. Maybe the social structure imposed by the community college they attended was rubbing him the wrong way.

Whatever it was, she decided to put some distance between the two of them. She touched her hand to her throat, remembering his very strong grip as he'd slammed her against the wall. Another man had done that, long, long ago. She looked at the thin scar near her thumb, rubbing it to quiet the memory.

Suddenly, Bastion was there, in the foyer outside the big living room, his face full of worry. He wore one of Russ's crisp white aprons. She stared at it while he pulled her into his arms.

"What happened?" he asked quietly.

Selena realized she was leaning into him, drawing from his strength, her arms folded between them. So much for wondering when the right time would be to come out to their team. Everyone was watching them.

"Nothing," she said, finally marshaling the strength to look at him.

Bastion touched her neck, then gave her a hard look. When Hawk came in the room, Bastion's hold on her eased as he sent the boy a narrow-eyed glare.

Selena fisted his apron. "Don't. Please. I dealt with it."

Bastion froze everyone in the area. "I know what he did. There are repercussions for harming my woman."

"He's a kid. His life is all mixed up right now. Cut him some slack. He challenged me and failed. That's punishment enough."

Bastion shook his head. He went to where Hawk stood in his trance and sniffed the boy. He closed his eyes, then shook his head again. "I don't like it. Something's not right." When he returned to Selena, he unfroze everyone.

"What isn't right?" Selena asked.

"I don't know. Stay away from Hawk."

She nodded. "I've been doing that."

Bastion kissed her cheek and took a long moment to stare into her eyes. "I'll just finish with the guys, then come out to join you. Grab a cup of coffee for me, *oui*?"

"*Oui.*" Selena laughed. When she headed toward the buffet, she sent an uneasy glance around at everyone's shocked faces. At first, she thought they were upset because Bastion had just tranced them, but then she realized it was because she and he had just shared a private conversation—while holding each other.

"What?" she asked them, throwing her arms wide as if to show she had nothing to hide. Everyone on her team had paired up with their loves over the last whirlwind year. Surely they wouldn't begrudge her finding her own love.

But maybe they did. Maybe they still felt Bastion and his Legion were enemies, and she was therefore a rat.

That made her sad. Her shoulders slumped.

Ace giggled, then gave a little clap. "We're happy for you, that's all," she said.

"I think the mighty Selena Irving has fallen," Val said.

At that, the women she used to guard hurried over to give her hugs. "We're happy for you," Mandy said.

"Never doubt that we're with you, whatever you choose," Ivy said.

"You've always been there for us," Fiona added.

"The guys just don't know what this all means," Eddie said. "They don't want to lose you."

"They aren't going to," Selena said.

"You're with a guy from another team," Remi said. "Something is going to have to change to facilitate that."

"Maybe." Selena looked at the circle of women she'd protected for most of a year, and though she'd often longed for a more challenging assignment, she was saddened to think the future might take her from them.

"You do you, Selena," Hope said. "The rest will work out."

"Things do seem to work out here," Wynn said, "even when it all seems lost."

"You're important to us," Addy said. "We all want you to be happy. And it looks like Bastion is a wonderful fit for you."

Val pushed his way into the circle of women and gave Selena a brotherly sideways hug. "What they said." He smiled at her, then stepped back to put an arm around Ace.

Selena blinked tears away. She hated crying, hated appearing weak. "Thanks, guys. You mean the world to me too. I don't want anything to change, but—"

"Change is the only constant in our lives," Owen said, wrapping an arm around Addy.

"*Eh, bien!*" Bastion roared, taking everyone's attention from Selena, which she totally needed. "We have a feast! Eat! We men need our strength for our training." He looked at her and Ace, then added, "And the little girls, too." Selena gave him a furious glare, which he answered with a wink. He looked at his watch. "We have less than an hour to prepare ourselves, so begin."

29

Selena was nervous as she waited for the rest of Bastion's crew to arrive. Shortly after breakfast, the house had cleared out. Lion and Hawk took Fiona back to Colorado. Usually, they would have stayed the weekend. She wondered if, after that weirdness with Hawk, Bastion had compelled them to go. The rest of the kids had left for their schools here in town. The women had gone to their different jobs. Maybe Owen had asked everyone to make themselves scarce.

It was for the best. Less chances for complications. At some point soon, the team was going to have to address the future they were facing with their families. Selena wondered if they could find a way to continue in the fight against the Omnis without having to take the human modifications.

A knock came at the front door. Max crossed the room to open it, then stood back to let Liege and Acier in. Owen joined them in the crowded foyer. "Would you and your team care for something to eat? Coffee?"

Liege took a moment to answer. "No, thank you. We're ready to get to work."

Owen gestured toward the hallway that led through the main portion of the house and out to the gym building. "We'll be in here. I wasn't certain what to expect from today's session. If we need a different setup going forward, we can put that together."

"It's fine," Liege said. "Today will be more of a demonstration than actual training. You need to know what you're up against before we can break it down into actionable segments."

Selena watched Liege pace in front of the group, his hands clasped behind his back. Sometimes he eyeballed an individual; sometimes he stared at the ground. Guerre and Acier kept to the right of the group. Bastion was on the left, close to Selena. He seemed nervous about how this would go, but she had the clear sense that Liege's men trusted him implicitly.

Liege stopped mid-pace. Still with his hands behind his back, he looked over the group. "Four of us were together in the same camp where we were trained in how to use our new mutant skills—and recruited to fight in the resistance. Acier's journey into life as a mutant was different from ours. But one thing is the same. What we were before being changed…who we were, what our lives were like, all changed after we became mutants. Telling you about those lives is unimportant, because the people that lived them are dead. Before we begin, I need to know about Santo."

"Why?" Val asked.

Selena felt a wave of tension wash through her. Santo was a touchy subject among her team.

"I understand you believe he's dead." Liege looked at Ace. "Tell me how that happened."

Ace sent Owen a glance, seeking permission. Owen nodded.

"I killed him," Val said.

"No, I did," Greer said.

"It was my fault," Angel said.

Before more of the team could lie, Liege held up a hand. "Only one person fought him that night. And never mind the details." He looked at Ace. "I can see the fight is still active in your memory."

"I wanted him dead," Ace said, her soft voice unwavering. "I'd earned the right to kill him, but during our fight, I changed my mind. I wanted him to just stop his tricks, turn himself over to the FBI. Surrender. He fell on a spike during our fight. He'll never face his crimes because he chose the coward's way out."

Liege nodded. "Without a doubt, Santo is a first-class bastard. He's also brilliant and doggedly focused. He told me in the training camps that he already knew about the details of his own death." Liege walked over to stand in front of Ace. "You fought valiantly that day, even with a broken arm."

Selena frowned at Bastion. Perhaps he'd told Liege

that little detail, as it had happened shortly before he'd begun stalking all of them at Blade's.

I did not tell him that, Bastion responded. *He is pulling the info he needs from her own mind.*

How is that possible? Selena asked.

I can read only limited thoughts from you, things you think urgently and clearly. Liege can read everything from everyone — if they are not shielding themselves from him.

"Santo is not dead," Liege said. "He's hidden himself somewhere in South America. I have sent one of my men for him." He looked around at the group. "And as for the rest of you, lies only delay progress. I appreciate that you wanted to protect one of your own, but don't do it again or there will be repercussions."

"Don't threaten my team, or this experiment of yours is done," Owen warned him.

"I have to be able to trust them. What's coming is so much worse than what you've yet faced." Liege sent a glance around at the group. "Let's have a demonstration. Bastion, step forward."

Bastion did as requested, standing near Liege, facing the group.

"On my word, you will throw your knives at Bastion," Liege ordered Selena and her team.

Selena gasped, but Bastion only smiled at her. "Don't worry, *mon amour*. They will not cause me harm."

Well, I'm not participating in this exercise.

"Selena, you will participate in this or you will be punished," Liege said.

"Fuck you, Liege. Not doin' it."

She is full of balls and courage, is she not? Bastion said to his team.

Acier busted out laughing. *Selena, yield to Liege. Do it if only to ease your own rage. Not one of us in this room can best him.*

"And fuck you, Acier."

"Go!" Liege shouted. Bastion took off at a run. Knives shot toward him along the way, but not one hit its mark...because Bastion had never moved from his spot in front of Liege.

Selena watched the shocked realization hit her friends. Their knives still hung in the air along a line that would have been lethal shots at his chest, neck, and eyes —had he been in the vicinity of their weapons.

Liege looked from the line of knives to Selena. As if motored on their own, the knives reversed course and returned to their prospective owners, hilt-first.

Selena felt a compulsion hit her, forcing her to step forward, stopping only feet from Liege.

Liege's brown eyes glowed a dim orange. "You disobeyed a direct order."

Selena did not shy away from Liege's fury. "Give me an ethical order, and I will comply. Order me to harm one of my own, and I will always fail."

"You think you have a choice in any of this? Any of it? Not anymore. Throw your weapon at Bastion."

Selena fought the urge to follow that order, an urge that was fast becoming a compulsion. She withdrew her knife from its holster, fighting herself, instinct against need. It was as if a hidden hand moved hers. She ground her teeth, every ounce of her strength focused on resisting. She managed to open her hand enough to let the knife slip through, but that force made her fingers close around the two-sided blade. The guys behind her gasped, but none were able to move forward to help her. It didn't matter; this was her against herself—they couldn't help.

With her right hand disabled, her left took over. Against her will, against everything she held sacred, her left hand sent the knife shooting toward Bastion. At the last second, Liege's hand shot between the blade and Bastion, letting the blade sink into the flesh of his palm. He reached over and slowly pulled it free, then handed it to Bastion to hold.

It seemed the fight had taken minutes, but when she had her own mobility again, she realized it was only seconds. She threw a punch at Liege's jaw. It was like hitting a slab of granite.

He grabbed her hand with his wounded one and squeezed their palms together. *You are Legion.*

Selena shook her head. Her lips bared her clenched teeth. "Like I said before, fuck you."

Liege's brows went up. Bastion laughed. "No, my love, you must mean fuck me, not him. You will learn, I hope."

Liege nodded toward Guerre. The healer gently took hold of Selena's wounded hand and clasped it between his. The throbbing pain stopped. Comforting heat slipped into her aching wounds. As she watched, an orange light seemed to emanate from Guerre's hands into hers. After a few moments, he took his hands away. Not only was her hand no longer bloody, it was no longer wounded.

Liege extended his hand, her knife flat on his palm. "Resume your place in the line. You did well. The example I wanted to show was that, while we mutants might compel a regular to do an action, resistance is possible."

"You made me throw my knife at Bastion."

"At first, yes. But when I ran into your resistance, I changed the compulsion. Instead of forcing you to send your knife into Bastion, I ordered you to stab me." Liege gave her a sad smile. "*That* you were willing to do."

The freeze he had in place broke, freeing the rest of her team. She held her hand up for them to see, wanting to keep them from experiencing the same awful lesson — whatever it was. "I'm good. I'm fine. It's all healed."

Owen took a step toward Liege, but a shake of Liege's head stopped him. Bastion's boss looked remorseful. "The lesson here is that, as regulars, while you are all highly trained warriors, you are not equal to the mental abilities of a mutant."

"Where does that leave us?" Blade asked.

"In a difficult spot," Liege said. "We can shield you so you can continue your work. We can sever your connections to the Omnis and the work you've already done, allowing you to disappear into the world of regulars. We can train you to fight the ghouls and hope Omni mutants lose interest in you. Or we can modify you so that you can become fully empowered fighters in this new and terrible war. We in the Legion had our lives stolen from us—that's not what we wish for you, so the choice is yours."

"None of that's a choice you can make now," Acier said, "so let's get on with our training. This time, we'll start with the ghouls."

Acier moved next to Liege. "You can take these things on. They're fast and lethal, yes, but barely sentient. The ghouls around here are being manipulated by this guy, who usually presents himself like this."

Acier produced one of those hologram-like images that looked just like a real person standing there with them in the gym. The man turned around like a model on a spinner of some sort.

Something snagged Selena's interest. "You said 'usually presents himself.' What does he really look like? Do you know?" Having the ability to shift their appearance was yet another level of hell. How would they ever know they'd encountered a mutant?

"He looks like this," Liege said. The projected image changed to that of a different man. From the back, he seemed as tall and muscular as his pretend self. Why bother projecting an image if vanity was his only defining factor? Selena waited impatiently for the figure to complete his turn so she could see his face, and when she saw it, the air left her lungs. Spots formed in her eyesight, giving her tunnel vision to the defining feature of the man in the projection: his scar. The scar she herself had carved on his cheek using a shard of shattered mirror, twelve years earlier.

Selena was only vaguely aware of Bastion coming to stand behind her shoulder, close enough to share his heat, but not quite touching her. She stared in horror at the ravaged visage of the Legion's prime enemy. The scar made a stretched oval on his cheek, in the center of which there was no flesh — it was open to his teeth.

Bile rose fast, clogging her throat. She covered her mouth and ran out of the gym, rushing into the women's locker room, where she was violently ill.

ACE GLARED at Liege and pivoted, but Bastion stopped her. "I'll go," he said. "She is mine." He jogged out of the room and hurried to follow her, finding her crouched against a wall near the sinks. Her beautiful green eyes were darkened with huge pupils; her hands were shaking. She was lost in a past that was as terrible as he feared. He slipped down to the floor next to her, touching her from shoulder to hip to knee.

"I lied to my team," Selena said.

Bastion remained silent. There wasn't enough info in that statement for him to put pieces together, so he waited for more.

"I told them that your enemy, who's now Brett Flynn, brought a friend to the school where I was and attacked me late one afternoon when everyone was gone."

"That wasn't a lie," Bastion said, able to discern that much at least.

"It wasn't the whole truth."

"It was as much as they needed to know. But why not tell them all of it?"

"You don't get it."

Merde. No, he did not get it. And she was not sharing her thoughts.

Selena shook her head, then got up to rinse her face. She scooped up cold water in her hands and buried her face in it long enough that Bastion feared she was trying to drown herself.

When she straightened, he handed her a towel. "I would like to get it, if you would take the time to explain it to me."

"No." She tossed the towel on the counter and headed back to the gym.

While her team did not focus on Selena, giving her the space to reclaim her composure, his team watched her curiously, all of them trying to read her. Bastion shielded her from them. Ace and Selena exchanged a long look, one that vibrated with energy and support. The two females understood each other on a level Bastion dreamed he'd one day have with the woman who was his light.

He'd fallen short of what she needed, and that put a crack in his heart, letting his demons out. He'd let everyone down—his mother, his brother. And now his light.

"I did not mean to shock you, Selena," Liege said.

"It is what it is," she said. She lifted her chin a notch. "I gave him that scar when he assaulted me. Afterward, my family brought charges against him. A couple of our court dates had to be postponed due to reconstructive surgery he was having. My parents told me later that he'd contracted a MRSA infection in his cheek. We ended up dropping the case for some reason that I never understood, and we moved shortly after that." She looked at her team. "We had to move several more times after that."

"He had that scar when we encountered him later in our camps," Guerre said. "For some reason, the modifications never healed it."

"Does he know I'm here? Am I why he's focused on us?"

"It doesn't matter, Selena," Owen said. "He's come for retribution, whether that's because of our role in fighting the Omnis, or because of you, or both."

"It does matter. If he's come for me, there is an easy resolution to this situation that protects all of you."

A chill blew its cold wind around Bastion's chest. "No. Giving yourself up is no solution at all."

"You don't know this bastard like we do, Sel," Acier said. "He's got a scorched-earth policy. If you surrender yourself, he'll not only torture you before he murders you, but he'll still come after everyone who ever knew you—everyone here, their families. Even your parents. Our only option is to end him. So the why of it doesn't matter, really."

"This all my fault. Cutting him that day put him on this path that's brought him here to us. I should have just let him—"

"If you say that, I'll punch you in the stomach," Ace snapped.

"We each make our own destiny, Selena," Guerre said. "He made his. You made yours. We make ours. We are where we are, so we go from here."

"You said you put a protection on us," Owen said. "Is there a way that Flynn could get through that?"

"Yes," Bastion said, forgoing his Franglish due to the dire situation. He didn't want anyone to misunderstand him. "There are any number of ways through it. He could take me out. Liege would reinstate the protection, but in the seconds between my incapacitation and Liege's recovery, Flynn could get in. Or he could turn his ghouls loose on the town. You would go fight them, of course. Even though, in an action like that, he wouldn't get all of you, he would get most of you. He might do something targeted, like send his ghouls to Ivy's diner, or to the school."

"I thought they didn't go out in the daylight?" Blade said.

"We haven't seen that happen yet," Liege replied. "Flynn's still hiding behind the mantle of darkness, where he gives his predations complete freedom. He could at any point decide to expose himself and the Omnis—and us—by making himself visible to the world of regulars. So far, his secrecy has benefitted him. I'm not convinced the Omnis have a handle on his activities."

"There's another way he could get inside," Guerre said. "Someone already inside could let him in."

"Everyone here is trusted," Owen said.

"Trust is an antiquated notion," Acier said. "It wouldn't keep him from possessing one or more of you, regardless of how well you're trusted or how unwilling you are to being taken over."

Liege looked disgusted. "All human constructs of legality and ethics are at risk in a world occupied by mutants."

Blade clasped his hands behind his head and cursed. He moved away from the group and walked in a wide circle as Liege's words sank in. When he stopped, he looked at Kit. "We're going to have to change."

"No. There is another way," Bastion said. "Most of the Omnis don't even know about the mutants in their ranks. It's why Flynn is keeping a low profile. You can still do what you're doing against Omni regulars and leave the mutants to us."

Liege appeared to like that suggestion. He looked at Owen. "Your dad has been changed. We can train him to do what needs to be done to keep everyone here safe from mutants. One of my men can stay with you to do the training and provide extra security. I'm hoping we can put down this uncontrolled spread of modifications. To do this with the best outcome, we need Santo."

"I don't want that bastard here," Greer said.

Liege lifted a brow. "That bastard may be your best shot at Owen's dad developing the skills we need him to have."

Angel crossed his arms. "Wynn's parents—the

researchers you've been looking for—warned us this could be an extinction event."

"They're right," Guerre said. "If this gets out before governance systems are put in place, every regular human becomes a *de facto* slave."

"Staring down a future like that, seems dealing with a bastard like Santo is the lesser of two evils," Blade said.

"I'm glad there's a way forward for us that doesn't require the modifications." Owen met Liege's gaze. "There's much still unknown about them. I'll be following my dad's progress closely."

Liege nodded. "It's good to leave your options open. I've sent Merc to retrieve Santo. Now, I think we would get the most out of our remaining time today if we focused on getting you ready to fight the ghouls."

30

When Bastion saw his team off that evening, it was about the time that everyone gathered in the living room prior to dinner.

Bastion sent his mental energy out through the sprawling mansion, searching for Selena's energy. She was in the gym building, working out. He headed that way. Ridiculous that he'd only been away from her for a little while, yet he already hungered for her.

As he entered that wing, Bastion encountered several of Selena's team coming toward him. Their energy felt like a wall, stopping him. The group made a half-circle around their team lead. Didn't they know that many to one were still fine odds for a mutant?

"You headed to the gym or the pool?" Kit said.

"Gym," Bastion answered.

"Don't bother, man," Greer said. "Selena's chased all of us out. She wants it to herself."

"That doesn't mean she doesn't want me there," Bastion said.

Max chuckled. "Doesn't mean she won't cut up that pretty face of yours."

Bastion met Max's laughing eyes. "My face is hers to slice. And her heart is mine to hold. Something is wrong if she chased you out. She needs comforting, not solitude."

Kit shook his head. "If you don't mind getting your ass handed to you, then go for it."

The guys left. Bastion approached the gym door, but Angel was stretched out in front of it doing push-ups, blocking anyone from entering.

"Why haven't you left with the others?" Bastion said.

"Just getting my reps in," Angel said. "Sel wanted the room to herself while she worked out, but it seemed to me she didn't exactly want to be alone, so I thought I'd hang around in case she needed to talk."

Bastion compelled him to get to his feet, then held a hand out to shake. "Thank you. It was considerate of you, but I've got this."

"Works for me. It's your head." Angel jogged down the hallway after the others.

Bastion stepped inside the dimly lit space. The ventilation wasn't entirely adequate for the number of men who worked out in the room. The stink of their sweat lingered. It probably wasn't something that bothered regulars, but Bastion's extra-sensitive nose smelled months of workouts.

Selena was over by the heavy punching bag. She'd

taped her hands and was wearing boxing gloves. She wore a skimpy exercise top and tight knit shorts. Bastion enjoyed watching her body flex and move as she shifted her weight and threw her punches, hits that got harder and more impressive as she became aware of him. Her face and back were moist with sweat—a scent that was fresh and sweet to him, unlike the stink in the rest of the room. He filled his lungs with it.

"I guess you didn't get the memo," she said.

"I got it, only mine didn't say what you said to the others." He steadied the long bag.

"I want to be alone."

"If that were true, I wouldn't be here."

"I have some things to work out. I don't want an audience."

"So work them out."

"Go away," she said.

"I'm not going anywhere, Selena. Why don't we talk it out?"

"Don't feel like talking." She landed a hard jab that shoved the bag into his shoulder.

"Then don't talk." *It's not like I need your words to know your thoughts.*

The violence inside Selena's mind was exactly the same as the violence outside of it. She was angry, confused, and scared. He knew her emotions, but he didn't know the why of them. So he just kept holding the punching bag and letting her work her emotions out until he could get to the heart of the matter.

After a while, she ripped off her gloves and tossed

them aside, then went over to a bare stretch of wall and slumped against it, sliding down cold cement blocks to her haunches. She whipped the tape off her knuckles and wrists, then sat there bunching it into a messy ball.

Bastion went over to sit with her. He didn't touch her, didn't want to crowd her. He left about a foot of space between them. He bent his legs and propped his hands on his knees, calmly waiting for her to speak first.

"It hurts, you know," she said without looking at him.

Bastion felt those words cut their way through him. If there was anything within his power that he could do to take the pain away from her, he would. Her thoughts were still so jumbled that even slipping inside her mind, which was open to him at the moment, didn't let him make sense of her distress. So he said nothing.

"I just got back here, but once again I can't stay, because my being here still endangers everyone."

"You can't leave now—you're needed here. Flynn knows you're here. It's possible he could come as an astral projection, prowling around the house and grounds as he looks for you. But it's also likely that he'll choose a more violent tack. Because the people here were part of your life, he'll cut them down. I've seen him do it many times. So your not being here will not spare the people you love."

She looked at him. "Then what do I do?"

"Go out to our fort. We may end up bringing everyone there."

"How can we tear up everyone's lives for this

bastard? Remi has an important job at the university in Laramie. She can't get down to Colorado. The young pride boys just got into mainstream schools. For the first time, they have regular lives. Eddie and Mandy both run businesses out of Blade's ranch. Ivy has a business in town. Hiding everyone at the fort is not the answer."

Bastion let the silence speak for itself. He didn't have a solution and didn't feel like telling Selena a lie, that everything would be all right. A war was coming, and he couldn't pretend otherwise. It was for her own well-being she get ready for it, whether it were to take place here or at the fort.

Bastion took long, slow breaths, sharing his composure with her. He didn't know if she would sense the calm energy he was sending her way and, if she did, how she would react to it. Contrary to his worries, she seemed hungry for the ease it gave her. He let her draw from him all that she needed. He couldn't see auras the way Liege could, but knew if he could, he'd see the angry colors of her emotions making way for the calming colors of his energy. Though they didn't touch, they were very much bound together.

At last, Selena sighed, straightened her legs out, and relaxed her hands in her lap. "Still, the question is, what do I do?" She looked at him.

"You prepare to fight. You and I can do extra training so that you develop your instincts and your perceptions are finely tuned to changes in energy."

"Is that trainable? I mean, obviously mutants can

learn it but their mental wiring is changed. You're different than I am."

"You can learn it, in time. Everything I do is a natural human ability lifted to an exponential level. None of it is nonhuman—it's more like extra-human. Do you want to tell me about the fight you and Flynn had?"

He had the clear sense that she wanted him to know, but didn't want to drag herself back into that hell by revisiting that day. "No."

"Would you open yourself to me so that I can see the story from your memories?"

"You can do that?"

"I can, only if you're open to me. Liege can far more easily. So can Flynn."

"How do we do this?"

"Let me hold your hand. Be still and quiet. This takes significant concentration from me."

Selena moved closer to him. He took her hand.

"Close your eyes. Relax. Think of something pleasant, a field of wildflowers, an ocean, the mountains—whatever gives you ease."

"Will it hurt?"

It would hurt him, but he didn't tell her that. "You won't feel a thing. If you become anxious, we'll stop. You may even feel a sense of relief after it's done, because, while you can tell someone a memory, this is experiential. I will know it as you do. It will become my memory too."

Selena wrapped her hands around his big arm and held him tightly to her. "Okay. Let's do this."

Bastion closed his eyes, centering himself. He opened his energy to hers until they vibrated at the same resonance level. Once they were connected, he called up her memory of that day, in just the same way he would call up one of his own memories.

He had to work to keep himself calm. Just seeing Flynn near Selena was enough to sever the link he'd opened. Second by second, he saw the whole event from her perspective, all of it downloaded to him at hyperspeed. He felt her fear, her absolute desire to live.

SHE WAS a freshman at her prep school. She'd joined a cross-country track team before the school year started, and to her surprise, she'd actually been enjoying it. But her focus on sports had impacted her academics, so she'd stayed after one day to do some catch-up.

The boys were in the library—the ones who'd been eyeing her since the school year started, staying as student after student packed up and left. She tried to ignore them, but they openly stared at her.

Unnerved, she gathered her things and left. She thought briefly about going outside, but her mom wouldn't be there for a while, and she'd be even more exposed waiting by herself.

Instead, she walked as calmly as she could, then turned down the hallway where the girls' bathroom was. It had a lock on the door, didn't it? She could wait out the time until her mom came to get her there.

She walked, then jogged, then ran to the bathroom. She

hadn't been fast enough. She saw the boys follow her as she stepped inside.

There was no lock on the door. She leaned against it, hoping they were just trying to scare her and would give up when they couldn't get inside. It worked for a moment, then they both pushed against the door, knocking her down.

She scooted backward, deeper into the bathroom as they stood over her, laughing. Though she'd never met the boys, she knew of them. They were on the football team. Their families were wealthy. They acted like kings of the school. Oliver Jensen had blond hair, deep blue eyes, an oval face. His friend, Toby Elliot, had dark hair and blue eyes with a face that was rounder.

Evil shone from their pretty eyes. Selena was terrified. She scrambled to her feet and swung her backpack at them, missing them. It hit the large mirror that spanned the length of the sinks, cracking it. That enraged them. One grabbed her neck and smashed her head into the broken mirror.

The impact left her stunned. They pushed her down and began ripping at her clothes. One sat at her head while the other destroyed her life. They took turns.

When she could get a breath from pressure around her neck, she flailed out to her side, searching for something to fight back with. Her hand grazed a big glass shard. She sliced up at the guy holding her head and neck, cutting him multiple times before slashing the shard down at the skull of the guy between her legs.

They screamed and let her go, but not before kicking and punching her, leaving her broken on the floor with all the mirror shards.

She wasn't certain how much time passed before she was able to gather herself up. Blood was everywhere, real and mirrored.

She was covered in it. Hers and theirs. She put her clothes back together. She couldn't stay in there. What if they came back?

She grabbed the big shard of glass. There was something next to it on the floor. A glob of flesh. She picked it up, not knowing if it was from the guy whose face she'd cut or from herself.

She caught her reflection in what remained of the big mirror. She was bleeding from a thousand nicks and cuts. And down there, between her legs. She was dimly aware of her body hurting, but the primary objective she had at the moment wasn't to tend to herself—it was to get somewhere safe.

But where would that be? The library was locked. The school would soon be locked down for the night. Maybe someone was in the main office, but God, it was long walk to that end of the school.

She opened the bathroom door and peeked into the hallway. No one was there. No one was anywhere. What if she was locked here in the school with them?

She was vaguely aware of crying as she made her way painfully down the long hall. When she turned the corner, a third of the football team was there, laughing and pointing at her, calling her terrible things. Rape bait. She looked for the two boys who'd attacked her but didn't see them. At least their cruel behavior wasn't a physical attack. Insults wouldn't kill her. She forced herself to walk past them. The first adult she saw was the janitor, wheeling his mop out of one of the classrooms.

He dropped everything and rushed over to help her. She collapsed when she saw him, knowing help was soon to arrive. He caught her and carried her, running to the office.

He was talking to her, keeping his voice steady and strong.

She couldn't really make out what he was saying, so she kept asking him to call her mom. He got her to the nurse's station. Sitting next to her on the bed, he tried to hold her hand, but both were clenched around the things she'd brought from the bathroom.

He and the nurse tried to get her to open her hands. She just gripped them tighter. Blood seeped from the hand that held the mirror shard.

Her mom was there suddenly. Crying and holding her face, checking her body with her hands. Castigating the school personnel. It was her mom who finally was able to get Selena to open her hands. She gently lifted the glass from her hand as the nurse stuck a wad of gauze there and squeezed.

And then her mom got her to open her other hand. Everyone encircling the cot went quiet. The assistant principal found a plastic bag and collected it from her palm, saying it would be evidence.

31

So that was where she'd gotten the term "rape bait" from. An innocent young girl, in a bad state of shock—of course she would internalize such an insult. It killed him that his beautiful, brilliant, resilient light thought of her body in such an awful way.

Bastion slowly separated himself from her, keeping their energies calm as he regained his own boundaries. The whole memory retrieval had taken less than five minutes. He'd seen everything in nonverbal knowings—the fight, the broken glass, the attack, the aftermath, the ambulance. Selena's persistent shock. Her mother's fury. He loved that woman too. If he ever got the chance to meet her, he'd give her a huge hug. She had stood by her daughter unfalteringly.

He let a few more minutes pass before taking a deep breath, signaling to Selena that the process was finished.

She looked up at him, her face pale. "Did it work?"

Bastion nodded. "I know why Flynn's coming after you."

"Because I scarred him."

"No. Because you lived. He's attacked a lot of women since you, but you're the only one still alive. What happened after the attack?" he asked.

"My parents sued Oliver—Flynn—his family, the school, just about everyone and anyone even remotely involved. Somehow, the whole town turned against us. I don't really understand how that happened. Evidence was lost. The DNA samples were corrupted. The case didn't go anywhere. My parents weren't easily cowed; something bad made them drop the case. We moved several times after that. My dad kept losing his jobs. My mom couldn't find work. It wasn't until a few months ago, when Greer compiled a stack of background info on all of us, that I learned the Omnis had been destroying my parents' lives—because of me. It's been twelve years since it happened, and the shadow of it has been with me the whole time."

Bastion was struggling to control his fury. "Do you know why you've been calling yourself 'rape bait'?"

"Because I am. Men look at my body like it's it an object they can just help themselves to. I'm disgusting."

Bastion scooped her up and set her on his lap. He brushed a bit of hair from her face. "You are beautiful. And any man with a functioning libido would of course find you attractive. But that's not where that awful term came from."

She frowned at him.

"When you were dragging yourself out of the bathroom, you went past a bunch of boys. 'Rape bait' was one of the taunts they threw at you. It has nothing to do with your beauty and everything to do with their pushing the blame on you for what Flynn did. And every time you look at yourself and reinforce that term, you are letting them attack you all over, like cutting into a wound so it never heals."

Her eyes turned to liquid pools of green.

Brutal honesty was a cruel friend. He should have kept his mouth shut.

"I've hated myself a long time."

Bastion nodded.

"I don't know that I can undo that."

"You can. It's just a habit of belief. Learn a new thought habit. Thank your body for protecting you that day and in all the fights that followed it."

She studied him, her mind closed to him. "I owe you an apology."

He gave her his half-grin. "Oh?"

"I underestimated you. I didn't think you'd be so philosophical."

"What did you think I was, then?"

Selena caught the sides of his beard in her hands then dragged her fingers slowly through the coarse growth. "A cave man."

Bastion laughed. "You do bring out the primal in me." He caught the back of her neck and brought her close. His lips barely skimmed hers before he bent his head and deepened the kiss.

When the kiss ended, she straightened. "I have pushed many lovers away. I didn't want them to get close to me."

He kissed her again. "Mm-hmm."

"What happens if I push you away?" she asked.

"You can't. I am you."

She squinted and shook her head. "What does that mean?"

"It means we're one. I'll know when you need space. And I'll know when you need company. As I did tonight. And what you need, whatever it is, is what I need."

She frowned. "It doesn't work like that."

"It should, *n'est pas*? It could, if we make it that way. Who's to say otherwise?"

She smoothed the wiry curls of his beard. "So you'd give up yourself for me. That's major concession. What do you want in return?"

"Why must this be a barter?"

"Everything in life is."

"Then I will give you the world if you fuck me—give you my world, anyway." He kissed her again. "*Dieu*, I will give you my world even if you don't fuck me. I will give you anything that is mine to give."

"I don't want things, Bastion, but I do want to fuck you."

He smiled. Perfect answer. He ground her hips over his dick. "Let's do it now."

She looked over her shoulder. "There are cameras in here—"

He untied her shoes, then removed them and her

socks as he said, "Cameras don't work around me. I have blocked this room; no one will be coming in on us. And no tech can watch us." He pulled the top of her sports bra down, freeing her breasts. He stroked the messy web of scars on the sides of them. "These marks are beautiful to me. They are a testament to your struggle and your survival."

"If I take the modifications, will they go away?"

"They may. Not all scars do. Flynn's didn't. Some of us are able to get lasting tattoos; some mutants' bodies reject the ink. Each of us is different."

He leaned forward to kiss the web of pain she'd carved into herself. He loved her. He had since the night he first saw her. Waiting for her had been hell on earth, but she was worth every second he'd been forced to surrender.

He held the heavy orbs of her breasts, pleasuring them with his tongue and teeth and hands. A wave of delicious pheromones scented the air between them, hers mixed with his. He kissed her neck, her jaw. He slipped his hands inside the hips of her tight knit shorts and began to push them down.

Selena stood, in a rush for what was coming. She removed her shorts and thong. Bastion got out of his socks and boots, then ripped his tee off. He pushed his jeans and underwear down his thighs, freeing himself. He was painfully erect—a reality that thrilled him. He'd been so long without any true desire that to feel such devastating hunger for a woman, this woman, was ecstasy.

He caught Selena's hips and drew her closer so he could bury his face between her thighs while she was standing. He slipped his tongue along her secret folds to circle her clit as his fingers entered her slick channel. She fisted his hair. He smiled as he continued sending her ever closer to an orgasm. When he felt her body tighten, he pushed her down over him, sliding all the way inside her.

Connected to her mind and her body, he knew just when to thrust and when to hold still, and he did it over and over again, prolonging her pleasure as one of her orgasms rolled into another. He loved the way her generous breasts bounced with her movement, the way her hips bucked against his. He sat up and wrapped his arms around her, wanting to feel all of her with all of him. When he sensed her peak had passed, he gripped her hips and pumped a last time, giving in to his own orgasm in a rush of hot release.

Spent, she slumped against him. Bastion loved the feel of her bare breasts against his chest. "You are a gift to me, Selena. A rare, wonderful gift. When I first ran into the Matchmaker, I wanted to kill him for stealing away my free will—and yours, though I didn't know who you were at the time."

She leaned up, resting her elbows on his chest. She was warm and languid, and he was already becoming hard again inside her. She smiled. He went fully hard.

"And now?" she asked.

"And now I would make him his own *Gateau St. Honoré*."

"What's that?"

"A delicacy of puff pastry, cream puffs, cream filling, and meringue."

"Mmm. I want one."

"Then I shall make one for you as well." He kissed her and made slow love to her again. Their gazes locked on each other, they finished together. He realized he could take her another dozen times before he felt somewhat satiated. "I think we should go to your room."

Selena sat up and glared at her shorts.

"You can shower in your room."

"Great. And I'll walk up there naked, in all my glory."

He smiled. "It is a fine glory."

"It's not happening."

"I'll grab a robe from the bathroom." He looked at her breasts as she was righting her sports bra.

"And everyone will see me in my robe."

"No one will see you. I will hide you. Take your bra off."

She narrowed her eyes. "Why?"

"Because I want to know you're naked underneath your robe."

He wasn't sure she'd grant his request, but after a moment, she conceded. "If anyone does see me, I'm locking you out of my room."

Bastion put his hand on his heart. "You wound me. I trust you implicitly, yet you trust me not at all."

The robe from the men's locker room fell in a heap beside them, startling her. "How did you do that?"

"I levitated it. Put it on so we can go."

She did just that, shoving her shorts and under-clothes in one of the pockets while Bastion pulled his jeans on and stashed his tee, socks, and underwear in his boots. She grabbed her shoes and socks.

Bastion took her hand. She looked hesitant as they stepped into the hallway. He smiled at her. "You are helping me see there are some benefits to being a mutant."

They left the gym building and went up the back stairs to the bedrooms in the southern wing. Ace and Val were coming out of their suite. Selena saw them and gasped, then ducked behind Bastion.

Ace frowned at his missing clothing and the boots he carried.

"Hey," Val said. "I see you survived Selena."

Bastion chuckled. "Yes. I survived her very well."

Selena punched his kidney.

"Come down for a beer before dinner," Val said.

"Sounds good."

The couple went down the stairs, and Bastion and Selena made it to her room without running into anyone else.

"They didn't see me?" Selena asked.

"They did not."

"What did he mean by that 'survived me' comment?"

"You scared the guys when you chased them out of the gym. They are fragile." He reached for the tie on her robe and loosened it, opening the terrycloth to reveal her nude body. He smiled as he took in her lush curves. "I want you again. *Now*. Turn around."

They were in front of her long mirror. He stood behind her, tall and broad. Her lean, taut body looked petite in front of his. He moved his hands over her luscious curves, from her neck, down her breasts, her slim ribcage, over her navel, to the trim triangle of dark hair on her mound. He slipped his fingers between her legs. She was still wet from their sex earlier.

He nuzzled her hair, moving it aside until his face was against hers. "It is all right to do it from behind, *oui*?"

Her green eyes had huge pupils as her gaze caught his in the mirror. She nodded.

Mirrors, nudity, and sex were triggers for her. He wasn't sure if what he had in mind would work, but if it did, there was a chance she could begin building new, pleasurable associations for those things.

"Lean forward and down." He flipped up the hem of the robe onto the small of her back, baring her ass, which was round and firm and divine. He guided himself into her channel as she braced herself on the wall, the mirror between her hands. She was just tall enough that he didn't have to crouch to penetrate her —spreading his legs more than hers worked fine. He watched her reflection in the mirror as he moved in her. She watched herself too, which he'd hoped she would.

Little by little, he wanted her to experience her body differently, not as something wicked that tempted men, but as something of incredible power that she gave freely to the one she loved.

Further rational thought failed him at that point. He was mesmerized by the movement of her breasts each time he pumped into her. He pumped harder and faster, getting close to his peak, trying to hang on long enough for her to get there first.

He leaned over her, bracing a hand beside hers so that he could tease her clit with his free hand. He felt her body tighten over his cock, gripping him.

He was close. So close.

One more thrust and she cried out, losing herself as she writhed and bucked against him. Her head dipped down, spilling her hair forward. He caught her hips and slammed into her, letting go of the tight restraint he'd exerted over himself. For long, wonderful moments, they spun out of control.

It took them both several breaths to settle down afterward. He withdrew, and she straightened. Her robe dropped around her, leaving a long column of skin exposed in her reflection. He wrapped his arms around her ribs and held her against him. "Let's skip dinner and stay in bed."

"No. We can't. I want to hear what the guys have to say about everything that happened today."

"I don't." He shrugged. "I don't care."

Selena turned and put her arms around his neck. She smiled up at him, melting away the bad temper overtaking him. "We have all night to be together."

"*Bien.*"

He lifted her, kissing her, penetrating her with his tongue and cock as he carried her into the bathroom. He set her on the counter. Her eyes softened and her lips parted as he moved in her.

He made a few more slick thrusts, then pulled out. "If we cannot stay here, then we must shower."

"Dammit, Bastion. Come back here and finish what you started."

"*Non*. Now is not the time for fucking, or so my light has said." He'd spent a decade pretending to enjoy encounters with women, trying to regain his lost desire, all for nothing. And now he had his light—and an unending flow of hunger for her. He resented the intrusion of social obligations, but none of that was her fault. Nor his. And as she'd said, they had tonight.

He reached into the shower and turned it on, then gathered a couple of towels near. He was already naked, but Selena still wore that robe. He lifted her from the counter, then pushed the robe off her shoulders, staring into her beautiful green eyes.

He loved her. And he owed the Matchmaker a debt of gratitude for bringing them together. Bastion caught her face in his hands and kissed her.

32

H awk couldn't sleep. He and Lion had argued on the way home. They never argued. What was his problem?

You shouldn't have left.

True. He hadn't wanted to leave the team's home in Wyoming. It was Friday. They could have hung out there the rest of the weekend. Odd. That had been their plan when they went home late the night before. So why hadn't they stayed?

Go home.

The urge to get in his truck and drive back to Wyoming was strong. But he never left Lion alone, and Lion wouldn't want to head up there in the middle of the night.

Hawk tossed under the heavy blankets, unable to get comfortable. He was hot, then cold. Maybe he was getting sick. He got up then pulled on a pair of jeans and a tee as he shoved his feet into his Chucks. He went down the hall to Fiona's room. Flattening his hand on her door, he listened for sounds from inside. Nothing. Of course there was silence—it was after midnight.

He opened the door. Ambient light from outside illuminated the big space. Fiona was asleep in the center of the big bed. It was wrong to be there, in her room. Geez, this was Fiona. Her boyfriend owned the apartment they lived in. She was off-limits for that and so many other reasons. She was like a sister to him.

Put your hand on her mouth, then get on top of her. That way she won't be able to scream as loud.

Hawk rubbed his eyes, trying to wake himself up. He must be sleepwalking. He'd never been in Fiona's room, so why be there now?

She's yours for the taking.

Hawk took a step into the room. Everything inside him rebelled. This was not right...whatever this was. He found himself actually struggling to resist his need to walk over to the bed.

You should have stayed in Wyoming.

That was true. He wouldn't have been as out of control there as he was now. Through sheer force of will, he made himself back up and leave Fiona's room, closing the door behind him. That cold sweat he was feeling earlier was back. He went downstairs, thinking he would just get some water, maybe make a sandwich.

Instead, he found himself at the front door, keys in hand. He blinked as he stared at the keys. He didn't want to, but he felt compelled to leave the apartment.

He took the elevator down, then went out the

hallway that exited onto the sidewalk instead of going into the garage. See? He still had control over himself. He put his hands in his front pockets and curled his fingers around the thin pocketknife he always kept with him. He and Lion weren't allowed to bring the knives they'd had in the pride with them to the campus. A pocketknife with a short blade was all that was allowed.

He might need it tonight.

He walked a few blocks, moving deeper into the heart of Old Town. It was past closing time at most bars, so the night was sparsely populated with drunken students. That was okay. He didn't need a lot of people. Just one would do.

One *female*. Any one of the young girls that were so plentiful in the college town. One who would be too scared to fight back. Hawk felt a shiver move through him, followed by a deep sense of love and appreciation. It warmed him on the cold February night.

He came to an alley that cut across the middle of a city block. It led to a maze of small, reserved parking lots, each belonging to a different establishment on the front side of the block. A breeze dipped into the shadowy space. Hawk sniffed the air, sifting through the different smells for the scent he wanted.

Oh, it was sweet.

A young human female.

Easy prey.

Hawk approached her, his hands in his pockets. Usually he was nervous around females, but not this time. She was going to give him the pleasure he sought.

Sweet, delicious fear. And an orgasm like he'd never experienced. He would be chivalrous at the end, staying with her as she took her last breath. He wasn't a monster, really.

The girl saw him. Her car was parked behind a bar. There were a couple of other cars, but the bar itself was quiet for the night.

Mmm. Maybe it was just as well he'd come back to Colorado. This was worth the delay his leaving caused.

The girl watched him nervously. Hawk gave her an engaging smile. She dropped her keys, then bent hastily to pick them up. She fumbled to right the key chain so she could hit the key fob. Hawk took the keys from her. "You don't need these."

The girl's eyes grew wide. She wanted him, just as he wanted her. Hawk leaned over her, pressing her back against the side of her car. He ran his fingers down her face. She was the perfect choice for tonight.

Well done, Hawk.

Hawk pressed his knees between hers. She had way too many clothes on. He retrieved his knife and opened the blade.

Fear broke through the girl's momentary panic, as it had to for this interaction to be as potent as he needed. Hawk put a hand over her mouth and slowly shook his head, and though he'd silenced her voice, her eyes still screamed.

Perfect.

Before he could even do so much as nick the soft

flesh of her neck, Hawk was yanked away from her. Some great force spun him around.

Lion. The meddling bastard.

He pounded Hawk with a right hook, then a left, moving him away from the girl.

Bent over, Hawk glared up at his friend. "What the hell's your problem, Lion?"

"*My* problem?"

"Yeah. Like, why can't you mind your own fucking business?"

"You are my business." Lion handed Hawk his hoodie.

Hawk grabbed it and jerked it over his head, suddenly aware of how cold he was. "What are you, my mother?"

Lion shoved his shoulders. "You know as well as I do we had no mothers. Geez, Hawk, you were gonna rape that girl."

Hawk stared at Lion, feeling something shift inside him. It was a crazy feeling, like he could finally get air to a part of his brain that had been suffocating. He looked back at where the girl had been, but she and her car were gone.

Never fear, my pet. I've erased her memory. I will keep you safe—no cameras in the alley have recorded you because none of them are working. We will try again another time. Don't be disappointed. Hunting was fun tonight.

Nausea made Hawk buckle over as he violently emptied his stomach. Some guy came out of the bar behind them, hollering for them to take off. Lion grabbed the back of Hawk's hoodie and pulled up, dragging him deeper into one of the alleys.

Hawk folded his hands under his arms and kept his head down as he ran-walked beside Lion. "I've never been with a female. I don't want my first time to be a rape." That sounded off, even to his own ears. "I never wanted *any* time to be rape."

"What's up with you?" Lion snapped.

"I dunno. I'm not myself."

"You haven't been for a while."

"I want to go back to the woods, Lion. This never happened there."

"We can't now, Hawk. The team has expectations of us. We can't let them down."

Hawk stopped him, a hand on his chest. "I don't have control over myself."

"Meaning?"

"I don't know. I need help. I can't go back to Blade's. I shouldn't even go back to the apartment. Lion—I went into Fee's room."

"I know. She told me. It's why I followed you." Lion pressed his lips into a thin line. "I'll call Max, see what he says."

"Don't call him. Please, not him, not anyone on the team. They'll kick us out. They'll kick the whole pride out. They can't know about this. Swear it to me."

Lion was silent a long minute. "I can't. You need to trust me. We've gotten through everything to this point. We'll get through this too."

33

onjour!" Bastion called cheerily as he entered the brightly lit and very busy kitchen the next morning. Jim and Russ worked together like a well-oiled machine—Russ calling out orders and Jim scrambling to respond.

"Morning," Jim said. Russ only grunted, his attention stuck on the sizzling pan on the stove.

The kitchen was filled with the scent of heavy American breakfast foods: meats, eggs, cheeses. There was a bowl of fruit and a covered basket of breads, but not a croissant or baguette in sight.

Bastion's motives for working his way into the kitchen routine were entirely selfish; he wanted to be sure there was good bread, premium butter, and quality jam. It appeared he'd have to make do with what was offered.

Instead of voicing his disappointment, he jumped in

to help Jim carry dishes out to the sideboard in the dining room.

"Do you think Russ would let me use the kitchen to make some bread today?" he asked.

"That man is territorial," Jim said, looking worried that Bastion, a newcomer to the group, would ask such an indulgence.

"I want to make some proper breads, maybe some croissants for the team."

"Sounds divine," Ivy, Kit's wife, said. "If he won't let you, I'd be happy to offer the kitchen at my diner, as long as you make extra that I could sell."

"*Bien sûr.* I could do that," Bastion said.

"Or you could use the kitchen at my house," Mandy, Rocco's wife and Zavi's stepmom said. "It's not an industrial kitchen, but you'd have the place to yourself."

"That would work as well," Bastion said. "I could make some chocolate croissants *pour les enfants.*"

Mandy's jaw dropped. She rubbed her huge belly. "Forget the kids. We need those for ourselves."

Bastion laughed.

"No. Seriously," Ivy said. "What do you need from us to make that happen?"

"Not a thing. I will go shopping for what I need."

A groan sounded from the living room entrance to the dining room. "Not another shopper," Selena said.

Bastion heard what went unsaid—that her buddy Val was big shopper. Bastion had seen that in the assistance he'd provided to the two weddings that had happened in the residence recently.

He grinned and opened his arms. "I love shopping. I love cooking. I love fighting. I love fu—" His gaze shifted to the two young boys coming into the room. "Fun. I love *fun*. I am an easy man." It was going to take some getting used to moderating his behavior around the swarm of children that lived here.

"He's promised us chocolate croissants, Sel," Ivy said. "We're going to have a problem with anything that gets in the way of that. So if he needs to go shopping, then shopping it is, feel me?"

Selena laughed. Ivy was beginning to sound like her husband. "Sorry to disappoint, but Bastion's going to be tied up in training today."

"Not the whole day," Bastion said. "And if I have to stay up late tonight, I will so that you have your treats this time tomorrow."

"Captain Hook!" the taller of the two young boys said as they flanked him. "You're still here."

"I am. Your papa has graciously asked me to stay for a while. But remember, my name is Bastion, not *Capitain* Hook."

Bastion turned his attention to Selena as the two mothers fixed plates for their kids. He checked her over, glad that she seemed rested. A slight touch of color warmed her cheeks as their shared gaze continued. He went around the table to her. Ignoring anyone else in the room, he caught her fingertips.

"*Bonjour, ma petite chou,*" he whispered as he leaned forward and kissed her. She stared up into his eyes, her

413

pupils dark. Bastion gave her a very male grin. Maybe they should go back up to her room.

Other members of her team were coming into the dining room, moving around them. Noise filled the long room. China clinked. Conversations started.

And still he and Selena stood locked in their silent exchange. *Do you want to go back upstairs?* he asked.

Yes.

Then let's not waste time here, he said.

But I'm hungry. And I've a feeling I'm gonna need sustenance.

It is true. You will.

When he pulled his attention from Selena, he realized many of her teammates were watching him with less-than-friendly expressions. He ignored them, but he knew that their reaction stung Selena a little. She didn't realize that their hostility originated not from a rejection of him but protectiveness over her. He respected them for that.

He led her over to the buffet table so they could get their breakfast. Bastion filled his plate.

There were no assigned seats, so they sat at the end of the table, leaving plenty of space for other couples to sit together.

The two boys, Troy and Zavi, moved from their seats by their parents to the end of the table where Bastion and Selena sat. He pretended not to notice their fascination with him. They exchanged several whispers, hands cupped to muffle the sound.

They reminded him of his childhood with his

brother. They were forever in trouble, forever getting into anything and everything they weren't supposed to.

Guess that was how they ended up where they did.

That was a sobering thought. He hoped these two had better sense than he and his brother had.

"Mr. Bastion?" Troy asked almost timidly.

"*Oui?*"

"Zavi doesn't believe you can disappear," Troy said.

There were many conversations happening. No one noticed the quiet statement Troy made…or the challenge it held for Bastion.

"Sometimes we know things that we don't have to prove to those who don't know them," Bastion said, trying his damnedest to sound like a mentor.

"He saw it, but I didn't," Zavi said.

"So you don't believe it can happen, is that it?" Bastion asked.

Zavi and Troy both nodded.

Bastion leaned toward them. "I can make you both disappear. Shall I?"

The boys' eyes got big. They exchanged fast whispers, then nodded.

Bastion smiled. "It is done. No one can see you. Or hear you. Or feel you."

"No one?" Troy asked. "Even if I shout?"

Bastion shrugged. "Try it and see."

"Hey!" the boys both shouted. No one at the table moved—except Selena, who turned to frown at Bastion.

"What are you up to?" she asked.

"You will see."

The boys stood on their chairs. "Hey! Hey look at us!"

Nothing. They exchanged shocked glances, then decided to step onto the table and walk toward their parents. They were laughing and dodging dishes. Just before they got to the far end, where Owen sat, Bastion removed their invisibility.

The boys stopped cold and stared in dread at Troy's dad. Their mothers squawked but were too pregnant to lift them down. Owen and Rocco swept their sons off the table.

"Bastion made us invisible," Troy said.

Owen glared down the table at him.

"That is true. But I did not tell them to walk on the table."

"You made them disappear?" Addy, Owen's wife, asked, alarm making her voice tremble.

Bastion wasn't the mind reader that Liege was, but he could tell that something terrible had happened with Addy and her boys, something that even now, in a room filled with loved ones, filled her with terror.

He sent her a wave of calming energy. He meant no harm in his little stunt. The truth was that it had been an important exercise.

Owen looked furious. "In the den. Now, Bastion."

Why do I feel as if I've been called to the headmaster's office?

Because you have. We had a no-trick policy, remember? Selena said.

It wasn't a trick. It was an exercise.

Both boys looked remorseful as he neared them.

Zavi was crying. Bastion put his hand on the boy's head. "Be at peace, boy. I have faced far worse than Troy's papa."

Zavi gasped some ragged breaths as he nodded. "I'm sorry, Mr. Bastion."

"It is I who should apologize, boy. Have no fear. All is well." Bastion smiled as he stepped into the hall. Yup. Those two were just like he and his brother. Trouble through and through. How he missed Simon.

Rocco and Owen were already in the den when Bastion entered.

Bastion was in the middle of the room when Owen said, "Close the door," so Bastion closed it telekinetically.

Owen jumped right into his ass-chewing. Bastion ignored him and wandered over to the sofa to sit through the storm. Rocco picked up the tirade when Owen quieted down. Bastion lifted his arms and rested them on the back of the sofa, waiting until their anger was spent.

It took many minutes. Finally, Bastion held up a hand, giving the two men a chance to breathe. "I understand family. Your boys were not harmed. Nor would I ever harm them. I understand the sacred care we have for our children. It is why I disappeared them."

Owen folded his arms. "I'm not following."

"When the ghouls come here—and they will—it will be when our defenses are down. They will spill into this house like boulders through the doors and windows. They will run throughout the house, sniffing out its occupants. They will shred every living thing they find —cat, dogs, men, women, and children. My team and I will train you to fight them. And you will overpower them because they are beasts, not strategists, but every being here who cannot fight will be slaughtered. All of them."

Silence met his words. He could see the anger leach from Rocco and Owen's faces.

"There is much you could do to fortify your home, but perhaps there isn't enough time for that. When the ghouls come, disappearing the civilians and animals is all that will save them. Out of sight, out of mind—ghouls are simple creatures. And though they may smell them, if we have disappeared them, the ghouls will not try to attack them. Your children, your women, they must become entirely comfortable being disappeared. They must be trained in what to do and how to act...how to survive the hell that will soon be here."

Owen and Rocco, who were standing in front of the big mahogany desk, now slumped against it, bracing their hands on its edge.

Bastion waved his hand over his torso. "I would show you the scars I have from fighting the monsters, but they don't stay on me. I heal too fast. They will mark you forever." He stood. "You can see the many scars on my pants." He lifted aside his tunic to let them see his messed-up suede trousers. "Your skin will look like this.

"Acier will be here in a half-hour for your training. Afterward, he will inspect your weapons and see what you might need." He started toward the door, but looked back at them. "Now, I am going to finish my breakfast. My methods are unconventional, but then, it is an unconventional war we fight."

Bastion could feel Selena's energy just on the other side of the door. He walked a little slower, giving her time to scoot away. She was halfway down the hallway when he left the room. She looked like she was just coming his way.

He smiled at her. "I heard you scurry away."

She bowed her head. "Dammit."

"You heard all of it?"

She sighed and nodded. "You really think those things are going to come here?"

"I do. And not just because you're here. Flynn sends them after the changed ones in the resistance, like me. Even if you and I left and never came back, the Ratcliffs will be here now and then. And Owen's father. Flynn will finally execute the revenge that he lives for when he destroys these fighters and those who aid them. And then the Omnis will burn the house. It happened before. To Merc. He lost his wife, his children, his whole fucking soul."

Addy and Mandy came into the hallway, blocking his access to the kitchen or dining room. If he thought their husbands were pissed, well, he'd never seen a protective mother before.

He put his hand on his heart. He was not lying or manipulating them; he was earnestly repentant for upsetting them. "I ask your forgiveness about my prank this morning. Your boys were in no danger at all, but only I knew that at the time. I am very sorry for frightening you."

Even if they forgave and forgot what he'd done, he couldn't. He'd lived so long a mutant among other warrior mutants that decent, regular behavior was never his natural state, and that saddened him, because he was losing his humanity in giant leaps at a time.

Still, he believed he'd done what he'd had to do.

"Bastion," Addy said, stopping him, "it was terrifying to see that you could make our children disappear. I'd like to know how to stop you—or find them—in the future."

Bastion slowly smiled as he looked at both women, then behind them to their husbands. "There are some things I can teach you."

Mandy nodded. "Good. Because if it happens again, I will disappear you."

Bastion laughed and gave them a brief bow. He really liked this group of fighters and their families. *Dieu*, how he hoped he could shield them from the worst of what was coming.

34

Bastion moved in a slow circle as he read the readiness of each fighter surrounding him. Eleven men, two females. Ace was a few inches shorter than Selena. The men towered over them, though that wasn't what mattered. Size wasn't a predictor of fighting prowess—lethal intent was a sole determinant of survival, and everyone here had a high amount of that.

Bastion opened an illusion in the center of the group of a life-sized ghoul, standing on his hind legs, then dropping to all fours as it walked around the inside of the circle, like an animal in a cage.

"The ghouls you'll face are unlike any adversary you've ever met," Bastion said. "They are predators. Their only purpose is to kill. In the heat of a fight, they'll even turn on each other."

"They aren't intelligent," Acier continued. "They receive their instructions from a handler, who may be near or far. He can redirect them at any point, calling them off an attack or refocusing them. They operate on pure instinct, as they aren't sentient. They have no fear. They can feel pain, but it only serves to fuel their frenzies. Being mutants, they heal fast. Not immediately, but fast. If you don't deliver lethal blows to them in a fight, you'll just have to take them down later, so it's best to finish them off when you have the chance."

"I'm going to show you a fight that we had with the ghouls inside Liege's girlfriend's apartment," Bastion said. "You'll see it from my and Acier's perspectives."

Bastion looked at Acier, coordinating the replay of the fight they had with the ghouls in Summer's apartment.

"Remember that what you're about to see is only a memory," Bastion said. "The ghouls aren't here in real life, this replay isn't live, and they can't hurt you." He nodded toward Acier.

Bastion walked in a slow circle inside the ring of fighters gathered around him. He felt the wave of tension that cut through Selena's team as they watched the scene unfold. Their eyes were open and fixed to the image. The scene played until all the ghouls were dead.

"Wait. How is that even possible, what you just showed us?" Kit said.

"I told you, it was a memory," Bastion said.

"Right, but no one here can see each other's memories," Kit said.

"We're mutants, remember?" Bastion asked. "Our minds have been enhanced. Our skills are always evolving. Everything we do, regulars can do—but with extreme effort. We've been enhanced to operate at the highest level of human capacity. Our memories are almost perfect. They don't fade with time. We can recall vivid details about every experience."

"But how are you sharing those with us?" Blade asked.

"Smoke and mirrors," Acier said. "It's just a matter of emitting the right electromagnetic wave frequency to convince your brain that it's seeing what it's seeing. What you call the 'real world' is your brain interpreting the inputs it receives of light and shadow, frequencies, all filtered through your own understanding of those things."

"This display is just us altering your sense of reality." Bastion looked around the group. "Those monsters are agile and strong. I would hate for them to spill out into normal human populations."

"It would be disastrous," Kit said.

Bastion nodded. "It would be the end of our secrecy —and of life as regular humans know it."

"These ghouls don't live long," Acier said, "which is why the Omnis are so lackadaisical about using them to take down enemies. They are tall, fast, and lethal, but they are not sentient, and they can be easily tricked. Their nails are razor-sharp, and their brains are so hopped up on adrenaline that they won't notice a fatal injury until they are physically incapacitated. It takes maybe four minutes for them to bleed out, and in that time, they will continue to fight. We've learned ways to trick them so that one of us could take down a small group. They often travel in small packs of three to five. My team and I can project images of ourselves across whatever fighting space there is, even make other monsters look like us so that they turn on each other and do our work for us."

"Again, how do you do that?" Blade asked.

"Mind games," Bastion said. "That's all it is. We can begin to teach you the same skills, but as you are regular humans, it will take a long time for you to conquer this ability. For our training to be successful, you must over-come your natural belief about your own limitations—otherwise, it will inhibit your growth." Bastion nodded at Acier.

The scene in the middle of the ring of fighters lit up with another memory. In this one, Acier showed himself projecting his image onto some of the ghouls. The group watched in fascinated horror as the monsters turned on themselves. When that fight scene had played out, it disappeared from the circle.

Bastion could feel Selena's tension and fear. Blade looked at him with a frown, clearly still not grasping how any of it was possible. Bastion cast her appearance on the group around her—but only made this projection available to her eyes.

She gasped.

"How many of you do you see, Selena?" Bastion asked.

Selena looked around at the group in disbelief. "We are all me," she said.

"No, we're all ourselves," Blade said.

Bastion released the illusion from Selena's mind and set the same illusion in Blade's mind, making everyone in the ring look like him. His eyebrows rose as he looked around at his teammates, seeing only his own face.

"And now I see all me."

"And now?" Bastion asked as he removed the illusion from Blade.

"Everyone is back to themselves."

"This is how we cause the ghouls to mistake other ghouls for us," Bastion said.

"And you think we can learn to do that?" Selena asked.

Bastion nodded. "It's not a quick lesson. It's what we will be teaching Nick, once he joins us. It begins with focus and concentration. Nick's progress will be faster than the rest of you will because his brain is actively being rewired."

"For now, to deal with the immediate threat," Acier said, "we'll teach you how to fight the ghouls."

"How does Flynn haul these things around?" Kit asked.

"Typically, in cattle trucks," Acier said.

"So he's got to be warehousing them somewhere," Blade said. "Maybe somewhere near a highway so he can move them around quickly."

Selena looked at Bastion. "What if we look for the ghoul warehouses while also searching for Flynn's hidey-hole? Hit him from both directions?"

Bastion and Acier exchanged looks. "It isn't as easy

as it sounds," Bastion said. "Everything associated with Flynn is under his protection—meaning it's covered with illusions and compulsions. You wouldn't even know if you got close to one of those."

"A protection is just a spin of energy, right?" Selena asked.

"Basically."

"Energy that you can sense?"

Bastion set his hands on his hips. "Not necessarily. Flynn's eluded us so far."

"I agree that we need to train to fight these ghouls," Owen said, "but we also need to work on finding Flynn. If we take him out, the ghouls end, no?"

"No," Bastion said. "We're not sure how much the OWO itself knows of what Flynn's been doing. Perhaps his work is a sanctioned activity—if so, they'll send a replacement for him. The only way to terminate the ghouls permanently is to destroy the labs making them, along with the specs used to formulate them. And we'll have to find the scientists heading the program and either bring them over to our side or terminate them. As for the remaining ghouls left without a handler, it's possible they'll turn on each other and kill themselves. But it's also possible that Flynn's got a backup who will pick up where he left off. Or it's possible that the Omnis will take control of Flynn's breeding program."

"And if that happens, we're up shit creek," Acier said.

"So it's monumental, but not insurmountable. We'll find a way," Owen said.

Acier grinned at Bastion.

"What?" Owen snapped.

"Nothing. You just sounded like Liege there for a moment." Acier laughed, Bastion didn't.

"It's the hope that keeps us fighting," Bastion said.

FOR THE NEXT WEEK, Bastion and his friends divided Selena's team into groups and went through drills on the basketball court. Blue gymnastic mats had been spread out all over.

Every now and then, when Selena had finished her rounds with the ghouls, she sent a look around at the different groups undergoing the same training. The room was filled with monsters—and her friends were covered with mock blood where real blood would have been if these ghouls were more than mirages.

The monsters looked every bit like werewolves from the worst B-movies she'd seen, except these weren't static masks made by third-rate costumers. The faces of these ghouls had full motion. They growled and snarled and squinted and flashed enormous canines.

The training was grueling. None of them were making much headway in learning how to defeat the ghouls. Sure, they got in good strikes, even some lethal ones, but not enough of them to take out a pack of the ghouls single-handedly.

That afternoon, Selena and Owen were the last in a late session in the gym. Most of the others had already finished for the day. Acier's focus and energy were inde-fatigable, so she took advantage of that as she pushed for another round.

Selena wiped her forehead with the back of her fore-arm. She was panting and sweating and covered with blood—the illusion of blood, anyway.

"Again," she said with a nod to Acier, who brought up a fresh group of ghouls.

"Enough," Bastion said. He'd joined her and Acier before the end of the last scenario. Selena straightened from her fighting pose. She caught an expression in his eyes that he immediately blinked to cover, but the ghost of it remained.

Fear. Sorrow. Disappointment.

He didn't think she could do this.

"Again, Acier."

"I said enough." Bastion nodded at her. "You're covered with the blood of your many deaths. This isn't working."

Selena was so tired that lifting her arms was a strug-gle, but she'd be damned if she gave Bastion the satisfac-tion. "It isn't working *yet*."

Before they could get into it further, a scream ripped into the room. Instantly, the monsters disappeared, as did the fake blood covering her and Owen.

Selena turned to see Addy, Owen's wife, standing at the hallway door, losing her shit. Owen rushed over and pulled her close, burying her face in his chest. "It's okay. I'm okay. It was just training."

She gripped his arms and leaned back to look at his face. "You were covered in blood."

"It was all an illusion. They were having us battle simulated monsters. It's a mutant thing."

Addy's hands shook as she patted his chest, arms, shoulders. At last, her crazed gulping of air slowed. Owen hugged her again and began murmuring low words of comfort, rocking her.

"Remember when I used to slay your dragons when we were kids? I'll soon have real ones to fight, but at least these ones don't fly."

Addy shook her head. "No. That was make-believe when we were kids. This is real life."

"It's something that we all have to face." Owen put his arm around her and led her from the gym. "I think it's time we called for a group meeting to discuss this." He looked back at Bastion and the guys. "We'll get together tonight, after the kids are in bed."

Selena looked down at herself, seeing that the blood-soaked clothes she'd been wearing were really only sweat-soaked. Now that she could finally take a full breath and didn't have keep powering through, she realized how tired she was. Her fingers ached from the tight grip she'd kept on her KA-BAR.

Bastion still stared at her, that hint of devastation returning to his eyes. "I know what she was feeling." He nodded toward Addy. "That fear of watching someone you love dying."

"It's been a week, Bastion," Selena said. "How long did it take you to learn to battle them?"

"That's not the point."

"It is the point."

"You're a regular. The skills you have can be fine-tuned, but they aren't going to evolve into anything more. At least, not quickly enough."

"You said humans could do anything mutants can."

"With time, Selena. Lots and lots of time. We don't have that."

She wiped her face on a gym towel from a nearby table. Her hands were shaking with fatigue. She fisted the towel to keep him from seeing, but as connected as they were, he probably already knew.

She and the Legion guys were alone in the basketball court. She met the eyes of each man, seeing if their assessment was the same. It was. She walked out, her legs rubbery, but her back was straight and her chin was high.

She'd be damned if she showed any sign of weakness in front of them.

BASTION SAT at the bottom of the stadium seats and dropped his head into his hands.

Acier watched him warily. "'Sup B?"

"You ever see the future?" Bastion asked.

Guerre frowned. "You getting premonitions now?"

"I hope not."

"Spill, Bastion," Acier said. "You look scared shitless. With all that we've been through, I've never seen you like that."

"I saw her die. She was cut from her throat to her gut."

Acier slumped to the bench beside him. Guerre looked away. Bastion opened his mind to his friends, letting them pull from him what he'd seen. It felt real. Like a memory. Like a knowing.

"How much time do we have?" Acier asked.

"Not much." Tears pooled in his eyes. "I've only just found her, and now I'm going to lose her."

"Not necessarily," Acier said.

"You saw what I saw."

"Maybe it's a warning," Guerre said, "not foregone truth."

"It's the Matchmaker's curse."

Acier lurched off the bench and returned to the blades laid out on the folding table. "Don't use that fiend as an excuse. We'll train her. We'll get her mind ready. We're not going to be leaving her here alone. One of us will always be with her."

"She's not a mutant. She's no match for the ghouls. Or Flynn."

"Then turn her," Acier said. "Bring her into our world. She's a helluva fighter. That will put her out of commission for a bit while we go after Flynn."

Bastion scoffed. "You want me to nuke her neurology when we know Flynn's coming for her?"

"I don't know a Legionnaire who didn't come through the fire like that," Acier said. "We didn't."

Bastion shook his head. "I'm not doing it. Besides, we don't even have access to the scientists who could do it. And if she chooses to go through that, I wouldn't let her until we have Santo. He could pull her through the shift."

Acier nodded, slipping another blade into its sleeve. "We need Merc to keep his shit together long enough to find him." Acier looked up. "I will protect your light with my life—you know that, Bastion."

"And I will as well," Guerre said. "I think we need to change up her training—you're a distraction. She looks to you for approval, and all she sees is your sadness. It says you don't have faith in her, robbing her of her faith in herself. Without that, she is for sure dead."

Bastion nodded. Guerre was right. Watching the simulated ghouls ripping her up was shredding him.

35

S elena was almost too tired to join the group for dinner. And she was still seething about Bastion's lack of faith in her. She hadn't let him in her head since his comments earlier. Resisting him was bringing back the old headaches she'd had months earlier.

She'd take a headache any day over a guy who didn't believe in her.

Bastion knocked on her door. Weird how she knew it was him. She yanked it open, but didn't stand back to let him in. His dark eyes had that lost-puppy look in them. "I can feel your anger," he said.

Way to confront the situation head-on. "Sounds like a personal problem."

"It is. I'm sorry and not sorry that I'm terrified of losing you."

"That's 'sorry not sorry.'"

He frowned, confused.

"The idiom. That's how you say it."

"But I am sorry. And also not sorry." His brows lowered. "Not sorry that I'm not sorry. It's different."

Selena couldn't help cracking a smile. She stepped back so he could get out of the hallway. She didn't want the rest of the team knowing he'd lost confidence in her.

"I haven't lost confidence in you," Bastion said.

He was in her head again. She must have dropped her blocks when she saw him.

"I've gained a need for you that is both dark and light. If I could put you in a bottle and keep you safe, I would."

"I wouldn't be safe in a bottle because being in one would kill me."

"I know. Which is why I must embrace both sides of you."

Selena stared into his big brown eyes. As much as he could, he was laying himself bare to her. "The dark—the curse you fear from the Matchmaker."

He nodded.

"I don't believe in curses."

"I don't fear my own death; I fear yours. And how can you not believe when you saw the Matchmaker for yourself?"

She put her hand on his hard chest, roughly over the area of his heart. "Because I'm not superstitious. I am going to die one day, but those motherfucking ghouls are not going to take me out."

He stared into her eyes for the longest moment. "Will you sit next to me at dinner?"

Whelp, apparently her blocks hadn't been working at all—she'd been planning to give him the cold shoulder tonight. Instead, she looped her arms around his neck. She had to stand on her tiptoes to do that, stretching her whole body against his rock-solid one. Maybe they shouldn't bother with the meal—he felt so damned delicious.

"I agree," he said, his mouth pressed against her hair. "Let's not waste the time."

"No, we aren't staying here. And yes, I will sit next to you. Owen has called for a meeting tonight in billiards room. We need to be there. Did Liege talk to him?"

"I don't think so. Maybe he's upset we scared Addy."

She looked at Bastion's mouth. He'd trimmed his beard neatly, baring the soft contours of his lips, curves she wanted to run her tongue over.

"Do it."

She stepped away from him. "Later." She took his hand and led him out into the hall.

I want to be on top…later.

She shot a look at him. *Maybe I'm not ready for that.*

I think you are. You do trust me, non?

She didn't answer that. Maybe it wasn't a matter of trusting him but whether she could trust herself to not freak out.

AFTER SUPPER, after the kids were in bed and the

household was settled for the evening, Bastion and Selena, Guerre and Acier, Russ and Jim, her entire team and their civilian partners gathered in the billiards room.

Bastion checked the energy signatures of the women. They were no fools. They knew something of the nature of mutants, from Addy's short stint being changed, as well as from the Ratcliffs and Owen's dad. Now, having a team of mutant fighters come visiting, it was obvious something was up. Bastion was glad that Owen had called them together. It was time to bring them in.

No one played pool or cards tonight. Some held small glasses of digestifs or mugs of coffee. The tension in the room was palpable.

Owen stood in front of the pool table and looked over the gathering of his team and their better halves. No children were in the room, not even the wild boys.

Bastion was glad he wasn't Owen, having to break the news to the women that monsters were real.

When Bastion first came out to them, Owen hadn't wanted to reveal any of this to anyone without a direct need to know. The Legion could have suppressed their memories of any interactions with the ghouls, but doing so wouldn't have stopped the nightmares as those memories fought to surface. And it would have left the most vulnerable among them ill-prepared for what Bastion thought was a certainty: the ghouls were coming. Fear always led to chaos, and chaos in a fight led to disaster.

It was time the civilians were told; he didn't want any of them to be unprepared.

He shut the double doors to the room.

Owen nodded at him. "I asked all of you to meet here tonight because I have some news that I wish I didn't have to share." He looked over at his wife's steady gaze, taking strength.

It amazed Bastion that as fragile as women often seemed on the outside, inside they had the heart of a Roman general. Humankind—and mutant-kind—would be lost without them.

"As you all know, we've been working with a security team from Colorado. They, like Addy once was and my dad still is, are mutants. We share a common enemy, and we've agreed to assist each other as we move forward in our fight against the Omni World Order.

"The OWO hasn't yet gone public with their mutant agenda. Fortunately for us, they prefer to work behind the scenes. I believe they're hoping to clinch their power before revealing themselves to the wider world. Their reticence is an opportunity we need if we're to stop them.

"Most of you were with us when the Ratcliffs explained how these human mutations could cause major shifts in power dynamics, destroying societies as we know them today." Owen checked Addy, seemingly to make sure she was up to hearing what he was about to say. "Humans aren't the only beings the Omnis are modifying. They've found a way to merge human and animal DNA, creating monsters capable of terrorizing and destroying any human or animal they encounter."

Eden, Blade's wife, frowned. "I don't understand. They've made a new species?"

"Not exactly," Owen said. "More like they've made monsters. These beings they've created are chimeras, an unsustainable mix of species, created to kill. I wanted to keep this knowledge from you. I never wanted you to see them or know about them or ever have your reality shattered by accepting their existence. But Addy convinced me that foreknowledge may be the only thing that can actually save your lives, should you have an encounter that we can't prevent. Bastion will tell you more about them, and then Kit and I will talk about what we're doing to protect you, the town, and all regular humans from them."

Except for Val, whose girlfriend Ace was in training with the team, all the guys reached over to hold the hands of their women. Bastion shut his eyes and sent a calm, centered feeling of strength to the civilians in the room before showing a life-sized illusion of one of the ghouls he'd fought. The women gasped in horror.

Bastion had it turn in a slow circle so that everyone could get a good look at it. "This monster is part man, part dog, sometimes part other animals. The only cognitive function left to it is what comes from the primitive part of its once-human brain that deals with survival. As you might imagine, the non-complementary sets of DNA don't let this ghoul live long. It has extraordinary strength but it cannot think or adapt. Being a mutant, it heals quickly, so killing it is somewhat difficult. It has extraordinary eyesight. Its olfactory senses are better than a bear's. There's absolutely no humanity left in these things, so killing or being killed is their only frame of mind."

Bastion sighed and looked at the ground, briefly avoiding the stricken faces of the women. "Remember when I disappeared Zavi and Troy?" He looked at their mothers. "I did so for a specific reason. These monsters cannot impose illusions or compulsions, but they do react to them. Even if they smell a target human, if they cannot see it, they ignore it. When these things come here, and I believe they will, hiding those of you not trained to fight will be our best defense against them."

Kit came up to stand next to Bastion. "We already run drills training you to get down to the bunker. We're going to tweak those drills to accommodate this new threat."

Kit's wife, Ivy, smoothed her hand over her distended belly. "Is it safe to be disappeared?"

"Completely," Bastion said. "Nothing actually happens to you. It affects anyone or anything observing you. They see the space where you are as it was before you were there. I will show you." He looked at Kit. "I'm volunteering you for this demonstration."

Kit nodded.

Bastion faced the group as he set the illusion over Kit, making it seem he'd disappeared. The women gasped.

"Kit, jump up and down," Bastion said.

"Fuck you, Bastion. Not doing that."

Bastion laughed, knowing no one could see or hear Kit. "What do you see?" Bastion asked the group.

"Nothing," Ivy said, a little fear in her voice.

"Tell us a secret," Bastion told Kit.

Kit let loose a string of cussing that would have made an Army sergeant blush. Midway through it, Bastion removed the illusion shielding him. The women gasped and his team members laughed. Kit actually turned red.

Bastion grinned. "That was just the tail end of his invectives. You should have heard the start of them."

Kit gave him a warning growl before reaching for his throat. Bastion froze him, leaving him visible and aware of his surroundings, but unable to move or speak. "You see, nothing happens when a person is disappeared. And nothing happens to those who would observe a disappeared person, except for a little distorted reality that's temporary." Bastion freed Kit, who gave him a narrow-eyed death stare. Bastion grinned in response.

"I know you have busy schedules," Owen said, "but I need you to make time to train with us so that we can get you and the kids used to what to do if we are overtaken by ghouls."

"What about our animals?" Mandy asked. "My horses, Eddie's dogs. Our pets here?"

"We will hide them as well," Bastion said.

"I don't mean to be morbid or anything," Ace said, "but what happens if you die?"

"That's an excellent question," Bastion said. "My protections will end with me. However, Liege and the others on my team will instantly replace them with their own."

"What if they're in Colorado when it happens?" Eddie asked.

"My team and I are always connected here." Bastion tapped his head. "If I die, they will make their own connections to you. Protecting regulars is what we do."

A FEW OF the team lingered after the meeting, though most retired for the night. Owen, Max, and Greer were there, as were Guerre and Acier. Selena was just about to head upstairs with Bastion when something pinged on Max's phone. He hit a button.

"Your dad and Jax are here," Max said to Owen. "I just let them in."

Owen looked surprised. He crossed the room just as the two men came into the billiards room. He gave his dad a hug, then shook hands with Jax.

"What's brought you guys down from the wilds?" Owen asked.

"We have news," Jax said. His gaze made the rounds in the room, settling on the three men he didn't know.

"So do we. Have you met Liege's men?" Owen asked.

Jax shook his head.

"Bastion, Guerre, Acier—this is my friend and brother-in-law, Wendell Jacobs," Owen said. "We call him Jax. And over there's my dad, Nick."

There was a tense exchange of handshakes. Nick

came over to Selena and gave her a hug. He stood back and took a read of her energy. "The problem's gone from your face."

She smiled. "And no more headaches."

"That's great. I mean that. I was really worried about you."

"I was really worried about me too."

Nick looked at Bastion, who had stayed close to Selena. "As long as you make Selena happy, you make us happy." The threat in that statement was barely veiled.

Bastion smiled widely. "As long as you have her best interests at heart, I am happy."

Nick laughed then grabbed Bastion's shoulder. "All right, then."

Owen went behind the bar and poured out three Balcones. He handed the newcomers their glasses, then took his. "What's the big news you have that had to be delivered in person?"

"We're clear to talk here?" Jax asked.

Max nodded. "We're clear."

"Doc Beck has the results of his analysis back. He'll be calling you in the morning," Jax said.

"But he told you first," Owen said.

"No. The Ratcliffs did. They helped him with the analysis. He sent over tissue slides and blood samples."

"And?" Greer asked, moving closer.

"And it appears that some sophisticated gene splicing wove elements of common canine DNA into specific areas of a human host's DNA, to the degree that the resultant being is its own new phylum."

"Can these things reproduce?" Greer asked.

Jax shook his head. "No. By their very engineering, they're incapable of creating their own offspring."

"We've been hearing urban legends about these monsters," Nick said. "It was too horrific to believe. Much of the news in the world of modifications is exaggerated, so we filed it away with other arcane and unverifiable discoveries."

"I guess this one's true," Max said.

"The Ratcliffs want to come see for themselves," Jax said.

Selena felt Bastion's relief and excitement. "They are welcome," he said. "But it is a dangerous time for them to come. Our enemy, Brett Flynn, is looking for them. I would only move them if they were heavily protected."

"I can go with you," Acier volunteered.

Jax looked at Owen. "Are you good with this?"

Owen didn't answer right away. He looked at Bastion. "To be honest, I do still have my misgivings. We've been working with the Legion for less than two weeks. They've done everything they said they would. They've opened their fort and their staff to us. But they also spied on us for two months."

"We did what we were made to do," Bastion said.

"It's natural to be cautious about forming alliances with those who come from stronger points of power," Nick said, "a lesson learned by colonized people everywhere."

Selena looked at Bastion and his friends, worried they were being insulted in this conversation. They didn't look concerned. They had deeper wells of patience than anyone she'd ever met.

"Selena and I will accompany them," Bastion said. "You trust your own staff, *non*?"

Owen looked from him to her. She spared him answering. "He doesn't. He thinks I'm under your control."

"Fair enough," Bastion said, meeting Owen's glare. "But I am not willing to lose these researchers. They're the only ones in the Omni resistance that we know of so far. They're key in any future we hope to build. Do what must be done to retrieve them safely."

At last, Owen nodded. To Jax, he said, "Stay for a day of training with us. I want you to see what these monsters are capable of. Then leave Nick here for training and take Acier with you to retrieve the doctors."

"I want to bring them to the fort," Acier said. "Every time we move them, we put them at risk. And we have the facilities and corpses for them to study—everything's already set up for them."

Owen and Jax exchanged a long look before Owen nodded.

"I've got it covered, O," Jax said. "Besides, I'd like to see this fort of theirs."

BASTION TOOK Selena's hand as they made their way

444

upstairs to her room. Her fingers threaded through his. Having him with her felt amazing—like he was the piece of her life that had always been missing. Her parents' marriage had always been strong—not always peaceful, but they'd pulled through every challenge together.

Selena had given up hope of finding something similar for herself. Being a soldier, and now a mercenary, with a past—and present—as violent as hers, well, none of that had lent itself to a stable love life.

When they stepped into her room, Bastion pulled her into his arms as he leaned against the wall. "Are your parents still alive?"

Of course he'd been listening in. "They are."

"Call them."

Selena looked up at him, trying to see where he was coming from. His eyes looked sad as he brushed a strand of her hair from her temple. "I could," she said.

"You should."

"Is there something you're not telling me?" She looked up at him. "Do you see the future?"

"I don't know."

"Really, that's a yes-or-no question."

"I've had a premonition. It's my first, so I don't yet know if I'm seeing the future."

Selena stepped away, backing up to the opposite wall, her hands tucked behind her. "What did you see?"

"I saw you injured in a fight."

She shook her head. "That might just have been you fearing the Matchmaker's curse."

"True. Losing you would kill me."

She stared at him a long moment. "It's late now. I'll call them tomorrow."

∾

BASTION WENT into the wider area of her room to strip for bed. She was an exceedingly neat person, so he gathered up his clothes and took them into her closet to the hamper. She was just pulling on knit shorts and a T-shirt.

Standing behind her, he slipped his arm around her waist. "You don't need clothes. You'll be out of them in just a minute."

She leaned against him. "I have to brush my teeth." Left unsaid was the fact that she still didn't like looking at herself naked.

He kissed the crown of her head, struck by another knowing that he was going to lose her. If they could have a normal lifetime together, he would have a chance to change her mind about herself.

But that was not going to be their fate.

He stepped away from her. They had the time they had. It was all any couple had. He couldn't waste it being sad. If these were her last days, he'd make them extraordinary for her.

"Do you mind if I go talk to Guerre and Acier for a few minutes?" he asked. "I want to get their take on the meeting tonight."

"Sure. And you probably need to update Liege. He'll be glad to hear about the Ratcliffs."

"No need to update him. He was with us today." He tapped his head. "In here. He was already patched in. He heard and saw what we did."

She wrapped her arms around his waist and lifted her face for a kiss. Bastion met her halfway. It was good he had perfect memory. He'd be able to revisit every single second of their time together. After her, he would live his entire life in the past.

Was that how Merc felt? Not dying, but not living?

He kissed Selena's forehead. "I won't be long." He pulled a pair of jeans on, then paused at the door. "What vista do you want tonight?"

She was brushing her teeth but smiled around the electric toothbrush. "An ocean," she mumbled.

Bastion smiled. "Done."

He walked down the hall to the room the guys shared. The door opened as he approached it. Guerre was sitting up on one of the extra-long twin beds. Acier was sitting in a side chair, his bare feet on the coffee table.

"Well, you look like an ice-cold drink of doom," Acier said.

Bastion leaned against the dresser. "I had another knowing."

Acier's face sobered. "Shit."

Guerre was silently watching him.

"You have knowings," Bastion said to Guerre. "Have any of them ever *not* come true?"

"No," Guerre answered.

Bastion's eyes watered. This had to be what Merc

felt day in and day out. How did he manage to keep breathing?

"It hasn't happened yet, Bastion," Acier said. "Think of it as a warning. We'll protect her."

"We don't have long," Bastion said. "The team has tried hard, but they are not ready for what's coming."

Acier dropped his feet to the ground and leaned forward. "We face the ghouls all the time. This is just another fight. There are three of us here."

Guerre looked at Acier. "This isn't just another fight."

"And there aren't three of us," Bastion said. "You'll be with Jax."

"Then I'll stay here."

Guerre shook his head. "The Ratcliffs need protection."

Bastion heaved a harsh breath, then swiped a hand from his forehead to his chin, trying to push his sorrow down deep into his chest.

He walked out of the room without another word. Liege was a master of control, but it had never been Bastion's strength. Somehow, he was going to have to make it his, because everything he did from this point forward mattered.

He returned to Selena's room. She was on the bed. Naked. Moonlight from the illusion he'd set on her ceiling washed her in a bluish light. She tore her eyes away from the stars and the tips of the palm trees to smile at him. With the distant sound of crashing waves, he could almost pretend they had forever, not mere hours.

He forced himself to smile back at her. He striped in the closet, leaving his things on floor. The illusion of moonlight covered Selena in a silvery-blue glow. He kneeled on the foot of the bed, letting himself feast on the sight of her. He picked one of her feet up, kissed the bottom of it, then set it beside him, widening the spread of her legs. He repeated that with her other foot.

He leaned down and kissed her ankles, one after the other, knowing his beard triggered shivery sensations against her skin. Slowly, he kissed his way up to her knee on one leg, then did the same on her other leg.

He was on all fours when he got to her thighs. He bent her leg, grazing his teeth against her soft inner skin. He raked his teeth along the same stretch of skin on her other thigh. When he was finished, both thighs were spread open, baring her core.

He settled himself deep between her legs, his shoulders blocking her legs from closing as he pushed his palms under her ass and brought his face to her secret center. He licked the sweet, sensitive skin from her opening to her clit, making her moan. The sound went right to his cock. He rocked himself against the mattress, wishing he were inside her.

He focused on her clit, making long strokes over it with his tongue. Her hips bucked. He gripped them, not ready for her to orgasm yet. He swept his tongue back and forth over her sensitive nub. Selena made a mewling sound, and when he gently sucked on her clit, she cried out.

Sitting up, she curled over him, wrapping her arms around his head, pressing his face even closer. "Bastion...please —"

He lifted his head. "Please what? This?" He penetrated her with his tongue. After a few soft, wet thrusts, he sucked her clit again. "Or that?"

"All of it. All of you. Now."

"Are you sure?" He licked his lips.

"Quit fucking talking."

He grinned as he crawled over her. He lifted her hips and entered her. She hadn't forbidden this position, and he was glad for that. It was one of the few that let him see her response to what he was doing. Her eyes were locked with his as he made shallow thrusts, hitting her g-spot. Her body responded as he knew it would, with an orgasm that hit fast and hard, ripping through her so that she cried out in shock and pleasure. He kept it going as long as he could before nearing his own release. He slipped all the way in and almost all the way out, faster and faster, until he was pounding into her. He held himself deep in her when his peak hit, letting her body milk his.

When it was over, he settled her back on the mattress and withdrew, then moved up to lie next to her. She snuggled into him so easily. He kissed her forehead, loving the feel of her warm body and luscious curves pressed against him.

"Bastion, do you remember when Liege was here that first day we were training? I cut my hand."

"I remember."

"Did you hear what Liege said to me when he grabbed my hand?"

"No. I remember you cutting your hand, but truthfully, I can't remember seeing him speak to you. He must have blocked it from us."

"He said I was Legion."

Bastion looked down at her. "Did he?"

"What did he mean by that?"

"It means he's accepted you into the Legion."

She pushed herself up to look at him. "Do I have to leave my team?"

"Not necessarily. We have Legionnaires all over the world. He said that to each of us as he accepted us. It's always a private moment."

"But you don't think I can keep up with you guys."

Bastion stroked the side of her face, wondering how to answer that. "You could if you were changed. All that you are as a regular becomes more so as a mutant. You're strong, resourceful, determined, brave, kind, brilliant. As a mutant, you would put all of us to shame."

"Then I want to change. Not to outshine any of you, but to be a better me."

Bastion leaned forward and nodded as he kissed her. Maybe it wouldn't be the ghouls that took her but the modifications instead. His premonition had become blurred by his fear.

Her lips were soft beneath his, so responsive. He slid

his hand into her hair, covering her ear as he deepened the kiss. She wrapped her arms around his neck, drawing him closer. He moved his hand down to cup a breast. That full, beautiful mound was bigger than his hand. He dipped his head to taste her peaked flesh. Impossibly, his cock got harder.

He kissed her collarbone, her throat. Her skin was warm and sweet. Slowly, he moved one leg between hers, then the other, moving his body so that he was lying on her. He slipped his hands under her shoulders as he gazed down into her tawny green eyes, then slowly entered her.

She opened her legs wider, shifting to accommodate him. He moved in her leisurely, letting them both feel him sliding in, and out, and in.

At one point, her shadows slipped between them. "Selena, take hold of my beard," he whispered, knowing that would anchor her here, with him, now.

She did that, pulling his face down to hers so she could kiss him. Her breathing was irregular. This was the first time they'd made love in this position. It felt divine to him, but was full of terrors for her.

He rolled them over so that she was on top. Instantly, he felt her body relax.

"Bastion?"

"Hm-mm?"

"Thank you." She pushed herself into an upright position and took over their movements, riding him in a beautiful rhythm. She arched her back. Her long, dark hair moved around her chest and shoulders.

He reached down to where their bodies were joined and pressed his thumb against her clit. Her tempo sped up with each rotation until she leaned over him and let go of her control. As soon as he felt her inner muscles clamping and releasing, tightening over him, he wrapped his arms around her, holding her close as he bucked up into her, thrusting hard and fast, prolonging her orgasm as he chased his. It hit him hard, exploding into her body.

After a long moment, she kissed him and said, "If you were a river, I'd be the boulders that shredded you into white water when you moved over me so that you could know what passion felt like."

Bastion smiled. "If you were a desert, I'd be the rain you were so hungry for."

"If you were a big evergreen, I'd be a nest of robins to keep you company."

Bastion used both hands to smooth her heavy hair from her face. "If you were mine, I'd love you forever."

"I am yours."

"Then I will love you forever."

"Do you?"

"Yes."

"Is that what this is? Because it kinda hurts."

"That's what this is."

"I love you, Bastion."

"I love you, Selena."

36

Selena was on her way to her room after breakfast the next morning, when she saw Hawk standing outside her door. He hadn't seen her yet. She had the strangest, most visceral reaction that she should turn around and slip away, fast, before he saw her.

She didn't. "Hawk. What can I do for you?"

He looked at her, then quickly looked away. His hands were fisted.

She frowned. Bastion had warned her to stay away from him, which hadn't been difficult with him away at school in Colorado. He and Lion didn't come home every weekend, so it was only a few days a month that he was an issue. "What's going on?"

He didn't meet her eyes. It was as if he was at war with himself, and she was the bystander about to get blown up. "I need to ask you something, and I don't want the others to know."

"Okaaaay. Let's have it."

"How did you know Bastion was visiting you?"

Not what she'd expected. "You mean when I couldn't see him or feel him or in any other way know that he was around me?"

Hawk nodded.

"He has a strong personality and a heavy French accent. Whenever he spoke to me, or even just slipped into my mind, he never hid himself from me. He would speak to me mentally, but always in his accent, with his words. Why are you asking this? Has someone been visiting you?" Selena thought of what Liege had told them all, that Brett Flynn liked to possess men who could do his dirty deeds.

"No. That would be crazy." Hawk shook his head too vigorously. "I just wondered how this all worked, with the mutants."

"Hawk, let's have a seat." She went over to one of the cushioned benches tucked into the hallway's wall and sat down. He reluctantly followed her. Close now, she could see the tension in his face, his red-rimmed eyes, his pale skin.

Everything was not all right. "Talk to me," Selena said.

He lifted his blue eyes and stared right into hers. His demeanor shifted. He squeezed his eyes shut, then grimaced as his eyes slowly opened, almost as if against his own will. He leaned forward and drew a long breath of her. Catching his throat in the crook of her hand, she shoved him away from her. He didn't fight back, didn't shake himself free of whatever had him in its grips.

No, he just started to laugh.

The sound was sickening, pulling at long-buried memories from a time when she was only a few years younger than he was now.

Bastion, I need you up here now.

"You smell so good, just as you did then." Hawk reached a hand out and almost touched her cheek with his fingers. "Too bad you've been marred."

Selena touched the faint scar Mouse's riata left that night last summer when the pride tried to kidnap Casey.

Hawk flattened his hand against his own cheek, pressing against his skin until it whitened beneath his palm. "Your scar is so much smaller than my own. I have wanted to find you and carve you up as you did me." Hawk smiled. "And now I have. And I will."

More sickening laughter.

Selena jumped up and backed away from the bench. Bastion was already coming toward them. He must have felt her reaction before she'd even summoned him, given how fast he made it up to her.

"Selena, go to the den and wait for me there," Bastion said.

Her hackles shot up. Okay, for one, she was not about to be dismissed. For two, Hawk was one of theirs, part of the pride. She wasn't about to leave him to face Bastion alone, despite whatever he'd gotten himself into that made him act like this.

The expression on Bastion's face was one she'd never seen, like he was trying to keep a rabid dog calm—whether that dog was her or Hawk, she wasn't sure.

He faced her. *It is for your own safety, Selena.*

Hawk isn't a threat to me.

No, he isn't, but he's two people right now. Hawk...and Flynn. I've summoned Liege to expel him from Hawk.

Should we lock him in one of the rooms up here? she asked.

He could get himself out of any restraint. Left free to roam here...he could do too much harm. He already has. Now Flynn knows everything about this house and its layout. Go tell your team what's happening.

You should do that. I don't fully understand it.

Bastion shook his head. *I'm the only one who can contain Hawk. I have him in a trance and will keep him calm. When Liege gets here, he'll get rid of Flynn. If Flynn jumps out of him and follows you, I don't want you to take him to sensitive areas in the house. Go. Keep everyone out of this hallway. And don't go to the bunker. We don't know where Hawk has taken Flynn, but if he hasn't seen the bunker or its secret entrances, all the better.*

How will I know if he follows me? Selena asked.

Chances are you won't, unless you're very sensitive to changes in the energy around you. You're making progress in that area, but you still need much more training and experience.

Flynn said he wanted to cut me.

Bastion nodded. *Flynn would say—and want—that. I've been afraid of this. Gather the others. I'll let you know if Flynn leaves Hawk.*

Selena turned down the hallway to go to the main stairs. Activating her comm unit, she said, "Kit, I need to see you in the den. Can you get the guys together?"

"Affirmative. What's up?" Kit asked.

"Big problem. We'll talk in the den."

"Roger that."

Lion was coming up the stairs, taking the steps three at a time. On the landing, he almost ran into her. She put a hand on his chest and stopped him when he tried to skirt around her. "Come with me."

"I can't. I have to find Hawk."

"Why?"

Lion stared at her, then rocked back on his heels as he chose his words carefully. "He's been odd lately. I don't think he's taking to school life very well."

"Odd in what way?"

Lion shrugged. "Quiet. Preoccupied. Distant."

"How long has that been going on?"

"Almost since we got to school. I talked to a counselor there. She said some of us have a harder time adjusting than others." Lion looked away from Selena, then lowered his gaze. "I don't think that's what he's going through. His personality is different. He's not himself. I thought, maybe, he got into some drugs, but that's not it."

Selena gripped Lion's sleeve. "I know what's happening to him, but we can't talk here. Let's go to the den. I've asked Kit to call the team together."

"No. I don't want to talk about this in front of them. They'll yank him from school and kick him, us, the pride, out of the house."

"That's not going to happen."

"If it's drugs, it is."

"It's not drugs. Trust me. This is a big problem, but he's not the cause of it."

Lion shot a last glance upstairs, then followed Selena down. The team was coming in from all over the house. Kit and Owen were already in the den when Selena and Lion got there. Val was the last one in. He closed the door behind him.

"You're up, Sel," Kit said.

Selena looked around at her teammates, wondering how to broach this subject. "Bastion's enemy, Brett Flynn, has possessed Hawk."

Silence met that revelation until Val said, "Yeah, like I said, we left Kansas long ago. We're in the Twilight Zone now."

"What does that even mean, Sel?" Kit asked.

"How could something like that happen?" Blade asked.

"I don't know how it happened or what it means, but it's something that Bastion isn't surprised about. Liege is coming over to get rid of Flynn." Selena crossed her arms. "I honestly don't know what any of this means, other than to state the obvious, which is that the Legion's enemy has been using Hawk to spy on us."

"For how long?" Owen asked.

"He's not been himself for a while now," Lion said. "Since shortly after we started at the community college. A month. Maybe less."

"You know, Lion, you can always come to us," Max said.

Lion's shoulders slumped. "I didn't know it was anything at first. I thought he was just having problems getting used to school life. And then I caught him following women. Stalking them. We started to fight. His behavior changed so much, I was afraid he was doing drugs." Lion looked at Max. "I thought you'd kick us out."

Max's smile was sad. "You and the pride are part of our team, for as long as you want to be. We aren't going to kick you guys out. You got problems, we'll figure them out."

"Lion," Selena said, "Hawk will be fine."

"What if he's been permanently damaged?" Lion asked, voicing the worst of his fears.

"We'll know after Liege is done," Selena said.

Max gave the kid a sideways hug. "Don't borrow trouble, Lion."

"The truth is that things have changed rapidly for all of us," Kit said. "With these human mutations, new skills and abilities have been brought forward, and they aren't all being used in ethical ways. We're still learning about these new capabilities, so we're as naive and unprotected as you boys. All I can say is that you have to be on the lookout for changes in personalities and behaviors—in yourself and others. Listen to your gut. Instinct is your best guide—now more than ever."

"We were trained to infiltrate and observe," Owen said. "But these new modifications are out-gaming us. So stay aware. If something doesn't make sense, don't ignore it. If something seems odd, pay attention to it. Bring it to the team." He looked around at the group. "That goes for everyone."

HOURS LATER, Bastion looked up as Liege joined the crew in the bunker, a cautious Hawk right behind him. The group had moved to the conference room to wait for news of Liege's work with Hawk.

"Hold it," Owen said, standing. "I don't want Hawk in here."

"He's clean," Liege said. "I've pushed Flynn from him. And I reinforced Bastion's protection on the house. Flynn won't be able to get back in. Nor will he be able to use Hawk again. He may, however, try to hit someone else."

Bastion was glad Liege had brought Hawk down to the group, though the kid looked shaken and fatigued. Lion waved Hawk over to sit next to him at the table.

"I'm glad you're better," Angel said. "Can you tell us what it was like? We need to know in case it happens to us."

Hawk looked around at the group. *Dieu*, he looked haunted as all hell. "I don't really know. It felt crowded in my head. I wasn't in command of my own body. I knew what I was doing, and I knew that I wasn't choosing to do it, and I knew that I was incapable of going to Lion or anyone for help. It's like Flynn owned me." Hawk looked at Liege. "If you hadn't pushed him out of me, I would have done something terrible." He shot a glance at Selena. "I would've hurt you. Flynn knows you."

The quiet that came over the room at that revelation held for a beat.

Liege nodded. "As I said, I put a protection on Hawk and on the house, but Flynn's coming for Selena."

Bastion was torn between what Selena had told him in confidence and what this team needed to understand for their own safety. "Flynn has attacked many women, but Selena's the only one who survived. He's coming to take care of that oversight."

"Then I have to leave," Selena said.

Bastion could feel the emotion behind her statement. He knew the sorrow that decision brought her — the isolation, the stress of being separated from friends. It was why he hadn't entered the service alone, why he'd talked his brother into following him. Why he brought his brother into the medical trials. He hadn't known they were going to be genetically modified, only that they were volunteering to test an intense new health regimen that would help their fellow soldiers. His need for connection had gotten his brother killed.

Selena's attachment to her team was exactly the same as he with his team. The relief he'd felt when he met Liege, Merc, and Guerre in the camps was huge. He wasn't wired to be a loner, and nor was she. "You can come to the fort with us."

Liege shook his head. "It won't matter. You are, of course, welcome at the fort. And I think perhaps it is where you belong now. But Flynn saw you here, and here is where he'll return again and again to find you."

"But you put a protection on our compound," Blade said. "Can he get through that?"

"He can't get through it, but he will track every single person who leaves here, watching where they go, seeing who they interact with. Flynn"—Liege looked at Owen—"as are all mutants like us, is wired for persistence. And while Bastion and I have a protection on Hawk and the property, he may find a way through. He hasn't yet—I have the same protection on my daughter's shelter, which he hasn't broken through. But you have to know that our skills are still evolving—he may find a way in."

"So what does it mean when you say you put a protection on Blade's property?" Owen asked.

"Everything is energy," Liege said. "You know that what appears as something solid is really a collection of atoms bouncing around at different frequencies. Whether that matter is living biomass or nonbiological, science has proven that what we think is solid isn't. You also know that there are different kinds of energy waves around us: cell phone signals, radio waves, Wi-Fi, microwaves. We are surrounded by energy that we either can't comprehend or don't see. Everything is energy, and the enhancements made to us help us see energy. We can observe it and use it to our benefit. Setting a protection over people and property is nothing more than creating an energy field using rules we define.

"When something that is specifically excluded from entering the energy field comes near it, all kinds of alerts sound—figuratively, of course—within the being who set the energy field. It isn't something the uninitiated would even be aware of. My team knows the feel of my energy and would know if I'd put a protection on someone or someplace. Energy fields are as unique to the individual as any other biometric measurement."

"So that should stop Flynn from slipping back into the house or the grounds," Greer said. "But what if he doesn't piggyback in someone he's possessing? What if he does what Bastion did and comes in as an astral traveler?"

"It should work for that as well. He hasn't been able to penetrate our protections yet, but it doesn't mean it won't happen. As mutants, our abilities are always changing, and he is a very strong mutant."

"So we need to figure out some sort of a sensor that can respond to a foreign energy entering the compound," Greer said.

Bastion shook his head. "There is no sensor yet created that can sense thought. Astral travelers are not as substantial as ghosts; they are nothing more than thoughts."

"But you can sense the energy another being projects," Blade said.

"We can," Liege said.

"So how do you do it?" Blade asked.

"It's different for each of us," Bastion said. "Some sense energy in a vague way that gives them goose bumps—this level of sensory perception is common among regulars. Others can see energy, like I can. Others hear energy—each of us emits an energetic sound that is unique. Some taste energy and can distinguish between different entities based on their flavor, as regulars can taste different apple flavors. By tasting, I just mean that that is how some mutants experience the energy, not that they actually taste someone." He shook his head as he looked around at the group. Trying to explain enhanced mutant senses to regulars was like teaching someone to tie a shoe when they had no hands.

"We were taught to use our higher-level senses after we were modified," Guerre said. "Training to master all of our new abilities was the purpose of the camps."

"Bastion," Owen said, "you are able to astral travel, right?"

Bastion nodded. "*Oui.*"

"I want you to work with Greer and Max to come up with a technological sensor that we can deploy so that we know when we are being visited."

"I mean no disrespect," Bastion said, "but there is nothing yet developed that can sense thought. Yes, thought is a vibration and therefore an energy, but it is out of the spectrum of human sensors. An astral projection is nothing more than a thought. It has no heat signature; it doesn't change light waves. And even if, in the future a tool were to be developed, an astral projection could disable such sensors in the same way that I disabled cameras when I was coming through the house."

"But animals are more sensitive to these types of energies than humans, correct?" Blade asked.

"They are," Bastion said.

"My wife, Eden, trains dogs. Could she train one to sense an astral visitor?" Blade asked.

Bastion smiled. "Indeed. I do think it would work. The dogs who live here did sense me, but I was able to assure them I meant no ill will. I think we could find a way to get dogs to patrol for unwanted visitors."

"That's an excellent idea," Liege said.

Blade checked with Kit, who checked with Owen, to see if it was going to fly. Owen nodded. Blade took out his cell phone and called Eden, who was at her kennel on the property. "Hey, babe. Can you join us down in the bunker? We need to talk to you about something. Right. Sounds good." When he hung up, he told the group, "She's just finishing up and will be here in a few minutes. So while I admit it's a great idea, I have no idea how to implement it. Or even explain it to her."

"Everyone on my team can astral project. We'll all be able to help as needed on this," Liege said. "It won't be a fast solution, but it should be a viable one. I like the idea of having a resource like this as we move forward in our fight against the Omnis."

A few minutes later, Eden came into the room. She looked around at the group, visibly working to keep her cool. Bastion supposed being summoned to the conference room rarely meant good news.

"Eden, we have a new project for you," Blade said. "We need you to train dogs to sound an alert when astral travelers are somewhere on the compound."

Eden started to chuckle. "Fuck you, Blade." She turned and headed toward the door.

"Eddie," Owen said, stopping her. "It sounds outrageous, but we're serious."

Eden was halfway to the door when she slowly turned back to face the room. "You're serious?"

In the time he'd been surveilling this group, Bastion had learned that Owen didn't have an ounce of humor in his body, so his assertion hit home.

Blade slipped an arm around her waist and walked her back toward the group. "You know that mutants have extraordinary mental capabilities. We've just discovered that the Legion's enemy, Brett Flynn, may begin visiting our compound while in a state of astral travel. There are no physical sensors that can identify anyone doing that, or at least one that couldn't be tampered with. That means we need a reliable source sensitive to certain energies that humans can't perceive. I was wondering if you could train some dogs to do this for us."

"I train them to sniff for ordnance and drugs. Not ghosts."

"Astral travel isn't the same type of energy as ghosts," Bastion said. "The dogs here sensed me when I was visiting. If they could sense me, they can sense Brett Flynn."

"How long do you think it would take to train dogs to patrol the house and the grounds for this new threat?" Kit asked.

Eden shook her head. "I can't believe we're actually having this discussion." She looked at Blade as if hoping he'd bust out laughing and tell her she'd just been punked.

No one laughed.

"Well, supposing we have access to astral travelers on demand, three to six months. I don't know. This is way out of my area of expertise."

"But it can be done, correct?" Owen asked.

"I honestly don't know," Eden said. "I'm willing to give it a go. I'll need to visit some shelters to find dogs that might fit this new agenda. It's not going to be a fast program, since it's new to me and filled with unknowns."

"Get started," Owen said. "Blade, go with her. Take the time you need, but be quick about it."

37

The skeptical vibe was heavy in the room the next day when Bastion began his astral travel work with a subset of Selena's team. He kept his amusement to himself, but he was really looking forward to this session. Stuff like this was second nature to all Legionnaires. He intended to have fun with it, while still demonstrating the power of astral travel.

He had the group push the long conference table off to the side, giving them room to work. "Let's start with the basics. Are you all familiar with what astral travel is?"

Greer was the only one who felt comfortable with the topic, so Bastion explained it to the others. "Astral travel is where someone's consciousness leaves their body to go to a physical destination elsewhere. That is about the only thing in common with most mutants, because every mutant can bring with them into their astral travel additional skills. For instance, I can still manipulate physical material telekinetically while in an astral state, though it takes some intense concentration. Some cannot do that. Others can do even more, like bilocate. They can split their consciousness into multiple instances, allowing them some level of continued activity in their physical bodies, while also manipulating their astral self in a way that simulates their physical bodies. Flynn can do the latter. A regular encountering him in his astral state might comprehend him as a physical being. They could touch him, see him, fight him. He is a very powerful foe."

"So how are you going to train us to do these things?" Kit asked.

"I'm not." Bastion shook his head. "Unless you take the human modifications, you will need years to conquer the ability to astral travel. Instead, I'm going to work on broadening your narrow perception of reality so that you can know when you are in the midst of a mutant in his astral state."

The guys swapped tense glances. Bastion wondered where they were in their discussions among themselves and with their families about becoming modified fighters. He wished he could talk to the Ratcliffs to see if Selena was right, that significant improvements had been made in the science of human mutations, making them safer. Nick had come through the change successfully, as had the Ratcliffs themselves.

If, and only if, it was much safer to do now than it had been when he and his brother took the changes, Bastion would be in favor of having these fighters undergo the procedure. And if Merc was able to find and retrieve Santo to oversee their mutant training, then it wouldn't all be for naught.

"Let's begin. It's important for you to understand that an astral body is not limited as a physical body. In my astral state, I can walk through walls, travel great distances at the speed of thought. I'll show you."

He took a seat at the conference table, choosing one that was stuck in the corner so it would be harder for his physical self to get in and out of. Everyone in the room turned to face him. He had to fight to keep his smile off his face as he closed his eyes. He just wished he could see their faces when he did what he was about to do.

In astral form, he popped up behind them, keeping himself visible. They stood in a semicircle, waiting for something to happen with his body in the chair. When nothing did, they got restless, thinking he was playing a joke on them.

"Yo, Bastion, wakey-wakey," Max said. "Lousy time for a nap."

Bastion's astral self laughed audibly, shocking them.

"Jesus, Mary, and Joseph," Kit barked, looking from Bastion's projection to his physical self, which was still sitting peacefully in the chair.

"Hi," Bastion said, laughing so hard inside that it was difficult to keep his concentration. Each of the four men came over to his astral projection and tried to touch him. Their hands went right through.

"Shit," Max said. "This is real."

"Or is it?" Blade asked. "Maybe this is a mass hallucination he's imposed on us."

Bastion nodded. "I could do that too. Such things are child's play."

"You said you can move physical things while you're like this?" Kit asked.

Bastion thought of those terrible moments in the shower with Selena and her box cutter. "I can, but for me it takes extreme concentration. For Flynn, it would be easy. Give me a test."

Max and Greer looked at each other. Greer whispered something to Bastion. He disappeared, then reappeared in the ops room, grabbed Greer's favorite pen, and took it into the bunkroom, dropping on the first lower bunk. He reappeared to the group.

"It's done."

Greer smiled. "I told him to take my green pen and put it in the bunkroom."

The group went out of the conference room, down the hall, and into the bunkroom. Blade grabbed the pen and handed it to Greer.

The four men returned to the conference room with a lot less bluster than when Bastion started the session.

Bastion had returned to himself and was sitting up, waiting for them. The guys sat at the table, stunned and so full of questions that they didn't know where to begin.

"Astral travel is the perfect vehicle for spies," Kit said.

"Correct. And that is exactly what we were specially

programmed to be. Allowing ourselves to be visible to regulars is a danger we've long avoided. Opening ourselves to you takes a lot of trust—on both of our parts."

He looked at the group, now lost in their own thoughts as they amended their sense of reality. It was something regulars clung to as the end all, be all that kept chaos at bay. He regretted having to tell them it was something that had never existed in accordance with their beliefs.

"Let's do an exercise to get a feel for how sensitive you are to energy," Bastion said. "It's important for you to know that your sense of energy is basically dormant and wholly undeveloped"—he looked at Greer—"except for you. But then, you received training from Santo when you were boy."

Greer nodded. "How did you know?"

"Liege read all of you when he first visited. Santo wasn't changed at that point, but his instincts were highly developed." Bastion nodded at Kit. "Come sit on this side of the table. The rest of you, sit opposite him."

They all took their seats. "Kit, I'm going to give you three orders to give your guys." Bastion looked at the three. "Each of you will do what Kit orders you, as he orders you."

Bastion compelled Kit to point to Blade and order him to say his name.

Blade looked at Kit, shaking his head once as if to clear it. He squinted, clearly seeing that Kit was talking to him but unable to hear it.

Bastion then compelled Kit to point to Greer and order him to say his name. Greer heard the order and shouted out his name, but no sound came from his mouth.

Last, Bastion compelled Kit to write an order down on paper and pass it over to Max. Max took the pad of paper, but just set it down, awaiting his own order; he'd lost his eyesight and needed an audible instruction.

Bastion removed those energetic blocks and smiled at the team's confused faces. "You, Blade, couldn't hear the order. You, Greer, couldn't speak in response to it. And you, Max, couldn't see the order."

Kit chuckled. "My three monkeys—couldn't hear, speak, or see evil."

"This is what you'll be up against when you confront a modified Omni. It's why I suggested you get out of the battle side of the fight and get into the support side of it."

"Or take the mods," Max said.

Bastion felt wrecked. He shook his head. "My brother—my best friend—followed me into the program. Neither of us knew what we were getting into. He didn't survive the changes forced on him. It is dangerous to be modified."

Max pushed his chair back violently and prowled around the room. "I have no one but Hope. No family. No children. Only my wife." He looked at Bastion. "I'm healthy, strong, mentally stable." Greer snorted, which Max ignored. "I'm a good candidate."

"All of you here are good candidates," Bastion said.

"But what happens to your body is major. My brother was as healthy as I was at the time, and he didn't make it through." He stared at Max a long moment. "If this is something you're open to, and if your wife is on board, then let's talk to the Ratcliffs. Their knowledge is better than mine. And they'd likely be the ones doing the procedure."

Max nodded. "I don't see a way around it. How can we contribute when we're up against mutants like you?"

"We'll talk to the Ratcliffs when they get to the fort," Kit said. "For now, our focus isn't on the mutant Omnis but the chimeras they've created—and on helping Eddie get her dogs up to speed."

AFTER LUNCH, the women and children gathered in the gym. The kids were boisterous, excited for whatever the security lesson would bring. The women were tense.

Bastion looked at Guerre, hating with a passion that he was going to have to scare them. "How do we do this? I don't even know where to begin. I don't want to do this. We're supposed to protect regulars like these, not expose them to our reality."

"These aren't normal regulars, Bastion," Guerre said. "These are the families of warriors. They know what their husbands do. They know the risks they face. Even the wild ones, maybe especially them, come from a side of life most humans could never understand. They are all strong enough for this."

"No one is strong enough for this."

"We do what we have to do," Guerre said. "You will find the strength for it, because what we're about to do will save their lives."

Bastion bowed his head and shut his eyes, trying to center himself. A slim, warm hand slipped into his. He looked up to see Selena standing next to him. *I think I'm having a panic attack,* he told her. *Doing this goes against everything I stand for.*

She nodded. *That's why I came over. Rocco and Kit will open this session and set the stage. They know the kids—they'll break it to them in a way that is not terrible.*

Please, have the pregnant women sit off to the side. I don't want them to faint.

On it. Selena went over and took Ivy and Mandy to the stadium seating. Both already looked terrified. He was glad that Selena sat between them and gripped their hands.

Calm yourself, Liege said, speaking via their telepathic link as he was monitoring the exercise from the fort in Colorado.

I'm going to vomit, Bastion answered.

It is what must be done. Better they experience this now among friendlies than during the heat of the moment. Keep it light, make it a challenge.

Merde, alors. *Liege, these are monsters coming for them, not a doughy purple dinosaur with a perpetual giggle.*

They will take their energy and response from you. Lead them.

Kit came up to Bastion and Guerre. "Before we

476

begin, can we somehow contain this information in their minds so that they can discuss it freely here but nowhere else? I want them to be able to talk about this and remember these lessons, but I don't want it slipping out in public."

Guerre nodded. "We will impose that constraint."

Kit held up his hands, getting the room to form a circle and be quiet. "You guys all know we've been working with a team like ours from Colorado. And you know that Troy and Augie's granddad is an altered human. I'm sure you've noticed that he looks as young as their dad. You also probably know that your teacher's parents, the Ratcliffs, are altered humans. You also know that we've been trying to deal with an anarchist group called the Omnis for a long time. What you don't know is that the Omnis have begun making other kinds of beings."

"What do you mean by 'beings,' Dad?" Casey asked.

"These are things that didn't make it through the modification process as expected. Whether that's intentional, we don't know. But the long and short of it is that the Omnis are creating...well...monsters."

Some of the younger pride boys moved closer to their brothers, some reaching for each other's hands. This was wrong on so many levels. He wanted to scoop all these civilians up and force them to go to the fort, where they would be safe and protected and would never need to know the ugly side of mutant life.

"Bastion, would you please show the group an example of what I'm talking about?" Kit requested.

"I cannot."

Bastion, it is for their own safety, Selena said.

It will fucking shred their young minds. He slapped a hand on Guerre's chest. *You will not show the ghouls either. But I have an idea. Follow my lead.*

"Let's make a game of this, *oui*? I have seen you play. You're favorite monster at the moment is a thing you call the wendigo. For our purposes, that will do nicely. In this game, let's say the wendigo is trying to catch you and eat you. There are ways you can escape him. Both involve getting down to the bunker. I know you've run drills here practicing that, so for our game today, let's say that blue tumbling pad to your right is the elevator that leads downstairs. And that one to your left is the access in the den. All of you are familiar with both of those, *oui*?"

Everyone indicated they knew the drill.

"Ladies, Jim and Russ, this exercise applies to you as well. When Guerre whistles, you lead as many of the kids as you can round up to one access point or another. All of you need to end up on one of the blue pads."

"Lion, come forward," Guerre said, taking over the exercise, as he was fully tuned in to what Bastion had in mind via their mental link. "You are going to represent the wendigo." Guerre looked around Lion at the kids. "I am going to give him a mask that will make him look like the monster you want to run from. Lion, they will see you as a monster. Roar and make terrible noises as you chase them to one pad or the other."

Lion nodded. Guerre changed Lion's appearance so

that from the shoulders up, he looked like a ghoul. But his arms and body were just his regular self, mitigating the impact. He slowly turned to face the group. The kids screamed in delighted terror. Guerre whistled.

The chase was on.

Lion often played with the wild boys, so this game was something familiar to them, although prior to this, they'd all had to imagine what a horrible wendigo looked like. Lion shouted. Women and children ran, bunching together on the different pads, laughing and trembling.

When Lion turned around, there was only one boy left on the court. The littlest wild boy of all, he was crouched in a small ball, his head tucked down near his knees. Kids from both pads shouted for him to come to them, but the boy was frozen in terror as Lion stomped closer and closer.

Bastion choked on a broken breath. This play was all too close to the reality of what might happen. He made the boy invisible — no one on the pads could see him. Lion had to look around, wondering where he went.

When the wendigo failed to get him, the little boy ventured a look up. Bastion nodded and smiled at him. "No one can see you. I've hidden you. You will be safe if you can get to one of the pads."

The boy slowly stood up, never taking his eyes off Lion. The boys had stopped calling him over — they didn't know where he'd gone. The boy took a step, then another and another, until he ran to the pad that represented the den. As soon as he stepped on it, Bastion allowed him to be seen again.

Everyone on both pads laughed and clapped, and the ones near the boy slapped him on the back.

Guerre removed the mask from Lion. "Very good. Well done, all of you. Now let's go over what happened."

"They need battle buddies," Rocco said. "Every one of them needs to be responsible for a friend."

"Good call," Kit agreed. "We can't have anyone left behind."

Bastion looked over at Selena, who was still holding the women's hands in a white-knuckled grip. She nodded. He nodded back. This had been a good exercise. If all went well when—and if—the ghouls came, the kids would get to their safe spots without ever setting eyes on the ghouls.

This was all right. It was going to be okay.

THE BIG BLUE gates swung open as Acier returned to the fort with Jax and the Ratcliffs. Bastion and Guerre were up at the Red Team's headquarters in Wyoming. Only Liege and Summer were there to greet them.

Acier brought them across the open courtyard and straight into the long living room. He could feel anxiety rolling off Jax and the researchers. Liege was genuinely excited, and Summer was happy to meet anyone living so deep in Liege's world. The two of them made a good pair. Summer was chatty with the newcomers, giving Liege a chance to read both of them.

He seemed pleased with what he discovered. "We've been looking for researchers like you for years now, ever since we left the training camps. I'm glad you're here. I hope you'll make the fort your home, at least for a while. We have a lot of ground to cover."

The Ratcliffs checked with Jax, who'd been responsible for their safety for several months. He nodded at them. "It's up to you. Owen feels you'll be safe here. And given the nature of this new threat we're up against, I think it's a good place to set up a war room and centralize our efforts."

Joyce looked at Nathan. "It would be nice to not have to bounce from safe house to safe house."

Nathan nodded. "We could get back to work."

"Why don't we go see the facilities they've put together here," Jax said, "see if there's anything else you may need?"

"Good idea," Liege said. "If you'll follow me, I'll give you the tour."

Summer waved them off. "I'm staying here. I'll have dinner ready when you're done. I'm sure you must be starving!"

38

Selena was curled against Bastion's side, warming her body and her heart. They'd had a few amazing rounds of sex tonight, then they'd played the "if you were" game he'd made up with that note he'd given her.

Now he slept deeply, peacefully, but she was up, worrying.

Acier had successfully brought the Ratcliffs back to the fort, so Selena knew they were out of Flynn's reach, which meant there was nothing keeping him from coming for her. And soon.

Bastion, Acier said, *come talk to us.*

Selena heard that summons through the mental link she shared with Bastion. He woke fast. They scrambled into clothes and hurried down to room Acier and Guerre shared.

"Do you feel it?" Acier asked. "The air is thick tonight."

Bastion nodded. He looked at her with sad eyes and pulled her close. "But then, I've been feeling this coming for weeks."

"Let's bring Owen in," Guerre said. "Tell him what we're sensing. Have him call a drill for the civilians so they get down to the bunker."

"There's a lot of them to coordinate," Acier said.

Selena was relieved that she wasn't alone in sensing something screaming toward them. At worst, the attack they'd been prepping for would happen tonight. At best, nothing would happen except a successful drill, and people would be tired in the morning.

It was a good call to make.

Bastion sent Owen a compulsion to join them. He knocked on their door a moment later, then entered, hair tousled, barefoot and shirtless, wearing only his flannel pajama bottoms.

Owen glared at them. "What?" he asked.

"We think it's time," Bastion said.

Owen frowned, then tilted his head as he slowly came awake. "Shit." He rubbed his face. "I keep hoping that all of this goes away, but every time I wake up, it's worse."

"Such is the truth right now," Guerre said. "Flynn and his ghouls are coming."

Owen was instantly awake. "How much time do we have?"

"Minutes. Or hours. We don't know," Acier said.

"Right," Owen said. "So we execute the plan. Acier, go get Russ and Jim. Guerre, you man the bunker entrance in the den. Bastion, you've got the elevator. Kit and I will rouse the rest of the household. Once the civilians are safe, we'll take up our assigned positions."

Bastion and Selena hurried back to her room. He went to the closet and came out a minute later, wearing his tunics and leather pants, then sat down to tie his boots. He stood and slid his sai weapons into his belt, two in the back, one in the front.

Selena was donning her own battle gear. He paused to watch her dress. She saw the worry in his eyes. This was it, the night that had been giving him nightmares for weeks. The thought filled her with dread.

"Selena."

She went over to him and held his hips, careful to avoid the sai.

He kissed her. "I love you."

"I love you too."

He put his hands on her face. She committed to memory everything about him. His dark, soulful eyes. His big, poufy hair. His beard, which she now loved.

He ran his fingertips over her cheeks. "I need to ask something of you."

"Anything."

"I need you to stay in the bunker with the civilians."

"Anything but that. I'm not a civilian."

"Flynn and his ghouls are coming for you."

"All the more reason I should be in the fight. I can't let you and everyone else put your lives on the line while I hide."

"You are an accomplished fighter, as is your entire

team. Guerre, Acier, and I should be able to handle this without your team coming near the ghouls. I'm not worried about them. And I wouldn't be worried about you if it were just ghouls." That was a lie and she knew it. "I am worried about Flynn. He's a sneaky bastard. He'll be using tonight to get to you." He took a deep breath. "Don't die for glory when you could live for love."

"This is what you've been fearing, isn't it?"

He nodded.

"Then I'll stay in the bunker with Greer and the civilians."

He pulled her into a tight hug. "Thank you."

WHEN THEY LEFT HER ROOM, the house was alive with people moving quickly to their designated entry point to the bunker. Their faces revealed the tension they felt, but no one was panicked. This evacuation had been practiced dozens of times over the last few days, in the day and in the night.

She and Bastion went past several women who were sharing goodbyes with their men. The guilt Selena felt putting them in this situation was tremendous.

Bastion took her hand and squeezed. You are not the maniac driving this. Flynn is. Keep your perspective right.

In the den, she kissed him. "Be safe."

He stared into her eyes, then smiled. "Always. I'll let you know when the threat is done."

Selena followed a group down the stairs to the bunker. Things were chaotic there. It was a large space, but a lot of people were moving around. Kit, Rocco, and Owen were hugging their families. Wynn was getting the younger pride boys settled in the bunkroom. There weren't enough beds for all the kids, so the older ones had pallets set up in the conference room.

A quick check showed everyone was accounted for. The bunker was secured. The house was secured. All that remained was the waiting—the part Selena hated the most.

Although there were many points of entry into the big mansion, Bastion's team took up posts outside so they could keep the ghouls from getting in. Guerre had the back of the house, Acier had the front, and Bastion held the entrance to the bunker tunnel. Selena listened to their check-ins via the team's comm unit. Her team was spread throughout the house. If the ghouls got inside, they'd have to go through the guys before getting to the civilians in the bunker.

Wynn came out of the bunkroom where some of the kids were riding out the storm. She was doing a second head count. When she finished, she looked at Selena with a frown. "Mouse is gone. He was here. I counted him before."

Selena nodded. "Let's check with Greer." They went into the ops room where Greer was manning the security cameras. "Hey—did you see Mouse go back upstairs?"

"No. Let me take a look." He flipped through the cams that watched the elevator and the den entrance. Mouse wasn't on any of them in the last half-hour. He went back to the screens he'd been watching and sat up straight. "Oh, shit. They're here."

Selena moved to have a better look at the screens. Bastion and his friends were each engaged in fights with multiple monsters. The ghouls' eyes were glowing orange, and they moved like a pack of wolves, each backing up the others.

Wynn gasped. Her face went white. She covered her mouth with her hand, but couldn't tear her eyes from the cameras.

Selena grabbed her arm and led her back to the conference room where the other women were, before returning to the ops room.

"Greer," Val said via their comm units, *"there's a kid up here. In the gym wing."*

"That's Mouse. I'm on it," Selena said.

"No." Greer stood up. "I got it. You stay here."

"Greer, you're our eyes on what's happening. I can't work the monitors like you can. I got this. I'll grab him and get back down here."

Greer glared at her. "Be quick about it."

Selena gave a last look at the screen that showed Bastion fighting the ghouls. She didn't tell him she was popping out of the bunker—she didn't want to distract him.

The first thing she heard when she exited the elevator was the sound of fighting—inside the house. She could hear furniture being smashed. Glass was shattering.

"You're clear," Greer said.

Selena hurried around the corner. At the doors leading to the gym wing, she saw Mouse pounding on the glass door, a look of terror on his young face. Greer unlocked the door. Selena pushed it open, but Mouse ran deeper into the building, disappearing into the workout room.

She didn't call out for him—didn't want to alert any ghouls who might be nearby that a kid was running loose. Instead, she jogged after him.

In the workout room, she whispered, "Mouse! Where are you? We have to get out of here." She heard a faint sniffling in the far corner and found him tucked into a tight ball, crying. The riata he always wore was nowhere in sight. She crouched and touched his back. "Hey. It's okay. I've got you. Why did you leave the bunker?"

He didn't answer her question. "I'm scared, Sel. There are monsters out there. Real ones. Not the pretend wendigos like we've been playing."

"I know." She grabbed his hand and tugged him to his feet. "Let's get out of here. We'll be safe in the bunker." They walked to the door. "Greer, I've got him. We're heading back."

"You're clear. Move it, Sel."

She looked at Mouse. "We have to hurry back to the elevator. Keep up with me, okay?"

Mouse nodded.

Selena opened the door from the workout room. The gym hallway was clear. Outside, she could see Guerre fighting the monsters. Several were lying prone around the lawn. She tore her gaze away and started down the hallway with Mouse.

The door to the pool room opened. Selena let go of Mouse to palm her knife. A man stepped into the hallway, blond, tall, muscular. She knew his square face from all the times Bastion and his team had shown him to her.

Brett Flynn.

Selena pushed Mouse behind her, but he scrambled free and ran to stand next to Flynn, smirking as he turned to face her.

"Mice make the best pets, don't you agree?" Flynn smiled at her as he tousled Mouse's hair.

Oh. God. This wasn't good. "Let him go."

"I don't think so." Flynn swept a forefinger along his own cheek, then gestured toward Selena. "This little monster tagged you with his riata. Only I am allowed to scar you. He took what was mine."

"He's a kid. He's not in this fight."

Flynn smiled down at Mouse. "But he's been so useful, driving my other pets onto the property. He was the only way in."

"You want me to be impressed that you used a child?" she scoffed. "I'm not." At least she now knew how Flynn got the ghouls onto the grounds, but not how he himself got in. Bastion had said Flynn couldn't get through the protections. That meant...Flynn wasn't really there. He was in his astral body.

Selena started forward. "Mouse, let's go."

Mouse was slammed against the wall, his arms and legs spread wide. He was a few inches off the ground.

"You think I'm not here, but if I weren't, could I do this?"

Mouse slowly slid up the wall. He was whimpering. "Sel, help me! Sel!" When his head hit the ceiling, his body bent and continued to move until he was standing over Flynn.

Selena watched as Flynn drew a knife from its sheath and held it up. "Come with me, and I'll spare the boy."

"Spare the boy, and I'll come with you."

"That's what I said."

"Do it, Flynn."

"Oh, very well." The force field holding Mouse must have vanished, for the boy dropped straight down, onto Flynn's knife.

Selena screamed and rushed forward to help him. But not only was he not breathing, he wasn't there. Both he and Flynn had disappeared.

Selena turned in a circle as she tried to grasp what had just happened. Bastion and the guys had spent most of the last two weeks introducing her and the team to the extreme mind fucks mutants were capable of. She squeezed her eyes shut, then opened them. She was still in the gym hallway, alone.

She walked out of the gym wing and back into the main hallway. All was silent now. She couldn't hear any sounds of fighting.

"Selena, what the fuck are you doing up there?" Greer asked, as if he hadn't been part of her decision to go after Mouse.

"Yeah, not digging the joke, Greer. Mouse was missing in Wynn's second head count."

"Um. No, he wasn't. He's here. Everyone except you is present and accounted for. Get your ass back down here."

"Flynn's here. In the house. As an astral projection."

"Hell. I'll alert the others. Get back here."

Selena ignored that. Something odd was happening. "Where did everyone go? No one's up here. It's all quiet. They were fighting a minute ago."

"Selena, come back here."

"No. Something's not right. I'm going to check it out."

"Dammit, Sel! I can't leave. Get your ass back here," Greer shouted into their comms.

Selena quit talking to him. Flynn was here; the others had disappeared — or had been taken down by the ghouls. Where was Bastion? Was he hurt?

She went down the hall, looking in each room, seeing neither her teammates nor their bodies. She wasn't so worried about Flynn now that she knew he was just a projection of himself. He couldn't hurt her... or so she hoped. Bastion had said he could still manipulate the physical world, but he couldn't be as strong in astral form as he was in person.

When she got to the foyer, Bastion stumbled into the room, tangling with two ghouls. God, those things were horrendous.

"Selena." Flynn's voice startled her. She spun around, seeing him standing beside the open front door. "You have a choice now. A turning point. The decision you make will impact everyone you love." He nodded toward Bastion. A ghoul was standing behind him, his clawed hand at Bastion's throat.

Even a fast-healing mutant wouldn't survive having his throat ripped out. The second ghoul was on all fours now, its distorted limbs making it move in a fiendish way as it sniffed at Bastion, rising on its hind legs to smell the blood pumping through his body.

"Selena, leave now. I got this. Go back with the others," Bastion said.

She shook her head.

"No, you can't. You know why?" Flynn asked. "Because you have a frail heart that feels far too much." He extended his hand. "Come with me, and I will spare your beloved mutant."

Tears filled Selena's eyes. She mentally pleaded with Bastion to understand. To save him, she had to go with Flynn.

BASTION WOKE in Selena's bed the next morning. Alone.

He sent his senses out, expanding in a widening field through the room, the house, the gym, the grounds.

She was gone.

Guerre, Acier—Selena's gone. She's not on the compound.

Bastion dressed fast and was just opening his door as the guys reached his room. "I never felt her leave. I would have woken up."

"Let's wake Greer and Max up, have them check the cameras," Guerre said.

Bastion texted the two ops guys to meet them in the bunker. It was early yet. Russ and Jim hadn't even come over to start breakfast.

They went to the den, then thundered down the stairs to the bunker. The ops guys came in from the weapons room looking bleary-eyed.

"What is it that couldn't wait until morning?" Max growled.

"It is morning," Bastion said. "Selena's gone. I want to see the security footage."

Greer sat at the bank of computer screens and played the footage from the previous night. They could see Selena leave her room. She went downstairs, but stood still, in a frozen state for several minutes. Then she walked to the foyer and left through the front door.

Guerre and Acier replayed the footage, but Bastion didn't need to see it again.

Flynn had come for Bastion's light. He'd taken her right from his arms.

39

Selena opened her eyes, shocked to find herself in the large bathroom of her prep school days. The white tiles were clean. The big mirror over the row of sinks was intact.

"Bet you never thought you'd come back here," Flynn said, leaning against one of the stalls.

Bastion, can you hear me?

"I felt nostalgic and wanted to bring you back here, where we began."

Selena faced Flynn, but didn't speak—she had no desire to participate in whatever sick fantasy he'd cooked up.

Bastion, please.

I hear you. Where are you?

In the bathroom where...

The scene blinked and changed. She wasn't standing there anymore talking with the devil. She was now on her back, lying on shards of glass. Flynn was on top of her.

She cried out to Bastion. *He's on me. It's happening all over again.*

It's not real, Selena. It's not happening. Flynn is incapable of sexual arousal. He's playing you against your memories.

Why?

He likes your fear.

Selena stared at the man moving over her. He wasn't the eighteen-year-boy, but the present-day man. He was enjoying her assault, now as he had then. Experiencing the event again, she realized she had no fear. Disgust, yes. Rage, yes. But he couldn't steal from her now as he did then. She reached over and grabbed the big shard of glass, the one she'd used way back then to cut him and his friend up. He'd reproduced the illusion exactly as it had been, minus his friend.

Selena sliced the side of his face. He stopped moving, looking at her in shock. No blood poured through the crevices of the hand he held to his cheek because all of this was just an illusion...and somehow, she'd wrested control of it from him.

She smiled at him, then kicked him off her. He punched her stomach, then slammed his fist into her jaw. Her mind went black.

BASTION WAS in the den at the Red Team headquarters,

surrounded by Selena's team and his. Liege had stayed at the fort with the Ratcliffs and Summer, but he'd sent a helicopter to them. They were all anxiously waiting to pinpoint her location, but Bastion hadn't been able to get a read on that yet. At least she was keeping herself open to him.

"He's torturing her," Bastion said.

"Can you see what she was seeing?" Owen asked.

Bastion nodded, then looked around the room. "Selena told you that Flynn and his friend assaulted her in the bathroom at school when she was fourteen. She said she fought them off. Well, that's true, she did, but they spent a half-hour taking turns with her first."

Owen looked crushed. "Christ."

"Flynn has taken her back to that point in time," Bastion said. "He's making her see it over and over."

"Are you sure he didn't take her back to that actual place?" Ace asked, her hands fisted.

Acier shook his head. "He doesn't need to physically be somewhere to project it to a regular."

"Flynn's modifications went haywire," Bastion said. "He can't get an erection, his facial scars never healed, and his sickness deepened. It's why he was riding Hawk, cultivating him for his own deviant purposes. He can only experience desire through possessing another man's experience."

Ace waved that away. "Whether it's happening now or not, she's in that mind space. We have to get her out of there."

Val put his arm around Ace and pulled her close.

"They're working on it. This isn't our world. They have to do it their way."

Liege had been in Selena's mind before, and he could go there again at will, except now Flynn was intercepting their connection.

"He's not blocking me," Bastion said.

Guerre nodded. "He can't. You're bonded. Can you reach her? Liege could follow you in."

I'm with you, Liege said. *When you get into her mind, I will too.*

"I can reach her, but she's not responding," Bastion said. Was she unconscious? What was happening?

SELENA OPENED HER EYES. Her body hurt. Her jaw hurt. That pain felt real—something surprisingly comforting, considering she was back in the nightmare again.

Bastion.

You're awake.

Got her! Liege said.

Bastion—stay with me.

I will. I am. We're coming for you. I need you to do something.

Anything.

Keep fighting Flynn.

He'll kill me.

No. He wants to relive your assault first. Every time you

don't play along, he has to start it over. He wants it replayed right so he can end it differently. Keep at it.

I love you. Were you hurt last night in the fight? she asked.

There was no fight, Selena. Your mind was manipulated.

But we talked to Guerre and Acier. Owen joined us. The ghouls were outside the house—I saw them on the security cameras. All the kids but one made it to the bunker.

Be calm, Selena. And stay focused. He's been messing with your reality. I will tell you everything soon. Keep fighting him. None of this is real. Not last night, not now.

It hurts like it's real.

Stay strong. We're close.

WHEN SELENA OPENED her eyes next, she was standing in the middle of the bathroom, frantically searching for a way to block the door or hide herself, a full reboot of the nightmare. The door slammed open. Flynn was there, with that same flat stare and lecherous grin he'd had twelve years ago. The effect was ruined by his new face. He was still hiding his appearance from her, which helped remind her that she was who she was and he was who he was—neither of them were the kids they'd been back in the day.

Selena had lost track of how many times this memory had been started over since he'd taken her. Enough that it was losing its hold on her. Odd, she thought, that the more he sought to terrorize her, the more she healed.

The memory jumped forward to when she was lying on top of all the glass from the smashed mirror. He crawled between her legs.

She was bored.

Bored.

She actually laughed. He slapped her.

This repeated simulation held less and less power over her. Like a lucid dream, she realized that she could move at will around the memory, be in different locations, react differently. Each little change she imposed on his illusion made him more frantic.

She had survived him then, and now—over and over.

This time, she reached to the ground and picked up a narrow chunk of flesh. Bloody and soft, it was the skin she'd cut from his cheek that day so long ago.

Flynn's face flickered like a malfunctioning TV, flipping back and forth between his old face and his new one. When he saw the skin she was holding up, he screamed and pressed it to his cheek.

"This is what you did to me. You ruined my life." He scrambled to his feet and backed away from her, his face still flickering between the two visages.

Selena got to her feet. She looked around the bathroom, then started to back up slowly, slipping toward the exit. This was just an illusion, and in theory, she should be able to exit from anywhere, but she didn't know where the edges of his fake reality were. Best to just stay with the mirage and head for the door. As soon as she opened it and stepped out, the bathroom disappeared. She was in a big, empty warehouse. Faint city light was streaming through its wall of cloudy windows.

Do you see that, Bastion?

I see. Be very cautious now. You hit a nerve giving him back his lost piece of skin.

He was right. Flynn was prowling toward her, holding the big glass shard from their fight in the bathroom. Gone was the new face he hid behind. In its place was the adult version of the boy's face, hideous scar and all.

He tilted his head twice, as if he was relieving a twitch in his neck. "I saw dozens of doctors, surgeons and specialists. They all said they could fix the damage you did. All of them made it worse."

Selena kept backing up. The cavernous warehouse held no place to hide, and she didn't yet know where the exits were. She hoped there was one in the corner behind her.

Flynn kept coming closer. "The last procedure was the worst. I contracted a MRSA infection." He moved his hand away. The piece of flesh he'd held to his cheek, though only a mirage, left it bloodied and terrible looking. In the middle of his cheek was a slug-sized hole, showing his clenched teeth.

Selena wanted to be ill.

"You see why I had to have you? An eye for an eye, a cheek for a cheek." He reached into his pocket to show a tiny glass vial. He laughed at the wave of fear that rippled through her. "Yes, you do understand."

The glass shard in his hand was gone, and in its

place was a wide, short knife.

"I'll tell you what I'm going to do—I don't want to leave you in suspense. I'm going to carve up your body, then your face. Then I'm going to pour this serum into your wounds. Know what's in it?"

Selena shook her head. She shot a glance around the room, searching for a door. There was one in the far corner.

"Live MRSA bacteria."

She had fifty-fifty odds with any normal man in a fight, but those odds dropped to nothing with a mutant like him. She couldn't risk getting close enough to engage him, now they'd broken free of his fantasy replay in the bathroom.

She took off in a pounding run for the corner, hoping the door wasn't locked. She'd gotten maybe ten yards closer to it before Flynn jumped in front of her. She looked back to where he'd been to make sure he wasn't there—she knew how mutants could fake so much. He couldn't be real—he'd moved too fast. She had to be looking at an astral projection, not the flesh-and-blood man.

She did a roundhouse kick, planting her foot in the middle of his jaw. He was solid. And he didn't lose his balance. He caught her ankle and slashed the knife along her calf laughing giddily at her cry of pain.

Selena crouched in front of him, prepared for hand-to-hand combat. She had no weapon and was a mere regular against his mutant superiority. Time was her only ally. Bastion would be here soon.

As Flynn advanced, she dodged and jumped here and there, avoiding his thrusts and slashes. At last she caught the wrist of his knife hand and, bending his elbow with a fast blow of her other arm, turned his thrust against him, stabbing him deep just below the collarbone.

He screamed at the pain, pushing a sonic blow at her that tossed her into the air. She landed hard on the concrete floor and slid a few yards, knocking the breath out of her. Before she stopped sliding, before she could even get her breath, he was on her. She was paralyzed, frozen by some trance that left all of her senses intact, but her body unable to move.

He laughed as he cut through her clothes. When her skin was exposed, he made a long slow cut down her body. The pain was excruciating. She couldn't move, couldn't escape what was happening, couldn't even scream. When he stopped the cut at the corner of her hip, he set the blade beside her and opened the vial. She was bleeding heavily. She felt cold and faint.

I love you, Bastion.

Hold on. We are here.

Flynn dripped the contents of the vial into her wound. Each drop burned like acid, spreading fire over and through her body.

She shut her eyes, surrendering to a strange peace that suddenly overtook the pain. Her last thought was of Bastion.

Their time together had been short, but it had meant everything to her.

40

The helicopter landed on the roof of the warehouse. Bastion and Guerre jumped out and hurried to the rooftop stairs. Bastion sent his energy out into the whole building, seeking Selena's.

He looked at Guerre. "She's not here."

She was, Liege said.

Either Flynn had taken her somewhere else, or he'd suppressed her energy. Bastion didn't want to even think about the third option—that she hadn't survived the bastard.

They split up; Bastion took the third floor of the sprawling warehouse, and Guerre took the ground floor. It was dark outside now. No lights were on in the abandoned building, but both men were able to see in the dark.

Bastion couldn't help but remember the last information he'd gotten from Selena—when Flynn was cutting her. He was terrified of what he would find...and terrified he wouldn't find her at all.

She wasn't on either of their floors, so they met in the stairwell on the second floor. Both sent their awareness into the room ahead of entering it, psychically checking for anything that felt like a trap.

There was nothing. No ghouls. No Flynn. No explosives. No trouble was lying in wait.

And no Selena.

They stepped inside. A pile of something was in the middle of the floor, absolutely still.

Selena.

Bastion rushed over. A dark pool of cooling blood encircled her. She looked at him, but didn't move or speak. Flynn had left her in a tranced state, frozen in place. Bastion knelt beside her and took her hand. He hadn't set the trance, so he couldn't release it from the outside in. He had to go inside her and break her out. He did that now, pushing his energy through her in an ever-expanding bubble until it stood between hers and Flynn's, breaking Flynn's grip on her.

Guerre was already working on her, stabilizing her wounds, keeping her vitals steady. When it was safe, Bastion lifted her and rushed her up the stairs and into the waiting helicopter.

Guerre continued working on her the whole flight back to the fort. A long, glowing line filled the wound Flynn had made on her. Bastion stared at his friend, but couldn't read anything other than his intense concentration.

After several long minutes, with the roar of the helicopter all around them, Selena looked up at Bastion. Her eyes were beautiful, trusting, and so full of pain. She caught the back of his arm as he bent over her. "Let's play the 'if you were' game," she whispered.

Bastion could barely hear her in the loud chopper. But he didn't need her voice to hear her. He smiled and nodded, blinking away a tear. "I'll go first." He sniffled. "If you were the sun, I'd be the flowers reflecting your beauty back to you."

"I like that," she whispered. "If you were the grass, I'd be a pack of rescued dogs rolling around on you."

"Good one." Bastion fought his emotions back. "If you were winter, I'd be the snowflakes, showing you the infinite ways you are unique."

She smiled and nodded, but her eyes swept shut. She no longer had the energy to speak, though she gave him one last line. *If you were mine, I'd love you forever.*

I am yours, Selena. I am yours.

IT SEEMED to take forever for the helicopter to make it back to the fort. Bastion covered Selena in a bubble of energy so the cold wind and dirt kicked up by the helicopter blades wouldn't worsen her condition. He ran with her into the fort.

A man he didn't know was waiting there with a gurney. Bastion set her on the bed, and the man rolled the gurney into the kitchen, where a makeshift operating room was set up.

No introductions were made—there was no time. Selena needed everyone's full attention. A man and a woman, both mutants, came over. The Ratcliffs, he supposed.

"Bastion, we have her now," the woman said. "Go wait in the living room."

No way was he going to leave his light in the hands of strangers, but Guerre caught his arm. "I'll be with her. Go, so we can take care of her."

Bastion sent Selena a last look, then walked backward out of the kitchen and into the living room. Liege was there with Summer. So was Acier. He knew Merc was paying close attention via their mental link.

Bastion sat in one of the armchairs. Everything about him hurt, from his heart outward.

Liege looked at Bastion from where he was standing by the bookshelf. "She's in the best of hands. Dr. Beck, the physician Owen's team uses, brought blood down for a transfusion—they got her blood type from her Army records. Between him and Guerre, she'll be patched up in no time."

That didn't prove to be true. Hours passed. Bastion alternated between sitting and pacing. The numbness he felt grew as Selena's energy weakened.

"Bastion?"

A woman's voice broke into his thoughts, the woman from the kitchen. Dr. Joyce Ratcliff. "I'm sorry—"

He stopped listening. His breath left him in a rush. He stumbled over to the armchair. His head was buzzing. He covered his ears and refused to look at the woman.

She didn't let that sway her. She crouched in front of him and grabbed his hands from his ears. Holding his cold hands in hers, she stared up into his eyes as she said, "I want to modify Selena."

"What?" Bastion blinked.

"We've brought several vials of the serum we used to modify Nick."

"You can't. It'll kill her. She can't survive something so traumatic now."

"I'm afraid it's the only option to save her at this point."

Tears spilled down Bastion's cheeks. He sent a panicked look at Liege. Guerre came into the room and sat on the coffee table behind Dr. Ratcliff. "Let them do it. I will help support her through the shock of the infusion."

Bastion got up and went into the kitchen. Machines were hooked up to Selena. Her blood pressure was dangerously low. She was on a ventilator. A bag of blood was slowly dripping into her arm. He stood beside her bed and held her hand.

What should he do? What could he do? She might not survive the transition. But she might not survive anyway. He kissed her knuckles. Closing his eyes, he tried to slip into her mind, to find where her spirit had gone while her body was so desperately wounded.

Stay here, Selena. Stay with me. I will be with you through every step of this change. Take my energy; take all that you need.

He looked over at the Ratcliffs, then at Guerre. At last, he nodded. "Do it."

∼

SELENA WOKE from a dream about standing in a freezing spring rainstorm, only to find she was actually in the icy downpour of a shower.

She wasn't alone. She was sitting on a bench with her legs draped over Bastion's. Though his arms held her in a tight grip, he was dead asleep. His mouth was open and long snores came from deep in his chest.

She smiled at him, then wondered why they were sleeping in the shower. That was when she remembered everything. The drill to get the families to the bunker. Mouse missing in the head count. Ghouls spread everywhere across Blade's property. Fighting in the house. Flynn threatening Bastion.

She shut her eyes. Bastion had said none of that had happened, that it had just been Flynn messing with her mind. It had felt so real.

She eased herself from Bastion's lap and shut the frigid water off. Stepping out of the stall, she grabbed one of the towels stacked near it. Before she could wrap herself in it, she caught her reflection in the mirror. She looked gaunt. Shadows circled her eyes.

Her gaze went lower, to her body, something she would have never done before. Now, she felt none of the panicky emotions that had been with her for over a decade. There was a new scar that crossed from one shoulder to the opposite hip, the wound that Flynn had carved into her. It was reddish and bruised, but it looked to have been months into its healing. How was that possible?

She touched that scar, testing the pain around it. There was none. How long had she been out of commission?

While she stared at her body, her gaze traveled to her breasts and hips. She turned to the side, checking the old scars she'd carved into her own body. Instead of the raised webbing she expected to see, there was just fading patches of discolored white skin.

Her scars were healing.

She huffed a disbelieving breath.

Bastion came into view behind her. He studied her, worry written across his face. He took her towel and wrapped her in it, then kissed her temple. "You're awake."

She nodded. She watched his reflection as she said, "You changed me."

His face tightened. He nodded. He lifted her and carried her out of the bathroom to her bed and settled her in the bed. The sheets smelled deliciously fresh.

"Summer has been changing the bed every time I bathe you," Bastion said.

"Why? How long have I been out?"

"Two weeks." Bastion looked reluctant to explain more, but he said, "You were gravely injured, Selena. Dr. Beck was here with blood for a transfusion. He, Guerre, and the Ratcliffs worked on you for hours, but you were dying."

"They had to change me."

Bastion nodded, then watched her closely.

She pulled on his hand, drawing him beneath the covers with her. "Am I going to be all right?"

He nodded. "I think so. You have a long road ahead of you now to acclimate to the modifications you received. But you're completely healed from your wounds."

"Flynn had a vial of something that he poured into my wound. He said it was live MRSA bacteria."

"It may have been, but in the mutation process, all toxins are pushed from the body. Whatever he poisoned you with would have been removed from your system. That's why we were constantly washing you and changing the bed linens. The cold showers helped with your fevers, too."

Selena kissed his knuckles. "Thank you."

"Don't thank me." Bastion frowned. "You don't thank your heart for beating or your lungs for breathing. What I did was selfish—I can't live without you."

Selena wiggled into the crook of his arm and wrapped hers around him. "My 'thank you' stands. You saved my life. And you made the difficult choice of the mutations for me. I wanted them, but I was afraid. Now we can have a proper future."

Bastion huffed a sharp sigh. "It was the only choice I could have made."

"Have the Ratcliffs been checking on me?"

"Several times a day. Dr. Beck sees you every few days. Guerre has been connected with you the whole time, monitoring you. He says you're healing very well." Bastion ventured a smile. "Your team has also been down to visit you. One or more of them is here every day. Ace has been relieving Summer in helping with your care. They love you very much."

Warm tears filled Selena's eyes. "I'm a very lucky mutant."

Bastion laughed. "I've called your parents."

"Oh. My. God. What did they say?"

"They will be here tomorrow."

"I can't believe you did that."

"If my daughter was gravely injured, I would absolutely want to know so that I could be there for her."

"Do they know I'm a mutant?"

Bastion grinned and shook his head. "No. There is no need for them to know that at this point."

Selena rubbed her cheek against Bastion's bare chest. "I love you. So much."

Bastion's arm tightened around her. "Good. Because I love you more."

THE NEXT DAY, they were in Summer's greenhouse, waiting for her parents to arrive. Acier had gone into town to pick them up.

Bastion could feel Selena's edgy tension. He decided to tell her a story to distract her from her worries.

"Did you ever wonder why our hearts are on the left side of our chests?" Bastion asked. "Not in the middle?"

Selena smiled. "No. But I'm guessing you have."

Bastion straightened the blanket covering her. They were sitting in a double recliner on the top tier, overlooking the lush rows of terracing that led down to the pool. He kissed her forehead, grateful her transition had gone as well as it had. He wouldn't have survived losing her, he knew that for sure.

The greenhouse was her favorite place in the fort. It was his favorite too.

"I have long wondered about this mystery of the heart. I think it comes from an error in the Bible. Maybe it wasn't on purpose. Maybe it was an error of translation."

"Bastion, you know I'm not a religious person."

"But God saved your life."

"No. Science saved my life."

Bastion waved that away. "Whatever. Believe what you like. I'm going to tell you about how woman came to have a heart."

Selena shook her head.

Bastion fought a laugh. "You see, in the beginning, God made woman without a heart, hence the expression 'heartless woman.'"

"Bastion—" Selena said, a stronger warning in her voice.

He laughed. He loved stirring the pot with her. "No,

it's true. Just hear me out, *mon amour*. In the beginning, God gave man two hearts, as he did two eyes and two ears and two arms and two lungs and so on. He gave no heart to woman because she took her strength from man."

"Bastion—"

He chuckled. His distraction was working. "Well, what did you expect? The Bible was transcribed by men, so of course it favors them. Anyway, God made man and then made woman his dependent, almost a sub-creature. But man said, 'I have two hearts and my woman has none. She cannot live without me.' To which God said, 'She is yours to do with as you will.' Man thought about this for a long time. Such decisions don't come easily, and there was much to consider. At last, he said to God, 'Give her one of my hearts, for then I will know, when I am born, that somewhere in the world is my other heart. I will not be alone because my heart and hers will beat with a single resonance and that resonance will help me find her.' God, being omniscient, knew what the outcome of this would be. 'If I do this, she will have her own hopes and dreams and desires independent of you.' Man gave this some thought. 'But you see, God, having been without a heart for so long, woman will now know what love is, and once she does, she will always be driven by her heart. Her dreams will give me hope. Her strength will strengthen me. Her courage will give me courage.' After this, God agreed to do what man requested, and both He and man saw what a better place the world was. It's why you and I have a resonance together, why your heart needs to be near mine."

Selena shook her head. She wiped her eyes before she turned to face him. "Bastion, that's not a biblical parable."

"Well, of course not. Early man feared the power given to women and tried to write them out of history. But it is true. It's why, when you stand with your body facing mine, your heart beats against where it once had its home in my chest."

Selena laughed and leaned her head against his shoulder. "You're crazy. You know that, right?"

"Well, I'm French, which makes me a romantic at heart. It's something you Americans will never understand."

"I guess your theory explains why some men have such a low opinion of women."

"Perhaps. Fools that they are, they like their women hopeless, dreamless, fearful. Me, I like my woman full of heart."

"I love your kind of crazy, Bastion."

"Of course you do. Your heart is mine." He smiled.

"So the world begins and ends with you?"

He shook his head. "It begins with me, goes through you, and ends with us."